# ABOUT THE AUTHOR

B.A. Crisp lives in Southwest Florida with her husband and her covert ops cat, Mr. Mew. Crisp earned degrees from Ursuline College and the George Washington University's Graduate School of Political Management. She attended the London School of Journalism and the University of Oxford's Summer Student's Writing Program. As an anti-human trafficking advocate she's worked alongside private military contractors, federal agents, strip club owners, and with other important people way too dignified to name here.

# X
# POINT
## B.A. CRISP

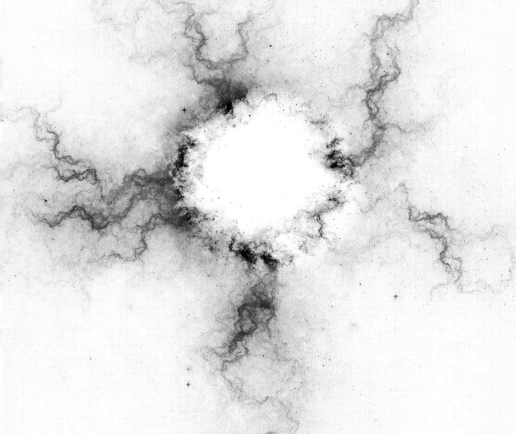

NAPLES, FL     WASHINGTON, D.C.     OXFORD, U.K.

Book II of the Quanta Chronicles Series

The characters and events in this book are fictitious. Any similarity to real persons, living or dead, is coincidental and not intended by the publisher.

Cover and interior by Ashley Ruggirello/cardboardmonet.com

2Portal Publishing

1629 K St. Suite 300

Washington, DC 20006

The publisher is not responsible for websites (or their content) that are not owned by the publisher.

2 Portal Publishing provides this author for speaking engagements. To learn more, please email: dcrisp@2portalpublishing.com

Library of Congress Cataloging—in—Publication Data

Crisp, BA

X Point: Port Meadow/BA Crisp.—First Edition Series Book II Quanta Chronicles

ISBN 978-1-7343087-1-6 (paperback) 978-1-7343087-2-3 (e-book).

1. Supernatural—Sci Fiction.

2. Adventure—Fiction. 3. Coming of Age—Sci—Fiction. 4. Self-Realization—

Fiction. LCCN: 2021930377

Printed in the United States of America

*In Memory of Sgt. Linda Pierre*
*KIA*
*April 11, 2016*
*Forward Operating Base Gamberi,*
*Nangarhar Province, Afghanistan*

# ACKNOWLEDGMENTS

To Macy, Mindy, Tyler, Cynthia, Monika, and Teri
for your ongoing support and encouragement

To Linda, Marc, Suzanne, Pauline, and Karen who will always be
"My Writer's Group"

Thanks to David Gatewood, Editor of Red Bird by B.A. Crisp and
to Cheryl Murphy of InkSlinger, Editor of X Point by B.A. Crisp

To Nikola Tesla and Dr. Harry Kloor, my muses and heroes

For the beings who feel alone and forgotten on this remote planet:

You're not. We're here.

"*Most certainly, some planets are not inhabited, but others are, and among these there must exist life under all conditions and phases of development.*"
—*Nikola Tesla, "How to Signal to Mars," 1910*

"*The day science begins to study non-physical phenomena it will make more progress in one decade than in all the previous centuries of its existence.*"
— *Nikola Tesla*

# ONE

## PASSWORD

THE SOUL of the sea is angry today, its mood choppy and restless. Staring over a cliff I think about those fortunate souls seized in her swirling embrace, centuries of ships, their passengers and crews, returned to brine, their wave shined bones sucked into the murky depths of a black portal only to be seen again as mirages on the horizon, or heard as deadly muses, a chorus of nautical ghosts, their nets cast for the living.

"What's the password?"

A little girl, maybe five years old, blocks my entry through a small gate to the crumbling castle. Russet ringlets meet the hem of her cardinal-colored cape, dancing in concert with an incoming breeze and the screeches of gulls. *Move out of my way,* I think. I want to jump over the cliff. I'm *compelled* to jump over the cliff. She stands defiant, hands locked on hips, the wind tossing thin rusty spirals about her cheeks as she searches my eyes for an answer, the *right* answer. I have no answers. I didn't know there'd be a test—I hate tests.

"What's your name?" I ask.

"I have no name if you have no password."

Her snarky retort sounds like one I might give. "I was at least twelve before I could launch such smart ass comebacks," I say. I offer her a thumbs up and the little girl cocks her head and crinkles her nose in confusion, as if she's never seen such a silly gesture and has no idea of its meaning.

Near the cliff's edge, a once commanding limestone fortress tilts, it's craggy exterior partially covered by ropey black vines that slither into undefended windows. The sagging estate holds weary watch over a vast and boiling blue-black ocean, one that hurls unrelenting waves against jagged bedrock. The water is reduced to frothy foam in its attempt to scoop away the bluff's foundation and rake it back to sea, a feat it will eventually, and soon, I think, accomplish. Late afternoon shadow meanders through untamed walls of thistle, stitching porous cracks with purple and thorn.

"Where are your parents?" I ask, looking around, unsure of how I, or she, got here. This place is too dangerous and desolate for anyone, especially a kid.

The little girl produces an oversized silver sword from beneath her cardinal cape and positions it between us—quite a remarkable feat for one so young—and again demands a password. "I take no prisoners," she says. Her too-big-for-her-hands weapon pitches a glint of light into my eyes.

I'm not sure how I missed the sword. It's just as big as she, but surprisingly, doesn't appear unwieldy in her tiny hands. The little girl's bottom lip juts out to blow a wayward ringlet from her eyes, a curl that repeatedly returns, against her frustration, to its original position.

"*Grrr*. Dad says I can't cut my hair or I'll lose my strength, like Samson in the Bible."

I've always had a soft spot for the underdog—this tiny *David* of a girl pitting herself against me, a gangly and suicidal female Goliath, quite proficient in the art of war and observation—or at least I thought so until I missed the sword—and the password. "Your mum lets you play with a weapon?" I ask.

"This isn't playtime," she says. "And besides, I don't have a mom."

Her golden-green orbs flicker with raw determination as she carefully measures me, her trespasser, eyeing me up and down, with pursed lips, a perfect clutch on her sword handle. Someone trained her well, I see. She's as comfortable wielding a blade as another kid might be cuddling a teddy bear—but she needs to move aside so I may jump.

A man crosses the lawn taking zero notice of our standoff. Surely, I think, we are a sight he can't miss. He strides toward an outbuilding, a stable, and threads a bridle through the mouth of a brawny gray steed. Seagulls glide overhead, their white and gray feathers a whir of flaps and floats along a shredded shoreline, calling to us. He is a tall man who radiates peace and contentment, two things I've always coveted but never achieved, hence the urge to toss myself overboard, away from Earth. The man firmly grasps a saddle, his carriage and rugged good looks, easy on my eyes. One curly dark ringlet occasionally skims his right cheek as a light swish of desire floats across my hips. An overwhelming sensation of familiarity sweeps through me.

*"Bennie?"*

I take a step around the girl to hurdle myself over the gate, toward the stables.

**KABOOM!**

The blast sucks the air from my lungs and launches me backward with a hard *thud* on a thorny patch. But there is no pain. There should be pain, I think. I detest pain even more than I do tests…and passwords…and failure, yet in this case, not feeling pain is painfully worrisome. Tiny footsteps draw closer. Her blade swings toward my chest…

…*"Ahhhhhhhh!"*

Beads of terror bubble up on my forehead as I freefall, arms extended, blindly reaching out for anything I might grab to save myself, earth giving way to a black abyss. The little girl, the man, the castle…*gone!*

Rattling off a thousand '*Hail Mary's*', I tumble and twirl through a stark, noiseless void, internally screaming. I've never really believed in prayer or God—or the Virgin Mary, but occasionally call on each, when I hope to bypass grave bodily harm. But I don't think God, or anyone else, can actually hear me from inside this endless vacuum, one that makes me think of Castalia's Blue Hole in Ohio, a seventy-five foot in diameter pond. It never sustained fish and was allegedly bottomless until scientists proved it wasn't. Then I realize...if there is a bottom here, landing will kill me!

I'm *so* fucked. I lied. I don't really want to die! I just think about it sometimes, what it might be like to die—not being dead, but the dying part. The *whoosh* of nothingness, an altered acoustic, and a metallic clicking noise overfills my ears. Heat intensifies. My body nosedives toward a pinpoint of expanding chalky light.

I close my eyes and brace for impact...for what I'm sure is Hell...

... ... ... ... ...

...am I...

...dead?

Confused, I roll to one side, tired and parched, eyes drawn back from the brightness because this I *do* feel and it stings. I curl rough sheets into bony fingers, momentarily fighting off the feeling of a hundred hornets in my head. I struggle to rattle my brain bearings. I'm awake enough to realize I've been asleep. Not dead. Eyes half open to a grayish hostile light. I blink away sleep grit. *Focus, Sam.* Thin strips of metal. White cork. Florescent tubes in the ceiling. The room treads in an out of focus. Bennie's gone, replaced by a sterile void, a squiggly-warped world I command my eyes to focus upon with little more than hazy success.

*Blip. Blip. Blip*—I hear.

An excruciating ache zips through my neck, along the base of my skull, until it stretches over throbbing temples to release a pent up cascade of pain. Gravity and a series of rubber-like tubes shackle me when I struggle to move but can't. I am whole, I think, if not healthy. *Alive.* Amber light recedes through a small crack in ugly green and yellow plaid curtains. It's late afternoon, sliding into dusk soon, I think—and those are institutional curtains.

No decent interior designer on this planet would ever dream of hanging such hideous drapery in any private residence. These are government issue curtains, in a government facility, some sort of hospital I think, and this is far from the perfect landing for which I'd hoped.

# TWO

# BLOOD OF UNKNOWN ORIGIN

TUBES DANGLE from an IV bag on a silver pole, which lead to small needles drilled starboard into my right hand. A black screen monitors vitals, blinking green dots and dashes similar to Morse code. I'm breathing too fast, too deep. *Slow down.*

Patient 001: Samantha Ryan Blake DOB 12/09/1967.

That's *me.*

Heart rate 35 BPM.

Blood Pressure 90/60.

BOUO Rh Negative.

*Shit!*

BOUO means, "Blood of Unknown Origin." I'm being studied, again, but by whom or what agency, I don't yet know. If I were in a *safe* facility, it wouldn't say, "*BOUO*", it would say, "**GB**" for 'Golden Blood.'

This is bad. My hybrid ass is in trouble.

**Blip. Blip. Blip**—goes the monitor.

*Think, Sam.*

Yesterday, or maybe earlier today, I trespassed into NASA Plum Hook Bay, my former foster home. That's when my left bicep took an unexpected bite from some exotic looking yellow-feathered insect, a flying bioelectromagnetic bug—a technological device similar to Bennie's robotic spider, Cutie Pie I. But this new bug? It wasn't Bennie's.

I've visited that kid's lab, aka *Silo #57*, about a zillion times and made a mental list of everything there: One pet cobra, a farm full of Brazilian bullet ants, various species of spiders, copious bones, wire, cable, chemical compounds, polished rocks, a wolf named Randolph, Amazonian plants, one weird laser weapon, and a pet cardinal named Edwin. Bennie had no yellow-feathered, sort of alive, sort of not, flying insects. The bioweaponry that poisoned my body and took me down was similar to something he'd build yet something else entirely.

"Ohhhh…" Every muscle in my body feels as if it's been repeatedly whacked with a meat tenderizer. My arms are cold… and numb. I take in a generous gulp of air and will my toes to action until they tingle and wiggle compliance but gravity still presses me down, driving a lightning rod of pain through my spine. I lean against the pillow. Maybe I should stop—just lie here and go back to sleep until I feel better, maybe head back to that cliff and find the little girl with the sword.

*No!*

A faint odor of medicinal ointment and pine cleaner jabs my nostrils. The rising tick-tock in my heart keeps pace with a growing concern I'm paralyzed—maybe that's why I can't move. I set heavy intention upon fingers, arms, and legs and will each into action. Nothing. A panic unlike any I've ever known sets in, a deep spring of helplessness bubbling up from the undercurrent of my heart. *Fuck, Sam. What have you done to yourself?*

Reggie warned me not to return to that God forsaken facility. I rarely listen—to him or anyone else. He says I'm smug, that I take unnecessary risks. And he's going to be super pissed I got caught, and even worse, disobeyed his order and wound up *here*, even though I have no idea where in the hell I am.

I couldn't help myself.

I needed to retrieve something very important behind those gates.

I failed.

Normally, I don't care if I upset people but Reggie's different. He took charge of me at Plum Hook Bay, got me off the streets and trained me to survive foster care—and he helped me avoid a murder charge. I met him soon after I killed a pig, the kind without hooves or a curly tail, one who preyed on kids. Reggie thought I had promise.

The small bones in my neck clack toward a wall clock, it's boring black-and-white face with a red second-hand ticking off marks between numbers. It's almost 4:30pm. Thankfully, I'm not completely paralyzed. I can turn my neck.

Maybe Reggie is right. Maybe I'm too unruly for clandestine work. It takes everything I have to will my arm to move. It doesn't. Actually, what Reggie said was, "You have talent," as long as I temper my temper. Going against his advice sucker punched me here. Unfortunately, my mistake provides plenty of free time for personal reflection, the latter of which I am *not* an expert. And it cost me my mobility. This is a much higher price than I expected to pay.

My pendulum swings toward rebellion because I have a serious problem trusting people, and if anyone lived through what I did, they'd understand. As a former ward of the court and foster kid, my 'best interests' got lost years ago, along with my case number and court file. According to the U.S. government, I don't exist. I'm *whitewashed* under *Project Bluebird*, operated by the CIA's Office of Scientific Intelligence, to determine if I could be trained, at sixteen, in 'natural' acts of assassination. I passed.

I was remanded to NASA Plum Hook Bay in 1984, along with a bunch of other *gifted* foster kids—but aged out at eighteen—ordered off property and bounced over to Langley, where I'm supposed to be trained as a clandestine operations officer. I start classes in a couple of weeks—if I get out of *here*. I am property of the U.S. government—well—not the regular government everyone sees on TV but a *behind the scenes* regime that likes to be left in the dark.

Reggie upskilled me in the art of self-reliance and survival using what he learned as a special forces guy and former Army Colonel. But he can't seem to reprogram my propensity for meandering around regulations and maybe all of this, my being here, is another hard lesson to teach me to listen. I despise rules. In my mind, authority always *sins*, its rituals and regulations, providing too many super glossy covers for deeply fucked up corruption.

This is an overly scrubbed room. No artwork, no television— no flower bouquets holding small cards that wish me a speedy recovery. It smells of bleach and antiseptic despair. Bright red and yellow, *"No visitors Allowed"* and **"Use of Deadly Force Authorized"** signs glare at me from bolted positions on a wall, which is bullshit. I'm not going anywhere!

Upon closer inspection, I notice my IV bag isn't *giving* blood, but taking it *away. Fuck.* This isn't a drill. I'm tethered to a BOUO-drip, kept alive just enough to continually produce new cells for whatever black ops agency put me here. *Damn it.* This wasn't supposed to happen. Reggie and Bennie both said my BOUO should remain one of the planet's best kept secrets. Whoever did this to me means *big* business—and I'm slowly drained as a rare commodity, kept alive *just enough*.

BOUO possesses traces of rare element 122, also known as *'una-tes-lium'*, which provides the U.S. military-industrial-intelligence complex, a necessary and unable-to-be-cloned plasma for fueling interstellar travel. It lies within an island of stability on the Periodic Table between muscovium and unbinilium. In simple terms, Bennie called it "Golden Blood". However, government officials with steep clearances know otherwise, that we, meaning Bennie and me, have at least one parent that comes from someplace else, and we are called Camaeliphim.

Bennie once told me Earth holds strategic intergalactic value because it serves as a repository between realms. It's piddly little orbit is responsible for keeping entire universes intact via a few portals that lead to alternate worlds with countless other interstellar gateways. I am the product of an otherworldly father and a human mother, biologically enhanced to ensure humans remain safe. Unfortunately for this planet, and for me, I'm not very good at my job.

The IV tugs at my flesh causing small ripples to flee up my forearm. On my left arm, a very strange looking platinum hospital bracelet lights up with a series of neon green numbers and symbols. It has two metal prongs, driven deep into bone through the underside of my wrist, a compulsory quasi-crucifixion. It doesn't hurt but the rest of my body does.

*Shit!* Someone's coming. I close my eyes and pretend to sleep.

A nurse checks a monitor before she stops to study me. Whoever she is—wherever I am, I don't want *anyone* to know I'm awake—at least not until I figure out a way out of here. She steps around an empty tray table and leans toward the wall before she pushes her palm against a metal plate above my head.

"Yes Lieutenant," a voice says.

"Major, I think you should come here," the nurse says. "Something's changed."

"What's changed?"

"Major, I think you should see for yourself."

*Think, Sam. What would Reggie do? What did he teach you?*

"Well?" The Major asks as she walks into the room and shuts the door, an impatient tone in her voice. "What's changed? She looks the same to me."

"Major, please look at her closely," the Lieutenant nurse says. "Her monitor blipped."

Through cracked eyes, I watch the Major hover a thin steel blue-light tipped wand over my body. "Heartbeat matches the monitor," she says, tapping my leg with the device. "No change. The QX-2 doesn't show a single cellular or internal atomic change and I've never known this thing to offer a failed reading. 001 remains in a coma, just as she has for the past four years."

*Four years?!*

*Breathe.*

*Reggie always says not to panic.*

*How can I NOT panic?*

A third person opens the door.

"Everything okay in here Major?" An MP asks, one posted outside my door, his brass and camo arm telling me that guarding a comatose hybrid has to be the easiest gig of his entire military career.

"We're fine, Sergeant" the Major says. "Shut the door."

"Yes, Ma'am."

"001 remains in a coma," the Major says to the nurse once the door closes. "Don't call me again unless she's dancing around her IV pole."

The Lieutenant lifts my arm to check the tubes and then fluffs a pillow under my head. "You take care, 001," she whispers in my ear, but it sounds more patronizing than sincere, as if my being in a four year coma barely registers a blip on her empathy radar, and I'm nothing more than a disconnected bundle of wire they aren't even trying to unravel.

Their voices fade with a loud click and lock of the door, sealing me off from escape. It's weird, I think, they'd lock the door of a coma patient—until I remember what happened last time…

…*Four years?*

*I've been here four years?!*

The air is leaden when I swallow. Swaying like a drunk, I struggle to sit up. Trembling, I set my mind to *moving* and barely foist feeble legs bedside, my body shaking, a ravenous hunger to move and to eat overtaking weakness. It's hard for me to accept how difficult it is to activate. Every finger curl is a struggle, every stretch of muscle recoils and screams in atrophied agony. What I want to do doesn't sync up with how this body fails to respond. I must *get up* if I don't want to *wind up* spending my life as a half-human fuel station. A wobbly set of crampy limbs bows under my weight like strained twigs. *Damn it!* The tray table rolls away…and down, down, down, I go…a feed loop of *Ring around the Rosie* dances in my head. The IV rips away from my arm and a catheter gets yanked from "down there".

*Breep! Breep! Breep!*

"Fuuuck me!" I try to yell, my throat not working. Everything in me that hasn't stirred in four years starts to gurgle and boil along with the jarring sound of the siren. Dark blue blood trickles down my forearm and drips onto the gray linoleum floor. Covering my throbbing ears, I accidentally smack myself in the side of the head with my government-issue bangle. A wave of pulsating vertigo ripples through my head but no way am I giving up now.

*"Stop!"*

*That's better,* I whisper to myself, welcoming a short-lived sliver of quasi-peace when the sirens abruptly cease and my throat cranks open for more air. Now, to figure a way to stand up and get out of here. Wait. I *moved!* If I did it once, I can do it again—*Come on, Sam*!

**MOVE!**

Sparky connections make contact between body and brain. Tingly fingers stab the bedsheets and rake the mattress, firing up every bit of willpower I have to clamp down and pull up on buckling legs. *We have lift off!*

Hobbling toward the window, I push my legs forward, *hup, toop, threep, fourp,* grabbing the back of a chair, the nightstand, anything in my path to stay on my feet. Twisted rusty coils of dingy copper hair dangle in my face so I divide my unruly locks into two fistfuls and knot it snug behind my neck, curious as to why my head isn't shaved. Whoever put me here doesn't seem overly concerned about my hygiene.

"001! Open the door!" The Major orders. She bangs and tugs on the handle.

Government agencies are notorious for bureaucracy bungles like sticky doors and this security glitch might be my way out—although I have zero clue how much time I have before this door rights itself and blows open to a swarm of military personnel. I also doubt my ability to put up much of a fight given I can barely raise a fist. The blood oozing down my forearm meanders lava slow to my elbow. I swipe it along the front of my hospital gown. It leaves a sapphire streak with gold flecks.

The window holds firm, not even a rattle or crack to push against. I pull back my left arm and fling the weird bracelet into the glass. The weight of it bounces back and slams me in the forehead. "Fuck!" I yell, and teeter backward, the window unbothered, not a single chard out of place. I should get a gold star for not falling down.

Every vertebrae in my spine teeters so I stagger-step back to the window and curl overgrown nails around the sill. Outside hums a vast and busy city that stretches as far as my eyes carry. I'm surprised such a high-clearance facility is hidden in plain sight but it's a perfect strategy on the part of whoever put me here. If I'm ensconced among skyscrapers, where highly distracted *at-risk* humans roam below, it makes my rescue or escape equally difficult, damn near impossible, really—and this, not being able to break out of here, trips my heart into sadness.

*Think, Sam...*

...The nubs between my shoulders ache as if someone's taken a hacksaw to wings I never had —nubs I try to reach but can't. These are Rosie's scars—the ones she gave me with a leather whip back at the Trail's End Motel, right before I was swept into NASA Plum Hook Bay. Rosie was my seventh foster mom in seven years but she didn't have a motherly bone in her body, foster or otherwise. She'd beat me for refusing to open my legs for men old enough to be my grandfather. She's dead.

I'm at least six stories above an urban street. A man wearing a colorful Rastafarian cap sells souvenirs from a vending truck. The sidewalk glows slick from recent rain, and people in gray, navy, or black suits scurry like Bennie's Brazilian bullet ants into and around crosswalks or cars. The sun's final rays bounce off glassy buildings, illuminating pieces of the city back unto itself through large rain puddles trapped in scattered potholes, a shattered mirror reflecting the collective lives of the damned and desperate below. Watching the world scurry by makes me feel *"sadgitated"*, a word I made up as a kid to describe feeling sad and irritated at the same time. Turning from the window I examine the room until my eyes ache, wondering what the hell I might use as a weapon. My feet make a swishy shuffle sound and baby steps deliver me to a sleek stainless steel cylinder near my bed. *Progress!*

*Bang, bang, bang!* **"001 open the damn door, we know you're awake!"**

A holographic dude's head pops forth all genie-like and I jerk back. He speaks with an echoing English lilt and advises today's date is Thursday, May 9, 1991, American broadcasting advisor, James Reinsch, who helped Winston Churchill with his "Iron Curtain" speech, is dead, aged 82, and…"your horoscope, under the sign of Sagittarius, says any relationships suffered from your harshness will be re-established this year."

*Fascinating.* Bennie never had one of these. Another flick of my hand and the news guy disappears. "You could at least have given me something I could use," I say to the gleaming tin can. It doesn't respond. "According to Earth's Gregorian Calendar my astrological sign is actually Ophiuchus," I say out loud—to no one. Only the most tuned in humans even know about this Zodiac sign, bestowed upon those born between November 30th-December 10th but I don't buy into bullshit like astrology.

What I do believe is that I don't make a good hybrid at all.

# THREE

# NOT WHO

A GLOWING SPHERE, an oversized egg about the size of a dresser, emerges from thin air just above my head. It expands and bifurcates. I'm too weak to run and the room too sparse to hide. The blubbery muscles on my legs jiggle and I'm not sure if it's from weakness or fear—or both. Flowy strands of white light sprout from each floating *egg*, and grow into limbs, a set of four legs now on the ground.

Two men in black stand before me, eerie chalk-colored skin, eyes so cold-clear blue I can't tell if they're peril or protection. They're unlike anything I've ever seen, even though I've seen plenty of guys in black suits—at Plum Hook Bay—Air Force intelligence they were. Reggie said those particular agents were "sheep-dipped", meaning they used to be military but got discharged and immediately brought back as private contractors so they can bend or break laws by intimidating private citizens who see things not meant for the majority of human eyes.

This weird looking duo in my room are not them—and I suspect, not even close to being human or hybrid. Now unscrambled, these black-suited beings stand shoulder-to-shoulder staring at me, each in possession of a red balloon tied around their wrist, the same sort of welcome balloon Barbara, Reggie's wife, once gave me back at NASA Plum Hook Bay, and Bennie stole.

Dread settles with a thud in my stomach as I rub my forehead, then my eyes. The men in black still stand, watch me, and say nothing. I must be sick like my mom. *Schizophrenia.* A complete break with reality. She's a guest of the Tiffin Ohio Lunatic Asylum. Reggie said someone slipped Avril too much LSD years ago when she too worked with the CIA, wanted to prevent her handing off some important file to her boss. My dad was no help. Not his fault though. He's still MIA in Viet Nam.

Grandma's church friends warned her this would happen. "The apple doesn't fall far from the tree," they said, thinking my mom a psycho loser, never knowing how much she secretly sacrificed so they could be free to judge her. After my grandma died, the church ladies wasted no time calling Cuyahoga County Children's Services for foster care placement and strongly suggested I receive psychiatric evaluation. When the first three tests came back *normal,* I was tested six more times. I was eight. No mom. MIA dad. No grandma. No family. "She won't grow up to be much," *they* said. Thus began my parade of foster homes, eight of them in eight years until I was sent to Plum Hook Bay.

To say I'm not comfortable with hospitals or bureaucracies for this very reason, *getting sick like my mom,* and then manhandled by strangers, is a grand understatement akin to describing stars as campfires. I hate institutions. Each has a way of making me feel guilty, frightened, or sick by simply stepping inside. I also carry a deeply embedded terror of having another quack shove me so far down a psych med rabbit hole, I might never return. A shiver skips along my spine remembering Dr. Evelyn Dennison. The beings in front of me still stand. If this is a hallucination, they appear solid enough to touch but I won't.

"You're definitely not hospital staff or in-house entertainment," I say, wondering if this is some sort of psyops test. "How'd you get in here?" I smack painfully cracked lips against a rusty throat and cautiously eye up this pair of overdressed icicles, wearing clothes without threads or seam but possessed of lines so perfect it would make a geometry teacher proud. They don't blink...at all!

"Use your brain to speak," the men in black say to me in unison, a telepathic communication, they're eerie faces completely expressionless, wiped clean of a single crease that might show me either kindness or cruelty. Good grief, give me some emotion, anything to let me know where I stand.

"Who are you?" I mentally ask, feeling queasy, and for some reason, ravenously hungry for strawberries. I shuffle toward them, playing a game of chicken, until they separate and move aside. I figure if they mean any harm, they could have exercised assassination options long before now. It's a lot easier to kill someone in a coma— who won't know it's coming. *They're real. They're here.* This is *not* a hallucination. I am not crazy, I tell myself, realizing I do have a few friends, doctors, and exe's who might counter my sudden declaration of sanity.

"Who are you?" I ask again, my back to them, trying to appear unafraid—but I am afraid. Since these 'men in black' understand the psychic complexity involved with telepathy, I do my best to bury the trepidation I feel—hiding it deep within the folds of my brain, where I hope it's too tight to tap into, something I was taught by Reggie when we studied *Remote Viewing*.

"Not Who," they mentally say.

"What?"

"I am Not Who, made manifest in a form you might understand."

I whirl around to face these freaks who now magically appear near the window. "How do you do that, move so fast?"

"We are Not Who," they answer.

"I hate riddles," I finally say. "Why do you use esco-tericism with me?"

The black suits look at one another and then rotate their heads in unison to stare me into intimidation, I think, until one of them finally says, "Esco-tericism? That is not a word of this planet. You must be careful. Earth beings already steal too much of our language and technology."

"Oh, so you *can* talk out loud," I say. "Good to know."

"I'd like to make you an offer," says the other.

"You've *got* to be kidding!" I huff and plop my ass bedside, annoyed, because those *exact* words once led me into a world of trouble approximately *six* years ago, when I initially agreed to accompany Dr.'s Dennison as their newest foster kid to NASA Plum Hook Bay. I had no choice. It was accept their offer or return to juvenile jail.

"Do you have a cigarette?" I ask.

"Smoking is not good for you," one says.

"Yea, okay," I say, averting my eyes. "I suppose waking up from a four-year IV junket is a good time to quit." I'm not craving a cigarette anyway. The nicotine rolled out of my system years ago, along with the THC and alcohol. Too bad. But the fruitless pounding on my hospital door, a desperate human exercise in futility and unnecessary noise, continues. "Can you make them sto…"

Before the words even leave my lips, **Not Who**, *finally* blinks…and then? Silence. It's as if everyone outside my door suddenly fell unconscious the way I did four years ago. It makes me think of a biblical proverb my grandmother once read: "*When you lie down, you will not be afraid; when you lie down, your sleep will be sweet.*"

My eyes zig-zag exploring every detail of these suited creatures, their shiny black shoes, pore-less, baby-powder colored faces, searching for answers to a lot of unanswered questions—but discover not a single one, as if Not Who's mind, if it even has a mind in the sense I understand a mind, has purposely gone "off air", their pale blue orbs a bright cloudless sky, never revealing depth or anything beyond the horizon of this moment.

"Fine," I finally say. "What *kind* of offer?"

"Your freedom in exchange for throwing Raga into the Source Vortex," one says.

"Oh, is that all? And Freedom from what?" I ask.

"Somewhere on this planet, Raga materialized. Earth is a particularly appealing place for Bezaliels like Raga. This planet's frequencies plummet enough for more of her kind to gain entrée and search for the Code of Everything."

Bezaliels. Vile beings. They roam realms and feed on planets. Usually, on Earth, people *feel* them as negative energy, but I've never heard of one crossing over, taking form. Then there's *The Word*, also known as *The Code of Everything*. It was split into a multitude of artifacts and writings, strewn like confetti all over this terrarium eons ago.

Humans had, over centuries, found pieces of 'The Word', sacred texts and such, upon which religions were established. But humans never thought to combine the unearthed codices, scrolls, texts or artifacts, they found. They hoarded, guarded, or killed each other for them instead, leading to a series of unfortunate events, and wars, that continue to this day. If humans ever did share their sacred discoveries, they'd learn to traverse black holes like turnpike tunnels—something Bezaliels hope to do—but the latter only wants it for the sake of gorging on other planets—not making them better, something humans would probably do too, Bennie said, if we let them. Hybrids like me are created to make sure the natives and the Bezaliels—and their offspring, the Nephilim, behave.

"Freedom from what?" I ask again, feeling less frightened, more in tune, as if this set of beings decided to turn my trepidation inside out and flip a switch in my head to bravery.

"Freedom from your humanness," Not Who says. "Freedom to travel among those of your kindred."

"I don't know what that means," I say, truthfully. The only thing I know and remember is *being human*, aside from some freakish otherworldly skill sets Reggie orders me to keep undercover. "Are you talking my certain death?"

The black suits look at one another quizzically, then at me. They shake their heads in unison but remain silent, looking down, literally burning a hole in the linoleum. There's smoke…

"Has anyone ever mentioned you are annoyingly creepy?" I ask. "Stop doing that!"

**Not Who** extinguishes the small flame with a dual foot stomp.

20

"I mean what I say," Not Who says. "You may travel freely among your kindred."

"What sort of form?" I ask, standing up again and reaching around to grasp the back of my hospital gown and keep it closed.

"Fully-fledged spiritual being," Not Who says. "Freedom to move about planets, galaxies, universes, dimensions, and perhaps, at times, to visit Ninmah's Portal, closer to The Source."

"My hybrid ecosystem is far from the epitome of health at the moment," I say. "I'm sure more worthy and stupid candidates roam the universe you might employ."

"You were specifically bred on this planet for this," Not Who says in unison. "If you don't want to help the multiverses, I can leave…"

The entities begin a steam-like fade.

"Wait!" I yell. "Do I have a choice?"

They, or *It*, returns to the form I understand, before uniformly and flatly answering, "You have free will."

"*Riiight*. We know that's a lie," I say. "Terms and conditions apply."

Not Who does the closest thing to a nod without a crack in face muscles. "Intransitivity, strategic dominance, or expected utility are superior to free will and present you with three additional choices."

"I'm not even going to pretend I know what you're talking about," I say. "But we still have a problem. How do I get out of here?"

"That's the easy part," Not Who says. "I'll split time."

"Split time?"

"Yes, but only for a fraction of a second because it warps the fabric of this reality."

"You can do *that?*" I ask.

"I slide two plates of time near a space boundary. It allows you to jump through, to somewhere else, but not here."

"Do you know Not Here too?" I ask.

"Who?" Not Who asks.

"Not Here," I say, satisfied by my clever joke and the fact I've kept pace with this creature's pure logic.

The men in black look at one another, simultaneously shrug, then look at me, cocking their heads in confusion.

"Never mind," I huff, blowing a red curl out of my face.

"Oh, yes, we know Never Mind," they say, as their lips tilt up. "Got. You."

"Your sense of humor is painfully sardonic. To where then?" I ask, trying to keep up with Not Who's modus ponens while my head spins.

"The technology is not perfect," Not Who says. "You will still be 'in the now', likely intact and not far away, but not here."

"*Likely?* Can you offer me better odds than *likely*, please?"

People stir outside my door.

"We have not much time to split time," says Not Who.

"How do I find this Raga thingy and get it to the Source Vortex?" I ask. "Where is the Source Vortex anyway? And what is it?"

"Find your Source Guide," Not Who says. "She will help you."

"You mean my fox?"

I feel a little guilty now. I never took the whole 'soul-guide' thing very seriously and considered it too much pressure for a wild red fox—one I named Hope and left behind the gates at NASA Plum Hook Bay—after Bennie presented her to me as a re-birthday gift. I couldn't exactly show up at Langley and tell the CIA she's my Source Guide. I'd be bounced out of the program faster than a comet and discredited as mentally unfit for duty.

"One should never leave behind their Soul Guide," Not Who says, uniformly shaking its heads, reading my mind.

"Fine. My freedom for this Raga bitch. Go!"

Not Who simultaneously reaches into a pocket of the other's suit, pulls out a silver pin, and pops it's red balloons...

# FOUR

## MAKONEN

SO, here I stand, six stories below where I woke up, on a busy city street, my ass hanging out from the back of a cheaply constructed 'Made in China' hospital gown. It's a cooler than expected afternoon, too chilly for my bare feet put to pavement. I tiptoe at first, pausing briefly after each step to feel dampness underfoot. I'm alive! *"Water is the most precious gift in the universe because it baptizes all sentient beings with life,"* Bennie used to say.

People gather, stare, point or otherwise look frighteningly appalled by my abrupt, disheveled appearance, compliments of two pale-faced, black-suited bozos, sent here from God only knows what realm. A wide-eyed little girl in hot-pink-bowed pigtails points at my strange bracelet and asks, "Mommy, what's that?" The woman covers the kid's eyes before they scurry down subway stairs faster than startled silver bugs. Other humans offer me wide berth, backing up along glass storefronts, mouths agape.

From around the corner of the building, four Army soldiers toting guns 'too big to miss', barrel toward me. "There she is! 001! Put your hands up! Get on the ground! Get on the ground right now!"

*001? Shit! That's ME!*

My legs sizzle with pain but that won't stop me. Soldiers bellow for me to stop or they'll shoot, which I know they won't, because whoever sent them knows that a living Golden Blood is worth a bazillion times more than a dead hybrid. The first alley I zig-zag through leads to a backstreet and onto a main drag. A rack of T-shirts hogs the sidewalk, and I slam into it cotton tees flying in all directions. Washington Monument looms in the distance less than a mile away.

Someone tugs on my flimsy dress, and without much effort, catapults me into the back of a vending truck. I land hard on a pile of soft clothing. The man in the Rastafarian hat crouches near as I raise a fist. "Shh." He says, gently wrapping two coconut-sized palms around my hands. "You need to trust me. You have no choice. Stay *dare* and be quiet."

He stands up and runs out of the truck flailing his arms. "Dis' crazy woman! She knock over my display, oh, mon. Look at dis dirt…ruined! Da wife, she will kill me."

Chatter from a soldier's radio, the stomping of feet, and then everything goes eerily quiet. Hand signals. I know that's what they're doing because I've watched hundreds of soldiers during training—and practiced alongside them at Plum Hook Bay. Through a narrow rusty crack that runs through the side of the trailer I notice one soldier's tipped down M-14. But an M-14 isn't Army issue, that's Marines, a selective fire, seven-point-six-two-by-five-one mm currently used as a marksman rifle. This is a Special Forces team sent to retrieve yours truly.

"Did you see her?" A Marine asks.

"Dis crazy woman wit her ahs hanging out of her shirt? She run into dee alley, dat way." The man says. "Go! If you find her, please, make her pay for dis' mess."

"Let's move! She's headed toward Federal Triangle! Someone radio Metro to shut down the trains. Not a single one goes out!"

The low hum of a helicopter—the same sort of repurposed Sikorsky MH-53 Pave Low the government used on the NASA side of Plum Hook Bay when it staged mock combat or search and rescue missions screams overhead. Burrowing myself further under a pile of clothes, the sound of blades fade so I listen for the Rastafarian man, ear up against the aluminum siding near the floor, and hear him a few yards away, speaking with another vendor, before he renters his truck.

"Why did you help me?" I ask, climbing out from under a pile of cheap t-shirts with bright letters that read, "Central Insurgence Agency" or "Federal Bureau of Ineptitude."

"You look like someone in need of help," he says, surveying the tumbled contents of his vending truck.

"I'm sorry about the mess," I say, not feeling guilty, and wondering if he's some new world version of a Black Panther who hates the government and hopes to overthrow it.

"No worries," he says. "Here, you look hungry." He extends a solidly sculpted right arm toward me, holding a gyro, one that overflows with freshly cut lamb from a spit, and oozes with onions, cucumbers, and yogurt.

"What makes you think I'm hungry?" I ask.

"From the looks of you, I tink you haven't eaten in a while," he says, glancing at the iron cuff on my wrist.

"Thanks," I say, not taking my eyes off of him. Lamb juice and tzatziki dribbles down my chin. He hands me a napkin. "Thanks," I say again, snagging pita and meat out of the foil like a wild animal, a few cucumbers falling into my lap where I leave them. "I can't believe those Marines didn't search your truck...just to be sure I wasn't here."

"Most times, people miss what is right in front of 'dem." He smirks and looks at the floor.

"Not those guys," I say with mouthful of food. "They're professionals."

"I would think 'dat Dr. Evelyn taught you better etiquette," he says. He points to a greasy spot on my chin.

My mouth comes to a complete stop. An urge to fight or take flight revs my nerves into action and sets my head to spin. My eyes search the depths of his pupils—to determine if I face a new and even worse sort of danger. Reggie always said you can tell a person's next move by looking into his or her eyes—that they'll give away a microsecond of intention on where they plan to strike.

"It's good to slow down or you might choke…or puke," the man says. He shifts his eyes and sifts through a pile of t-shirts, carelessly tosses the lot into black garbage bags, the exact same kind I was handed in 1984, to shove my limited possessions into, before being transferred, without notice, to NASA Plum Hook Bay.

"How do you know Dr. Evelyn?" I ask, slowly realizing that this, him being here, isn't some random event. Laying the wrapper aside, it takes little effort for me to stand this time, and move toward the back door of his vending truck.

"It's okay," he says. "I'm not going to hurt you. I promise. I only know *of* her. I am Makonen." He uses a napkin to sop up some of the sauce that runs down my wrist but I jerk back. He looks at my metal bracelet and shakes his head.

"Are you some sort of black rights activist?" I ask.

"I am a Buddhist. You want dis ting off?" he asks.

I nod, his copper-colored eyes growing warm when he looks at me again. My ability to read auras, I admit, feels more than a bit rusty.

"Hold out your wrist, like dis," Makonen says as he shows me.

I tentatively offer him my wrist. "Do you know what this is?" I ask.

"This," he points to the bracelet, "is a Dream Stealer."

"A Dream Stealer?"

Makonen lifts the sleeve of his tunic and flips his wrist toward me. Two puncture wounds, one on each side of a protruding tendon runs into his coffee-colored palm. "The DOE siphons memories and dreams of hybrids. It uploads them into ether systems for storage."

"You're hybrid?"

"From Alphion Proximal C," he says.

Floodgates of relief wash over me because Alphion Proximals are warrior empaths who's code is built upon duty, trust, and loyalty. Buddhism is their usual Earthly philosophy of choice but they aren't born here, they sneak in and out to help Camaeliphims and humans.

"Why does the DOE steal our memories?" I ask.

"To learn from us," he says. "There exist many types of hybrids...some manmade, or as we might say, 'biotechnical', and others created between man and what humans might consider otherworldly beings...some of us are even created between beings from other worlds."

Bennie told me years ago that the Atomic Energy Commission changed its name to DOE (Department of Energy), in order to throw off politicians and the public, to sound less foreboding after people protested against its nuclear programs. The clever nomenclature is meant to hide heinous experiments behind ultra-boring electrical data or complicated engineering projects.

"What does the DOE do with our memories and dreams?" I ask.

"It destroys them," he answers. "It steals and stores our ancestral memories, codes of time, or any celestial knowledge hidden within cell membranes. But the DOE's retrieval process is faulty when it comes to hybrids. It's Dream Stealers upload mostly misinformation."

"How is this possible?" I ask.

"Hybrid cells mutate and this keeps the DOE in the dark," Makonen says with another chuckle.

"Good," I say, adding a heavy frown for measure. "But why are you working in a souvenir truck?"

"I've been waiting for you to awaken. It is an honor and a privilege to meet a noble Golden Blood. Now hold still and don't be frightened. You must not move a muscle. Can you do dis for me?"

I feel far from noble at the moment. I'm a grunt birthed here in half-human form because the 'Nobles' in this spiral galaxy, some of them my own relatives, refuse to dirty their proverbial robes. "Did you send the black suited beings to my room?" I ask.

"I did not," Makonen says, a look of astonishment crossing his face. "*It* visited you?"

"Yes," I say. "Who is it?"

"Not Who," he says. "This is a rare event indeed to have Not Who directly intervene."

I look at him confused. "Wha…"

Makonen puts up his palm to me like Reggie used to do when he was finished answering questions. He refocuses on my bracelet and takes a deep breath. His eyes go royal blue and remind me of the Astral Weavers I once met at Plum Hook Bay. I thought they were dead the day I stumbled over them in a cave, until their eyes glowed with the exact same phosphorescence. Astral Weavers are tasked with patching rips and tears in this universe, holes that threaten balance between realms.

Makonen opens his left hand, spreads his fingers wide, and hovers it under my clandestine cuff, his energy pleasantly warming my forearm. Wisps of shimmery spirals rise up from his palm to encircle the bracelet until it glows molten orange, drops off, and disappears. Not a burn or mark on me, save for two painless puncture wounds on my wrist, which match Makonen's.

"We are now twins," he jokes.

"That's awesome! How did you do that?" I ask, cupping and turning two fingers and a thumb around my relieved skin.

"It takes centuries of discipline," he says, tossing me a satisfied smile, one born of quiet, studied enlightenment, and possessed of way more patience, and probably smarts, than I have. "You must precisely tune your inner frequency toward the Source. I am only capable of influencing small objects. Some of my elders are able to part oceans, even planets."

"Wow," I whisper, studying my arm more closely, looking for any delayed signs of injury. "Do those of my kindred possess this ability?" I ask, hoping I might learn how to do this.

"All beings possess such abilities," Makonen says. "Even humans. But few have the discipline to learn secret knowledge held within the Akashic Record."

"Akashic Record?"

"A compendium of universal history, knowledge, thoughts, emotions, energy, and intent," he says.

"Oh, is that all?" I say with a laugh. But I do file his answer away for later research. "What about my memories and dreams? Can you give them back to me?"

"'Dis I cannot do," he says. "But there is a being on Earth able to help you. Shh, listen."

"I don't hear anything," I whisper.

Makonen holds up a palm again. "Precisely. It's too quiet..." he whispers. "...When the street dis' quiet...Samantha, you must go."

"But they won't kill me," I say.

"They will not kill you," Makonen says. "They will re-contain you for further study. Head to the Tidal Basin and cross into Franklin Roosevelt Memorial Park. You will be met. Go, now..."

"But..."

Makonen tosses me a t-shirt and sweatpants. I hurriedly slide the loose clothes over my frame, the black sweats too short, so I push them up to my knees—and stuff a lone pocket with a buckeye he gives me. He shoves me through the back door of his trailer where I stumble backward, stunned for a moment after landing with a hard thud on concrete. He leaps over me and lunges at a soldier.

I struggle to my feet as Makonen pulls a grenade from his jacket.

"No!" I yell.

Makonen releases the pin.

***BAM!***

Shots fired.

Alphion Proximal down.

People scream, duck, and scramble.

Charred skin dust settles over me as I bolt toward the river, adrenaline pushing my pencil legs with renewed energy, through narrow streets pockmarked with dented garbage cans and dark green bags spilling over with Styrofoam fast-food containers, and drained coffee cups, past a bus stop, and a crumbling lot where gang graffiti marks territory with a rainbow of spray paint, over a small bridge traversing a concrete courtyard full of trendy restaurants and shops catering to overworked lawyers and lobbyists who amble out of nearby high-rises.

I wish I could have gotten to know Makonen better, this hybrid who gave his life to save mine, and maybe even this world too. Sweaty ash grime sticks to my arms, grit I don't even bother to remove, a solemn reminder of human-hybrid mortality, repentance, and our rapid return to dust.

# FIVE

# VIGO

HOW AM I supposed to cross the Tidal Basin?

I can't fly—at least not yet. I dip my big toe into the water, spinning it until little ripples form undulating rings of expanding waves. "*BRRRRR!*"

I have no idea who my contact is on the other side because I never had the opportunity to ask Makonen. It's even more unsettling he's gone from this world, *poof*, just like that, and I never got to know him. I suspect any creature willing to die for another must be damn decent.

Streetlights bring a soft glow to this cozy shoreline park as people go about their business, paying me little mind, generally averting eye contact, I suspect, because my unwashed appearance, shoeless feet, and greasy hair screams homeless, drug-addicted stereotype, one who might beg for help or a handout. I squint across the basin into a dense silhouette of trees, searching out the best entry point. A crew of recreational workers line paddleboats against the shoreline...

...The pedals smoke, which burns a hole in the bottom of the craft, it takes on water, and I churn my legs as if trying to win the Tour De France.

Some guy launches another paddle boat to come after me as people onshore shout and gesture, a storm line of protest loaded with nothing resembling brotherly love, but instead, spittle loaded cheers or jeers, the more conscionable voices drowned out by base suggestions.

My little boat slowly goes under, its yellow plastic frame and big red inflexible tires melting into the murky tidal basin, a sluggish descent of *clug clug clug...*

...I hover two inches above water.

A flash of light from shore nearly costs me my balance. I shield my face with a hand.

"Damn," I whisper. It wouldn't be DC if tourists or reporters weren't camera ready to snap a monument or scandal, or in my case, a monumental scandal. "I'm going to catch hell for this." People onshore drop their jaws, their ropes, their kids, and lift pointer fingers, gasp, scream, or stare. The first rule of Septum Oculi is I'm not supposed to let humans without the proper 'cosmic clearance' witness my skill sets. Why? It fucks up everything they've ever been taught about *God* and leaves them to grapple with leftover confusion.

Humans learn about angels in the mythological sense, but when confronted in person, complete shock almost always supersedes faith. I suppose that's because Camaeliphim look rather human and humans can't fly...allegedly. And contrary to myth, Camaeliphim do not walk around with big white wings attached to our backs that flare open like peacock feathers for dramatic effect. The cherubim and seraphim are the only *angels* outfitted with built-in pinions, but, unfortunately, they're almost extinct. They were hunted as a delicacy by Xoogs, creatures that my kind exterminated thousands of Nibiru orbits ago.

The guy in the paddle boat completely tips his ride into the water, and thankfully, performs one of the fastest breath strokes I've ever witnessed, safely back to shore. An old lady in a floral skirt and yellow cardigan sweater, who'd been feeding a gaggle of ducks, makes the sign of the cross. Others run screaming. The rest of the humans gawk at a levitating half-hybrid freak rocking every foundation they know about the logical order of physics and religion.

Humans *can* train themselves to levitate, translocate, or see auras. A few humans succeed in such feats, no guru, manual, or steering wheel required. Unfortunately, they too, like me, are swiftly whisked away by secret agencies for further study, discredited as charlatans, or put away as mental patients. Or worse —they wind up dead. *So,* keeping humans controlled, I've learned, is the order of this planet's rotation. Religion and politics are the most frequently used methods of domination because each requires an enemy to fight in order to thrive, something humans conjure in abundance.

I lower my head and float across the river wondering what Barbara would think of my water-walk lasting longer than Peter the Apostle's. Unfortunately, I'm too weak to gain altitude and crash-land short of the opposite shore, getting baptized by the unholy waters of the DC Tidal Basin, a fall that would make her laugh and say, "That's what you get for showing off!"

"Fuck my life," I say, the human part of me feeling angry and fearful I'll be recaptured. Reggie always said fear causes people to sink fast.

*"Grrrrrrr..."* Squinting into darkness I can't locate what is attached to the menacing growl. I remember White Bigfoot back at Plum Hook Bay, but this new snarl sounds less menacing and there's no Sulphur-like scent in the air that used to accompany the creature I spotted roaming NASA's woodland, munching on pine-cones, and scaring the crap out of us kids.

Again, I'm caught between two yucky-no-good options. I can't go forward and I can't turn back. A decision must be made—the lesser of two evils, Dr. Evelyn would say—and I'm sure as hell not returning to a coma-induced 'no-life' of inanimation at some non-descript hellhole passing as a covert pseudo-quasi-military hospital.

My mind wanders to what Dr. Evelyn and Dr. Sterling might be doing right now as I try to figure out what's next, a light fog drifting into the woods and through my head. Barbara told me Dr.'s Dennison left Plum Hook Bay after their respective commissions were cancelled, that they retired to Oxford in the U.K. with plans to travel the world. I don't buy that. Both of them worked for Septum Oculi (SO), the eyes of the world, even though I found Dr. Evelyn's methods and motives suspect. There's no way SO would send Drs. Dennison. Inc. out to pasture, they're too valuable.

I creep through the labyrinth of trees, dodging and peering around bulky dampened trunks. I drop for a belly crawl and slither along the ground, the same way Reggie taught me to reach the juiciest blueberries from under a bush. He also tutored me on the art of remaining motionless but I find it difficult to sit still, unless maybe my life is at stake. Reggie told me human snipers train themselves to remain statue still for hours, a finger settled on the trigger, in order to 'make the kill'. He said if they could do this, so could I. It will probably take me as long to learn stillness as it did for humans to build Notre Dame. The sniper skills elude me too. I'm not very good with guns.

Picking at a small piece of tree bark that crumbles like cookie dough in my palm, I wonder about my Jiu-Jitsu skills, how rusty they might be. It's been years since I grappled. Maybe martial arts is like learning to ride a bike, where it isn't be completely forgotten. Still, I highly doubt my ability to disarm a highly trained soldier or take down a threat after an involuntary four-year nap.

*Breathe, Sam.*

Something is out there. I *feel* it—near me—but see no aura. I *sense* it searching, hear it rooting around. My human instinct is to put my head down, close my eyes, and hope it goes away—but I realize that any decent beast will eventually fetter me out—so I stand—to fight—or attempt to fight and get confronted by a monument, upon which, is carved a quote:

**"The structure of world peace cannot be the work of one man,**

*or one party, or one nation…it must be a peace which rests on the cooperative effort of the whole world…"*

"*Grrrrrr…*" It's behind me. I rotate my spine, turn my feet toward the danger, heart galloping in my chest, the hair on my forearms at full attention, waiting for whatever it is to attack.

"*Sarge?*"

It can't be.

Sarge is buried at Plum Hook Bay under a huge willow tree. I remember how he wanted a piece of Dr. Evelyn the first day I arrived, barking, growling and sliming up her side of the car window. This German Shepherd standing less than ten feet away, sure looks like Sarge. He whines—a low whistle sort of song, before he lets out a lengthy high-pitched howl.

*Shit! I'm in trouble!*

*Run!*

*No. Don't. Don't panic, Sam.*

*Breathe. Don't run.*

"Hey boy," I say. "*Shhhh…*" I pat an index finger to my lips before holding up a palm the way Rakito, another Plum Brook foster kid once did with a wolf named Randolph, a calming gesture, he told me. Rakito, regularly used this approach on lions in Africa—to steal their meat.

"*GRRRRRRRRRR…*"

"It appears I'm no Rakito…" I whisper to the animal.

The dog snaps at the air but doesn't strike. He's huge, his head almost reaches my chest. Muscles ripple beneath glistening rain-wet black and tan fur. I'm not sure why this military dog hasn't latched his jaws into my forearm the way most K9's are taught to do when hunting down perps. His long pink tongue hangs out one side of his snout, his shockingly yellow eyes trained on me like a laser target. He barely moves another muscle in his well-bred shiny fur body, except to pant, exuding an almost Zen-like calm before he slowly turns in a circle. "*Woof,*" he quietly barks.

The dog approaches me, bends his front legs to the ground in front of me, and rolls over, exposing his belly. *What the hell?* I've never seen a military dog suddenly turn docile. Reaching out a shaky hand I scratch his fur-lined underside. He seems to like this but his bizarre behavior as a military animal confuses me. These types of dogs rarely make friends outside their handlers. They're taught to clamp their jaws around flesh and not let go, unless an arm comes off, potentially making a newly chewed off limb ripe for playing fetch.

The German Shepherd bolts upright and trots away from me into darkness. But he stops, turns around. All the muscles in my body tense when he gets behind me. I feel his snout on my back. Tightening my fists, I control my breathing. I got this far. I am not going back to that awful facility. The dog nudges me forward in the direction of the road.

"Really? We're going to have a *Lassie* moment?" I ask, shaking my head in disbelief. He wags his tail and licks my face. "You must be my point of contact. Okay, okay, stop!" I stuff stiff, cold-stung fingers into the thin pockets of my sweatpants. "Okay, big boy," I say. "Where do you want me to follow?"

Through the park, around boulders and benches, toward a lonely street we go until the animal stops near an empty utility road. He's young and majestic looking under the low light of streetlamps—a fine breed of animal. No wonder German Shepherds are the dog of choice when it comes to military operations—but this one? I'm skeptical about this lug of a dog. He seems *off*...too nice for police work. The dog squats beside me.

"Really? You can't take a piss someplace else?" I ask, leaning into his fur for warmth. He whimpers, looks at me funny, and pulls away a little bit.

"What?" I ask.

The dog stares ahead and ignores me...waiting...for something. Headlights the size of fireflies slowly amble toward us until they grow to double flashlights and I shrink inside, hoping to disappear. Then I stand, readying my legs for another run but the dog firmly bites into the waistband of my sweats, shakes his head, and tugs my ass down, into the road. "What the hell are you doing?" I ask. "I didn't make it this far for a damn dog to set me up as roadkill!"

A van stops. It's side door slowly slides open. "Need a ride?" A familiar voice asks.

The hair on my forearms involuntarily rise.

"Reggie? What in the hell are you doing here?" It's one of the few times I'm overjoyed to see him but won't tell him that.

"We don't have time for reunion mush, you hi-falutin' city girl…you want a ride or not?" He asks, face forward, eyes on the road.

"Yes. I may need to phone a lawyer."

"Is that so?" He grins at our old joke between friends.

"How the fuck did Makonen signal you I'd be here?" I ask. I climb into the passenger side as the dog hurdles a seat and settles behind me.

"Whew!" Reggie says waving his hand in front of his face.

"What?" I ask.

"You need a shower," he says. "You stink!"

"It's the dog," I say, glaring at Reggie.

"No," Reggie says laughing, "I'm pretty sure it's *you!*"

"What's up with the dog?" I ask.

"That's no dog," Reggie answers. "That's Vigo—my soul guide."

"*YOUR* soul-guide? *YOU…you* have a soul-guide? I never saw this dog at Plum Hook Bay…"

Reggie showers me with a disapproving stare. "That's because you were blind to him," he says. "He's the protégé of Sarge. Damn good companion, too. And, unlike some careless hybrids I know, I don't make a habit of leaving *my* soul-guide behind."

# SIX

# VERITY LANE

"LIFE IS about to get a whole lot worse for everyone," Reggie says.

"Why?" I ask.

I towel dry my spirally hair in front of a rusted barrel, one that now doubles as a fire pit. Between the curl and its color, my unruly locks draw about as much unwanted attention as a blowtorch. I consider asking Reggie to borrow his knife to cut it all away—until I remember what Barbara, his wife said, about long hair being a woman's 'crowning glory'—and realize—I'm too vain for such drastic measures. Instead, I cram what I can of my red nest into a camouflage cap.

"When people get scared, they do crazy things," he says. He hands me a cup of hot chocolate, no sugar, just the way I love it.

"People have *always* been scared," I say, fighting off the distinct feeling of being watched, even though we conducted an 'all clear' and found only a few chatty rats and one shaken raccoon. "Fear is seeded into mortals."

Vigo meanders over and nudges his muzzle on my lap after I settle into a dilapidated office chair. I glide a palm over a soft spot between his yellow eyes. He glances around guilty-like, eyeing up the mug with elevated hope. "No can do," I say. "Colonel Reggie taught me years ago that dogs are deathly allergic to chocolate."

A scowl skitters along the top of Vigo's fuzzy caterpillar eyebrows.

"We have an unprecedented number of beings who wind up dead, particularly among this planet's remote tribes," Reggie continues. "Every first world country is firing blame toward every other country and nobody knows why it's happening, why these indigenous populations are suddenly the target of unseen, unknown death squads. Vigo! Go lie down!"

The dog whimpers but does as he's told, giving Reggie a disapproving 'whisper-woof' as he saunters into a corner.

"Don't get smart with me, Vigo. You know what happened last time you showed your ass."

The dog rolls his eyes and body in a semi-circle, then plops on a crumpled pile of khaki colored wool blankets. He turns his back from Reggie, letting loose with a disgruntled snort.

"You still don't make friends, easily, do you?" I chuckle. "But...what's your take? On all of this?"

Reggie turns off the hotplate inside this abandoned space somewhere outside of Fairfax, Virginia. This 'building' is actually wedged into a mountainside, obscured from a dirt road by hordes of tightly packed pines that surge and swell over wide ripples of Appalachian foothills. A mishmash of steel beams and old timber rafters are tightly sewn together overhead to brace against the weight of the mountain, which bears down from all sides.

"This decommissioned facility was used to store weapons and to train soldiers in the art of battlefront triage," Reggie says.

I nod, remembering how he trained me to do the same thing. I mentally push back on the sound of squealing pigs in my head.

"I think we have very unwelcome, uninvited visitors to this planet that mean everyone, hybrid or human, harm..." he says, poking a piece of rusty rebar into the flames until cinders swirl above our heads like disturbed hornets. "Dr. Sterling Dennison registered something very strange when he split those neutrinos back at NASA," Reggie says. "I don't understand it all, but I'm trying."

"What did Dr. Sterling find?" I ask, feeling uneasy.

"I'm not sure but I think..." he sucks in a breath. "I think some damn demons broke through another dimension when he oscillated those particles and now a band of them are here."

"Reggie," I say, laughing. "I think you're wife's sermons are wearing on you. Maybe you should invest in earplugs."

"Hear me out," he says. "Everything at NASA Plum Hook Bay happened *after* Dr. Dennison figured out neutrinos change form after they're split. That's when all the weirdness began. He couldn't risk his clearance or my cover by talking with me, so I went to Bennie, to ask him some questions. You remember that light in the sky?"

"Of course I do," I say. "How could any of us forget *that*? I couldn't eat or sleep for days. Did you ever find out what it was?"

Reggie shakes his head. "No," he says. "Except that it wasn't NASA's. The DOE had no idea what it might be either and that, I could tell, made all those high clearance folks real nervous."

"Why did you go to Bennie?" I ask. "I'm surprised you'd solicit a kid for debriefing."

"He's not '*just a kid*' and you know it," Reggie says, poking the fire a bit harder now. Angry molten embers rise until the crisp air cools and calms each one into ashy carcasses, which drift to settle on a pile of tossed bricks. "He was the most intelligent hybrid within a three galaxy radius."

"Bennie was the weirdest kid I ever met," I say, thinking about how his words and mannerisms seemed decades older than the thirteen year-old I so now miss. "Dr. Evelyn told me Bennie was a super genius, that his indefatigable mind was the result of trauma. He rarely played, slept even less, and spent most of his time alone, cooped up in his lab."

"He was forced to work," Reggie says. "Once the DOE figured out he was hyper-intelligent and a hybrid, he became the property of the US government and was labeled 'above top-secret'."

"His lab was above top-secret too," I say. "It was far advanced from anything I've ever seen with its holographic quantum computers and high-grade off-Earth chemicals."

"Dr. Sterling shared a lot with that kid," Reggie says. "Bennie was like a son to him. When you rolled into Silo Fifty-Seven, it caused the DOE a lot of heartburn."

"Why?" I ask.

"I'm not sure," Reggie says. "All I do know is that Bennie demanded you not be harmed and allowed to continue to visit him. He threatened to stop working if Project Blue Bird remanded you to a cage below the nuclear reactor site."

"I had no idea," I say.

An involuntary shudder forces its way along my spine. The underside of the NASA Plum Hook Bay nuclear reactor was a place no human being would ever want to visit, located more than two miles underground.

"No one told you," Reggie says. "After you came face-to-face with a Nephilim down there, and killed it, the DOE stamped you as its property too."

"Bennie took me there," I said. "We found his sister and those other kids too. They were…" I can't continue because the lump in my throat grows too big. "We were all government property the moment those gates closed behind us."

Unpleasant memories from that god awful place flood my brain, ready to swallow me up. I close my eyes to keep the pain from seeping through. *Turn it off! Turn it off like a faucet!*

Reggie's palm touches my forearm, a rare show of empathy that brings me back to now. "You're not going in that direction," he says. "You may be government property but you're an adult now, you have some say so about your life."

"But I'll never be free," I say.

"Someday you will," he says.

And we both know he means not in this lifetime.

"Bennie was the 'go to guy' for us foster kids at Plum Hook Bay, the 'imperfect eleven', he called us," I say. What I don't say is we appealed to Bennie whenever we required explanations for supernatural events. His answers rarely strayed from the technical except for an occasional foray into paranormal expositions. Bennie could be drier than a drained camel hump during a Saharan high noon, or as animated as a laser light, depending on the day, and his mood. "What did Bennie say?" I ask.

"Goofiest shit I ever heard," Reggie says. "He told me that a couple of Bezaliels took form here under the leadership of Basaseal."

"Who's Basaseal?" I ask.

"A demon briefly mentioned in the *Book of Enoch*," Reggie says.

"I know the book," I say. "But I don't know the name Basaseal. Verity told me about Enoch when we were kids at Plum Hook Bay. She said Enoch was allegedly given secret sacred knowledge straight from God. She warned me that the Book of Enoch is apocryphal. Bennie was there. He disagreed. He said humans didn't have the clearance for Enoch's canons and that he and I could speak the mutating language of Enochians, that we could decipher the book—but Verity, being pure human, could not."

"Angels of God," Reggie says as he rocks back a bit on his black lace combat boots.

"I don't buy the whole angels of God hype," I say, "but Bennie did lock Verity in a steamer trunk so we could converse, in Enochian. I could speak the language…it just came to me that day, which I found weird."

Reggie's lips curl. "You mean you don't buy the fire and brimstone God you were taught as a child?"

"I mean I don't believe in *any* God," I say. "What could God possibly find interesting about our piddly little lives in the grand scheme of a cosmos?"

Reggie shakes his head. "Still got a grudge against God, huh?"

"Can't keep hard feelings about something that doesn't exist," I say. "We're like amoeba to any real god, I would think."

"You speak Enochian?" He asks, discarding the rebar and turning away from the fire.

"I can't remember a single word of it right now."

"Hmm," Reggie says. "Verity Lane sounds as if she'd be useful about now. Wasn't she your best friend at Plum Hook Bay?"

"She's still my best friend," I say. "Well, I think of her that way. A lot of years have passed. I'm sure she has a new best friend by now. Do you know where she is? Did she go to law school? Did she get her dad out of the brig?"

"Slow down," Reggie says. "I thought you wanted to hear what Bennie said?"

"I do."

"Bennie told me Basaseal is rarely recorded among sacred texts, a fact Bezaliels count upon to keep their kind hidden among humans," he says. "We don't know much about Basaseal except he's beyond redemption. Bennie said that even chaos cringes when Basaseal is near."

"Where is the Book of Enoch?" I ask. "I never actually saw it at Plum Hook Bay."

"Fragments of it were found in a Qumran cave about 1948 and are in the custody of the Israel Antiquities Authority," Reggie says.

"Have the fragments been deciphered?"

"Once," Reggie says, "before the language mutated. The book is…"

"Scattered all over the globe," I say, cutting him off. "It's part of a code that includes artifacts and places too, damn near impossible to find, let alone decipher—but it must be done—or this planet is fucked."

Reggie purses his lips and nods.

I think about Plum Hook Bay, and how, for a month, Mother Nature went on some histrionic rampage, turning midsummer leaves gray-crunch dead overnight and it snowed—in August, in Ohio, in 1984. The Huron River froze solid and hundreds of cardinals showed up, which somehow kept me sane and offered small comfort, their bright red feathers like checkmarks against a white-out landscape. I've never felt that sort of fear, before or since, an evil so rancid and palpable, firing up every nerve fiber I had. Something was closing in on us behind those NASA gates, hiding just on the other side of our realm, waiting...

...I shiver back to reality and glance around at empty ammo cases, tank parts, pipes, thin stockpiles of sheet metal, and various tools rusting in organized compartments under decades of dust. I can almost hear the clank of metal, the battered sighs of soldiers, and the noise of war, mingling with the scent of stale blood and pig shit, the sort of place a Bezaliel might find homey. I hover my nose above hot chocolate to quell the unpleasant. I fight off a gnawing, creepy feeling that Reggie and I are not alone. Vigo stares down a pitch-black hallway, registering dim concern, perhaps over a rat or wayward squirrel, so I try to relax.

"This site was used to wound pigs," Reggie says, sensing my edginess.

"Smells about right," I say. "I never really understood why you stabbed or shot pigs in the barn at Plum Hook and then expected me to save them."

"It's a soldier's job to calm the pig and secure its wound before it bleeds to death," he says. "It's good training."

"I was a kid," I say, peering at him accusingly over the rim of my mug. "Why would I ever want to save anything I plan to kill?"

"The skill isn't learned for what you plan to kill, but for those who get hurt along the way you might be able to save."

Our eyes meet in standoff until I relinquish my stare. I take a sip and study him. "Where's Barbara?" I finally ask. "Is she in the area?"

"No. She's safe—with a guy I know," he says. "He owns a defunct underground nuclear missile site just outside Plattsburgh, New York."

"Oh, wow—*he* has to be hating *that*," I say, feeling sorry for anyone held captive to one of Barbara's relentless sermons.

"He's fine," Reggie says smiling. "The silo owner invested in earplugs. My wife feeds him daily doses from the Bible and three squares a day in her effort to save his soul."

We both laugh out loud and it lightens my heart.

"Barbara believes everyone on this planet should be saved by

Jesus Christ," I say.

"She claims it's her personal responsibility to ensure a sinner's blood is not left on her hands," Reggie says. "Metaphorically speaking."

Barbara serves up her sermons alongside heaping helpings of homemade chicken and dumplings, which makes the former a hell of a lot more pleasant to digest. Most people and hybrids, including me, can't help but like her. She's a good wife to Reggie and they're the happiest couple I know—unlike Dr. Evelyn and Dr. Sterling, they're marriage more of an aloof arrangement of tolerance bolstered by busy careers and long absences.

"From what does the missile silo guy need to be saved?" I ask.

"Himself," Reggie answers. "Like most of us."

My mouth involuntarily salivates when I think about Barbara's homemade biscuits and gravy served up with lightly seasoned wild polk leaves. Best damn food I ever had in my life. I'd never even heard of 'polk leaves' until Barbara pointed them out to me in the woods at Plum Hook Bay. We gathered up as many as we could and she simmered a small batch, using a dash of vinegar and her favorite seasonings, a hodge-podge of dried wild herbs, her secret recipe, she'd said. "But don't eat the buckeyes," she warned me. "They're poison unless properly prepared." The *hetuk*, the "Eyes of God," she called them, and I always carried one with me—until I lost it. I finger the buckeye in my pocket Makonen gave me right before he blew himself up.

Reggie and I sit in silence for a moment, hearing nothing but the sound of our breath and the occasional scurry of rodents—just like old times. So much of my past is foggy—like my dad's face or how I came to be born of a human mother, or what exactly happened to me after I took a poisoned dart. But other parts—the *otherworldly* extensions of my existence, occasionally reveal themselves within snippets of subconscious—blurry ghosts and sneaky shadows momentarily recaptured in visions—of something hauntingly familiar but just out of mind reach…a former life or two…or three…or four hundred.

"Did you know Makonen?" I ask.

"I posted him outside that building to keep watch."

"He gave his life to save me," I say.

Reggie pulls a joint from his shirt pocket, lights it, and then passes it to me. "Makonen has returned among my kindred," he says. "Here, this will help your cells heal."

"*You?* You're an Alphion Proximal?" I inhale deeply, enjoying the smoky pine-tar taste before I cough and cough again. "Damn, Reggie, you grow the best shit."

"I've got human in me too," he says. "Let me see your wrist."

I knew there was more to Reggie and suspected as much back at Plum Hook Bay. I'd watch soldiers become visibly shaken if they pissed him off—the hair on their necks and forearms stiffen, just as it does for me—and for Vigo too. I once watched him take a soldier down with a quick pinch to his neck nerve.

I fling my wrist at Reggie and search his face for any sign of grief over Makonen. If he's sad, it doesn't show. Reggie doesn't talk much and hides his feelings under decades of special ops training. He's sturdy and reliable, a loyalty born from hard fought honor and loss, his skin the color of dark walnut, loaded with scars and dents, but indispensable as a warrior, mentor, and friend. Reggie curses so low I don't hear what he says. "They were looking through your blood."

"I know. Makonen told me," I say. "Did you send Not Who to my room, too?"

"Not Who?"

"A being in matching black suits," I say. "At least I think it was a being—or creature. It split time and pushed me through its gap so I could escape from that god-forsaken high-rise. It's how I wound up near Makonen."

"It came to see you?" he asks, an unusual micro-quiver of whistle surprise escaping Reggie's lips. "*It?*"

"Come on," Reggie rises from the ammo trunk he's been using as a bench. He tosses me a rucksack. "Makonen told me he wasn't strong enough to split that building to get you out. It seems we have another visitor on this planet besides Bezaliels."

"Where are we going?" I ask.

"You want back what the DOE took from you?"

"You mean my dreams and memories?"

"Yes."

"You can do that?" I ask.

"No," he says. "Your mother can."

"My mom?" My heart kicks up a gear. "But she's locked up in some Ohio looney bin, right? How can she help?"

"What humans view as her insanity..." Reggie says, "...more advanced civilizations know as her illumination to higher realms. I think it's time the two of you become reacquainted."

"She can undo what the DOE did to me?"

"No guarantees," he says. "She might shed light on *Not Who*. Would you like to see her?"

"Of course, I would," I say. "It's just that...well? I'm..."

"A little nervous?" He asks.

"Yes. Will she remember me?"

"I don't know," he says. "Would you like some social support?"

"No offense Colonel but I don't think you're right for the part," I say.

"Oh, hell no..." Reggie protests, folding his barrel arms across his chest. "I didn't mean *me!*"

He lets loose with a low bird whistle that causes Vigo to come to full attention, his eyes still focused on the pitch-black hallway.

From the innards of this building, a shadow stretches toward us, the *click, click, click* of heels to cement. Reggie cups a palm over my right shoulder, but I, out of habit, ready a defensive posture. Someone rustles past unkempt parachutes—a woman my age, silk blouse, black skirt, confident posture—and all the memories of our sixteen-year-old selves flash through my head, except this time, the formal, self-contained vision before me doesn't quite match my candid snapshots of henna tattoos, colored rosaries, purple gloves, or mixing Paganism with Christianity because, as she used to say, "Shit happens."

"Hello, Ti-fi," Verity Lane says.

# SEVEN

# THE EYE OF PROVIDENCE

ROOM 355 of the Tiffin Lunatic Asylum—that's where I'm headed. It angers me that officials still use the term *lunatic* in 1991. My mom is not a *lunatic*. She's the victim of a covertly administered LSD overdose, compliments of someone/s moving within deep government circles who wanted her dead.

"They used to lobotomize female patients here to combat 'menstrual' issues," Verity says, laying a palm to her belly with a wince.

"You're not helping," I say. "I brought you with me for moral support, remember?"

"They say this place is cursed," she adds. "I wonder if Bezaliels lurk."

"Verity, we aren't Bezaliel hunters today."

She clutches my forearm for correction. "We are *always* on the hunt for Bezaliels."

Reggie leads us through security on another part of the grounds. It's far from main campus and looks like a park, except I don't see a single patient outside...and that makes me suspicious. Fresh air and exercise must be better therapy for spooled up minds than a slow roast brain simmer percolating between the confines of sterile walls, psych meds, and zip-ties.

"This side of the asylum is highly restricted," Verity says. "It's reserved for the *criminally insane* and not open for visitation without prior clearance."

Soldiers in fatigues, their backs at ease against endless white hallways, project dispassionate glances when we pass. It isn't difficult to discern this facility is actually a clandestine military hospital nestled inside an asylum. It reminds me of Jade Sokolov's babushka dolls, stackable wooden figures she hid inside one another, a sneaky way for the government to save faces and space. Jade was practically catapulted back to Moscow after the lid came off Project Blue Bird. A real psycho, that one. What sort of person launches an arrow into a wolf's leg just to watch it suffer? If anyone deserves a room *here*, it's her. But that's another story...

...We glide through metal detectors and endure robotic wand scans after Verity flashes an ID. Caramel spirals bounce when she walks, a fashionable bob set atop soft-focus café-au-lait skin. Her lime green eyes still pop with startling radiance, the only detectable show of spunk left of her, insofar as I can tell. She ditched the hoop earrings and henna tattoos from our adolescence, replaced them with overcooked solemnity accompanied by periodic micro-frowns. The minted demeanor is a byproduct, I suspect, of working at Langley. Verity's alien carriage feels both impressive and awkward. She's completely dismantled the skittish Haitian foster girl I knew, cast it aside, along with her sense of wonder, like a double summer rainbow fading too soon.

Verity fiddles with her silver Phidias Vacheron Constantin watch, turning it so the white clockface is topside. She talked practically nonstop the entire road trip, something that hasn't changed. "Enoch was taken to Heaven and appointed guardian of celestial treasures, chief of archangels and immediate attendant to the Throne of God," she'd said in the car. "He was alive when called up. Most Christians, except Ethiopians and Eritreans, don't believe Enoch is a chief of angels or treasure keeper. Do you know he was Noah's great-grandfather?"

Verity finished Harvard ahead of schedule, testing out of most of her classes, which doesn't surprise me. NASA Plum Hook Bay took charge of twelve 'highly gifted' foster kids between 1983 and 1984, including me. She passed her bar exam, one of the youngest in the school's history to do so. She's holds a doctorate in theology too and works "of counsel" for the CIA. But the most astounding news of all…she's married. Seth Sahin, her husband, is a master gunnery sergeant in the Marine Corp. It's weird for me to think of Verity as someone's *wife*. "We met on my first diplomatic assignment in Greece," she said. "My husband is overseas for eighteen months near the Turkish border."

I process her personal news flashes with edgy, envious apprehension. Verity always stuck close to Barbara when we were at Plum Hook, while I got tagged for farm chores with Reggie. I prefer the outdoors, far away from meds and therapy, while Verity favored amenities and an oversized kitchen. Despite our pastoral differences, our 'best friend-ness' grew from a mutual affinity for reading, MIA fathers, and copious unanswered questions about what brought us into this strange covert world of high weirdness. She used to blend an exhaustive collection of religious beliefs and rituals into a fruity shake back then, mixing Paganism and Voodoo, with Christianity, a concerted effort to understand our seriously fucked up childhoods. She called her odiferous clouds of essential oils and sage a 'soul smoothie', while her various candles, crystals, and consecrated salt acted as our 'psychic armor'.

Upon closer scan, I'm not so sure I like the newly improved Verity. The timid girl I constantly plucked from spells-gone-wrong is erased and I miss her. She's still friendly—just different, so grown up and serious. The transformation feels like a permanent splinter between us I can't extract, one that hurts but I can't pinpoint where. Maybe it's because our remote and unconventional foster home was one supersized unethical scam and I'm bothered Verity plummeted headfirst into its spooky chum. She mentioned too, that she still hasn't located her dad. He's lost in a brig somewhere, having defied some orders in Viet Nam.

Reggie said during our ride here he was vehemently opposed to governments rearing foster kids, or any kids, behind the gates of nuclear reactor testing sites like NASA Plum Hook Bay. "The optics were horrible," he said. He didn't mention the experiments, the ones he fought to keep me from as best he could.

------

I stand before an imposing gray metal door with big black numbers.

**355**

Next to mom's door is a handwritten sign that reads, '*611 days without incident*'.

On the other side, my mom.

It's been fifteen years.

No contact allowed.

Too dangerous *they* said.

"In some circles, your mom's considered an *oracle*," Reggie says. "Some of us believe her LSD overdose unlocked a portal in her subconscious, one that enables her to '*see*' things."

"Doctors on Earth call her *schizophrenic*," I say, pitching him an eye roll. I'm not sure what to think. Who wants to be associated with *crazy*?

A guy in white scrubs slides fingers around prongs sticking out of a wall. He nestles his palm on a steel plate until it lights up blue. The first door to my mother's room buzzes before it pops open, making a deflated balloon-hiss sound. He unlocks the second door with a key. His nametag reads, *L. Smooter* and this pint-sized-plain-looking 'blend-into-the-fabric' fellow sucks his cheeks so tightly he gets fish lips and appears passively annoyed we've disturbed his peace.

"Your mom," Reggie says putting a hand between my shoulders, "isn't easy to manage. She's driven away at least a dozen nurses."

"She's misunderstood." L. Smooter says. "Avril isn't a danger unless provoked. It's the thing paying her periodic visits that presents a problem."

"Who visits?" I ask, sort of pleased this guy so readily defended her.

"I'm not sure how to answer that," Smooter says. "But don't touch her. She doesn't like to be touched. I'd like for us to make it to day six twelve without incident." He points to the paper sign taped to the wall.

"You require debriefing before you go in there," Reggie says.

"Debriefing?"

"Have a seat," he says, patting a bench that's chained to the wall. "Some things you need to know."

L. Smooter relocks the second door, releasing a pent up sigh as he shuffles away. "Why didn't you say so before? Let me know when you're finished."

A sharp glare bounces off Reggie's silver rimmed glasses from the fluorescent lights above our heads. "In an oddly captive and self-serving way, the CIA secretly cares for your mom," he says. "But only as long as she takes care of them."

"How?" I ask. "How does my mom take care of the CIA?"

"Avril provides the CIA with coordinates to our nation's top secret allied and enemy bases, prison camps, factories, level 5 biolabs, or military technology," he says. "Or at least she did."

"She does all that while locked up in this place? How? Does she have access to a computer like the ones Bennie had or something?"

Reggie shakes his head and looks at the floor, then at me. "She has visions and speaks in riddles. People no longer enter her room to decode what she says. We used to send in 'cosmically cleared' HHUMINT (Hybrid and/or Human intelligence) to decipher messages. We tried to send robots...but she uses her mind to blow them up."

"Her mind? What pisses her off so much she blows up robots?" I ask. "Is it being locked up? The loss of freedom? I'd be mad too if a bunch of shitheads ruined my entire life with a botched assassination attempt and then made me live *here*."

"The deal was, they'd leave *you* alone, to live your life," he says.

"But the CIA broke their deal," I say. "Not surprising. Why?"

"The man you murdered in your motel room…"

"He deserved to die," I interrupt, blotting the vile memory as best I can. "He preyed on kids. He had every intention of slaughtering me too. But that doesn't explain the broken deal between my mom and the CIA."

Reggie nods an understanding. "You tore his manhood to shreds…with your hands. You left a blood bath behind."

"I used my teeth too," I say, looking away, staring again at yet another ugly colored Pepto-Bismol speckled linoleum floor, not liking one bit where this is headed, stifling an urge to puke. "But what's your point?"

"I get it," Reggie says. "You did what you had to do. You hit Septum Oculi's radar the day you tore that man to shreds. We moved in fast to scoop you out of the court system and over to NASA Plum Hook Bay. A deal was struck with the CIA. We had no choice."

"What sort of deal?" I ask.

"The CIA was to oversee most but not all of your training," he says. "In exchange for allowing us to keep you there."

"How did I show up on Septum Oculi's radar?"

"Our Arctic based antineutrino detectors registered off the charts when you killed that creep," Reggie says. "Whatever energy you manifested in your motel room when you were sixteen triggered alarms at multiple agencies, including NASA, the DIA, JSOC, DOE, NSA, DARPA, the CIA, and a host of others you've never heard about. We thought Armageddon had begun, that someone, somewhere, pushed launch codes on nuclear missiles. But the coordinates led directly to the Trail's End Motel, which made no sense. You left a bunch of engineers, military personnel, and intelligence officers scratching their heads. Higher-ups ripped everyone a new asshole."

"How is my mother involved?" I ask.

"We suspect your mother kept some sort of psychic tether on you, sensed your distress, and helped *something* cross dimensions to save you. The transfer almost killed her and seriously weakened, we think, whatever she let through," Reggie says.

"Your incident led to an interagency task force reopening Project Looking Glass," Verity adds.

"I don't know what that is," I say.

Project Looking Glass sees future probabilities and also into the past," Verity says. "It involves a collapsible cube and timeline wars."

"So? What does this Project Looking Glass have to do with my mom?"

"It enables a person to see and re-experience a memory first hand," she explains. "For example, a person could encounter past entities, travel to physically altered spaces, visit those spaces in their past form, and meet or interact with people that occupied the past, who have been long dead. The CIA requires the cube to manipulate laws of nature. We want to figure out what she let through."

"Why? So all these agencies can fuck up this world even more?" I ask. "What does any of this have to do with me?"

"We think part of this technology was somehow built into your blood and becomes doubly powerful with the cube," Reggie says.

"And to think, I merely thought of myself as a breathing fueling station," I say, feeling angrier by the minute. "Where's the cube?" I ask.

"We have a copy but not the real deal," Verity says. "The copy cube, if I get this right, screws up probability and rearranges laws of nature. We're unable to control the timelines to our advantage because probabilities randomly change once human influence is injected.

There's more..." She hands me a manila folder. "Unfortunately, a few of our best case officers spontaneously combusted in your mom's room, lost their flesh, or mysteriously drowned in their own lung fluid—even if they're sent in wearing advanced hazmat suits. You're mom...how do I say this, Sam?"

"Spit it out," I say.

"Your mom has killed a lot of people," she says. "She's pissed."

"Will she kill me too?" I ask. "Reggie, you always told me you weren't sure if she'd recognize me, that she wanders in an out of lucidity. Why would today be any different?"

"We don't know," Reggie says. "We're hoping she'll talk with you."

"Why? Has she asked for me?"

Verity shakes her head.

"Your mom," Reggie says, "is a wheel-chair confined weapon —property of one of the darkest black ops agencies within U.S. government."

"No wonder she's pissed," I huff. "You assholes consider her property, not a person. Who owns her?"

"Nobody really knows who 'owns' her," Verity adds, as if her statement somehow lessens CIA culpability. "Her contract is lost in a maze of coded paperwork—but this, her being here, is how Reggie keeps her safe."

"Reggie? You mean *YOU* put her here?" I ask.

"Septum Oculi ordered her here. I had no choice," he says. "She's too dangerous for a regular prison and this is the best the government had."

---

L. Smooter reopens the door open wide enough for me to turn sideways and slip through but not before he narrows his eyes at Reggie. "Are you sure about this?"

"Not really," Reggie says.

"That doesn't give me a lot of comfort."

"That's part of my job," Reggie says. "To see that you don't get too damn comfortable."

My red heels click unescorted into near darkness, shoes that used to be mom's. I hope she notices. I took them from my grandmother's house years ago, stuffed them into a backpack while church ladies boxed up grandma's stuff after she died from cancer, before they dragged me kicking and screaming to my first foster home. I was eight. The shoes finally fit.

A security lock echoes in my ear, *phhhht.*

I'm sealed in this room with Avril, a hollowed out weapon-woman capable of mass destruction…and she's my mom. At first scent, it's clear we possess completely polarized tolerance levels for hygiene, although Reggie and Vigo might disagree.

I'd rather have a long needle jabbed in my ass than linger too long in this piss-and-body-odor abyss. I step further into her space, a chilly cave of stale cigarette smoke; it clings to my clothes like an infestation of ticks and mingles in a funky way with institutional disinfectant and stale cafeteria food. I pretend it doesn't affect me but my stony façade is a lie.

"Hi, Mom. It's me, Samantha."

Avril's shadowed silhouette sits back-brace straight near a shaded bay window.

Lights out.

A can of Bugle Boy Tobacco keeps her company on a tiny wooden table. Stacks of rolled cigarettes lie in wait, ready to march one by one to an ashy death of chain-smoking consumption. A lamp, an old clock radio, and a military-grade twin bed on wheels, one with a metal railing to hold her in at night, *I wish they had one of those for her mind, too,* hold court. A plastic water pitcher rests on a rolling tray. A dusty TV hangs in a corner. Piles of books and newspapers teeter near the ceiling on a large dresser against a grayscale wall. A nightlight strains from the adjacent bathroom. No pictures of Dad, Grandma, or me—nothing to indicate family or people who might care about her. Does she even know she has —*had*—a family?

In the middle of the room rests an easel, the kind master painters use for creating seascapes or stills of fruit. It cradles a blank canvas, awaiting inspiration. I never knew my mom liked painting and it makes me feel sad…for all I never learned about her or the woman she was before free falling into insanity. No piano here, either. It was she who taught me how to play when I was only three. "You have longer than average fingers," she'd said. I stopped playing after grandma died. I wonder if mom stopped playing after they put her here. She's lost weight too. Her thick terrycloth robe can't conceal she's about as wide as a fishing pole. If I hung her on a porch, her bones might clatter. I try to rid the unpleasant vision of my mom doubling as a human windchime.

"Who's with you?" It's sounds more demand than question, her raspy smoke residue voice inflated with what I think is anger living large in a barely there frame of mind or body.

"Just me, Mom. No one else."

"Are you sure?"

"Yes."

"Are you here to kill me?" She asks.

"No. I'm your daughter."

"Did they plant a device inside you?"

"No, Mom."

"They make them the size of a grain of rice, you know. Slip it right under your skin or up your nose, all the way into your brain, and you wouldn't even know it was there. Bastards. What do you want?"

"It's me, Mom. Your daughter. Samantha."

She waves a hand in the air, swatting at nothing in front of her face, and cautiously rolls toward me in her wheelchair. She gives me a sideways, one-eyed-pirate-once-over. Avril looks much older than her early forties; lines of loss and injury deeply etched into her forehead, as if a thousand ghostly ships pass through her locks but she's unable to stowaway on a single one of them. Seeing her like this causes the hurt in my stomach to swell over into my heart. We experience no sappy movie-like mother daughter reunion moment. No wide smiles of recognition. No hugs. I always imagined this would go differently—better—that there would be instant recognition, joyful tears, tight hugs.

"You can't be Sam," Avril says. "You're too big. Sam is four."

"I grew up," I say, folding my arms across my chest for protection, wondering how I might fend off potential spontaneous combustion or a pulmonary edema, should she decide I'm not worth taking another breath.

Mom inches closer, conducting a thorough inspection. "They got you too, huh?" Her eyes drill into mine. Without warning, she wheels around and skids across to the other side of the room. "No escape. Blood demons! Don't go with them! They're here! Go away! I have a guest. Stop talking to me!" She rattles her head back and forth and smacks the side of her face, trying to force phantom voices, I think, out of her ear.

I pretend my body is a fortress. Impenetrable. *Focus on your breathing, Sam.*

Reggie says deep breathing helps calm the soul enough to figure out what comes next. I fight back involuntary tears but there's a breach and *drip, drip, drip* to the floor. *It was not supposed to be this way!* I crumple up my anger and mentally toss it into my gut, forcing it down like a rotten meal. Years of pent up trauma molded me into something shatterproof, as tenderized as steel. *Turn it off like a faucet!* But I can't.

"I hear your tears," mom softly says as she spins around and scrutinizes me again, head cocked, rolling closer. "You remember much more than you let on to the others."

I'm not sure that she likes what she sees—her intense stare reminds of me of how Bennie once peered into my soul, "to see what is in there", the day he rescued me from his pet Cobra in the dining room at Plum Hook Bay. I did this to my mom. It's my fault. I shift uncomfortably and look away. I was born and it ruined her life.

"So… the fuckers…." Mom trails off. "Be careful, Sam. You're right to be suspicious." She finger wags a warning. "They aren't what you think, dear girl. Monsters need to be kept in cages. Perks come with high prices. By God, I know your face! You've grown into your skin. Don't let them use you up like a jar of peanut butter."

"Peanut butter and jelly on Samantha's smelly belly," I say with a gulp.

Mom cackles and the loudness of it causes my spine to vibrate. That last little refrain used to be our inside joke when I was a kid. "Trust no one," she warns. "Not even the person you see in the mirror. Mirrors never tell the truth anyway. Want a cigarette?"

I bob my head and don't take my eyes off of her.

Avril wheels backward, picks up her rolling papers, and shapes a fag in about two seconds. "I was in high demand at Woodstock," she jokes.

I finally unlock my jaw and lower the tension along my neck long enough to laugh. Somewhere within the crackling compartments of her mind spark occasional glimmers of lucidity and humor, something I remember, something that once made me feel safe and mentally cozy around her.

"Had to make you a fresh one," she says as she hands it to me. "The others are loaded with poison. Government pays me good money for these cyanide loaded stags. See?" She waves an arm in the air like a Sears Catalog model. "I live the life of Riley in this shithole. Someone came to see me. He's evil. Looking for you, this collector of damned souls, this son of perdition. Plans to take you to hell. I couldn't kill him. I tried. Careful. He wants the bride. I gave him a cigarette."

"Who came to see you?" I ask.

My eyes adjust to the dim space, a room leaden with sadness and anger—as if mom took on this entire planet's mistakes and tightly folded it inside. She rocks back and forth in her wheelchair without answering. Avril used to look like a classic Hollywood movie star, but that's all over now. Years ago, voices in her head kicked up record-breaking dust storms. And ghosts no one else could see came calling, phantoms that refused to leave, and I'm terrified of one day sharing her fate.

Sometimes, I see them too, these hazy, photonic-looking-half-there spirits, which fade and reappear—always out of reach yet trying to communicate with me. Sometimes they speak to me in chirps, whistles or growls, or mentally transfer packets of coded concepts with strange symbols, directly into my brain, a strange but efficient sort of language where nothing gets lost in translation. Other times they appear to me as light beings, emitting packages of photonic information.

"I tried to change the trajectory of your life," she says. "To keep you safe." Avril takes a long, slow drag from her cigarette and surveys me again. She blows a cloud of smoke over her head in perfect circles. "Your father came to see me too. He brings light just like you. Light bearers is what you are!"

"Shh," I whisper. "They'll hear you outside."

"Your dad, he saved you," Mom says. "He's a guardian angel, you know. Down he soars with a scepter! You're healed!"

"Dad is dead," I say. "He went missing in Vietnam in 1971, when I was four, remember? Shh, please keep your voice down."

"Is that what they told you? Lies! He watches over us through seven veils of the Sumerian Seals. Take a step, step, step to the other side before you're ripe and poof," she snaps her fingers. "You're gone!"

"Shh," I say again.

I'm hard to kill, I'm told—but I sense I've met my match where mom's concerned. She pushes a palm hard against her forehead and pivots her neck as if smacked by some supernatural force. I lower my head, avoiding eye contact, because I once read, it's a protective stance lesser apes resort to when facing off with alphas. Unfortunately, Avril will never be the mom I always wanted. This is more of an 'ouchie' than I expected, but would she try to kill me, her daughter, as she's done to others? I edge toward the bay window and peer through a small crack in the curtains to change the subject. The snow outside is half melted and makes way for light green buds of Spring, the season finally slipping into something more comfortable.

"May I please open this window? No offense but it sort of stinks in here. We could both use some fresh air."

Mom laughs a bit softer this time. I suppose that's a good sign. A whoosh on the wheels of her chair and she's behind me. Every muscle fiber instinctively tightens on my bones. "Yes," she says. "We'll be okay under the eye of God."

The windows are protected with wide iron bars fused like giant crosses into the panes. Light comes tumbling through anyway, a fading day's rays illuminating the glimmer of distant beauty around mom's weathered face.

"Will you be home after the war?" she asks.

"What war?"

"The war where all the children are stacked into piles, their skin peeling away from their bodies and their eyes stolen—empty black sockets. You find me disgusting, don't you?"

"It's not your fault," I say. "You weren't exactly given a choice in this tragedy."

"Hmm. At least your blunt. Your level of truthfulness is hard for humans to both reach or take. It's a gift and a curse. And this?" Mom runs her palms over the front of her robe. "This human form is but an illusion to which this world applies useless labels, tonics and potions. I could clean the skin or plump up the muscle but such rituals eventually prove futile. Oh, some of us will plead with God for youth and immortality, try to buy Earth time, but the answer is always no. And don't you fret my dear—I hardly spend any time in here."

"What does that mean?"

"Just what I said," Mom replies. "Look!" She points at my feet. "Sam! My baby girl, look at you! You're here! You've grown into my shoes! Do you like them? Ready to save the world? Oh, no." She wheels away from the rays of the window to conceal herself again in shadow. "The dark ones come. Leather hands, leather hands, leather hands."

Mom hangs her head and switches off. Greasy gray hairs catch on her shoulders like crunchy mop strands. A switch flips in her mind. "You're God's little angel," she finally says, smiling in a freakish *one-off* sort of way, her voice an echo of smattering marbles against crackling sheet metal. "Golden Blood, hunt you, we will."

"Who are you?" I ask.

Mom wheels closer . I don't dare flinch. She's her but not her —I *feel* the negative energy in the room expand—its frequency and vibration humming through my center. "*The air is different,*" Fensig used to say. I wonder, briefly, if he returned to Greenland—

to his nomadic lifestyle just inside the Arctic Circle where he used to care for a reindeer herd. He said he'd do that once Plum Hook Bay cut us loose and he finished four years of duty with the Marine Corps.

"If, they find you..." Mom snatches my right forearm, slamming me head first into her seriously fucked up unreality. I instinctively tug to pull away from her vice grip but can't, my heartbeat kicking into overdrive.

And that's when it occurs to me...it isn't my mom that kills people—it's something else. Something that bounces back personal demons, sort of the way a mirror reflects close but not exact versions of a 'self'. I'll bet, based on what I learned from Dr. Evelyn and Bennie, that my mom absorbs and channels negative energy in a similar way plants uptake carbon dioxide. This creates a sort of inside-out cosmic flow that engulfs everything in its path. Maybe my mom's personal grid is full, and stuff like evil, uses the cracks in her system to leak out, its tendrils reaching for anything *alive.*

I stop fighting her—or it—and move into my mom for a long hug, taking on some of the hurt and pain she holds, sharing her burden. The bulbs in the room light up and burst. Branches from the large oaks outside scratch at the windows, warping the iron crosses and glass until a booming voice comes through Avril— something she channels, I think, because it doesn't sound like my mom at all.

**"Into the bosom of no time, the Viking holds the Isle. Engross a blood diamond as cleanly as a wolf passes through a compass. The clever fox outwits wickedness, to attain the password. Seven Rays and Seven Seals, the Balancer must X an eye to realize the point of the Gods..."**

I brand this riddle into my brain for later retrieval. Strange symbols bombard my head, thousands of pin-prick pains piercing my chest—packets of information—concepts of space, time, travel, and light—uploaded into synaptic networks and plumping every cell in my head until the information makes me collapse. Mom's skeletal fingers trace a path from the top of my head to the base of my skull. She slaps her palm hard on the back of my neck, plunging an ethereal bolt into my carotid artery. My body stiffens as memories, dreams, and visions break the dam in my brain. A swirling portal appears, a dividing line between realms... a figure walks toward me but doesn't cross over...a man, I think.

"Bennie?" I reach for him with a free arm. He disappears. "No! Wait..." I scream.

"No grasping," Avril says. "He's not *here*."

I let go...and so too, she.

And that's when I see them...

...on the inside wall of her window enclave where they'd been hidden to my left. Taped to almost every surface, one on top of another, taking up every bit of space like some otherworldly wallpaper... mom has painted...eyes. Her subject matter reminds me of Dr. Evelyn's necklace and Reggie's goofy gold eye ring. And my Mom's necklace too—though it isn't around her neck anymore, a symbol denoting some highly specialized sect of Septum Oculi for which I had no clearance or 'need to know' and wasn't 'read into'. Avril releases a low whistle like she's impressed, as if seeing an exhibit of her art for the first time.

"Mom, what is all of this?"

"The Eye of Providence," she says. "Soul portals." (If her smile got any brighter, I could use it as a floodlight.) "Which one is your favorite?" she asks.

I point to a colorful oil on canvas leaning against the baseboard. It's tiny compared to the rest, perhaps a foot by foot wide, but very detailed, a hazel eye surrounded by shades of orange, with blobs of purple flowers in the background, and a swish of red paint that I recognize as her symbol for a cardinal, it's beak a sharp curve and it's gaze cast into the void of the black pupil, a masterful and confident swipe of red, over an eye staring into nothingness.

"Ah, you're an abstract sort of lady. It's my gift to you," she says, plucking it off the floor and handing it to me. "See? I even signed it, right there on the back. It's your soul portal, for my granddaughter."

*Avril Ryan Blake*

"I'm your daughter, not your granddaughter," I say. But I'm happy to learn I share my mom's middle name, a new piece of information about my shredded past.

"Good grief, you don't think I know that?" Mom scolds. "Your daughter, my granddaughter, has hazel eyes and russet hair. Your unruly curls, your temper, and your stubbornness too—just like your father—but thankfully my granddaughter will have your soul mate's intelligence."

"Soul mate? I don't believe in such nonsense." I check my arms and chest just in case my verbal challenge displeases her. I'm not scorched. I inhale. I don't seem to be drowning either.

"Camaeliphims mate for lifetimes once you grant him the friendliness of your thighs," Mom says. "Thank God my granddaughter will have his brain."

"Really, mom?" I shake my head and frown. "We've been reunited for like, what, five minutes and you're already criticizing my intelligence level?"

"*What?*" She backs up and rolls away into the dark innards of the room. "I never said you *weren't* smart. Our middle name means 'illustrious wisdom'. You are smart. But you're also impulsive, hard-headed, and fail to listen—to your own detriment. Your father is the same. Stubborn angel is he. But this—what we're able to do with the right training, is not a game. It's a matter of vibration, frequencies and energy—maintaining life, not only here on Earth, but elsewhere."

"Whose brain will my daughter have?" I ask.

Now it's my mom's turn to roll her eyes at me. "His brain. Your life mate. Woof. He's big in other places too. Keep yourself fresh."

"*Mom!*"

I wonder if it will be Genin's baby— a trace of foolishness blows through me because I know my brain is bigger than his and I haven't heard from him in years. Like Verity, he could be married now too. Finding and then mating with another Camaeliphim hybrid is about as likely as aliens publicly outing themselves at

Madison Square Garden. Besides, I'd make a horrible mother. I misplaced my Source Guide. If I can't keep track of a fox, how on Earth would I ever manage a child?

"One should never leave behind their Source Guide," Mom says.

"So I've heard," I say. "Geez, I need to find a set of friends and family who *can't* read my mind."

The door peels open with a whoosh and L. Smooter peeks in. "Everything going all right in here, ladies? We heard quite a ruckus."

"Oh, you darling boy," Mom says. "My glorious and faithful keeper!"

Smooter holds the door with one arm and bows before her, a gesture of learned professionalism that no doubt calms the natives. I guess he does possess a tiny spark—one I feel my mom trusts and appreciates. She likes him. He looks around the room and laughs. "I see you've been redecorating again, Avril. I like what you've done with the place." His smile nosedives as someone new pushes into the room.

"*Dr. Evelyn?*" I say, crossing in front of my mom. "What are *YOU* doing here?"

# EIGHT

# DREAM HEALER

"*YOU!*" Mom yells, pointing a skeletal finger at Dr. Evelyn. "You're a *thief!*"

Dr. Evelyn looks exactly as she did four years ago—same gorgeous ivory cashmere ensemble, swingy platinum-bobbed hair and freshly pressed high-end label newness, a complete dichotomy of the woman I call mom, who sits behind me now, shriveled in a government-issue wheelchair—and I can tell, Avril's not liking her new visitor one bit.

"Hello, Samantha," Dr. Evelyn coolly says, as if we just passed one another moments ago in the hall—all eyes on mom. Sweat trickles down my neck and the small white hairs on my forearms rise but not for the same reasons this happens when Reggie barks training orders at me. Dr. Evelyn Dennison was my Plum Hook Bay psychiatrist who preferred *medication management* and solitary confinement over talk therapy and outdoor exercise. She also accepted a lot of deliveries on the NASA side of the farm, mostly oversized yellow body bags.

Mom puts her wheelchair between Dr. Evelyn and me.

"You can't be in here," Smooter says to Dr. Evelyn. "You know what happened last time!"

"Last time?" I ask. "These two *know* each other? What happened last time?"

"I'll cover you, honey!" Mom yells. "Make a run for it! Don't let this bitch inside your head! She'll invade your brain cells like millions of little hermit crabs! Don't let her steal your jewelry, either!" Mom grabs a book from a low shelf and hurls it at Dr. Evelyn. Then another. She wheels over to her bedside tray and throws the water pitcher at her too.

I stand in the way to stop mom from doing more harm but she gathers speed and I crash on her lap. She pays me no heed and rolls over to Dr. Evelyn anyway. When Avril applies the brakes to her wheelchair, I roll off. Mom spins around and does an unexpected wheelie, which, truthfully, is sort of impressive and my initial urge to laugh is quickly stifled by the realization she could actually kill Dr. Evelyn, so I quickly get back on my feet. Smooter tries to block Avril as if he's playing defensive tackle but she easily dodges him too.

"Let me at her!" Avril shouts. "Get the hell out of my way! Give me back my necklace, you pompous pilferer!"

"What the hell is going on?" I ask Dr. Evelyn. "What did Smooter mean, 'like last time'?"

"She doesn't live in reality," Dr. Evelyn says, before she dodges out of the way.

"That doesn't answer my question," I say. "She *knows* you. How?"

Smooter finally grabs the back of Mom's chair and she comes to an abrupt stop. To my surprise, she stands. "Hi-yaaaaaa!"

Mom rushes us, pushes me to one side, and lunges at Dr. Evelyn.

The two of them careen to the floor in the middle of the room and begin rolling around. Ju-jitsu. Of course. Both of these grown ass women have lost all decorum but each has been trained to fight. Dr. Evelyn pulls up mom's robe, exposing her white granny-panty clad ass. Mom rips the buttons off of Dr. Evelyn's silk blouse revealing her expensive black La Perla lace bra. An arm twist here, a flip there...Dr. Evelyn wraps Mom in a headlock, but not before

Mom punches Dr. Evelyn in the jaw and rips the eye necklace from Dr. Evelyn's chest.

"I wonder when Avril will conjure up lung-blocking plasma or perhaps order the wall ivy now running down the walls to strangle Dr. Evelyn," I say to Smooter.

"Not today," he says. "We've gone 611 days without incident."

"What about this?" I ask, throwing a palm toward two women rolling around together on an asylum floor. "Doesn't this, along with the warped windows and ivy now growing down the walls, meet your criteria for *incident*?"

"Not unless Avril kills her," he says. "The windows and ivy? It's normal. But I should probably call an orderly." Smooter cracks the door to get help.

Reggie and Vigo pounce into the room. Reggie calmly strides over to the two women, lifts both from the floor, and separates them like two naughty schoolchildren. He plants mom back in her wheelchair with a gentle thud. Vigo barks and growls at Dr. Evelyn...just like Sarge used to do...until Reggie shouts, "*PLATZ!*" in German.

I find it difficult to trust people even dogs don't like. "Would one of you please tell me what in the hell is going on?" I ask. I'm still trying to figure out too, why my mom hasn't *killed* Dr. Evelyn.

Mom whimpers, bent over, arms folded across her stomach. It's like she's trapped in this body—as if it doesn't belong to her, never did, and I wonder for a moment if she has contained so much energy inside this biological vessel of hers that she may be depleted of cells, like a wilted plant in desperate need of water.

Dr. Evelyn yanks her necklace out of mom's hands and I see that Evelyn has a bloody bottom lip. This isn't funny, but a small tug at the back of my brain says, *Way to go, Mom!* It's sort of awesome to see Dr. Evelyn bleed like the rest of us.

"I'll trade you one of my premium cigarettes for the necklace, you know, to perk you up a bit." Mom finally says to Dr. Evelyn, looking at my former psychiatrist with more scorn than I think I've ever seen anyone throw out.

"No thank you," Dr. Evelyn replies as she brushes her slacks with her palms, returning the same stink eyes to my mom. "I've already inhaled my daily quota of poison from you."

"You sure about that?" Mom says. "You look like you could use a good whiff of cyanide."

"And you look as if you could use a bath...or four," Dr. Evelyn pipes back. Dr. Evelyn clasps the eye necklace around her throat, straightens her hair, and snatches a tissue from a nearby holder to wipe the blood from her mouth.

"It's you..." Mom says to Reggie, losing all focus on Dr. Evelyn.

Dr. Evelyn and I quizzically look at one another and then pass glances between Reggie, Smooter, and my mom. Vigo too, cocks his canine head, ears up, looking just as confused as me. Mom, for whatever reason, decides to change the stations in her head and turns down the volume. She stands again and ambles over to Reggie. He doesn't move but watches her. She gently places pencil thin fingers to his temples. Tears float down her face and settle into little puddles on the lines of her cheeks.

"Don't let the devil drain her blood," Mom says to Reggie. "The beast looks for the Viking through the bride. Keep seven eyes on her. Promise me. You are my daughter's keeper. A Chosen."

"I'll do my best Avril,'" he says, tenderly kissing her hand in a show of respect.

"You two know each other?" Dr. Evelyn asks.

Mom stares at Reggie in eerie awe, the look of a transfixed mental patient on too many meds, as he helps her, for the second time, back into her wheelchair.

"Yes," Reggie says.

"How?" Dr. Evelyn and I ask in unison.

"Long story," Reggie says. "She returned my memories to me." He holds out his wrist, unlatches his watch, and shows us two scar prongs, like mine.

"I didn't give you all of your memories back," Mom corrects him. "I left off the painful ones. But I see life has recently brought you more." She lightly pats the top of his hand, looks at Evelyn, then turns her attention to the dog. "Vigo! How are you? Good boy!"

Mom whistles and Reggie's Source Guide, barrels over to say hello, jumps on her lap, licks her face and wags his tail, hopping from her knees to the floor before he dances in a circle. "There, there," Mom says. "Good boy!" She slips her hands into a bedside drawer and offers him a treat. "Sit." Vigo does and she allows him to take it with his teeth. "Sam will need to borrow your Source Guide since she can't keep track of her own," Avril says to Reggie.

Vigo stops chewing on his steak bone and tilts his head toward mom. He lets out a low series of whimper-whines and one long "ARRRROOOOH".

"I like this about as much you do," I say to him, folding my arms across my chest, wondering now, just how many of *my* memories mom purposely withheld.

Reggie winces and begins to protest until Avril stops him. "I know, I know," she says putting two fingers to her lips. "But since Sam dislocated her fox, she must use Vigo as a surrogate until she's strong enough to summon Hope."

"How do you know *her?*" I interrupt to ask, pointing at Dr. Evelyn.

"She's my sister," Mom says without hesitation. "And she took what is mine!"

"*Sister?* Dr. Evelyn is your *SISTER?* That means…Oh, no. This can't be true!"

"Yes, she's your Aunt," Mom says matter-of-factly. "And if you didn't need her, I would have killed her traitorous ass long ago."

Stunned, I sit in the only other chair in the room. "How are you…? Evelyn, why didn't you—why didn't you tell me?"

"I couldn't," Evelyn says. "We share the same father. I grew up in London and your mom was raised in the U.S. We met for the first time at the University of Oxford." Dr. Evelyn looks at my mom. "I saved her, Avril. I found her. We're sisters. I paid my penance. What happened to us was a long time ago and has nothing to do with Sam."

"It has everything to do with Sam!" Mom yells. "She was denied her rightful place because of you."

"That's not true," Dr. Evelyn says. "It is true that I had to watch her from afar but I always protected her like a daughter."

"Fuck you," Mom says, practically snarling. "You did not put her bests interests before yours!" She rolls right up to Dr. Evelyn and stands to look her directly in the eyes. "There can only be *one* mother, do I make myself clear?"

"Yes," Dr. Evelyn says looking down—but I don't know what my mom means because Evelyn *never* treated me like a daughter.

"Now, give me the fucking necklace," Avril says, her tone so loaded with hostility it makes me glad I'm not the source of her anger.

"I was…I was only holding it for Sam until she was ready," Dr. Evelyn says now looking at Reggie, pleading for help with her eyes, I think. He offers her none, then looks away, out the window.

The tension between Avril and Evelyn is as palpable and raw as the prong scars on my wrist.

"She's ready *now*," Mom says through gritted teeth. "Hand. It. Over."

Dr. Evelyn grudgingly drops the gold eye necklace into mom's palm and backs up against the wall. I *feel* mom's rage against Dr. Evelyn—the madness it contains too, but what I fail to discern is why.

Mom's aura swiftly moves through a spectrum of black, red, gold, and indigo, perhaps a symptom of her mental illness or perhaps something more—I can't tell. Mom turns to me. "Where is that friend of yours?"

"You mean Bennie?"

"No. Not him. The other one, the young woman you think of as your 'best friend'. She's here. I *feel* her—she's a receptor too, like me."

"You mean Verity?"

"Yes. Bring Verity to me. I need to speak with her."

"But…" Smooter says.

"Relax Louie," Mom says. "I won't kill her. She'll do that on her own—or not."

"Mom," I say. "No harm comes to Verity, got it?"

Mom dismissively flips her hand toward me as she lights a cigarette.

Smooter cracks the door and motions for Verity to come into the room.

"I haven't had so many visitors since Viet Nam," Mom says smiling before she suddenly turns her lips down. "I don't like so many people in my room. Everyone leave except this one. Verity is it?"

Verity nervously looks around at the rest of us before she recovers and tips her head back and forth.

"I need your help," Mom says. "You've trained yourself in the art of 'Luminescensy'. I could feel your power on the other side of the door."

Verity fiddles with her watch, her hands shake.

"You once put a photonic circle of protection around my daughter," Avril says. "This pleases me. From one receptor to another, do you accept my request for help?"

"But I..."

"No," Mom interrupts. "I know what you're thinking. You had little choice in a matter once set before you."

"I accept your request," Verity says.

I have no idea what my mom means about Verity having little choice in a matter—unless she means Verity being forced into Plum Hook Bay. Dr. Evelyn made us both 'offers' to go there but we had no choice. It was agree to her training by signing an integrity contract or go to jail for our respective crimes, mine being murder—or so I thought—until Reggie told me that what I did was actually self-defense.

I bob my head back and forth like a rallying tennis ball between my mom and Evelyn. Dr. Evelyn Dennison is my *aunt*. She and my mom look nothing alike. Where Dr. Evelyn is pale, smooth, and white-haired with blue-gray eyes, my mom is olive-skinned and wrinkled, with dark curly hair and hazel eyes. This is too much information in one damn day.

"Be gone, all of you," Mom says with a wave of her hand to dismiss everyone except Verity.

"May I remain?" I ask.

"No distractions," Avril says.

*Distraction?* Geez, I haven't seen my mom since I was eight and now she's throwing me out of her room. I'm envious too, that she asks for Verity's help, while I'm forced to step aside. What the hell is Luminescency anyway?

Louie seals the door behind my mom and Verity. "You should get lunch," he says, hurrying back to his desk to pick up the receiver on a red phone—one I've seen Dr. Evelyn and Reggie use back at NASA Plum Hook Bay when things got serious. "And get dinner too…come to think of it, you guys should just rent a hotel and come back tomorrow. This will probably take a while…"

# NINE

# EBIANS

IT'S 5am when we return to the asylum.

Reggie said last night over dinner that sharing one's Source Guide is a *BIG* deal and that he's not very happy about me borrowing Vigo. Vigo doesn't seem happy about it either.

I shouldn't have left my Source Guide behind but Hope is a wild fox and loves the outdoors. She could traverse cave tunnels and woodlands better than a homing pigeon. I thought if I left her at Plum Hook Bay she'd watch over Bennie's lab with Randolph, maybe take care of Edwin, his cardinal, too. Nothing worse than fucking up and realizing it too late. "I've never met an animal quite like Vigo," I say, as we drive through the gates of the asylum. The sun peeks over a series of low hills as I try to make conversation—although I don't know why. I've never been much of a talker and neither is Reggie.

Vigo gives me the cold paw when I reach out to scratch his ears, along with a low-grade unenthusiastic 'woof'. He tosses his muzzle sky side and plops it into Reggie's lap.

"Snob," I say.

"I want you to break into Plum Hook Bay and find your Soul Guide," Reggie says, staring through the windshield, as if breaking into a nuclear reactor testing facility for a second time, after getting caught the first time, is somehow no big deal and I won't be expected.

"Are you kidding me? Um, *hello!*" I wave my arms at him but he pays no attention. "You were the one who said never return to Plum Hook Bay. I just lost four years of my life over that trespass and now you want me to go back there?"

"You didn't have anyone covering your *six*," he says. "You violated my order and flew solo. Verity and I can help you this time."

I huff and push myself back on the leather seat and silently stare at passing trees. We bump along a wide utility road running parallel to the river, buffered by tall pines so thick it's like trying to peer through curtain cracks.

Dr. Evelyn didn't join us last night. I don't know where she went, probably not far. I have questions for her, lots of questions. I spent years in her care—as an involuntary patient and a reluctant student, but never as her niece. She could win an acting award for keeping our familial ties so top secret and it pisses me off she never told me.

Reggie said he didn't know what the drama between Dr. Evelyn and my mom might be—but that it had to be serious. He's disappointed too, that Dr. Evelyn failed to disclose she is my aunt. Reggie looks more troubled than ever. And this troubles *me...*

We round the turn on the other side of the hospital and wind through the park-like setting. Reggie slams the brakes on the van. Vigo and I lunge forward and I have to grab the dog's collar to keep him from going through the windshield. Plumes of smoke rise from my mom's building. But there's something else...

"What are they?" I ask.

"Don't know..." Reggie responds, pausing briefly, looking just as puzzled as I feel. "These are similar to that glowing ball of light back at Plum Hook, the one that snatched up Saratu."

*Saratu.*

"I haven't thought about her in years," I say.

Saratu had gone missing for weeks at Plum Hook Bay after a

glowing sphere uploaded her from the front yard with a light beam. With Bennie's help, Jade and I made it to the underside of the nuclear reactor to find her—but we didn't find her. She wasn't there. What we stumbled into instead was a world of horrors, a complete shit show I wish I could scrub from my brain and should have asked my mom to remove.

I always wondered how Saratu managed to escape the freaky glowing orb. It didn't belong to the government because anyone with any rank whatsoever that day, flew into high-alert, screaming orders, banging phones, and flipping switches. Multiple generals showed up on scene too, alongside private sector spooks. Soldiers threw punches at physicists and physicists blamed the engineers. Something had gone holy fuck wrong at NASA Plum Hook Bay.

Reggie told me back then I rescued Saratu, that she was airlifted over NASA's razor-wire fence and whisked to an undisclosed location for her safety. I briefly remember seeing her near a fence line with Lozen before I passed out, wondering how she escaped—or if the orb let her go. But *I* didn't save her. Saratu didn't need saving. If I recall correctly, and I usually do, she rescued *us*. And now that I think about it, she went willingly into that craft, whatever it was. After that, the entire place was decommissioned and we were ordered to leave.

White orbs lope gracefully in a series of slow-moving, snake-like *S* patterns and they're smaller here than the one that plucked Saratu. Reggie presses the gas pedal but the van sputters and stalls. A rush of wind rattles the windows and rocks the vehicle. I feel about three seconds of intense heat.

"What's happening?" I ask, tightening my grasp on Vigo's collar.

"The engine refuses to turn," Reggie says. "Whatever those things are, they're throwing off some sort of atmospheric field, I think, disrupting the van's electronics."

We're forced to get out and jog. Fire trucks and ambulances scream past us followed closely by a black Cadillac with tinted windows. The emergency vehicles stall too, just yards from our van. The Cadillac does not.

Intense gold-red-orange orbs, five of them, cast a glow so bright it causes mass curiosity on site, but no hysteria. Hospital staff and patients alike pour out of the building's front doors in semi-disorganized, fire-drill fashion, shaking their heads and pointing up in awe—yet no one registers alarm.

"I don't see Avril or Verity," I say, cupping a hand over my eyes and sweeping them over the sea of people.

Soccer-ball sized glowing balls settle over the heads of certain patients, defying all known laws of gravity because none of these little crafts, if that's what they are, have propulsion systems. The undersides and exterior shell are glass-like and house spinning neon blue plasma that sometimes glows red. A faint fizz and crackle causes the air to vibrate and lifts the hair on my arms, neck, and head. These strange spheres are much smaller than the one that snatched Saratu—too small to be piloted. But whatever they are, it's as if they watch, gather data—or perhaps scramble people's brains—although I don't *feel* muddled.

"Do you see the angels?" A patient asks, staring up at the weird lights in raptured awe, rocking to-and-fro on his tiptoes as if he's high. "They're soooooo beautiful."

The orbs align in V-formation, shoot themselves straight into the atmosphere with astonishing speed, and disappear in less than a second. Given what Dr. Sterling taught me about rocket propulsion, my immediate calculations make no sense. These orbs travel faster than the speed of light and perform impossible maneuvers. G-forces would splat humans like bug juice if any could fit inside. Such instantaneous ariel acrobatics aren't possible on Earth with even the most stealth technology. Einstein's hair would flatten if he were alive to see this.

Pandemonium erupts behind me.

Patients run in every direction, chased by orderlies and security. Some try to climb over electrical fences but get zapped and fall to the ground. Their bodies seize with a series of jerks and twitches, which is uncomfortable to watch, so I don't. Others run down a hill and jump into the river, and still others are tackled and dragged screaming toward the smoldering building, or handcuffed to tree limbs, or sit or stand, staring at the sky, lost in catatonic oblivion to the break out chaos.

"We have to find Avril and Verity," I say, pushing through a small throng of patients and staff toward the doors.

One officer recognizes us from yesterday and waves us through a clear side door. Medical charts, bandages, and hundreds of papers lie strewn in hallways like multi-colored confetti. It's eerily quiet—too quiet. A thin layer of smoke floats through the corridor. A wayward strobe light blips by an exit sign. Further into the bowels of this asylum, the scent of ozone and earth invades my nostrils.

"You have another weapon?" I ask, fearing the worst for my mom and Verity.

"Always," Reggie says as he clears halls. "Brought it for you just in case."

"A sword?" I ask.

Reggie tosses me a gun.

"I hate guns," I say, flipping the safety off with a click of my thumb on his 1911 semi-auto .45.

"That's because you're a lousy shot," he says, and he's right.

"I prefer my sword," I say.

"You can't 'conceal carry' a sword," he says. "And it's not appropriate in 1991 to walk around with an oversized blade dangling from your hip. Besides, swords require getting up close and personal…learn to shoot."

L. Smooter lies motionless in front of the nurse's station. I squat to check his pulse.

"Avril," he weakly mumbles. He points over his head to her steel-reinforced door—now twisted like taffy and barely attached to its hinges.

Vigo barks nonstop and even Reggie's German commands don't shut him up. Reggie stops me from running into the room with a firm hand press to my chest. "Vigo first," he says. "Go boy! Howl if it's safe."

Vigo clamors over the door.

"He could die," I say, panic bubbling through my blood.

"Vigo's fate will be worse if he's stopped from doing what he was born to do," Reggie says.

Sparks buzz and spit from the security circuit board...

...We wait...

...And wait...

...And wait...

"*Arrrrrroooooooooooo!*"

---

While institutionalized chaos and pandemonium reign outside, mom's room is a peaceful paradise inside. Literally. Reggie and I roll eyes toward one another in disbelief and holster our weapons. Ivy sheaths the walls and large palm trees punch through the roof. The trickle of a narrow stream, from what was once mom's bathroom, cuts a gentle path through the center of what is left of Avril's space. Fresh moss and ferns completely cover the linoleum floor, and orchids, thousands of species, hang in colorful bloom, their pale green-gray roots dangling—and that's when I spot Verity, ensconced upside down, eyes closed, arms crossed over her chest, like a slumbering bat!

I pull a small knife from my waistband.

"No," Reggie says. "We'll have to untangle her with our hands. I've seen this before."

"Where?"

"Viet Nam. Seven miles west of Khe Sanh about halfway to the Laotian border. Shortly after midnight, an NVA force attacked our camp. Some of my unit was found in the jungle, trapped in oversized orchids like this. Anyway, a few of the guys cut away the roots, except for one guy, Private Pierce. He untangled himself and lived to tell the tale. By next morning, every other guy who'd taken a knife to those roots was dead."

"Poison?" I ask.

"I'm not sure," Reggie says. "We went back to collect root samples with the intelligence guys. We couldn't find a single orchid. It was as if the jungle swallowed up the evidence."A shiver ripples along my spine. I'm sad for the soldiers who didn't know any better and lost their lives to vanishing orchids. "That deeply disturbs my sense of fairness," I say.

Reggie gently runs a palm up the length of one of the roots. "Ignorance can get you killed just the same as evil," he says. "Whatever this is, it's alive in more ways than one."

"You mean it's intelligent?"

"I think so," he nods.

Verity moans, coming to, before she begins to struggle against the vines.

"Shh," I say. "Don't wiggle. We'll get you out of here but we have to do it gently. Don't tear the roots."

Twenty minutes later, Verity stands upright, a bit disheveled but not hurt in any way that I can tell. I scan what's left of the room looking for Avril.

"She's not here," Verity says.

"What do you mean she's not here?" I ask.

"They took her."

"Who took her?" I ask, my voice rising.

"The Tall Whites. They took her."

"*Who?*"

"Ebians. They came in through the window in formation. At first, I thought it was an electrified horse floating toward us, until I realized it was actually a group of tall beings in horse-like formation."

"*Ebians?* You mean the creatures from Bennie's weird story?" I ask. "I thought he was making that shit up."

"I didn't believe it either until I saw them with my own eyes," Verity says clutching her elbows with a shiver.

"What are Ebians?" Reggie asks.

"Back at Plum Hook, Bennie told Sam and me this story about how some group called Ebians were the original Earth seeders," Verity says. "He and I got into a huge argument because I believed the Bible's creation story. He said Ebians helped the Source enhance Camaeliphims, to counter Nephilims and their creators, the Bezaliels—and that Ebians dismantled the Code of

Everything, aka the Word, here on this planet, to prevent perpetual multiverse chaos."

"I've heard the Code of Everything is strewn all over this planet," Reggie says, inspecting a large banana leaf. "I never knew about Ebians."

"Avril told me Sam is a 'pet project' of the Ebians," Verity says. "Bennie claimed they're the most advanced beings anywhere—and closest to the Source—or what we know as God."

"Why would they take my mom?" I ask.

"*GRRRRRR,*" Vigo growls.

Metal clatters and crunches. The three of us raise our weapons toward the twisted door.

L. Smooter helps Dr. Evelyn over the debris.

"Where's Avril?" Louie asks, a look of alarm planted on his face.

"They took her," I say, lowering my weapon.

"Shit!" Louie yells. He scrambles up the debris and back out of the room about as fast as he came through, failing to ask *who* took her.

"I'm surprised you came back," I say to Dr. Evelyn.

"I have a duty to my sister."

"And that might be?" I ask.

"I have a message for you," Verity interrupts, pulling up her hair and securing it with a clip. "From your mom." She brushes her slacks and adjusts her blouse. From her front pocket she removes Avril's eye necklace. If Dr. Evelyn is upset when Verity clasps the jewel around my neck, she doesn't let it show. The white sapphire and opal eye surrounded by gold and diamonds glitters against my pale chest when I check it in a sliver of mirror disappearing on a wall, covered over by ivy.

"It was given to your mom years ago, to be passed to you," Verity says.

"Why?"

"She wouldn't tell me," Verity says. "I thought the ring signified those who work for Septum Oculi but she said no."

"Reggie, you wear an eye ring," I say. "Want to share its meaning?"

"No," he says, sticking a revolver back in his waistband. He twists the ring on his finger and shoves both hands in his pockets.

"Why not?"

"Because we have enough curses and fury entering this world," he says. "I'm not adding to it…"

"Verity? You're schooled in this stuff," I say. "What do you think?"

She looks up at the ceiling, to gather her thoughts, I think, before she responds.

"Eyes are probably the most prolific symbol on the planet," she says. "They can represent clairvoyance, omniscience, or gateways to the soul. Some cultures view them as wicked, as in the 'evil eye' or blessed, like the Eye of Providence."

A few steps to the right, one swipe of my hands against the foliage, where mom's wall of painted eyes hang…and they're gone. All of them. "We'll be okay under the eye of God," she'd said, but I don't repeat her words to the others nor mention her paintings have been torn away. Avril used the term *Eye of Providence*, meaning divine, as in, I think, God watching over humanity.

"Your mom did say only a Camaeliphim can properly wear this specific eye necklace," Verity says. "Otherwise, it's just a piece of jewelry. Activation is only possible when two receptors, like your mom and me, stand in agreement, to draw down energy from the Source into the eye—for the Balancer."

"Balancer?"

"That would be you," Verity replies. "Balancer between realms. Manager of Chaos."

"We're all in trouble," Reggie says.

I pitch him a disapproving look while touching the necklace. Dr. Evelyn glares at Verity for a split second, long enough for me to notice and quick enough for her to think I didn't. The eye necklace doesn't make me *feel* any different—but I always admired it when Dr. Evelyn wore it—even planned to steal it when we lived at Plum Hook Bay—but she never took it off.

"Did you know this?" I ask Dr. Evelyn.

"I knew it had power but I was never able to activate that power," she says. And for the first time since I've known her, I notice dark half-moon circles under her eyes.

"But you tried, didn't you?" I ask. "You stole this necklace from my mom after someone attempted to murder her."

A tear spills down Dr. Evelyn's cheek but dries before it hits her blouse. "Walk with me," she says. "Over here..."

We take a seat together on a wide log as I wonder how in the hell Verity and my mom created some otherworldly jungle in a hospital room, unless it's some sort of holographic trick and the rest of us have climbed into a weird matrix just on the near side of reality.

"I'm going to tell you our story, your mom's and mine," she says. She sucks in a deep breath then heavily sighs. "We both attended Oxford—Exeter College to be exact. We didn't know we were sisters. We roomed on opposite sides of the quad. Each of our dorm rooms faced a chapel. Once particular evening, the singing and the chants separately beckoned us, the voices angelic. We arrived at the Chapel nearly the same time. But it was completely empty...and dark. It gave us quite a fright. In our rush to leave, I spilled my purse. Your mother stopped to help me gather my things, including a small picture of my father. We were both gob smacked when she asked why I carried a picture of *her* dad. "

"Who was he?" I ask.

"Ian Windsor was an electrical engineer who went missing in 1945. He'd been working with Nikola Tesla on some specialized plasma. Your grandfather, in addition to being a celebrated electrical engineer, led quite a domestic double life, keeping two wives and two daughters on different continents."

My mother and my grandmother never talked about Ian Windsor. In fact, outside of my father, I don't recall either woman ever mentioning *any* of my relatives. "What happened?" I ask.

"The Chapel lit up," Dr. Evelyn says. "Your mum and me cowered in absolute terror. Yet these *beings*, they calmed us. They claimed we'd both been called—but only one of us would be chosen."

"Chosen?"

"To be inseminated."

"In the *Chapel*?"

"The chapel was saved from demolition for this very purpose —to bring the Source closer to the people and prevent perpetual galactic chaos—but no, nothing consummated in the chapel, it was a wedding of sorts. I figured I was a natural choice, believing myself mentally and physically superior to your mother. I'd gone to boarding school at St. Andrews. I'd been groomed for royal marriage, and I was 'legitimate' under the eyes of both the law and our Lord. Your mother had a formal education and etiquette training but wiggled out of high society, fancy clothes, and duty whenever she could. Avril preferred isolated pursuits, walking in the woods outside of Jericho, or reading for hours about plants among the stacks at Blackwell's. She even refused to have a debutante ball. My sister was always a strange girl."

"But you weren't chosen," I said.

"No." Dr. Evelyn shakes her head. "Your father was completely enchanted by her. I was called to *serve* your mother instead, sort of a lady-in-waiting to the incubator of celestial hybrid nobility."

"And you resented this?"

"Very much," Evelyn says. "Your mother had the very thing they required that I lacked."

"A heart?" I ask.

Dr. Evelyn flips a hand at me. "No silly, your mum was humble yet perceptive and open to experience, a gifted child— always able to see things no one else could. I was furious they chose her, an American yokel."

"Do you hate her?" I ask.

"Quite the contrary," Dr. Evelyn says. "We don't see eye to eye where you're concerned. She hoped to stop fate but that's impossible. Your mother completely lost the plot. Avril was very angry with me for plucking you out of foster care—but that was *always* the plan. She feared for your safety and tried to go around fate using the juvenile court system to lose you in its cracks and mold you a new identity. Samantha isn't even your real name."

"What is my real name?"

"To hell if I know," Evelyn says, as if my name means nothing and doesn't need to be known. "Avril wasn't wrong to be concerned but she lost everything to have you, including her career, her mind, and her love, your father."

"I see why she hates you," I say. "Why'd you take my necklace?"

"I thought I could train myself to take your place, prove my worth, and figure out the necklace."

Verity approaches us and none too soon, I think. I was about to push my aunt over this log. "Avril also told me you must find Genin."

My heart leaps a bit at the sound of his name and the same feelings of warmth whoosh across my hips. "Genin? Why?" I ask.

"He's in danger. She said the war has begun."

"Oh, no," Dr. Evelyn says drawing a palm over her mouth.

"I have no idea where Genin might be," I say. "Last he'd written, he was training for some Navy Seal program in California. That was years ago. Where did the Tall Whites take my mom?"

"They didn't *take* her," Verity says. "She went with them."

"Could my mom survive their dimension?" I ask.

"She can now," Verity says. "She tri-located."

"Tri-located?"

"She shed her form—entered a total light state."

"Can my mom return?" I ask Verity.

"No." Verity lowers her head.

An involuntary tear cuts a path down my cheek.

"I know where to find Genin," Reggie says, walking toward us. "He can't come to us, but you can go to him."

"Where is he?" I ask.

"Overseas," Reggie says. "He's part of an international task force gathering field intel on those tribal murders I told you about. I can find a place for you on his team."

"But I don't have the credentials or training," I say. "My DOE-induced side-trip to coma-land locked me out of GWU and a career with the CIA, remember?"

"Not exactly," Dr. Evelyn says, folding her hands and putting two pointer fingers under her chin when she stands to pace. "The reason you were brought to and hidden on Plum Hook Bay in the first place is because Septum Oculi thought something like this might happen. While Reggie wasn't "read into" me being your aunt, we both had a 'need to know' when it came to your training..."

"I don't understand," I say.

"You actually have a degree, a Doctorate in Strategic Foresight with a concentration in exobiology, that you remotely earned on Plum Hook Bay from The University of Oxford's Future of Humanity Institute," Dr. Evelyn says.

"A Foresight degree? Seriously?" I ask. "How can I possibly have a degree in *Foresight* when I know nothing about it? Is that even a real degree?"

"Oh, but you do," she answers. "Do you remember your lessons on philosophical foundations and philosophy of the mind?"

"Yes, but..."

"Do you also remember our lessons on biosecurity, prediction, and human enhancement, and forecasting through imagination and dreams?"

"I can't believe that any university as renowned as Oxford would remotely offer a degree in "Foresight"," I say.

"You remember Dr. Sterling tutoring you in biology, neuroscience, astrobiology and natural history, right?"

"Yes."

"Remember the exam I gave you?"

"You mean the one that lasted five days and took me eight-hours a day to complete?" I ask.

"Yes, that one," Dr. Evelyn says with a light laugh. "And the thesis you had to write and defend?"

"You said it was for my high-school diploma."

"I lied," she says, tugging and straightening the cuff of her blouse. "You were too smart for your own good. We had to keep your mind occupied and we weren't sure how much time we'd have. Septum Oculi made a decision to begin your training immediately. You have a degree."

"And this Future of Humanity Institute…at Oxford…they're okay with this?"

"Not exactly," Dr. Evelyn says, adjusting her hair in what is left of another mirror disappearing under a bush. "We had to make a rather large donation, Dr. Sterling and I. Plus, there was someone at MI-6 we knew, who, you know, tugged a few strings."

"Where is Dr. Sterling, anyway?" I ask.

"I don't know," she says, showing a slight slice of sadness in her eyes. "He's been missing for about as long as you were in a coma."

It's not like Dr. Sterling to leave Evelyn's side, I think, wondering what might have happened to him.

"Okay, fine," I say, hardly believing what I hear about being degreed. "But I don't have any military or CIA training…"

From out of nowhere, Reggie flings his Army knife at my head. I catch it in my hand, handle side, without even looking, before my brain catches up to what happened, an instinctive reflex. "You do have such training," he says. "I taught you and so did Sgt. Major Lynch."

"But…"

"Do you know Jujitsu?"

I nod.

"Do you know Krav Maga?" He asks.

"Yes."

"If I dropped you in the middle of nowhere and gave you coordinates or not, could you figure out where you are, survive in the wild, and find your way back?"

"Yes."

"How many languages do you speak?" Dr. Evelyn asks.

"Seven," I respond.

"Can you hunt, kill and take down an enemy if needed, or enter a facility undetected to gather intel? Can you walk one-hundred miles with a fifty-pound rucksack strapped to your back?

Are you able to handle torture, disguise yourself, and deflect attention to save another soldier?" Reggie asks.

"Yes," I say. "But I'll avoid it if I'm able."

"Are you willing to take a bullet for your brothers and sisters in arms?" He asks.

"Of course," I say.

"Will you never tell a soul about your clandestine service or seek public accolades for serving the United States?" Verity asks.

"No," I say. "People would never believe me if I did."

"It's also considered treason under the Espionage Act," Verity says. "A One-hundred-thousand dollar fine and ten years in prison."

"Are you capable of flying without the aid of technology?" Evelyn asks.

"Sometimes," I admit. "I wouldn't exactly call it going airborne. I'm look more like a flying squirrel."

"Well then, Dr. Blake, I'd say you're ready for this assignment," Reggie says.

"To where?" I ask.

"Indonesia," Reggie says.

*Dr. Blake. Hmm. I do like the sound of that. Dr. Samantha Ryan Blake.* It isn't *'all hail her royal highness'* like I'd once daydreamed about at Plum Hook but it will do, a tiny scrap of painfully earned credibility to lean against my tattered and troubled backdrop.

Vigo growls and barks again at the door.

"001 won't be going anywhere but with us," someone says.

Two men in black suits amble over crumpled steel, their micro-expressions registering more than a bit of surprise by the mini-jungle, before they recover. They don't resemble or even *feel* like 'Not Who', the *'It'* being that showed up in my hospital room back in D.C. These men, I sense, are just that…men…Air Force intelligence hired as private contractors on behalf of DOE to remand me back to being a comatose fueling station.

"Who are you?" Dr. Evelyn asks, crossing in front of them, her arms folded.

Vigo places himself between the men and the rest of us and bares his teeth. ***"GRRRRRRR...."***

"You have no need to know," one of them says before he looks at me. "Come on. We'd rather not hurt any more people today than we already have."

Verity brushes some moss from her hair and rolls her eyes. "Ted. Dan." She says. "What an unexpected, blood-curdling surprise."

"Verity Lane?" One of them asks, blinking in disbelief. "What the hell are you doing here?"

"I'm *her* lawyer," Verity says, pointing at me. "*Dr.* Blake is not going anywhere with you."

"Under Title Ten—she belongs to the DOE and we have orders to bring her straight to them," one of them says.

Reggie, Vigo, Verity and even Dr. Evelyn, stand in front of me, blocking Ted and Dan's path.

"I'll take your Title Ten and raise you Title Fifty or Title Eighteen, take your pick." Verity says. "Dr. Blake is now officially in CIA detainment by order of Septum Oculi for reasons of national security."

"But...you can't do that!" Dan says.

"Where are you taking her?" Ted asks—I think its Ted. Verity didn't, thankfully, formally introduce us.

"I can and I will," Verity says. "Step aside gentlemen, although I use that term loosely." She takes my arm and gives me a wink. "Tertia Optima coming through—and *you* have no 'need to know'."

As we climb out of what's left of my mom's room, a teary-eyed L. Smooter balances precariously over the rubble and hangs another handwritten sign beside the naked door frame.

*'0 Days Without Incident'.*

# TEN

# PLUM HOOK BAY

FIVE YEARS HAVE PASSED since I last stood, and collapsed, on this land.

Peeking out from the shadows, meticulously tended orchids, thousands of species, bloom in a kaleidoscope of color, suspended in rope netted hammocks, reaching multi-fingered roots toward the forest floor. First seen by Reggie with his unit in Viet Nam, then in my mom's room, and now here, at NASA Plum Hook Bay, I experience mixed feelings.

A tsunami of memories forces me to lean against the welcoming trunk of a thick blue spruce. I think about Pa Ling and Fensig swimming in the Huron River, Tetana pushing me in for a swim, Genin and my ayahuasca trip to the caves under the river. Jade with her bow and arrows. Saratu used to stroll through the gardens near the house in a hand-woven wrap, which reminded me of bed sheets. And Bennie. Words do no justice to how much I miss that freaky thirteen-year-old whiz-kid twerp who, along with Saratu, saved our lives.

The horror of this place creeps into my head, a million little hermit crabs of distressing recollections, kids in cages, locked rooms, and macabre experiments. I stuff it all back into a dark corner of my brain and try to hum it to rest but it doesn't work.

The sixty-foot boulder, nestled in the middle of the Huron river, a massive obelisk of limestone is still as imposing as I remember. I spent a summer swimming around this thing and a few nights watching vortexes expand and contract within it. Sometimes *beings*, Astral Weavers, I think, used this obelisk to catapult from here to there—wherever *there* might be. This mysterious rock denotes spiritual significance for the Iroquois', and before them, Fort Ancient Peoples.

Native burials and thousands of artifacts rest in a multitude of caves under my feet too. It is my hope they remain at repose and undisturbed. Given the fact this acreage was a governmental land grab, my hopes are razor thin. Reggie said, "Get in and get out!" He plastered me with an earpiece and a small camera to record "goings on". It will be dark soon and I need to hurry.

The general public and the media were told NASA Plum Hook Bay got decommissioned in 1985 and closed. But classified documents reveal a private defense firm, Sky Wolf Technologies, poured millions of dollars into NASA Plum Hook Bay. Lurking beneath this mote of legal paper is U.S. Army command, and DOE, which still run the show, so little has changed, except a few coats of paint and an epic upgrade to its underground optic cables, something Reggie says they'll use for advanced computer systems, all wirelessly connected, something Bennie once shared with me he worked on—even showed me his bioelectric magnetic spider and some handheld GPS thingy.

Sgt. Major Brock Lynch, my former weapons instructor, is the newly crowned Lt. Colonel here. Reggie tells me that's quite a promotional jump in the span of just under five years. He said Lynch likely deserves it for the shitshow he survived on the front lines of the Gulf War. I was never a favorite of Lynch. I can't shoot worth a shit and I think he views missed targets as proof of human weakness. He used to say my intense stare could laser cut concrete and that I suffered from a serious lack of discipline. Part of our problem, I think, is we both harbor personal war stories, afraid if we share too much with the world, others might consider us ripe for pillage, so yea, he was right, I have attitude.

Tangled vines, leafy ferns, and well-placed tree trunks spill over to provide great cover in the woods where I avoid the paths. I weave my way through searching for my fox. It's too dangerous to fly, a costly risk that put me on radar last time. I squat near a fallen log, tilt my head back, and let loose with a perfect whippoorwill call and some low growls.

No Hope.

Either my fox is well-hidden or she's been relocated—or worse. If my Source Guide is dead, my Earthly demise is practically imminent—perhaps days or months away, and if I'm lucky, maybe a year.

Reggie's rusted over John Deere tractor sits covered in wildflowers near a newly installed razor wire fence. A herd of feral horses, released decades before I arrived, roam overgrown fields. This land was, according to Dr. Sterling, subject to eminent domain during the 1940's. Two-hundred farmers lost property that had been in their families for generations. The government came in with court orders and guns, seized ten thousand acres for 'deep black expansion'.

The lone conifer in the cornfield no longer stands. It's one I used to read under, protected by puffy fans of pine needles from having to attend therapy, falling snowflakes, or bright sun. It's spindly branches are sawed away, leaving a toppled half-rotten log leaking tarry sap. For what purpose this tree was struck down I don't see. An underground cave near the tree's tangled root system is covered with two massive slabs of bedrock that remind me of laser-cut pyramid stones, placed here, I suspect, to keep out trespassers, or perhaps, seal in escapees. I've been trapped under there with dozens of other kids. Some of us made it out. An involuntary shiver rattles my body as I struggle to sew up this gaping mind wound. It's best to move along...

An American flag still sways on the flag pole in front of the estate but now a new black flag joins it beneath, a yellow-gold moon with a howling wolf. And the sun just surrendered to dusk.

Down by the oversized red barn near the bottom of a small hill, Reggie's blue Ford is resurrected. Lynch barks orders at some soldiers as I creep by unnoticed, and then climbs in to zoom off. Wait until I tell Reggie that Lt. Colonel Lynch commandeered his beloved truck for 'official Army business'. I'm sure that won't make Reggie happy, particularly since we spent months meticulously rebuilding its engine and repairing its body, sanding, polishing and scrubbing away all the wounds—kissing the boo-boos, Reggie called it.

The willow tree where Sarge lies buried is now an empty stump. The regal queen with delicate limbs of shaggy blue-leaf splendor that once tumbled down to meet plush grass is laid to waste. During summer, I used to hide beneath her skirt of branches searching out four-leaf clovers. I'd stare up through the limbs and daydream about stowing away on a Lake Erie barge, maybe sailing to India's Golden Temple. It seems silly now—the immature and fruitless hope of a child-woman trapped in a cloak-and-dagger world.

Everyone said Sarge died of natural causes, but he was deeply disturbed by some unseen threat the day I arrived. Like him and the willow tree, and the conifer in the cornfield, I too, feel cut down. It takes a considerable amount of fortitude to withhold tears. Change has arrived, as it always does, and there is little I can do to slow her axe.

I bid Sarge a silent greeting. "Hello, fella."

"Goodbye your majesty," I say to the nonexistent willow.

A red cardinal swoops onto a pine branch a short distance away. He wobbles his head and chirps a greeting before flying off toward the river, his beautiful red wings gliding him onward and it makes me think about Bennie and his pet cardinal, Edwin. Edwin wasn't his Source Guide. Bennie had a wolf named Randolph too —although I always felt the wolf didn't suit him as well as the cardinal, and now I wonder, did he too borrow someone else's Source Guide?

I swipe a tear from one cheek when I reach the NASA side of the farm, but another lands on the ground beside what used to be

Silo #57. It's a small hill now, completely covered over with a grand buckeye tree, from the Hetuk seed I tossed, right before being stung by poison. The irony for me is that hetuk seeds like the buckeye are toxic to humans. If not properly prepared, Barbara said, they can cause paralysis or death, but if correctly roasted, the seed heals a host of injuries. It hides Bennie and his story under its roots. And I can't decide if paying respects again to Bennie paralyzes my heart or heals my inner wounds.

*"...in all our woods there is not a tree so hard to kill as the Buckeye...denoting to all the world that Buckeyes are not easily conquered, and could, with great difficulty, be destroyed."* Verity once read me those words by Daniel Drake, an Ohio arborist. It's too bad Bennie wasn't so hard to kill. I like to think this tree cradles his spirit, tending to him through mother nature, especially since he never really knew his mom. None of us did.

I lay a palm over the Buckeye tree's sturdy roots and hope to feel a pulse, even pray to the Great Spirit for a weak one. I sense a vibrating energy and stealthy communication snaking its way through grass, root systems, bacteria, bugs, and nearby trees. I hoist myself onto a lower boughs and climb as high as I can for a wide lens view of NASA Plum Hook Bay. Standing on a beefy limb, I scour the vista to Lake Erie.

Thankfully, the part of the river near NASA's retention pond no longer runs rusty, a good sign that nature and man work in conjunction to detoxify this place—allowing it to breathe again as it did before humans arrived to split neutrinos and spill chemicals.

*Shit!*

Soldiers suddenly emerge from a congregation of conifers to pass right below me, at ease, joking, and talking, their guns sloppily banging against camouflage hips as they scope out a comfortable place to smoke weed. I imagine this semi-rowdy crew found Reggie's old stash in the barn or along a fence line where his once carefully tended crop now grows wild and hidden within thick bundles of bull grass and blue thistle. Major Lynch would have these soldiers balls nailed to boards if he knew they were 'polluting their GI soul' with MJ.

Still as an owl looking over its prey, I size up each soldier's aura. A couple have real problems—health or mental—but Lynch wouldn't have it any other way. He thrives on *'hardcore fixer-uppers'* as he calls them—soldiers with violent pasts looking for a cause. Lynch sparingly doles out praise too, which he told me, keeps soldiers from going soft and getting killed in action. I suppose he's right—can't have a bunch of pansies prancing around in uniform —or the United States will become a divided nation, perfectly seasoned for plucking. But then again, what a great way to confuse the enemy—give them hugs and flowers instead. The soldiers head toward NASA, near a cliff I know, unwary of my trespass.

The NASA Plum Hook Station, as it used to be called, still buzzes with activity, but not nearly as loud as I remember. Armed guards roam watch towers but smokestacks send no signals and the nuclear reactor is *off grid*—decommissioned after a staged 'accident'. It was something right out of the intelligence playbooks to cover over a multitude of sins that included uninformed experiments on human and hybrid children. Government officials 'took' foster kids into their care because we had no family—no one to report us missing or to consider our 'best interests'. Less red flags.

Polished metal and stone glare back at me, just as I remember, a stark futuristic city where swarms of soldiers in dark uniforms skitter here or there. Tanks growl and small planes on the landing strip provide the eerie audible hum of electro-magnetic propulsion. Thankfully, no one unloads yellow body bags from long black vans today. I scan the acreage the best I can using the crystal optic 'binoculars' Reggie loaned me, but still no sign of Hope. She could be hiding underground, I think. But Source Guides typically *sense* their charges and come running.

Reggie and Verity are probably eating ice cream back at Toft's Dairy, about ten miles away, expecting at some point to hear from me so they can scoop me up from our agreed upon rendezvous. Since I can't locate my fox, there is something else I must do, something I haven't shared with a soul—not even Reggie. Shoving myself deeper into a woodland embrace I meander along the river bank, searching every fox den I find but come up empty. My Source Guide is elusive. Darkness matures.

An expanding chill supplants the summer sun and the landscape drifts in and out of focus, going from clear to blurry, then clear again, almost like a holograph. Since I'm used to Plum Hook's terrain and mind games, I continue on, even when it starts to snow—in May 1991, just as it did in August 1984. A white layer of loose powder covers the ground, complicating my fox hunt and it leaves visible tracks—mine. Raising my frame a few inches off the ground, I smirk at my cleverness.

*Whack!*

*"Damn it,"* I whisper. "Bitch-smacked by a rogue branch."

A steep ravine catches my fall along with a small avalanche of snow, dirt, and leaves. I stretch my arm muscles and latch onto a tree root where I dangle and then drop. Thankfully, my landing is leafy soft. Pearlescent swirls of stars—millions of them—meet my eyes.

The expansive space above me makes me miss something I used to know and sadness throws a dark cape of longing over my heart. Even though I exist on Earth, I'm imprisoned in this biological vessel, fully dependent on its water, gravity, plants, insects, animals, and this atmosphere, for survival. On the flip side, this tiny planet is connected to an infinite span of multiverses, interdependent and intelligent, and I, and the rest of the humans and hybrids, part of it.

---

Sweat gallops along my forehead and spreads out across my chest. I tiptoe into the massive library. Precisely carved vines, miniature angels, and a solitary cardinal rest upon weighty branches that stretch across the entire ceiling and fade above the grand piano into a cloudy universe of galaxies. This used to be my favorite room, too beautiful to destroy or demolish, the craftswoman lost to history like most other females who get replaced with dick-slinging fables that get passed off as accurate historical narrative.

I'm disappointed Zitkala Sa's books are gone from the shelves and replaced by dime store versions of aviation and astronomy magazines. Verity told me Zitkala Sa means *Red Bird* in Lakota. Zitkala Sa's poetry and stories were some of my favorites. She'd been forced to give up and change almost everything about herself to help her people—to adapt—to assimilate into a world that expected it of her but one that would not fully accept her. The ladder to reach the highest shelves is missing too. But I won't need that.

The first time I ever barely spoke with Bennie he'd hidden himself here behind the autographed Mark Twain series, to spy on Verity and me. He scrambled when I caught him, from a shelf to under the grand piano, a rare D-274 Steinway Alma Tadema built in 1883 bolted to the floor. I followed him. "They *hear* you," he'd said. Bennie planted a quick kiss between my eyes and dashed out in a flurry, leaving me to wonder what on Earth he ever meant.

Tapping fingertips to forehead I still feel his smoochy peck on my soul. Crawling up under the piano, my eyes scan its underside. And there it is, wedged between the wires and the soundboard, just where I left it almost six years ago—the flat 'key device' everyone involved with Project Looking Glass would love to get their hands on. I gently unweave its finery from the piano innards and tuck it in my bra under my left breast.

Stepping outside, the air grows warm again. Oh, hell no! Automatic weapons sputter a ricochet of bullets. Ducking down, I'm trapped by a 'live fire' training exercise, caught between two practicing counter forces. A small unit of soldiers barrel toward me, weapons drawn. If I fly, they'll shoot. If I stand here, they'll shoot. The only thing left any screwed hybrid like me can do is...

...*Run!*

I blow past the window to my old room on the backside of the mansion. So much for the stealth tactics Reggie taught me. I inelegantly plunge into a ditch. *Crack!* Fuck! I broke the night goggles and camera. *Damn it!* Reggie warned me each pair costs Septum Oculi about fifty-thousand dollars and made me swear I'd take good care of them. Hugging my arms around a pile of old leaves, I draft them over me for camouflage and lay stick still.

Five minutes...

Ten Minutes...

Twelve Minutes...

No sound. Not even crickets. Something isn't right here. The leaves float away up and out of the ditch. I raise my head and sniff the air. I'm in a lost space, on the farm, close to the soldiers but on the other side of some freakish one-off sky veil. With my hands, I feel the dirt beneath me, the grass in the ditch, the coolness of the evening. This isn't a dream. No. It's not a hallucination either. I feel oddly detached but still part of reality. Lifting my head barely above the rim of the trench, nobody is here. Time to go! Foisting myself over the rim, I sprint toward an adjacent cornfield, one of the best manmade labyrinths around. Good luck to anyone trying to find me there!

Something flickers from the corner of my sight. "Ahhhh!" Thump. Hybrid Down! Tucking and rolling, I land on my feet and pull a small blade from my hip, combat ready. A female laughs. I recognize her voice although it's been a long time. This is the voice of someone who used to visit my crib, and occasionally, my lucid dreams during the smoky gray dawn of a new morning, but I've never actually met her in solid form.

"Lozen?" I straighten my battle crouch.

"Need some help?" She asks, her face creasing into a smile.

"Yes, I do—but what are *you* doing here?" I ask. "I mean, *in the flesh?*"

"Lets' see...in the Earthly language called English, I'd have to say, 'saving your ass'."

Twelve giant-sized Astral Weavers, their strong chests layered with black pearls, stand before me sporting copper armbands with red feathers, which strain to contain swollen biceps. Their arms reflect ancient charcoal-colored tattoos and their bright yellow-green eyes and reddish hair glint under a half-moon.

Lozen is a cunning battle strategist and guardian of the twelve gates of the Portals of Ninmah, able to traverse dimensions—that's all I can remember. She stands almost seven-feet tall and playfully taps her tantalum spear on the top of my head. I swat it away and frown. If she wanted, she could turn that thing on and I'd be flash broiled. We share her realm's customary greeting of placing a hand palm between the neck and chest of the other in a show of warrior-hood and friendship. "We have much trouble on this planet," she says. "But we have no Earth time to discuss. You must leave this place and find the Raga."

Army soldiers search behind the ditch I just left.

"Shit," I whisper. "We have to hide."

"They can't see us," Lozen calmly says, checking her fingernails.

"Of course they can! We're only a few feet away!"

"No," Lozen says. "We see them but they're blind to us."

"How?"

"'Opticom'."

"Opticom?"

"It's a mind manipulation technique," She says, waving her hand across the rest of her unit. "We focus our electro-magnetic density ranges to absorb certain widths of broadband, rendering us invisible. The drawback to this weaponry is that when we move, it generates distortion and risks a hormonal cascade among humans."

"What happens if they get too close?" I ask.

"Oh," Lozen says. "It drives humans into intense but temporary fear, nausea, perhaps some yelling and diarrhea—and on occasion, they faint."

At that moment, a soldier drops his weapon and runs in the opposite direction screaming. "Just like that," she says, as his unit retreats into the woods, leaving their guns behind.

"Okay, Princess," she says to me. "Time to get you outside these gates."

"How?" I ask. "I'm sure by now they've set up a perimeter."

"Hold still," she says, pulling something out of her waistband, a stick-thick wand made of what looks like selenite crystal, except it has jagged edges at the top that remind me of small sharks teeth. "This may hurt just a little."

"What is it?" I ask.

"Time ranger," she says. "Set your intention on where to go—hurry—stare into it and set your intention—but don't go far in time or you'll be lost even longer than you were the first round."

"Why do extraterrestrials get all the cool shit?" I ask.

"Hurry! I can't have my unit under so much stress holding humans under virtual veil," she says with a stern look. "Plus, it's not polite to tease the humans. Set your intention and close your eyes."

"Fine," I say. "When you see Nemain, please tell her I miss her—and thank you. I've set my intention…"

She smacks my ass so hard with her spear I whirl around…and just like that, I find myself standing before a very surprised Reggie and Verity, who immediately drop their ice cream cones in front of Toft's, along with a boy, an onlooker about seventeen, I'd guess.

*Shit.*

"You…" he says, "Y-y-y-you *appeared,* from like, out of nowhere."

"I have no idea what you're talking about," I say to the boy. If I maintain denial, most people conclude they're mistaken.

"I know what I saw and you just materialized from nowhere! Wait a minute. I remember you! You were the girl who stood up to my grandfather a few years ago inside Toft's. These two were with you!"

"Damn," Reggie mutters.

"You mean that prejudice old coot who called my friend here awful names?" I ask, ready for another confrontation, because bad apples usually cling to dysfunctional trees until they rot. "It was not a good day for ice cream six years ago."

I completely lost my sixteen-year-old mind that day—fell apart in front of everyone, including, evidently, this kid, but that's another story. "How is that bigoted butthole, your grandfather?" I ask.

"He's dead," the boy says. "He died a few years ago…"

"I'm sorry," I say, but not really. This kid's grandfather was a total dick.

"It's okay," the boy says. "My brother Caleb and my dad was

with him—grandpa pointed to the barn ceiling hollering about some angel in blue robes. They didn't see a thing. When they checked on grandpa again he'd slumped over dead. Heart attack."

I sway a bit feeling light-headed. The boy catches me when I wobble and smiles at Verity. "Whoa. You should probably sit down," he says. "You fainted last time you was here."

Who wouldn't faint if they found out one of their best friends was murdered? But I don't say anything, don't tell the boy why. He would have been around ten or so, at the time, I think, when Katie died. "What's your name?" I ask.

"Freeman," he says. "Are you an angel?"

Reggie, Verity, and I trade glances. "Her?" Reggie says with a big laugh. "She's got about as much angel in her as a day old cow patty rotting in the sun."

"You seem a lot nicer than your grandfather was," I say, twisting my brows at Reggie.

"I loved him for sure," Freeman says, scratching his blonde buzzcut with farm-work-weathered fingers. "Even if I didn't like him much. He was a rabid cruel old man. Learned some things from him though, like how *not* to treat people."

I rub the side of my ass cheek to ease Lozen's sting.

"Why you rubbing your ass?" Reggie asks.

"An unexpected swat to the backside before tele-transport," I say.

"I *knew* it!" Freeman says. "Are you guys aliens or something?"

"Where's my night-vision goggles?" Reggie asks.

"I broke them," I say. "It was an accident."

Reggie looks at me way too calmly but I can tell he's super pissed. "Sam," he says, "I told you..."

I hold up my palm in front of his face. "I saw your blue Ford."

"Yea, it was destroyed by that funky orb and is nothing but a pile of scrap behind the barn," he says.

"No it's not. Lynch refurbished it. It's now his personal vehicle."

"Oh, hell no!" Reggie says. "You telling me he's driving *my* truck around Plum Hook Bay?"

"Yes."

"Vigo," Reggie says as the dog muzzles his knee. "God as my witness, we're getting my truck back…"

"I can help you," Freeman says. "I know a secret way…"

"What secret way?" Verity asks. "To where?"

"NASA Plum Hook Bay. It's a hole in the ground that leads to a tunnel system. It's a labyrinth but I figured out how to find the other side. I hunt rabbits there."

"You telling us you trespass into restricted government property and bypass the use of deadly force and don't trip any alarms?" Verity looks incredulous, a hand on her hip as she swivels her head and eyes the boy up and down.

"Not exactly," Freeman says. "The soldiers caught me. They started to cart me off to the FBI office there."

"And?"

"I told them if they told on me, I'd tell on them. So they turned off their body cameras and radioed headquarters that my breach was a rabbit, to disregard the false alarm."

"What could you possibly have on *them*?" Verity asks.

"They smoke weed from wild pot plants growing along the fence line near the woods," Freeman says. "And they wave vans full of contraband through a back decoy gate that looks like a hill. It opens up and vehicles go through. They just loaded a fox up and took it out of here a day or so ago, although that was kinda weird. Why'd they go to that trouble I can't figure. I mean, they could have just shot the varmint instead."

"Shit," Reggie says under his breath. "If a kid can figure this out, just imagine what our enemies know."

*They could have just shot the varmint instead,* I think. But they didn't.

# ELEVEN

# DARK ANGELS COMETH

LOOSE DIRT COVERS some of the corpses.

"What do you think?" Genin asks. "Tribal dispute? Jumiat-Ulema? Russians? Or someone else? Private contractors, maybe?"

"I figure there were at least five of them," I say, looking over the crime scene. "Their tracks are still visible in the mud where the monsoon hasn't completely destroyed evidence. And they were wearing boots, so that rules out a tribal dispute."

Bamboo arrows lie scattered like hundreds of spent matchsticks around our team. None hit their targets, which is surprising for a tribe so skilled in archery. I poke a small branch into the mud to uncover a partial skull bearing a small hole. A child. A girl about ten years old, the traditional wrap of her people still on her head. We've arrived a few weeks too late. This was a massacre.

The Sentelinese are a protected but *not* peaceful hunter-gather tribe on a very remote Bay of Bengal island chain between India and Thailand, in international waters. No one, until now, has ever gotten this close to them and lived.

The Indian government issued a 'no contact' order two years ago in 1990, prohibiting curiosity seekers from coming ashore, after native spear attacks resulted in wounded boats and planes limping back to civilization looking like porcupines. Can't say I blame the natives for wanting to be left alone. But the Sentelinese possess nothing anyone might want enough to kill all one-hundred-ten of them. And if they did have anything of value, it could be taken without murdering mostly kids—although the Sentelinese *would* put up a deadly fight. From the looks of this, it was a professional ambush, the tribe woefully unprepared and decimated.

"It can't be a Taliban type 'convert or die' situation," says Genin. "Whoever or whatever killed these people moved through their ranks faster than a surprise tsunami."

Genin rests his weapon across his broad chest and stretches a bulky leg over a fallen log. Tan biceps, slightly damp with sweat, bulge beneath his sleeveless camouflage. His thick beard makes him look as if he's been stuck here fighting a war that ended decades ago and someone forgot to tell him. Yet I know it's not true, because we flew over here from India yesterday in *Hercules*, a Lockheed C-130 military transport unit, specially built to land on the beach.

Higher-ups at Langley ordered us in, which tells me someone from our government knows more about this island and its purpose than they share. This 'need to know' bullshit is both a blessing and scourge in the realm of covert ops. The weird thing is that satellites show nothing—no ships, submarines, or planes coming near or making landfall at this off-limits island.

Genin hardly changed since our time together at Plum Hook Bay. He lost his mullet courtesy of the U.S. military and he's filled out in all the right places—quite the alpha-male, actually—and has the personality to go with, which sometimes irritates me. Seeing him again feels as if he never left—that my being 'in-animated' for four years never really happened, except for the fact that he and Verity appear grown up—changed their appearances and gained some advantageous skill sets. We work together now, thanks to Reggie, but none of us are privy to each other's true mission, which is good and bad. Good because I get to see Genin, but bad, because when I do, it usually means a lot of people in the same place are dead.

For the past year, Genin and I have reported similar "M.O." in a Brazilian rainforest, the mountains of Mongolia, and in the Central African Republic. Other members of our team said they found the same type of massacre in Papua New Guinea about six years ago. What any of this has to do with strange orbs, NASA Plum Hook Bay, or my mom's ethereal flight off this planet, we aren't sure. What we do know is that a small variety of new creatures, interdimensional or otherwise, pay visits to Earth.

We've been able to gloss over the evidence to the general public with counter stories, retrieval ops, discredit campaigns, or excuses. The CIA is a master at compartmentalizing, I've learned—good for our base of underpaid thrill hounds but bad for the health, welfare, and safety of its country, I think—and potentially detrimental to national security given our government's newfound affinity for swiftly replacing HUMINT (human intelligence) with co-opted artificial intelligence through the private sector. Bennie once told me there was grave danger in such compartmentalization. Too many unknowns.

After having my microchip and Dream Stealer removed, I never take for granted just how perceptive Bennie was all those years ago, and how valuable my privacy. This planet's national security reminds me of a political pyramid scheme with too many cracks and quacks in the system. Verity told me too, that our government keeps nosy journalists or conspiracy theorists in the dark when they file FOIA (Freedom of Information Act) requests because most of this stuff gets run through private contracting companies. She slings around words like 'proprietary information' or 'trade secret' against civilian vault crackers.

"What are you thinking?" Asks Genin.

"Gangs from China, Thailand, or Burma?"

"But why? And how in the hell would they get here?" He asks. "This place is surrounded by miles of ocean. It takes an entire day of jungle busting with machetes just to find this village. Why waste so much money and resources to slaughter people who don't stand a chance in hell of escape?"

I stumble over a broken branch.

"Walk much?" Genin jokes.

Vigo is beachside, back at the plane, and just like Reggie, he doesn't like being told what to do. He barks his displeasure, which we all hear. Reggie and his dog are not happy Vigo's stuck with me since I can't locate my Source Guide, likely the exact same fox removed from Plum Hook Bay, out the back way, months earlier. But that Freeman kid was right, why go to so much trouble for a fox? Unless, and this is what I figure, the person who gave the order knows about all about the value of Source Guides.

All this death. Bodies lie everywhere. Sometimes I think I sense Raga when I'm surrounded by extinguished lives but I'm not sure how to contain such an evil spirit, or virus, or whatever the damn thing is, let alone throw it into a Source Vortex, a place that can't be on Earth, which doubly complicates my cosmic clad contract with Not Who.

I reexamine the ground. Bullet casings. Lots of them…1911's, M9's and M4's, U.S. Military weapons, likely stolen and sold on the black market. One of the killers also used a Russian Vityaz-SN, a standard issue semi-automatic, handed out like candy canes to every military branch behind the Iron Curtain. Too many spent casings but no pockmarks on tree trunks. If every bullet found its target, this means there wasn't a single miss. Professionals.

Surprise.

Kill.

Vanish.

But why here?

"Professionals usually pick up their casings—every last one of them," I say. "Which tells me that whoever did this, purposely left a trail of confusion."

Genin nods as he scours thick mangroves a few yards from the Sentelinese community camp. The waters surrounding this northern Andaman Island are rough and continuously beat the shoreline and smooth jagged rocks until they resemble crystal.

Angry waves echo into the heart of the jungle, followed by flocks of yellow-breasted togians, which squawk and settle upon a tall Padauk tree over my head. They open and fold blue wings under a strong sun as sea breezes burst through the canopy, knocking large palm leaves and bamboo together. It resonates a pleasant natural wind chime to the tune of the bird's song. Ancient spider leg-like footpaths crawl out in eight directions into the dense jungle from the swollen body that is this camp. Vigo continues to bark, a non-native disruption contrary to the island's natural rhythm and flow.

Our forensic analyst, Dr. Monica, yells at some of the Seal team members. Well—they *were* Seal Team members. Since we aren't at war with the Sentelinese, American military is not permitted to conduct any ops here, so the CIA recruits these people as temporary private contractors with Top-Secret clearance. We *borrow* them from our military and redress them in uniforms void of any identifying insignia.

"For bloody Christ's sake, stope steppin' so hard 'round the evidence ya clumsy diggers."

Dr. Monica is a 6'2" cigar smoking, whiskey tipping forensic doctor who serves in TAG, a tactical assault group out of Australia. She was raised by a survivalist single mom who protected Aboriginals near the edge of the Outback on a vast cattle farm. She's one of many women I've met on my clandestine ops journey who commands complete respect from her unit. Frankly, I think she'd rip the balls off of any man with her bare hands if he dared make the mistake of demeaning her contributions because she has a vagina.

Women in our line of work frequently take periodic fire from the semi-auto of misogyny. It's unwarranted as far as I'm concerned. I think women make much better case officers or federal agents than men. We aren't as easily sidetracked from a mission with sex, booze, or cash—what we call *MICE* motivations (Money, Ideology, Cash, Ego). More importantly, people typically overlook females as 'spy material', a data point the ladies definitely exploit.

Discarded tools, handmade fishnets, and crude clay cook pots lie scattered. Someone was looking for something and wasted no time with the natives. Three huts are leveled to piles of kindling. Neatly lined pebbles and small rocks sit undisturbed in the mud along the border of this rudimentary community, the remnants of what looks like child's play. Wild boar bones are stacked in a long-extinguished fire pit.

"Stroooth. Jesus foking Christ," Monica says. "This is heaps bad."

Genin and I trade knowing looks as Dr. Monica steps through the bush. With Dr. Monica, most things we encounter are 'heaps bad'. She eyes us both up and down suspiciously. "It's nah good to have the hots for a teammate," she says. "It could compromise us all."

"We're friends, that's it," Genin says.

I nod but feel a little irritated by his too quick response.

"Aye, mates if ya say so—but we all heard you two '*friends*' (she uses finger quotations to drive home her point) smashing your back out in the tent on mainland last nigh'. Lemme know when you nut ou' your weddin' tackle."

Some of the SEALS from our unit rustle through ferns and enter our clearing. Dr. Monica steps halfway through the bushes and motions me. "Mate," she says. "Ya gotta come int' the bush and see this…" Monica holds back branches as we step into thick folds of tropical forest. We pace about twenty yards before I see what looks like a neatly stacked pile of Lincoln logs—only it isn't.

"Oh my God," I whisper.

Flesh hangs in strips from about twenty corpses, mainly children, their eyeless Modigliani sockets a vacuum of extinguished emptiness. I suck in my breath and turn my head. Monica takes her pen and lifts up some skin with a gloved hand from one of the corpses before she cuts it into a plastic evidence bag. "Aye, ya never gets used to seein' this typo cruelty," she says. "Strangest bloody thing I ever witnessed."

Genin stares at the pile of bodies for a moment before he continues ahead into an even thicker part of the jungle, where I think even mosquitos belly crawl through. I lose sight of him and it makes me feel uneasy but Vigo, thankfully, stops barking.

"They ain't rottin'," Monica says.

"What?" I ask.

"They ain't decomposin', there's no rigor settin' in. Even the maggots and ants won't go near 'em."

"What about their eyes?" I ask. "They rotted away, no?"

"Afraid not," she says. "The orbs on these poor carpet grubs been plum plucked out o' 'em. And that ain't all. Whoeva' did this also took all thay innards, haut, lungs, kidneys, spleens and livahs. Cut 'em clean out fina' than any scapel job I eva' seen. The surgeon eitha has a han' steadia' than a pa'fect level or a state o' the aut laysah. I'm goin' with the last 'un. Mate, toss me my Sullivan's Cove."

I reach into Dr. Monica's rucksack and soft pitch her flask. She unscrews the top, tips her head back and takes a long swig, no doubt, to help her dim this horrid crime scene. She's right. The smell of death is not here. I creep closer to the bodies and take a sniff where a pleasing odor of ozone rises. That's weird. I easily lift a corpse arm and it drops back into position upon release.

"Want some?" She asks.

"Yes."

"Here's the otha thing," she says, tossing back her flask. "Eva single one o' these battlers took a bullet after they was already dead."

"Why waste so much ammo?" I ask, taking a long sip to calm my growing anger. I lost my nervousness back in the Amazon. I guess it was the last straw, piled on top of all the other bullshit I deal with, that finally broke my fright and queasiness over this sort of shit show.

Monica shrugs as I hand her back the flask.

The trees behind her thrash wildly. She drops her drink. We draw our weapons. *Click, click.* Genin rushes into the clearing, pale as a puffy summer cloud under a dark crop of beard. He drops to his knees. My blood turns icy with concern as I move toward him to help but Dr. Monica yanks me back.

"Poison?" I ask, panic in my voice. Genin holds out his hand to wave no. He looks at me with tears in his eyes. He swallows hard. I've never seen him cry, but cry he does.

"Not poison," he says. "Worse. Doc, go take a look."

"Wha' could be warse than murdered carpet grubs?" She asks.

Genin doesn't answer.

Dr. Monica looks at me quizzically but stomps toward Genin. He rises to his feet and holds the palms back, backing in and spinning around, weapon ready, leading us.

"Sam," he says. "I don't want you to see this. Please stay back."

"Like hell," I say. "We're a team."

Genin steps around Dr. Monica and grabs my upper arm in an attempt to yank me back to where we've been, which is completely out of character for him and a ludicrous thing to do. He may be a Navy SEAL but he doesn't stand a chance against my hybrid skill sets. I flip him unto his back with a thud to the ground. He registers a look of total surprise but he doesn't let go of my arm and sweeps my legs, until I too, am off my feet.

"Get yer hand off o' 'er this instant or I be puttin' a bullet in ya," Dr. Monica says, her weapon trained on Genin. "That ain' na way to be treatin' ah laydee. She's a grown ass woman. Let. Her. Through. Now."

Genin releases my arm and lowers his head. "There's a reason I don't want her to see this, Monica." Tears trickle from both of his eyes into his beard.

I've never seen him act this way, not like this. The guys on his team joke that Genin has a titanium heart and nerves forged from hallow point bullets. Dr. Monica and I exchange 'he's out of his mind' glances.

"Please," Genin says, shaking his head. "It's. It's. It's not...this can't be happening." He staggers a little and then tries to recompose.

"What is it?" I ask, able to *feel* the grief welling up inside of him, sudden waves of sadness he desperately tries to contain. I duck under his large arm to keep him from collapsing again after we stand and his aura turns thunderstorm gray.

"Not what. Who," he finally says, hugging me close.

"Who?" I ask, dread streaming through my veins.

"Pa Ling and Fensig..." he whispers.

"What?" I shake my head to sweep out cobwebs and abruptly extract myself from Genin's embrace. "Did I hear you correctly?"

"Yes..."

"Are you sure?"

Genin takes my hand in his. Together we walk toward what I hope doesn't exist.

"No. No. Oh, God, no," I whisper, staring in disbelief as my heart sinks to my toes and I drop to my knees.

Side by side Pa Ling and Fensig's corpses are nailed on makeshift crosses, nearly naked, except for pigskin loincloths, suspended by spears driven through their forearms and stomachs. Carved on Pa Ling's chest are the letters "SCAT", while Fensig's chest has the letters "HACH".

Scathach.

That's *me*. *ME!*

My heart pounds in my ears.

Scathach (pronounced Scay-How) is a name Bennie called me when he gave me Hope as a re-birthday present. My hands tingle until they go numb. A torrent of grief smashes through my tough exterior. *Breathe Sam. Breathe.* What I usually do when confronted with unexpected death but perfectly timed inhales and exhales are of little comfort here. A rustle startles us from behind, the sound of snapping palms. We train our weapons, *click, click, click,* ready to shoot. Sweat trickles down my forehead and burns my eyes.

"Vigo!" I yell. "You almost got yourself killed!"

Reggie's Soul Guide sits at the edge of the circle, cocks his head, and waits for my comrades and me to stand down before he ambles to my side. He licks my hand and I slide a palm through his damp fur. Vigo is notorious for not listening when he's ordered to "stay" but I'm glad, at least this time, he disobeyed my order. His presence is a small tonic to my jagged nerves. Dr. Monica circles the oddly staged spectacle of double cruelty. She pulls a small pen camera from her chest pocket to take photos.

"How lon' ya two been knowin' these puh blokes?" She finally asks, her voice softer, almost maternal.

"We used to know each other," Genin trails off... "But that was a long time ago..."

I know Dr. Monica won't ask more questions. She can't. It's part of our security code under this human intelligence world in which we've been drafted to work.

I sink further into to my knees and focus on rotted palm leaves. I rock back and forth. Genin kneels and puts his arm around me, a small but treasured comfort under the harshness of unexpectedly discovering the Pa Ling and Fensig, our friends, so grossly mutilated in a remote jungle, hundreds of miles from the nearest civilization. These men were Genin's best friends at Plum Hook Bay. The three of them were inseparable as teenagers and would traipse through the forests for hours, hunting, swimming, camping or otherwise doing what guys do. Fensig came to Plum Hook from Greenland while Pa Ling was from—Indonesia!

"Pa Ling is from Indonesia," I say. "As Bajua, or sea nomad, he *had* to have known about this island."

"You think he was here on assignment?" Genin asks.

"Maybe," I say. "Maybe he showed up to warn the tribe."

"You think the Sentinelese killed Pa Ling and Fensig?" Genin asks.

"They're known for violence," I say. "But I'm not sure they'd understand the meaning behind a crucifixion. Then again, nobody's ever been able to get close enough to them to ask."

"What's tha' caaved on their stomachs?" Dr. Monica asks.

I force myself to look at the corpses again.

*SCATHACH.*

"It's one word carved on both abdomens," I say. "Scathach was a mythic Scottish warrior who trained the legendary Cuhullin in the art of combat. Legend says she guards the Fortress of Shadows and is a daughter of Bryce of Agarthia."

"Oh, cripes," Dr. Monica says, looking confused. "Is that all? Why didn't ya' sigh so before?"

"Sounds as if you *know* her," Genin says.

"Verity told me about her," I say, which is half true. "Remember how she used to read all those books on religion and history? She told me Scathatch's story was never written, save for an oral footnote or two."

"Figures she got thrust outta the lime," Dr. Monica says. "Lemme guess—some bloke got all the credit for slayin' her dragon somewhere, ri'?"

"Something like that," I say.

"What do you think it means?" Genin asks, slowly circling the corpses, a look of revenge smoldering under his now cool exterior. "Did this Scathach kill Pa Ling and Fensig?"

"No," I say. "I don't think so. It's a call-out. A warning or challenge."

"What sort of challenge?" He asks.

A sudden headache forces me to pin my palms against each temple. Dizziness throws me again, between two worlds, where an astral tether keeps me bound to Earth but capable of bilocating. I lean against Genin to keep from falling over and feel Vigo's fur against my thigh, bolstering me from the opposite side as I take an involuntary ride through a series of geometric shapes and equations, symbols, and packets of concepts unraveling within the folds of my memory...

"...Scathach, great warrior, martial arts expert and instructor of the battle gifted. She trains only the best of soldiers, men and women who pass her tests. Those who cannot complete her training, die— impaled upon hubris. She is a goddess of balance between natural order and entropy."

"What did I do?" I ask the lady in blue robes, the one who appears in my vision.

"You ensure deserving beings pass into the Land of Ni. You are a sister of the Valkyries, known as Norns, in most galaxies," she says without speaking, touching a small tubelike device to her throat.

"I didn't die during the last war," I say. "Not the way humans do."

"You were saved by an interdimensional sister, Nemain, and taken to Xirnan," she says. "It took the Ormian Council centuries of Earth time to find a human female suitable for your enhanced DNA, hence your mother being chosen."

"Who is Raga?" I ask.

"The fiercest tyrannical warrior known to any civilization. She helps Bezaliels conquer planets from the inside, using Nephilim as navigators."

"Where do I find her?" I ask.

"Discard your pride. It is weakness embedded in your human flesh but not part of your blood. Instead of looking up, try looking under..."

"Why is my celestial name carved upon the flesh of my friends?"

"To dampen your fortitude," Blue Robes lady says. "To draw out the Viking and to find the bride."

"Who is the Viking?" I ask.

"One of Golden Blood, hidden here, like the Word."

"I thought I was the only one left," I say.

"You were the only one found," she says. "There are others..." She taps a long digit to her neck, tilts back her head, and fades away.

"You okay?" Genin asks. He's used to my astral forays but only knows them as 'seizures of service', a cover story to blanket his 'need to know' because neither he nor Dr. Monica have that sort of clearance and do not work with Septum Oculi.

"Genin, how many underground cavern systems exist on this planet?" I ask.

"Thousands," he answers. "Why?"

"How many of them are tunnels leading to underground bases or linking continents together?"

"I don't know exactly," he says. "I just know they exist—some as far beneath the surface as 165 miles with a catacomb of tunnel entrances all over the planet, mostly camouflaged."

"What in bloody hell?" Dr. Monica says.

Genin and I swivel our heads as Dr. Monika presses on a small bulge protruding from Pa Ling's stomach area. "Feels like this bloke's swallowed a fokin' grenade or somethin'. Ah, ya two may want to loo' away and take some cover."

"You're not cutting into him," Genin protests as he steps forward.

I gently tug at his forearm. "She has to do her job," I say. "Even when it's one of our own."

"But…"

"Genin," I say. "What's hanging there is no longer Pa Ling. It's his shell. He's not there."

"I promise ya' lad, I'll sew 'im up right so he may have a propa' gatherin'," she adds.

Genin nods and waves his hand for Dr. Monica to proceed. He doesn't look or back away.

Drawing her forensic knife Dr. Monica cuts through Pa Ling's torso with careful precision to avoid disembowelment. Years of skinning animals post hunt on her mother's ranch has made her one of the top forensic coroners on this planet.

Pa Ling's fluids and blood spill onto the ground below her feet making a gushing splash sound but his innards remain intact. Dr. Monica is forced to puncture a portion of his stomach at the juncture where it meets the small intestine. The sound and putrid smell float over us, but we're so used to it we hardly flinch. She slowly punches her fist into the opening, turning it clockwise.

"I've got it," she whispers, slowly removing her hand from Pa Ling's torso. She opens her palm, stares at the item in disbelief and makes a face.

"What is it?" Genin asks.

"A compass," Dr. Monica replies. "It's ol' too—looks like a military compass from the 1960's. But why woul' he swallow a fokin' compass? I don' thin' the bloke coul' get it down his throot an it's go' an engravin' on tho back o' it."

"May I see?" I ask.

Dr. Monica shrugs and drops the compass into my hand. I turn it over and wipe some of the fluids away to reveal an inscription.

*From BB.*

A jolt of adrenaline courses through my system as I stare at the compass—*MY* compass—the one Reggie gave me back on Plum

Hook Bay when he taught me how to catch and kill chickens for dinner. The needle slowly spins in a circle refusing to settle on any direction, but it's not nearly as schizophrenic as it was at Plum Hook Bay, where I could never, except maybe once, get it to work.

"What is it?" Dr. Monica asks.

"This is *my* compass," I say, feeling completely bewildered. "How did Pa Ling wind up with *my* compass in *his* stomach? It's too big to swallow," I say.

"You like it that much? I suppose you can have it once it comes out of evidence...in about fifty o' so yeers," she says as she reaches to snatch it back.

"That's not what I mean." I say. I turn toward Genin. "Remember the compass Reggie gave me back at Plum Hook?"

Genin nods.

"What was inscribed on the back—you remember?"

"It read, *From BB*," he says. "Wait. Are you saying...?"

I hand the compass back to Dr. Monica. "Turn it over."

She reads the inscription, looks up at the sky and silently curses before looking around and handing it back to me. "It's yours," Dr. Monica says. "But tell no one. I could see heaps o' trouble for not baggin' this evidence. Come on, let's cut these poor blokes loose and get 'em in our best bags."

# TWELVE

# SARATU THE DORJE

THE SUN IS TOO bright and the air too humid for a funeral.

I thought it might be cooler at such a higher altitude but weather offers little respect to the living...or the dead. A pager hooked to my underwear vibrates. It's an inopportune time to check it now. I scan a multitude of solemn faces. Oil lamps and high-quality Baieidō incense burn nonstop around a large bronze image of Buddha. A pleasant scent of agarwood tickles my nose when I spot Tetana's corpse riverside, in state, ritually placed atop stacked branches. Her friends, people I've never met, present at intervals for prayer service.

My arms and legs feel like pillars and my mind is unable to conjure any daydreams for temporary escape. First death first took the 'Tweedles' then it came for Tetana. Her absence from this Earth leaves me empty inside, unable to wail, and as silent as the reddish dust that seals itself over my sandals. Priests chant in unison from religious texts, ring small brass bells, and lightly beat drums or blow into long tuba-like instruments. Its music vibrates against canyon walls and rumbles low through my chest.

Death.

I can't seem to influence its choice of souls these days and I'm unsure how to turn its course. Tetana was killed four days ago enforcing a "no fly zone" in Iraq under an advance directive for implementation of *Operation Vigilant Warrior.* She experienced mechanical failure of 'unknown origin' in her F-16. She'd radioed the flight deck that something was up there with her but the command information center saw nothing on radar. I listened to her plane's black box at Langley. Her 'last words' were a calmly uttered, "*Fuck.*"

I stuff my grief further into the folds of my robes and try to focus on some faces here. But I have a serious case of 'monkey-mind'. My thoughts swing wildly from one synaptic brain branch to another.

I'm relieved Joe Abar, my boss at Langley, insisted I take a break. I need this downtime after traipsing for months through dense jungles with Genin and Dr. Monica. We are no closer to solving the mystery of the tribal murders, nor am I any closer to finding Raga or my Source Guide. Abar temporarily separated and reassigned our team weeks ago—says it will refresh our heads. I sent Vigo back to Reggie. A third funeral was not part of my vacation plans.

As a newly crowned NOC (No Official Cover), Langley secured me a fake temp job. It comes with cool perks but zero diplomatic immunity. If I'm caught on foreign soil extracting classified information, Abar told me the punishment is execution or an extended stay at one of our adversaries finest and most remote zero-star prisons. My new position is a trojan horse, I think, because I'm based in London. I don't suspect the U.K. is in the habit of executing or imprisoning allies, especially since my work has everything to do with helping us all. I left the U.K. yesterday. I never dreamed as a child I'd actually come this far. It isn't India or the Golden Temple, but it is Nepal.

I'm *employed* as an executive for Harrington Technologies, a global defense firm. The entire company is privately owned by some guy with alleged ties to a multitude of highly important people, including the Royal family. Never met him. Not many people have. I was briefed his outfit works with the CIA to help secure global peace. I think that's one big crock of crap. Harrington Technologies, like any other private defense contractor I've worked with, poke hornet nests, mostly in third-world countries. It's done to score lucrative contracts and legal passes for human rights abuses under the guise of 'war', a business model, which requires constant feeding.

One of Tetana's Air Force comrades redraws my attention as she places a "Tiger Shark" patch over Tetana's chest, along the red border of her black sari. Tetana resembles a serene ninja, especially when her placid face is illuminated by late afternoon sun, which finally dips a few rays behind a mountain to offer everyone a break.

*Rest in peace, baby girl. I'm going to miss you.*

I place a customary offering of wooden prayer beads and incense on the steps leading down to the wide muddy river as I wipe away a tear. I cover my head with a veil like most of the women here, as is their custom, a fortunate and ancient tradition enabling me to go mostly unnoticed. Some of Tetana's Air Force friends stand together in prayer with the Lamas.

Three out of twelve former Plum Hook Bay foster kids are dead —within weeks of one another. Not good odds for the rest of us and way too coincidental. For all I know, the number could be higher but I hope not. I need answers, preferably from those I trust.

*Who* do I trust?

They've arrived…two people I desperately hoped to see again but wasn't sure if they'd show…

…Priyanka dabs a tear from her eye with a handkerchief. Rakito holds her hand. He gently drapes one lanky yet muscled onyx arm across her shoulders, pulling her small praline frame into protective comfort. A basket handle rests over Priyanka's left forearm, gently banging against a hip under her sari. A red dot, like a target in the middle of her forehead, signifies she's married. First Verity, now Priyanka. Both fall prey to legally sanctioned prostitution, or what others call *marriage*. Pity. I will *never* marry. Women give up too much of themselves when they marry…their dreams, goals, fitness, and mental health…and for what? Priyanka makes lemonade while Rakito builds lasers. *Pffft*. Not for me.

I learned in their files that Rakito and Priyanka tied her knot after Priyanka fled Plum Hook Bay and followed Rakito into the Peace Corp. This unsanctioned act pretty much wiped out their futures in covert ops. From the looks of it, I don't think they care. They have five children including two sets of twins and a robust fair-trade organic coffee plantation in Burundi. Unlike the rest of us, who opted for a life under the knuckle of bureaucracy, Priyanka and Rakito fled into ignorant civilian bliss. I wouldn't have thought so then, but perhaps they made a better decision.

I'm within five feet of the couple but go unrecognized. They descend steps toward me, then pass, standing before Tetana's body, to pay their respects. Priyanka places her tear dampened handkerchief in the basket and pulls out a small round neon pink container. She unscrews the lid and brings a plastic wand to her lips. Rakito helps her blow bubbles over Tetana's body. Some of the smaller children screech and point in delight, clap their hands or poke soapy orbs. My tears finally fall and I let them go, washing my face and heart with broken tenderness, remembering…

Blowing bubbles was Verity's thing, *holy bubbles,* she called them. Priyanka brought it here because she remembered Tetana loved bubbles too and thought of them as 'angel tears'. I'm moved by Priyanka's thoughtfulness. At Plum Hook Bay we were all once full of bubbles, bacon, and Barbara's daily sermons—before our lives were irrevocably changed. I've lost some of that I think—the ability to lighten up, live, and clap after bubbles. Priyanka places the little bottle in the crook of Tetana's arm on the opposite side of the Shark patch.

What I wouldn't give to spend an afternoon with Verity in this beautiful place reminiscing about our lives. Verity wasn't permitted to come. She works in an office full of paper pushers who err on the side of severely limited resources. We talk on the phone occasionally, but our jobs and top secret clearances severely handicap quality 'catch-up' time.

Rakito kisses his fingers and touches the pile of wood

supporting Tetana's body. Heads bent close, the couple whisper prayers together. Once finished, they turn to ascend, Priyanka's head again tucked into the security of Rakito's armpit, tears softly falling on the stone carved steps in front of her, drops I count in her wake. I follow eleven steps behind.

"Priyanka," I softly say, but loud enough for her to hear.

They both freeze slightly, then slowly turn around.

Priyanka's eyes spark as if someone just flipped the switch on a new set of Christmas lights. "Baap re baap! Arey! *Sam!*" She practically flies back down the steps before she flings her arms out and gathers me into her sari for a tight hug.

A floodlight of joy escapes from Rakito's perfect peppermint Tic-Tac mouth as he smiles wide, patting my back and taking both of us into a lion-hearted embrace. Priyanka sobs leave a wet patch of smeary tears on my shoulder. She releases me and rears back to get a better look.

"You're here! Oh my God, we thought we'd never see you again!" She says, wiping red-rimmed eyes. "You look fantastic! Your arms feel like bricks—so strong—we could use you on the coffee farm. You're so tall and skinny! Look Rakito! Sam has 'fire hair'! Your tribe would think her a witch!" Priyanka stands back holding my fingertips in hers as she dances us around and laughs.

"We try a couple of times to find you, but couldn't," Rakito says.

This doesn't surprise me. I live mostly as a ghost compliments of the American government. I can't share this with either of them. Once they decided to 'get out' they were 'out'—as in zero clearance. Civilians. No need to know. Lucky bastards.

"I remain pretty much 'off grid'," I say. "Not much of a people person. You both look wonderful. Marriage seems to work in your favor."

"Thank you. Are any of the others here?" She asks.

"Not that I've seen," I say.

"We try to notify Pa Ling and Fensig, but we do not find them," Rakito says. "You see them, our Tweedles?"

Here is where I must tell an outright lie. I haven't seen

anything of what made Pa Ling and Fensig the Tweedles, but I have seen what is left of their corpses… too many times.

*SCAT-HACH.*

"I have not talked with them in years," I say, settling on a lie of omission and redirecting the conversation. "Wow. Who'd have thought all those years ago, you'd still be together, and married! Children?"

"We knew," says Priyanka as she takes her husband's hand. "He is my life."

Rakito looks at his wife with complete admiration. Their reciprocal intimacy is elusive and foreign to me, like a visit to the ninth planet, Nibiru. While I recognize what commitment to my country feels like, I've never been able to accept a diamond and sacrifice myself as part of a couple. Most men can't adjust to my federally mandated disappearing acts. My romantic relationships usually skim the surface of superficial, the way slate skips over river water. I give Priyanka and Rakito credit. Civilian or not, their commitment is impressive.

"You see Genin?" Rakito asks.

"No."

Genin.

Another lie.

Genin is the one man I trust enough to share my body with but our 'moments' are more like nostalgic reunion trips to the amusement park. If it gets too emotional, we both slide back into our clothes and slip away. Genin's now in the Middle East on a special ops assignment I know nothing about.

"We have five children," Priyanka says.

Rakito stands a bit taller—straightens his shoulders like a proud chief. "Dis woman," he says, striking a fist to his chest. "She strong. She bears us two sets of twins. Two daughters and two sons —and another daughter too. They, and she, are God's gift to me."

Priyanka winks and leans into me. "Yes, and he's not allowed to touch me ever again," she jokes. "I swear this man could make me pregnant just by giving me a bite off his plate."

"I would love to meet them someday," I say.

"We would consider it an honor of greatness to open our home for you," Rakito says as he slightly bows.

"We live in Burundi," Priyanka says. "Rakito worked until his knuckles turned to knots to build a life for us. We own a fair-trade coffee plantation. I take care of the business side while he climbs mountains all day, checking and tending the crop."

"Partnership is better for coffee business," Rakito says.

"Sam, enough about us, what have you been doing all these years? Married? Kids?" Priyanka asks.

"Oh. No. Never married," I say.

More activity takes place at the bottom of the steps.

"They're getting ready to begin the procession," Priyanka says. "It is customary for Tetana's husband to light the first fire."

"She's married too?" I ask.

"That's what we heard," Priyanka says.

"We learned about Tetana's death through telegram," Rakito adds.

"Who sent the telegram?" I ask.

They look at one another, then me, and shrug. "We don't know," Rakito says. "No signature, just a request to please attend the funeral of our friend."

Rakito's words put me on high alert. I too received a telegram in London. I assumed it was from Genin or maybe Reggie. I haven't talked with or seen either of them for more than a month.

A figure in traditional men's clothing lights a torch from a nearby fire and descends parallel stairs. This must be Tetana's husband, except there was no mention of him in her file. I checked. There was no marriage license or record of children, either. The man's head is covered with a wide-brimmed hat made of dried palm leaves, rendering his features difficult to discern. He greets Tetana's Air Force friends. Throngs of people file in behind Tetana's husband when he abruptly stops and turns around. He flips up the brim of his hat with one hand and uses a torch in the other to motion us to join them.

"Oh my God!" Yells Priyanka.

"Shhhhhh," says Rakito, trying to hold his wife back by her waist. "Shh. Shh, woman."

"Don't you shush me!" She says, yanking her arm from him with a hard twist. "That is our friend!"

Rakito's jaw is almost in the dust at our feet and I'm just as speechless and open-mouthed as he. It's Saratu.

How in the hell did she get here? How long has she been free? Feeling dazed and confused, I watch this effusive creature named Saratu lay hands over a multitude of monks, nuns, and military, no worse for wear, it seems, after doing hard time at Plum Hook Bay. Her aura emanates waves of static electricity through my body and it takes everything I have to calmly and gracefully descend the steps again and act like a grown ass woman. It may be Tetana's funeral but now I suddenly burst inside with childlike joy.

*Saratu is alive!*

She leads our quasi-casual procession of Lamas, friends, and "family" to the corpse. She still walks barefoot and I feel grateful for this simple unchanged part of our past. Saratu was *always* barefoot at Plum Hook Bay because she said it helped her connect with Earth's energy.

Saratu arrived at NASA with an established ability to locate water under desert sands in her Sahara homeland. As I study her now, handwoven robes have been replaced with 'regular' clothes, muddy trousers under a relaxed nondescript neutral tunic—a change I don't like. I miss her colored wraps—the ones I ignorantly referred to as "sheets" when we first met, a kaleidoscopic cacophony of sashaying color that made her look like an African angel painted by the breath of Gods. She touches torch to wood under Tetana's body in five places. Fire wraps itself around the offerings until it envelopes Tetana too, reducing her body to a few ounces of ash within minutes. What is left gets entrusted to the slow flowing river, which eventually runs into the holy Ganges.

*I will miss you Tetana.*
*Thank you for your service.*
*10-4.*

An Air Force Lieutenant hands an expertly folded American flag to Saratu. I had no idea these two, Tetana and Saratu, maintained a connection and I'm unsure how that's possible. Tetana was special ops and had a limited military clearance as far as I knew, and although she wasn't as far down the rabbit hole as Genin or I, she too, would have had to limit personal ties.

Four F-16's fly in formation over our heads in a V-shape, a gap in their second command to honor our friend, a special dispensation for airspace granted by the Nepali government. My fingers work like windshield wipers against my eyes. I don't like to cry but I especially loathe crying in public.

Funeral rites concluded, Saratu whispers in an old woman's ear, someone she appears to know well. The sage lady is unnaturally bent by years of what I suspect is physical labor and osteoporosis. She steadies a bright purple cane under twisted dye stained knotty fingers and slowly approaches me. Saratu walks with a small crowd of followers, moving further away. She disappears behind the boulder thick walls of a well-protected monastery.

"Please," the old woman says, looking deeply into my eyes (hers are friendly and calming), "The Samding Dorje Phagmo invites you to her home for a feast in honor of Tetana, and to thank all who come here."

"What's a Samding Dorje Phagmo?" I lean over and whisper to Priyanka.

"Seems our Saratu now holds court as the third highest-ranking member in Tibetan Buddhism," Priyanka says. "My God, only the Dali Lama himself can bestow that sort of attainment. Come on, let's check this out."

Priyanka moves ahead with Rakito in tow. I follow after them with a cacophony of people, searching the crowd to see if I notice anyone else of our ilk. I do not. No Jade. No Genin. No Verity. Reggie and the Dr.'s Dennison are not here either—and it makes me sad that they either weren't invited or perhaps ignored the invitation.

Our procession enters the monastery through gigantic iron gates. Monks in orange robes mill about an oversized veranda above us as we're led to a stone courtyard near the top of this building. Nuns covered in bright pink robes, their hair completely shorn, ready a feast. Each lays red, orange, and yellow print block cloths on the ground. A bounty of rice, goat meat, cheese, dumplings, and mixed peppers settle over delicately detailed hand-sewn or woven fabrics. Below us rests a large pool of water. Lotus flowers bounce like fish bobbers, tightly closed, save one that bursts white, opening wide its symmetrical petals skyward. This dynamic and diverse combination of people, the precision applied to details, and the relaxed complexity surrounding us, resonates with so much meaning and story, it oozes from the pores of every leaf, stone, lotus and today's saffron sunset, which now melts the sky into a soft amber glow and enters my heart as gratitude.

"Sit," a Lama says to me, patting the orange cushion beside his.

I kneel beside him, next to Priyanka and Rakito, while another monk leads us in prayer and offers a blessing. The humidity is replaced by a creeping chill as the last of the sun slides below distant powdered mountaintops.

I do not see Saratu.

A nun approaches before I'm able to nibble the first bite of this glorious feast. "Please follow me," she says.

We rise.

"Please," she says, "Dorje seeks only the one called Sam."

"Go," Priyanka whispers in my ear. "We'll wait for you here." She pokes me with a light elbow nudge and a smile, the same 'at ease' composition of sturdy river rock attitude she always possessed at Plum Hook Bay, one that doesn't fight or give in to the current but rides it through with thought and grace. She would have made a great federal agent, I think.

The vast corridor is supported by immense round blood-red columns. The nun doesn't offer me her name or attempt conversation and neither do I. A crisp breeze sweeps through a wide-open hall, a welcome cold front tiptoeing through the monastery. It lightly tousles wisps of my hair and causes a natural shiver. As we pass a screenless window I gawk at undulating waves of green hills and distant black snow-capped peaks that crowd into one another and stretch their peaks vying for the attention of misty clouds.

"Please, no shoes," the nun says.

I kick off my sandals, leaving them in the hall among many others.

The stone steps feel cool under the soles of my feet, a welcome invitation to walk this way more often. Maybe Saratu is onto something with her disdain for footwear. The pager in my underwear buzzes again. No. It's my compass. I pull it from the belt on my sari. It spins again, directionless, like always. I think Reggie gave me a dysfunctional compass that loathes its purpose in this life. I roll my eyes in irritation and stuff it away, secretly grateful to have it back, but unhappy about the deadly circumstances in which it arrived.

Ceremonial paintings of deities ripple above my head as we climb higher in the tower around a winding set of stone carved stairs. Thin silk tapestries gently swing, pushed by our passing. Small lanterns and a variety of orchids hang suspended by their roots in glassless windows. Somewhere in the distance I hear a wooden flute. I smell patchouli, sandalwood, and oranges. Water trickles but I don't see the source. I feel surprisingly at ease and mindful—the serenity of this place gently washing away my tension. We arrive at a large crackled green double door decorated with heavy brass knobs. Two monks, one on each side, pull thickly braided ropes.

Slowly, it creaks open…

…and Saratu the Dorje is here.

She's changed into a gold and green robe, seated atop a wooden altar, her svelte frame supported by a large ivory pillow. Upon her head, a gold crown. Copper armbands grip each bicep. She's bedecked in layers of black pearls. Candles litter the floor and lead up five wide steps ablaze with the soft glow of hundreds of small oblong paper lanterns. A sea of saffron seated monks chant on each side of this incandescent path. Lotus flowers and 'holy water' fill large crystal bowls at her feet. Saratu sits cross-legged, one hand in the air in front of her, a thumb touching two fingers. She motions me to approach.

"*Om tare tuttare ture svaha*," the monks say.

Here Saratu sits as the Goddess of wisdom and universal compassion made manifest. Is she for real? I stifle a laugh at this overwhelming spectacle of reverence. Saratu appears to be imitating the White Tara painting that hung in my room back at Plum Hook Bay, one she daily meditated upon, and insisted, when we were sixteen, that it be brought to hang in my space.

Dr. Evelyn always said if Saratu was left to wander the world, she'd either be crucified by depraved jackals within moments, or make so many friends so fast she'd realize her own religion—but—how *in the fuck did she pull this off?*

Saratu rises when I reach her. "Jampa," she says to a monk three steps below us.

He bows with palms pressed together over his chest. "Yes, Dorje," he says in his native Tibetan tongue, a language I still struggle to master despite Reggie's teachings.

My pager vibrates during a pause in chanting and echoes loudly through the chamber. *Damn it, Abar. What could you possibly want right now?* Everyone looks at me quizzically. I rub my stomach.

"Excuse me," I say to the crowd. "Gas pains."

Most of the monks have no idea what I just said, because they don't understand English but Saratu chuckles.

"Have you found Tinley?" Saratu asks the monk.

"No Dorje."

"This is the way, then. Walk with me, Sam."

Saratu was practically mute at Plum Hook Bay—traumatized after her family was murdered and she was brought to the states by Dr. Awoudi, our former psychologist. I wonder what happened to *him?* Dr. Evelyn said he located 'promising souls', that was his specialty, but he wasn't like Evelyn. He was kind and remained *outside* Plum Hook's gates, finding me in foster care before I even met Reggie or the rest. It seems Saratu found her tongue…and her place. She's still the same serene person but different—much more assured and definitely in charge.

We disappear into private quarters behind the altar. Thick purple cushions sit plump under a sheer ivory canopy. Beyond this, I'm surprised to see an opulent room housing enough amenities to infer the jealousy and wrath of Gods. Hundreds of hardcover books line her shelves. Golden chalices embedded with gemstones hold court on a teak table. Colorful paintings and bronze figures adorn walls or mantels. A hand painted prayer table, soft reds, gold, and painted with white lotuses, rests beneath a detailed tapestry of some ancient mountain city. The nameplate under the tapestry reads, *Shambhala* and it looks like a place I now want to visit more than the Golden Temple.

Saratu removes her crown and places it on a gleaming boxwood desk, its intricate legs boasting delicate mandalas and saffron robed Buddhas. "Samantha. I have missed you many days and nights," she says, embracing me with a hug I don't refuse.

"I have missed you too," I say. "You certainly seem to be doing well."

"Ah," she says, "Do I hide my pain so flawlessly? Wine?"

"You drink?"

"No. It's for you, my dear friend."

I take the glass of red she pours. She chooses water for herself. We clink our hammered brass goblets. I sniff the wine but don't take a sip when I bring it to my lips. Spy Craft 101—although these days, with new gadgetry, its rather easy to in-animate or kill a nemesis with tasteless and/or odorless concoctions. Old hyper-vigilance habits and obsolete tradecraft die hard for me, I suppose.

A lone tear zig-zags down Saratu's cheek. "I loved her very much.".

"We all did," I say. "Tetana will be deeply missed. You rarely spoke a word when we were classmates at Plum Hook. I'm glad you talk now."

Saratu sighs and smiles. "More than a monk probably should," she says. She dabs a tear with a small corner of her robe. "Tetana was my wife...."

"Your *wife*?"

"Our monks knew."

"I don't understand," I say. "You and Tetana? I didn't think Tibetan monks would be open to that sort of thing—you know, like Christians, they'd be vehemently opposed to same sex unions —or even marriage among monks for that matter. Isn't sex taboo for religious people who take vows like yours?"

"A body is a vessel of limited illusory matter," she says matter-of-factly. "Enlightened consciousness understands what sleeping beings cannot, that love transcends labels beyond gender, sex, or dogma. Your words are singed with Westernized thoughts of 'sin'. But such burdensome ideologies and swift judgement confound paths to illumination."

"I'm sorry, Saratu," I say, and I mean it. "I spent most of my time getting into trouble at Plum Hook Bay and having to take detention with Miss Barbara. She preached a lot of Christian sermons while I polished silver. Sometimes her Bible verses run for hours like a feed loop through my head."

We laugh in unison and it releases some of my tension.

"There is much Light in Christianity, Judaism, and Islam," Saratu says. "People from different religions can learn from and should share their respective beliefs. Loving-kindness is a universal language."

"But you didn't bring me here for a religious discussion," I say.

"No," Saratu says. "Tetana's soul is now free." She lets out a deep sigh and continues. "Mine is troubled. I celebrate her path to nirvana. I mourn mine without her. Time and meditation will heal my spirit but in this moment, how wilted I feel with Tetana's kiss extinguished."

"How long were you lovers?" I ask.

Saratu traces the outline of a small golden Buddha statue on a shelf. "She brought me here, not far from what used to be her village, a few years ago. I'd been kept in an unground military installation near Blue Diamond Hills in your Nevada, U.S.A."

"How did she *find* you?" I ask.

"Reggie asked Tetana to be part of my relocation escort to

Nepal," she answers. "Septum Oculi thought I'd spent enough time helping your country. Your government had limited interest in advanced technology for enlightenment purposes. They cared only for re-engineering beings to build greater weaponry against their own Earth cousins on other continents. The love between Tetana and me blossomed, like the Lotus, from mud to sun."

"You're not human," I say.

"No."

"What are you?"

"Cietan," she says.

"Fully-fledged?" I ask, staring at her with a look of shock but knowing its true.

"Yes."

"How?" I ask. "I mean, how can you be here in your true form?"

"I'm able to adopt a physical appearance that mirrors cultures from across the universe. We call it 'multiplicity of universiality' to expand from spark to form and back again," she says.

"Your kind," I say. "You assist mortal journeys to other realms and deliver curriculums of light to planets ready to rise out of duality."

"I see you're recovering some of your memories," she says, lightly tapping my forehead three times with an index finger. "Duality is but a label humans apply to differentiate between good or evil, up or down, yin or yang. True opposites do not exist despite the compelling illusory appearance of separation. Carbon-based beings cannot become more or less coal or diamond than they already are—that is why I'm here."

"This gives me hope," I say. "If you're assigned here, it means human growth is still possible."

"Perhaps," she says.

"How did you become the Dorje?" I ask.

"This is a story to be told another time," Saratu says. "Someone left a message for you with one of my monks."

Saratu unlocks and reaches into the top drawer of her desk. I'm ready to throw a good right cross if she pulls out a gun, a blow dart, a cobra or whatever else I suspect fully-fledged celestial ninja monk goddesses might use if they plan to kill an enemy. She hands me a boring legal envelope and wags her finger at me in reproach. "Sam, I do not believe in violence," she says with a raised eyebrow. "You should recognize your cohorts. Our universal essence is the same even though we fight a different way."

I bow my head, feeling foolish for my extraordinarily short-lived vow to act less hypervigilant among those I consider friends.

"A man came yesterday," she continues. "How he knew you'd show, I cannot say. Tinley presented this to me. It was not sealed."

She hands me the envelope with my name on the front. It also reads: "*Poison. Do not smoke!*" I recognize the writing. It's my mother's hand. I open the flap. It contains one of my mother's eye paintings, an Egyptian Eye of Horus and six hand-rolled cigarettes in a small plastic bag.

"I need to use a phone," I say. "*Shit.* I can't. The lines are likely not secure."

"International call?"

"Yes."

"Follow me."

Saratu walks deep into her bedroom closet and pushes a row of robes aside, exposing a panel of black dots that blend nearly perfectly into the dark paneling. She tap dances her fingers over them until the back of the closet wall opens into a large secret space, her *real* office. A single red phone sits on a small round table. She shuts the door behind us.

"Are you serious? I thought these only existed in highly classified government facilities," I say. "Why would *you* have a safe line, a red phone?" A trickle of sweat races down my spine.

"Not mine," she says. "It belongs to the Dali Lama. Here in the middle world, he accepts his position as a diplomat regarding many issues of interest to governments all over the globe—and beyond, just like the pope does at the Vatican." She glances up then down again and smiles wide at me. "I'm not sure how this phone garners so much trust."

"Nobody can crack a red phone," I say. "The outgoing

numbers get scrambled so the call can't be traced. Pinning the location is impossible too because it looks as if someone is dialing from the middle of an ocean."

I rap on the walls. "It's at least two feet thick with concrete. The Dali is a genius."

It's 4pm here, which means its 6am in Ohio. And Louie, I've learned, is not permitted to leave the hospital because my mother's room is considered a crime scene, and he, a witness.

"Third floor nurses station please."

Louie picks up after the ninth ring.

"Smooter here, what do *you* want?"

"Really, Louie? Your professional greeting could use some polishing," I say.

"I have no time for pleasantries, Dr. Blake. You left me quite a mess to clean up. Literally."

"I did no such thing," I say. "My mother made that jungle when she decided to check-out of your four-star hellhole. Can you talk? If you can't, just say, 'I think you have the wrong floor, let me transfer you.'"

"What? I'm fine. For Christ's sake, get on with it. What do you want?"

"Did my mom have any other visitors before I arrived?"

"She wasn't allowed any visitors unless it was cleared by Septum Oculi, you know that."

"Are you sure?" I ask.

"Hell, yes, I'm sure...wait a minute..." Louie says with a pause. "...there was this kid."

"What kid?" I ask. "How could a kid get clearance to visit an asylum for the criminally insane?"

"He didn't," Louie says. "He was a patient in a room down the hall."

"Locked up like my mom?"

"No. He earned permission to roam the floor," Louie says. "He'd visit the nurse's station sometimes but when he did, he *always* stood in front of Avril's door, like he was in a trance or something. I figured it was the meds. The kid was on some pretty heavy stuff."

"What's his name?" I ask.

"I was never told," he responds. "We used a number, 6-1-1. He refused to talk."

"Oh." I say.

"Cute but creepy kid," Louie says. "Well, he wasn't exactly a kid…he was eighteen, I think. Or was he nineteen? I can't remember."

"What did he look like?" I ask.

"Cute but creepy," Louie says again. "Pale skin and brown eyes — a mop of dark ringlets that kept falling in his face."

My heart jumps into my throat and its beating hammers my ears. "Where is he now?" I ask. "What room?"

"He's not here anymore," Louis says, to my extreme disappointment. "He was transferred months ago. You know how this place works they don't tell me a damn thin…"

"Louie, you there?"

"I have work to do," he finally says. "I think you have the wrong floor, let me transfer you."

The line goes dead.

*Shit!*

I stare at the envelope on the table. It's my mother's handwriting and this is her drawing. How did the *deliveryman* know I'd be here and how did he get hold of *her* cigarettes?

My pager vibrates again. "Hold on a second," I say.

I lift up my sari to check my beeper.

"Need to use the phone again?" Saratu asks.

"No thank you," My heart plunges from throat to feet when Abar messages S.O.S.

"I must return stateside."

Saratu and I descend the steps toward the altar. Three monks and two nuns swiftly shuffle toward us, their robes smacking at their calves like rough waves. They repeatedly bow to Saratu. We bow back.

"We find Tinley," one says. "He has broken his vow. Looks like asthma attack."

Down the corridors we go, a little quicker this time, headed to a small alcove nestled nearby.

"Who is Tinley?" I ask.

"Chinese Triad mafia member trying to pass as a monk," Saratu says. "He's been sent here to kill me."

"Why?"

"The Beijing government has never been a fan of the Dali Lama or Buddhism," she says. "It feels that both are too progressive. When the Dali Lama blessed me, a foreigner, with the high rank of Dorje, this was viewed as a great threat. They hired a thug because I am considered too vile for them to touch."

"You're vile because you're a foreign monk?" I ask.

"I'm a threat because I have breasts," Saratu says with a light laugh. "That's a big deal around here."

"Are you worried?"

"I'm Ceitan," she says.

"They can't kill you," I say. "They can't even *wound* you. You have the ability to regenerate. Only another of your kindred could kill you. But humans could 'inanimate' you, no?"

Saratu stops, turns toward me, and takes both of my hands into hers. "Congratulations," she says.

"For what?" I ask. "I didn't do anything."

"You have a daughter," she says.

"I don't have a child," I say, rubbing my stomach and looking down to see if she sees something I don't. "Do I *look* pregnant?"

Saratu registers a micro-look of concern.

"My mistake," she says. "I usually do not get such things wrong."

"Okaaay," I say. "I'm not sure what's going on here. I don't see myself as a mother, ever. I'm not the motherly type."

I don't say so to Saratu but if I were a mother, I'd probably be the sort Dr. Monica had—one that flexibly raises her kid in the Outback so mini-me would learn to fend for itself and I wouldn't be bothered with soft-boiled whining or attitude.

"You will be a wonderful mother," Saratu says.

Tinley is at our feet, collapsed in an orange heap of robe, his blue face contorted, and his lifeless eyes open skyward. I squat beside him and look up from his pre-death vantage point. A perfect circular hole punches through a cloud, as if a hand of God reached through and personally smote this mafia-monk.

"Oh," says Saratu. "I almost forgot. You *had* seven cigarettes in that envelope. Tinley is Chinese. He doesn't read or speak English. I borrowed one." She winks at me.

"You mean these cigarettes are actually poison loaded?"

"I guess so," Saratu says as she tilts her lips into a soft smile. She lifts her robe and lightly steps over a very dead Tinley. She instructs the monks and nuns to prepare his body for purification.

"You just told me back at your room that you don't believe in violence," I say.

"I don't," Tetana shrugs. "I gave Tinley a cigarette for bringing me the envelope. A postulant on the path to enlightenment always has free will. I guess he inhaled. I'll see you at the banquet in Tetana's honor."

Saratu winks at me, turns on barefoot heels, and calmly retreats back to her quarters.

# THIRTEEN

# LOSING HOPE

JACK MEADOWS, the assistant agent in charge of our division at Langley, stands in front of the door leading into Verity's private ICU wing at Inova Hospital in New Falls, Virginia. When I come charging up the hall, he continues his deep discussion with our boss, Joe Abar.

"Hey, Sam," says Jack. "I'm sorry we had to call you back for this."

"Is she...?"

"She's alive," he says. "Someone roughed her up pretty good. Took quite a blow to the side of her head. Three surgeries since Tuesday to relieve the fluid on her noggin."

I won't allow tears or a fallen face give up the fact I've known Verity a lot longer and more closely than these two are aware. "Hi Sir," I say to Agent Abar, our Special Agent in Charge (SAC). I'm surprised to see him here. Big bosses who have their mugs on walls at Langley usually don't make public rounds.

"Hello Dr. Blake," he says. "I'm sure you're wondering why we're both here."

The palm of his hand rests on his neck just under his baldhead.

His red tie looks as if it chokes him. He despises ties. He told me so. As a former military man who took assignments in some of the most dangerous places on Earth, he'd rather break knuckles than drag his own through mountains of yawning paperwork that sit piled on his desk. Most people, including federal agents, and especially criminals, initially think Abar's rather dumb. But he's actually what I call, 'Colombo' smart, based on an old 1970's detective show I used to watch. Abar observes. He listens better than an owl in a tree, and then, if any of his targets make the mistake of thinking they're 'all clear', he'll turn around and say, "Just one more thing…" before he jackhammers his prey with hallow pointed questions.

Down the hall, a doctor and a lab technician wave to Meadows. The technician takes a clipboard from the doctor and walks past us to sit down behind the nurses station. She picks up the phone to make a call and too quickly looks away from me when our eyes meet, as if she has something to hide. What are my bosses up to?

Agent Jack Meadows is less brass with rolled up sleeves, no tie today, or most other days, either. His disheveled bleach blonde hair looks as if it's been zapped by a solar flare. He surfs during his off time and takes a more Maslow approach with case agents like me, occasionally inviting underlings out for craft beers at his favorite pubs or for walks around D.C.'s monuments and parks. He *talks* with us to learn our motives, fears, or interests. Put Abar and Meadows together and it makes for the best 'good cop, bad cop' duo I've ever encountered. No way they'd *both* show up here 'just because' or to offer me hugs.

"I don't see you two carrying a 'care package' or balloons," I say.

"We've got a problem," says Abar. He extends his arm toward Verity's closed hospital door. "A couple of days ago lawyer Lane in there began semi-consciously repeating your name . She hasn't stopped. You two never worked together as far as we know. She blurted out something about a Plum Hook Bay and a Dr. Evelyn?"

Both men look at one another before looking at me and I know exactly what their facial exchange means because I've shared it with colleagues. It's a glance that silently screams 'we don't trust the person in front of us' or 'we already have secret or sensitive information about you but want to test if you'll lie to us.'

"You didn't train together at Langley. Did you cross paths on the remote tribal murders?" Abar asks.

"No, Sir."

"There's more," says Meadows. "Her husband was killed by sniper fire three days ago near Turkey. We'd given her some time off to make arrangements and…"

"And?" I ask, after Meadows grows silent.

Both of my superiors exchange glances again but this time I get a 'how much should we trust her with' look.

"Verity had been working another angle of the tribal murders," Meadows says. "She was attacked in her home two days ago and fought like hell. Whoever did this absconded with highly classified files and also took the baby."

"Baby? What baby?" I ask, trying to hide my astonishment. "Boy? Girl? How old?" This news stings my heart. Verity is a widow. And now I learn, a mother too, a detail she neglected to mention when I saw her a few months ago—although, to her credit, she may not have known at the time she was pregnant, which I find doubtful given her 'receptor' capabilities. Something doesn't add up.

"Two-week-old baby girl," says Abar. "The FBI has not intercepted any ransom calls and NSA has picked up zero communication signals indicating who might be behind this or why."

I remain calm, faking detachment. *"Learning Farsi is easy…I can teach you…"* Verity slaps the pinecone back into my palm, *"…It's bad karma to drop your third eye…"* *"You didn't leap, you flew!"* I push back my former foster home memories and bring forward *'soldier face'.* "Any leads?" I ask.

"Maybe," says Meadows. "As you're aware, the CIA is notorious for compartmentalizing cases. We all work on a 'need to know' basis. But there is another angle to the tribal murders."

"What angle?" I ask.

"Not all of the natives are dead," he says.

"What do you mean?" I ask. "Every place you've sent Genin and me, the natives are dead. All of them."

"Some anthropological teams conducted a census on remote tribes *before* the 1989 slaughters, just ahead of the Gulf War," Abar says. "Verity was part of that academic outfit as an intern and third year law student, to ensure the agency stayed within legal bounds. Sort of a test run for her current position. She's great with languages too, so the tribespeople responded well to her. Every single indigenous person she interviewed had the same story about how some of their members went missing. Tribal leaders and shamans swore it was the work of their respective gods, punishing them. The data shows many women and children are probably unaccounted for."

"Probably unaccounted for? How many?" I ask.

"Approximately forty-five hundred," says Abar.

"Why do you think they're missing?" I ask. "Academics make mistakes. That's a relatively small number when you're counting indigenous people all over the globe. We know how data gets skewed to increase Congressional funding for black ops agendas... and people move or die of disease, accidents, or old age."

"She didn't make a mistake," admits Abar.

Meadows shifts his weight from one leg to the other, body language that tells me Abar made an executive decision to 'read me in' and tell me more than Meadows thinks I should know. But his too obvious throat clearing will also keep me from getting "*the rest of the story.*"

"We have a Delta Team in a remote region of the Middle East," says Meadows. "They're conducting recon on illegal chemical and weapons sales, hence your ancillary work at Harrington Technologies. This Team witnessed a very bizarre incident six months ago."

This would be Genin's team, I suspect, although no one has said so. It's the only reason he'd be in the Middle East at a remote outpost doing recon, probably very near where Verity's husband was killed. Maybe that bullet was meant for Genin instead, a thought that strikes me suddenly anxious for his safety.

Meadows looks at Abar, then me, then back at Abar. These two are struggling—volleying about who knows what and how much each can or should share...

"Go on," says Abar. "Tell her."

"It's not uncommon for tribal villages in the Middle East to engage in the slave trade using people they capture during territorial disputes," Meadows says. "Except this particular trade was different. The women and children one Delta Team saw were not locals, not even close. A child about eight, was shot in the head, her insides cut out in front of the others."

"Oh my God," I say, feeling revulsion and anger. "*Why?*"

"The Operator claims the arms trafficker, who Delta seems to believe is a British national, told the tribal chief that this victim had special blood because her organs would not rot, even in the sun," he says. "They left her liver, spleen, kidneys and heart on a rock for a week. They did not decay. The tribal chief bought all the slaves and resold them at quite a profit to terrorist groups in the region. They killed most of the women and children and drank their blood or dined on their organs, thinking it would make them invincible during battle."

"*Jesus Christ.* Did it work?" I ask. I consider the barbarity. Human beings doing this to other human beings—a form of cannibalism viewed among my hybrid peers as heinously primitive.

"No, it didn't work, not as far as we can tell," says Meadows. "Seems most of the natives are just that, normal humans who die and rot like the rest of us. Some terrorists feel duped when they filet a corpse and it quickly decays under the heat of the desert. Others, the opportunists, view it as a gift from Allah to transact in organs, decaying or not. And some, the smarter ones, keep victims alive, subjecting them to gang rape or slavery, until they figure out how they can reap the most blood money for their victims."

"If you know this, why not send in para teams to extract the victims?" I ask.

"We have reason to believe that a couple of global medical research facilities may have purchased some of these victims for covert cloning or other experiments, " says Abar as he looks at Meadows.

"You mean our own?"

Abar nods. "In some cases, yes…Fort Detrick has a couple at the National Interagency Confederation."

It takes every molecule of energy I have to keep my blood from boiling out of my ears and to act nonchalant, as if trading unwilling humans like a deck of cards is *normal*.

"They were already dead," Abar says. "We didn't take any victims alive, but the optics sure as hell don't look good. We got them back here for study because, frankly, there are a few corpses that don't decay and the Pentagon is screaming at us to find answers—is it some sort of weapon or poison or enhanced genetics? A virus? As Dr. Monica shared, not even scavengers will touch the bodies, they're odorless and don't decay. Every test we conduct drives us further away from answers."

"Why don't the bodies decompose, do we know?"

"We don't know," says Abar. "We've never witnessed anything like this. There is no trace of chemical, viral, or bacterial tampering, but the corpses do have one thing in common."

"What?"

"They all have RH negative blood," says Meadows. "Whatever is being manipulated only works with an RH negative host."

I feel a growing ache in my stomach. About ninety-five percent of the global population possesses a D protein, or positive RH factor in their blood. Roughly five percent of the remaining population has RH negative blood. But there are a few others, like me, within that five percent of negatives, that are something else entirely. *"Did you know governments put Golden Bloods on secret registries?"* Bennie had asked me when we were kids.

"You all right?" asks Meadows.

"You just told me women and children are being sold as sex

slaves or breathing organ donors," I say. "Terrorists feast on their insides hoping to gain superpowers and someone is targeting rare blood types for sketchy experiments. Yea, I'm perfectly fine…just another day in the foxhole. You think Verity stumbled onto something?"

"We don't have that answer," says Abar.

"Verity's daughter is RH negative," says Meadows. "Only five percent of the global population has this blood type."

"*Euskari, Samantha.*" Bennie had said. *Welcome to Earth.*

"Again, what does any of this have to do with Verity or her baby?" I ask. "Why take such a risk and draw so much attention kidnapping a CIA officer's child?"

"We don't know," says Meadows.

"What *do* you know?" I ask. "All we have are a bunch of dead ends and dead people."

Meadows pinches his eyebrows and puckers his lips together but doesn't say a word. He rubs an index finger against picket fence straight teeth.

"We know you have Rh negative blood," says Abar.

*Shit.*

"You're still not giving me the entire story," I say, trying to recover. "The medical lesson is all very interesting but will you *please* stop shooting around the orange dot?"

"Verity and her husband are both Rh positive," says Abar. "And they don't have the recessive gene, either of them. It's impossible for these people to be the biological parents of this child."

"So. Maybe they adopted." I say. "Or they hired a surrogate."

Both men shake their heads in unison.

"Verity gave birth to her," says Meadows. "Right here in this hospital."

"Then she had an affair?"

"This is what we originally suspected," says Meadows. "But not what happened. The baby's blood? It's not entirely human."

"What?"

"It's BOUO, blood of unknown origin," Abar says. "We only

have a small sample taken from the infant's foot shortly after birth —the hospital phlebotomist thought he was going senile when he looked at it under a microscope. He called in a colleague to take a look. We intercepted. Have you ever heard of BOUO?"

"The blood is deep blue with gold flecks and aspects of plasma that resemble chlorophyll," Meadows adds. "We think this baby was biologically engineered with Verity's consent or changed in utero without her consent, we're not sure. What we do know is that it likely won't survive long in an Earthly atmosphere —unless..."

"Unless what? Someone *knows* what they've got?" I ignore Abar's question, hoping it, and he, will both go away.

Both men nod.

I search the memory banks of my mind and arrive at only one answer based on everything I've learned as an exobiologist; Verity was the surrogate parent for a hybrid-human couple and this baby inherited dominant extraterrestrial DNA.

When I was born, I was lucky enough to develop a recessive gene, which allows my 'body' to filter and process almost any planet's atmosphere thanks to una-teslium—hence, my 'Golden Blood'. Verity's baby, unknowingly to Abar, Meadows, and even Dr. Monica, may be able to survive on this planet. Maybe.

"And this is where you come in," says Abar. "We don't know how Verity knows you and perhaps you can't tell us for good reason. But since she's calling out for you by name, we thought maybe she'd be comfortable confiding in you...if she wakes up."

Abar waves the lab technician over, the one who hangs up the phone, the one who looked as if she earlier had something to hide. My heart does a mad dash toward the exit but my feet keep me in place, facing them, acting as if nothing is wrong.

"One more thing..." he says.

*Here we go.*

"You mind giving us some blood for Dr. Monica to work with?"

"Can't she get it from the corpses?" I ask, folding my arms, which immediately gives me away to Abar and Meadows as guarded. I stall to buy myself time, to think, to get out of this. If I knock over the lab tech's equipment, it's too obvious. They'll just order another. If I run or try to fly out of here, I'll be apprehended, dragged back, and forced to give blood. Either option keeps me out of Verity's room or delays my entry.

"She did, but we want to compare what she has with blood from a living Rh negative," says Meadows.

I don't trust either of these men. Bureaucratic spooks won't hesitate to throw their subordinates at a pack of hyenas if they sniff a promotion. Entire intelligence careers have been burned to ruins with underhanded trade tactics like this. And these two are on a fishing expedition likely brought on by one of Abar's 'hunches'. My problem is that he's rarely wrong.

"Isn't there anybody else living within an eighty-mile radius who has this Rh-negative blood?" I ask.

"You're the only one, we suspect, within a galaxy radius," says Abar.

So, he and Meadows know about my blood. I'm so fucked. "Seems I have no choice. Do I?"

"It's an order," Abar says. "You know, just a formality."

Both men smirk when I grudgingly plop down in a gray metal folding chair outside Verity's door. I roll up my sleeve. I know what they're going to find. Most CIA case officers give blood on the Farm. They keep it in an agent's personnel file at OPM. I bypassed that protocol because I never roomed at Quantico or Langley but studied at Plum Hook Bay, where Dr. Evelyn simply copied O- blood into a new and phony file she created. Since most federal agencies are weighed down by too much paper, and admins aren't permitted to read intelligence personnel files, no one likely noticed my skewed, incomplete blood type, until now. These two? They're onto me.

"I go in to see Verity alone," I say. "No listening devices, hidden cameras, or bullshit. If I catch even a whiff of surveillance, I'll climb over your heads and go straight to the Director."

The lab tech finishes drawing my blood into a tube but I don't see any gold flecks, which is unusual.

"You have my word," says Abar.

"How much is that worth?" I ask, pissed off, refusing to look at either Abar or Meadows.

The lab tech's nametag reads *L. Smith*. I don't look at her either.

"Your current assignment is to remain with Verity until she talks," Abar says.

I know Abar's not telling me the entire truth. The listening device and/or cameras will be hidden in the ceiling vents or in the room next to Verity's—technically not a lie on his part, that's how the CIA works. I'd do the same thing.

*L. Smith. L. Smith.*

Why do I recognize that name?

The lab technician looks up at me briefly enough to wink but doesn't say a word.

*Of course!*

This is the same name as the nurse who took my blood for Dr. Awoudi at juvenile jail when I was sixteen—right before I entered Plum Hook! She isn't the *same* nurse—but she wears the same nametag, the *exact* same nametag. Did Louie Smooter have something to do with this? No. He couldn't have. Reggie checked on him as I flew back from Nepal. I was concerned after he used our safety tagline to get off the phone. Reggie said Louie was placed under lockdown at that very moment, as a suspect in my mom's disappearance. Reggie's working on getting him out— although Reggie did admit Louie's freedom would come a whole lot sooner if Verity were conscious and working.

L. Smith walks down the hall carrying an entire tray of blood tubes, one of which she uses to replace mine, a clever sleight-of-hand trick, like making a coin disappear and reappear, before she hands it off to a lab tech.

---

Verity's face is thinner. Her frizzy blondish-honey hair is shaved under mounds of white gauze wrapped turban-like around her head. She reminds me of a mummy angel in her white gown, tucked into white sheets in a white room. She'd hate this and no doubt would want to be clad in purple—if that's even her favorite color anymore. Her flawless face is the only warm accent in this otherwise cold and antiseptic landscape. It kinda reminds me of the blizzard we experienced together back at Plum Hook Bay—in August.

Bittersweet feelings creep over the fence of my memories, like a wall of climbing roses, thorny yet beautiful. I pull up a plastic chair, which feels as rigid as I do. Bureaucracies and hospitals, I think, are masters of institutional ugliness designed to induce discomfort rather than promote healing. Ugh, I do not want to be here—but more so, I don't want Verity to be here.

Verity's heartbeat blips on the monitor. Eyes closed. I imagine she's dreaming about Prince, her favorite musician. God, I've missed her, my 'best friend'. My heart pushes up toward my throat as I watch her breathe. I lean in and slide my arm through the guardrail, taking her hand in mine.

"Hey, kiddo," I whisper. "Heard you put up one hell of a fight. But honestly, you really should stop sugar-coating this entire coma thing and wake up so you can tell me how you really feel."

No response. I look at the monitor. I listen for a hopeful increase in her heartbeat.

Silence.

"Hmm. The best friend arriving to save the day always works in the movies," I say out loud, hoping she'll hear me and maybe curl her lips up just a little.

Nothing.

Verity's lost a husband and a baby. I wonder, briefly, if she stole her baby—maybe found one alive in a remote forest or on an island, after its parents were killed, and brought it home using CIA back channels. I discard that thought because I think Abar and Meadows would have known. I consider joking with her about getting married. She said she never would. But the timing is horrible. Her husband is dead. She must feel completely devastated. What do you say to someone who's lost both a husband and a daughter within days, and now fights for her life? How do I tell her that three of our Plum Hook classmates are dead too? I wish I had magic words to heal Verity, but clever epiphanies go unrealized. I'm unable to fix a single one of her internal wounds or external injuries and it leaves me feeling isolated and helpless.

The black and white clock on the white wall reads 11:07pm.

Without warning, Verity grips my forearm and I jerk awake. She moans, says my name, stirs a bit, and retreats into the relentless recess of shadowy unconsciousness while I think about old times at Plum Hook Bay and thumb through dated magazines to slow my heartrate. I accidentally drop a periodical about sacred geometry bedside her bed and lean over to pick it up.

Two tear-filled lime green orbs lock on my face when I raise my head. She doesn't blink. I sit at attention, my back ram-rod straight leaning into her. "Verity?" I whisper near her ear. "You in there?"

"You came," she softly whispers as her lips stretch upward a little and she tries to lift her shoulders from the bed. "I knew you would."

"It's okay," I say. "Prince had another engagement but sends his regrets."

She tries to laugh but winces instead.

"Don't try to sit up," I say. "Geez, it's about time you're awake. I don't have all day, you know."

Verity tilts her head back on the pillow. "Ohhhhh."

I rub her exposed carmel arm, sliding my fingertips back and forth from wrist to elbow, hoping it provides at least a little comfort. "I'm afraid I'm not a very good bedside companion," I say, feeling awkward and unsure what to do.

Verity swallows hard and presses her head again into the pillow and closes her eyes.

"I'll call a nurse," I say.

"No nurse. No anybody…and definitely no Abar or Meadows. No bosses," she says.

I huff through my nose. Verity was coherent enough to know

Abar and Meadows paid her a hospital visit, which means she's likely been in and out of consciousness longer than they suspect.

"You want some water?" I ask.

She shakes her head, opens her eyes, and raises her opposite arm to show me her IV. She has fluids. I knew this. I just don't know what else to say or do at the moment.

"I could add some vodka to that plasma bag," I say.

"Maybe another time," she says. "It's good to see you, Sam... but you have to find her."

"I was briefed you have a daughter. And its good to see you too, although you could have done better with a choice of venue." I glance around the room and then give her a wink. "I mean, come on, we should be in the Bahamas right now tipping back rum and smoking kick ass weed."

Verity smiles but her tone is serious. "They also know the baby isn't mine."

"Yes."

"What they don't know, yet, is that she's yours," she says.

I hold back a laugh for her sake, she's been through so much.

"Verity, your morphine must be talking."

"Listen," she says, turning on her side to face me. "She's *your* daughter."

"Verity, look...I will do everything possible to find this baby but you have to stay with me, here. She can't be mine. I'd know if I'd ever been pregnant," I say.

"But you wouldn't know if Dr. Evelyn took some of your eggs."

Time.

Stops.

**Bang.**

"What the fuck do you mean, I wouldn't know if Dr. Evelyn took some of my *eggs*?" I remove my hand from Verity's. The tick-tock of my heart moves faster than the second hand on the wall clock.

My head bolts from its starting blocks and gallops toward rage. "You wouldn't make this up," I say.

"No," she whispers, barely audible, but there. "You had a surgery," Verity says. "The day you found out Katie was murdered. A doctor came over from the NASA side of the farm. They knocked you out cold with a sedative because you were so upset. I couldn't sleep so I went to your room to check on you. It was the first time Bennie ever actually talked to me."

"Bennie?" I ask. "Bennie was in my room?"

"Bennie slipped into your room post-op, with Randolph, his wolf," Verity says. He asked me to leave you alone with him that night so he could watch over you. He was very upset. He cried."

"I feel sick," I say.

The distant memory comes zooming back into a clearing as if it happened yesterday. I *had* hurt "down there" the day after Katie's murder. I thought it was a late period. I dreamt Bennie and Randolph were in my bedroom. But now I realize...it wasn't a dream. I'd been drugged. Dr. Evelyn and Verity were there, before Bennie. My aunt wore blue scrubs and a surgical mask.

"Oh my God...she..."

"Sam, I'm so sorry..." Verity says.

"Your daughter is two weeks old," I say. "I haven't seen you in almost five years except for our reunion outside Fairfax. This doesn't make sense. Explain that."

"Seth, that's my husband...was my husband. We couldn't have children. I had a perfectly good uterus but not so good ovaries" Verity says. "Dr. Evelyn shared this bad news after one of our annual health exams at Plum Hook. She made me an offer, one I declined."

"What sort of offer?" I ask.

"Dr. Evelyn offered me the opportunity to carry *your* child."

"You initially declined," I say. "But you changed your mind," I say. "Why?"

"Seth and I tried in vitro, we considered adoption...we even talked about him getting another woman pregnant. When Dr. Evelyn showed up at the asylum, I asked your aunt if her offer was still on the table. She said yes."

"And you didn't feel it necessary to tell me?" I ask, not even hiding my contempt.

"I couldn't," Verity says. "I signed a non-disclosure."

"Why would Dr. Evelyn make such an offer?"

"Evelyn offered me the chance to give birth to your child using a special embryo kept under heavy guard NASA Plum Hook Bay," Verity says. "I knew she had a reason for doing this and I think it had to do with preserving your elite DNA. Dr. Evelyn forged the paperwork and arranged for the birth to look like a miracle. I didn't even tell my husband, made it look as if "we" got pregnant. He was deployed when I gave birth."

"You made a deal with the devil," I say. "God, didn't you think about what Dr. Evelyn might expect from you in return?"

"I didn't think that far ahead," she says. "I swear to God, I love our daughter as if she is my own. Please, please find her."

I practically drown in shock. The sudden helplessness I feel of having a child, a wee one, 'out there', in this world, compounds my worry and my job mulit-fold. "Tell me about the day you were attacked," I say, stuffing down my anger and burying my shaking hands under the folds of her bedsheets.

"I was home," Verity says. "I was supposed to be on leave after Seth's death but I began to go a little stir crazy and decided to look at some files again."

Verity touches her fingers to her right temple and scrunches her eyes.

"Go on…" I say.

"I got clobbered at my desk but I didn't hear anyone breech the perimeter. I'd turned on the alarm. They were professonals," she says. "Two men fought one another for the baby. One killed the other. The guy who survived sounded Russian so I used the language, which surprised him. I was shocked he let me live. He even propped me up and covered me, wiped some blood away from my temple, said we have big job to do, bigger than dislike. I have no idea what he meant by that, if he even said it at all, I was fading pretty fast. He fled with Hope when we heard sirens."

"Hope?" I ask.

"I named your daughter after the fox Bennie gave you at Plum Hook for your re-birthday."

"Who was the dead guy?" I ask.

"We don't know," Verity says. "No trace of him anywhere when the police arrived. I passed out. I heard Meadows tell Abar that neighbors heard the ruckus and called the cops. Meadows said one lady saw a newer black suburban drive away."

"Government vehicle?" I ask.

"I think so, but we can't be sure. Hope's records are missing too. All of them. It's as if she never existed."

"You prepared a report on the tribal census before your husband was killed," I say. "You'd planned to show Abar."

"No," Verity says. "I secretly compiled something else."

"A file?"

"Bennie was right," she says.

"About what?" I ask.

"The Code of Everything, the Word," Verity says as she winces again. "I created a file but not the kind you think."

"Go on," I say.

"It's a list of geocaches someone else started, along with a map —I traced the tribal murders and cross-referenced them with sacred structures and artifacts all over the world..."

"And this man who took Hope made off with that geocache file?"

"No. He didn't," she says.

"You still have the file?" I ask. "Oh my God, Verity, where?"

Dewey tears lodge in her lime-green eyes.

"I begged my husband to take it with him to the Middle East," she says.

"What?! Why in the hell would you do *that?*" I ask.

"I thought it would be safer," she says. "Nobody would think to check a deployed Marine's rucksack, especially a master sergeant."

"Shit," I say. "Where is Seth's rucksack?"

"The Pentagon has it—but the file isn't there."

"Damn it, Verity. Where's the file?"

"Seth hid it in a cave in Turkey…"

"Which cave?" I ask.

Verity shrugs, visibly exhausted, dark circles under her eyes. "I didn't ask because I didn't want to risk giving away the information or his unit if I ever came under interogation."

"Who is my daughter's father? Do you know?" A tear trickles down my cheek as I push back on jetlag. "Tell me, Verity," I say. "If my body has been breached for my eggs so you could carry a kid, I fucking deserve to know who her father is…is it Genin?"

"It's Bennie," she finally says. "You and Bennie are the parents of this child."

"*Bennie?*"

"*I'm so sorry.*"

"No. No!" I squeeze my eyes shut in a futile effort to block out her words. "This can't be true." I fight an urge to crawl in bed beside her, to cover up forever. I have a daughter, carried to term by my former best friend, and fathered by a hybrid I've never so much as kissed, who died years ago, saving humans.

*Humans.*

I think I'd hate homo sapiens completely if I weren't half human myself. If this fucked up turn of events doesn't qualify me for an extended stay at the Tiffin, Ohio Lunatic Asylum under the care of L. Smooter, I can't think of a better qualifier. "Does Reggie know Dr. Evelyn did this?" I ask.

"Reggie? No," she says. "He and Barbara have no idea. I don't think Dr. Evelyn even told Dr. Sterling. She was completely *off grid*. She said our little secret was a win-win, because someday this baby would do great things."

"Bennie knew," I say.

"I believe so…after the fact," she says. "He was super pissed at Dr. Evelyn and it was the first time I ever felt frightened by him, that's why I left him in your room…to get away."

Sometime during my medicated stupor at Plum Hook Bay, I vaguely remember Bennie sitting at my bedside. He laid a palm on my abdomen that night and I felt better, almost immediately—

likely due to his salve—that stuff he cooked up from Ayuhausca bark inside Silo #57.

"Is Bennie alive?" I ask.

"He died at Plum Hook Bay," Verity says.

"I'm not so sure about that," I say. "Dr. Evelyn played us all. Where is she now?"

Verity coughs.

She coughs again.

She shakes her head.

"Please find Hope," she says.

"Damn straight I'll find my daughter," I say. "Verity, where is Evelyn?"

"Verity? Verity! I'm calling a nurse," I say.

"No." She shakes her head again and shivers. "I would die to protect Hope," Verity says. "That's what real friends do. We take a bullet for each other. I was proud to know Hope was your daughter—*our* daughter."

"What does she look like?" I can't help myself.

*Blip. Blip. Blip. Blip Blip.*

"Verity!"

Her body jerks then tenses before she releases my forearm and flops over on her back unmoving. The heart monitor eratically thumps, like tragic classical music and then she goes completely limp. I slam my palm over a red emergency button and pull her up into my arms.

"Verity," I say. "Please don't leave me…"

Medical staff rushes the room and a nurse shoves me out of the way. I can't bear to watch, a race against death, to save my best friend but watch I do. No emotion flickers across Verity's face, no fear, anger, resignation or pain…my chest pounds so hard in my chest I'm unable to move.

"You going to call it?" A nurse asks.

"She's gone," says the doctor.

It's 3:55 am Friday, May 15th when Verity Isabelle Lane is pronounced deceased.

I'm numb. Everyone around me carries on as if nothing

dramatic just happened. Charts. Papers. Dictation. Practiced pity and rehearsed condolences. Business as usual. Verity can't be dead. If she's gone its Dr. Evelyn's fault. Verity never asked to be placed at Plum Hook Bay. I hold Verity's memory so tightly in my head it hurts, thinking of the candles, spells, and herbs, she'd once shown and shared with me—but nothing in her arsenal of magic to bring her back to life. *Poof.* We were close once…best friends.

# FOURTEEN

# ALL EYES ON DECK

I'M NOT Agent Abar's favorite person this morning and haven't been since we buried Verity two weeks ago. Privately, I've sobbed myself empty of tears since we lost her, but publicly I must act as if her death is just another day at the office, a sad but inevitable part of our job. The autopsy report shows Verity died from an aneurysm.

Abar walks to a bookshelf on one side of his desk and turns his back to me. He lightly dusts his fingertips across the top of his extensive collection of challenge coins. He's kept me practically chained to a cubicle next to his office since I refused to share the details of my final conversation with Verity. I suppose he thinks he can break my resolve using mind-numbing paperwork as mental torture but my decision has nothing to do with CIA principle (that's practically nonexistent), and everything to do with finding my daughter.

I haven't yet figured out how to maneuver around Abar, but I'm working on it. While I need agency resources to find Hope, he needs me to figure out how everything ties into the tribal murders and I've told *no one* about Verity's MIA geocache file.

Meadow's is on the opposite side of Abar's desk. He leans

against the wall, his hands in his pockets. He occasionally looks out the window at the courtyard, to stare at Kryptos, a sculpture made by some local artist that continues to baffle our analysts because its secret code is only partially solved. He hovered close to Verity's ICU practically the entire time she was there, which kicks up my respect for him.

Marvin, a secretary, brings in three steaming cups of coffee from the newly opened Store 001 on campus, a Starbucks. Even the baristas must undergo high security clearance to work there and no one is allowed to talk, except to call out aliases when orders are ready. Marvin nods at me and places the beverages on a small table opposite of Abar's desk.

Meadow's sweeps the tray and cups with a wand before he gives Marvin the 'all clear' and resumes his position holding up the wall by the door.

Twenty-seconds of silence follows. It's an old military tactic designed to make me feel awkward and uncomfortable—to get me talking. My lips remain bolted. The three of us can sit here in silence all day as far as I'm concerned.

"Dr. Blake," Abar finally says. "We have terrible people out there selling vulnerable humans to the highest bidder. How would you feel if more people get killed because you're withholding information?"

"I can't give it to you," I say.

"I am the director of this division," he says. "I hold a much higher clearance than you do."

"No, you don't," I say. "At least not in this area. If I share sensitive compartmented information, I break the law under the Espionage Act."

Abar loosens his tie then decides to toss it on a shelf. He places an arm on each side of my chair and bends over, his placid face inches from mine as we lock eyes. I'll bet this guy wins at poker every time. "If you withhold information we require to crack one of the most heinous terror rings in history, I will have you charged with obstruction...or worse," he says, slowly and deliberately, so I'm sure to understand he's serious. "I find it funny that some of our best case officers, all connected to you in some way, are now dead, but here you sit, alive and well in my office." The dark circles under his eyes look like new moons but damn this guy has nearly perfect pores.

Meadows told me last week that Abar is in line to become the next CIA director. He needs us to get our shit together so he can get his promotion, but Abar's advancement is the least of my worries. Most knuckle draggers I know care more about their place in the government hierarchy than they do about national security or their subordinates. Yet, I do notice today, that Meadows seems more concerned about Abar's promotion than Abar himself seems to be.

"Are you threatening me with treason?" I ask.

"Yes," he says without a flinch. "People are getting killed and this hits way too close to home. You're loyalty to your dead cohorts, although admirable, is misplaced and suspiciously inconvenient. You're a highly respected and decorated case officer, Dr. Blake. I suggest that you carefully consider your career over protecting the last words of your dead friend, who we believe, committed criminal acts…"

"Fuck you!" I say. "Verity was no criminal. I see where the agency is headed with this."

The Firm (the CIA training facility is the Farm), is distancing itself from Verity. It's typical spook play to kickstart a discredit campaign for any questionable actions she may have taken under its orders. Besmirch her name to save the factory. But—Abar struck a nerve and I instinctively reacted, just as he expected. *Damn it.* I will not be able to walk that outburst back to my brain, where it should have stayed. Reggie taught me to control my temper so much better than this. Abar turns away from me, clearly taken aback—or pretending to be. It's hard to tell with him. I may have played back the notes of this tune just as he hoped.

*Get control of yourself, Sam.*

"Sir, Verity was every bit the patriot and would never betray our country for some sort of payoff," I say. "And neither would I.

Anything we do is a commitment to make things better and keep people safe. We're not criminals."

"Is that temper of yours how you handle yourself in the field?" Abar asks. "If so, maybe the FBI is a better fit for you."

The FBI—that's considered a joke around here. Agents within that bureau can be spotted from space. Why? The FBI suffers a serious lack of diversity. Almost every federal agent within that agency is an ivy-league, corn-bred college graduate that resembles a Ken doll.

"I'm sorry sir," I say. "I know you want information, but I can't…at least not yet. I'm a good case officer. Get me back in the field. It will get us closer to answers."

An awkward silence permeates the already stiff air in Abar's office.

"Sir, if I may interject," Meadows says, stepping away from the wall he's holding up. "Dr. Blake is a valuable officer. Her 'legend' is she's an international executive for Harrington Defense Technologies in London. For the past year, she's collected evidence on the tribal murders using this company as a cover with the blessing of their human resources department…"

"I'm listening…" says Abar.

I'm listening too. Where is Meadows going with this?

"What if we put Sam closer to the intel we have in London regarding Luca Harrington's alleged role in illegal weapons and chemical sales?" Meadows asks.

"How does that help us here?" Abar asks.

I agree with Abar. I don't want to go 'off task' because it puts me farther away from finding my daughter and my Source Guide.

"The agent we have in place can't get close to Harrington," says Meadows. "Field Ops tells us Harrington's made several trips, not to, but very near where the remote tribal murders took place. Every. Single. Time. I'd certainly like to know why."

"If the field agent can't get close to this guy," says Abar. "What makes you think Dr. Blake can?"

Meadow's sly smile causes me discomfort but I'm intrigued so I lean forward to hear more about how Harrington might be connected to the tribal murders. This Harrington character makes the UK papers now and then, but it's always in regard to some acquisition or donation he's made to help kids. He's a billionaire. Scratch that—he's a multi-billionaire, a self-made empire built on the blood of people who die in battles all over the globe. Every case officer who's ever mentioned Harrington tells me what a decent hearted prick Harrington is.

"The case officer we planted there," says Meadows, "the one trying to win his attention, isn't having any luck."

"So?" I ask. "What does that have to do with me?"

"Harrington prefers redheads," Meadows says smiling. "And the more of a challenge for him, the better."

"Oh, *that's* not sexist," I say, folding my arms over my lap. "How are Harrington's proclivities tied to the tribal murders?"

"We have reason to suspect that Luca Harrington may be much more involved in the tribal murders than we thought," says Meadows. "But he's smart. He covers his ass and has friends in high places. He keeps nothing incriminating at his office. We've bugged his buildings, and the NSA remote sifted some of his files. His multiple holdings and estates appear clean too, save one we haven't been able to breach. On paper? He's cleaner than bleach."

"Maybe he is squeaky clean," says Abar. "It's rare, but possible."

Meadow's shakes his head. "But not likely…"

Both men nod at one another in agreement.

"So, you think placing me within Harrington's trusted corporate circle will do the trick?" I ask. "Do you actually think Harrington is stupid enough to be so thunderstruck by my hair he'll confide his crimes to my phony persona? Maybe chase me around his desk? Good god, only a *guy* would come up with such a bullshit idea."

"Harrington doesn't trust anyone who works for him," Meadows says. "You'd have to make contact and win him over another way."

"What do you propose?" I ask.

"The guy hardly sleeps," says Meadows. "There is a place he

frequents on those long, cold, London nights, where he occasionally socializes."

"I don't like the sound of this," I say. "Are you saying you want me to 'honey trap' this guy in some whore house? You want me to seduce him?"

Abar smiles at me for the first time in two weeks.

I narrow my eyes at Meadows enough to sharpen steel.

"Yes," he says. "But it's not a brothel and you don't have to bed the guy, just get him to trust you. If you go to bed with him, he'll lose interest. He likes the chase."

"If it's not a brothel, what is the place he frequents? Pool hall? Pub? Late night loom weaving class?" I ask.

"It's a nightclub," says Meadows. "A very popular place with three floors and a lot of live entertainment."

"Musical artists or comedians?" I ask.

"Strippers."

Abar doesn't even bother to stifle a laugh.

"Oh, hell no! I won't do it!" I practically pole vault out of the chair. "I didn't swear an oath to serve my country for you guys to park me as a stripper. The other female case officer you convinced to do this should dye her damn hair. Find someone else."

Case officers slowly pass by the open door, taking their time, trying to listen. Abar walks over and slams it shut.

"Who?" Asks Abar. "Who else should do this?"

"I don't give a shit who, but it's not going to be me! Get Fred over in Illicit Finance to do it," I say.

"Fred is not Harrington's type. He's a brunette," Meadows jokes. "The agent we have there now, she just isn't able to make a connection with this guy."

"And you think Dr. Blake here can play warm and fuzzy?" Abar asks Meadows rolling his eyes. "That's a tall order, in more ways than one."

"Well, Harrington is drawn to stature too," Meadows says as he winks at Abar. "I'll add that 'warm and fuzzy' isn't his thing, or doesn't seem to be."

"You guys really do need to hire more women around here," I

say. "This is bullshit. If Harrington's so smart, he'll figure me out within minutes, if not seconds. I will not do this."

"Strippers make the best covert ops agents in the world," Meadows says.

"Oh, now I suppose you're going to sell me on the fact that women who expose themselves for a living are master spies?"

"Most people can't get past 'stripper' to even consider that you might be employed by the CIA," Meadows says. "It's a more perfect cover than a thong!"

"You're an ass," I say, glaring at both men.

"Sam, strip clubs are a cornucopia of intel. Do you have any idea how many cases we've closed thanks to help from the strip club industry?"

"I can't believe I'm hearing this," I say.

"He does have a point," says Abar. "Women who work in the sex industry are stigmatized, which works in our favor because it detracts prying eyes from your true mission."

"Is this conversation *really* happening?" I ask, feeling disgust, and throwing up my arms. "You're both hurting my ears."

"We can arrange to have Sam fired from Harrington Tech," says Meadows. "She's stuck in London, without work, and economically desperate but bull headed (I frown). She can use her newly unemployed status as a reason to go off on Harrington at the strip club. He'll be intrigued because *everyone* is intimidated by him."

"*Hello?* Can either of you hear me? I said, 'no way'. I'm not doing this."

"Harrington. Didn't you tell me a couple of days ago this guy had some sort of secret partner?" Abar asks Meadows.

"Did I just become invisible?" I ask.

They ignore me.

"We believe so," says Meadows. "Except we can't find him...or her. Someone breached our mainframes to pull everything we had on Harrington and left NSA with nothing but a repeating video of a howling wolf under a full moon."

I perk up because I know that logo.

"The Russians were hit too and got some German version of a music video about 99 red balloons," Meadows continues. "We're working with Russian agents now to try to figure it all out but Yeltsin is on the reorganization warpath, which offers moles in our agencies some cover. FSK is about to be renamed FSB."

Is it within reach that Bennie somehow made it out of the underbelly of NASA Plum Hook Bay's nuclear reactor *alive?* Nobody ever saw or heard from Bennie again but that doesn't mean he died—there was no body—and all of this, I feel, bears heavy resemblance to his unique set of skills. I don't say anything, but I wonder if Bennie might be Harrington's silent partner. But God, an undercover stripper? Really?

"Put on your best poker face Sam, you're going back to London," Meadows says.

"Sir, may I *please* go back to my cubicle now?" I ask Abar. "This chat has been a lot of fun for the two of you, but I've got real work to do."

"You're going to London," says Abar. "The separation will do us both some good."

"I don't want to go to London," I say. "I'm not going to work as a stripper for the CIA. Find me another cover. I don't even know anything about the stripping business and I'm damn sure not taking off my clothes in front of a bunch of perves. And if you bring it up again, I'll file a lawsuit against the agency for your even asking me to do this!"

"Would you like me to get the EEOC on the phone?" Abar asks. He lifts the receiver and acts as if he's about to help me lodge a sexual harassment complaint.

"Dial," I say. "I dare you."

Of course, nothing happens, because Abar's being a smart ass. "It's not an ask," he says. "It's an order..." And for the first time, the way he says this, the deepening of his voice and the flicker in his eyes, cause the hairs on my forearms and neck to rise—just like Reggie.

"Actually," says Meadows, rubbing the back of his neck, "It's called adult entertainment and it's known as a Gentlemen's Club."

"And I'll bet there isn't a single *gentleman* to be found within a fifty-mile radius," I say folding my arms. "And how would you know, anyway? Favorite hangout of yours?"

"Sometimes," Meadows says. "It's actually a very classy place."

"Riiiight," I say. "And little green men are real."

Abar walks over to the window, says nothing. He turns his back to us again, staring into the courtyard. "You'll be fine," he finally says. "I'll have one of the MI6 agents pick you up at the airport." He twists his gold band with his thumb until I notice his eye ring facing me. "A Russian man with dual citizenship." I maintain poker face in front of Meadows as Abar places his hands back in his pockets. "So, it's settled," says Abar. "You're going."

"Yes, Sir."

# FIFTEEN

# RICK'S TEAHOUSE OF THE DANCING LADY

HE'S LATE.

I lean against a wall at Heathrow Airport near baggage claim and wait for my contact, a small black suitcase propped against my hip. Throngs of summer crowds, business travelers and tourists, pull, contract, and stretch again in all directions as if milling through an oversized taffy machine. Teenage laughter, the cries of disgruntled toddlers, and the pleadings of overloaded parents, as they steer uncooperative offspring toward taxi's or terminals, invade my head space.

One little girl with springy ringlets drops her Beanie Baby at my feet. She reaches for the toy as her mom yanks it away to brush off the microscopic germs of international travel. She's pulled down the terminal looking back at me, the edge of her little pink blanket dragging behind her along the floor, picking up dirt and grim from here to Hannover.

Ever since Verity's deathbed confession, I pay much more attention to kids these days. In every child, I look for a piece of my daughter and consider what she might look like or where she might be. I try not to think about the possibility she's already dead, her body parts used in some bizarre bullshit ritual to enhance the battle powers of an over radicalized terrorist. Or maybe her blood is slowly drained while she lies in a coma somewhere like I did, her plasma used for its Una-teslium. I slap the worst thoughts away, but like pesky mosquito's, they come back to uncomfortably buzz around dimly lit corners of my brain. It's kept me awake and dropping Rolaids down my throat for days. Me. A mom. I haven't reconciled the fact Bennie is Hope's father. When I find "Aunt" Evelyn, and I will, she'll never be able to punch her stamp of approval on anything this heinous again. How many other eggs did she snatch from the fallopian baskets of unwitting test subjects?

"Samantha?"

I tip my head to him and we shake hands.

"I am Konstantin Kurunov. Sorry to be late. Traffic."

Impressive grip. He's about cruising altitude taller than I and too pasty-looking for my taste. His leafy green eyes surmise me under a shag of fuzzy golden unkempt hair. He's neither handsome nor ugly. Konstantin looks like the type of 'nice guy' women could ask to pick up tampons at the drugstore. If I were to compare him to an animal, he'd be an Iberian lynx. His tailored clothes and polished shoes reveal pride and appreciation for nice things but his unkempt hair and easy smile tell me he's also adaptable, comfortable in his skin.

He takes my bag with one pole-vault like arm and extends his opposite elbow to me as if we're characters in some black and white movie and he's the male lead. I shoot him a 'you've got to be kidding' me feminist glare. He drops his elbow back at his side with a slight shrug. "You travel light for lady," he says, jiggling my suitcase handle.

"I don't like to lug around dead waste," I say.

A driver steers us down the wrong side of a road toward a strip club on Great Queen Street in downtown London. I'm not a fan of this city. The traffic is always a bitch. The tube is either hot and crowded or freezing and crowded. It's just fucking crowded here. Plus, it's hard for me to find a good meal, unless its foreign food. I had the best meal of my life once in London, an Eritrean restaurant, the owners taking time to share pictures of their country, one nestled between the sea and unrest beside Ethiopia. Our car is now lodged between two double-decker red buses and moves about as fast as ants wading through molasses. My mind speed bumps through a series of to-do's and how I might get out of this sexist assignment while Konstantin's low-level body odor invades my nose.

He offers me a stick of gum.

"No thank you."

Konstantin chews with his mouth closed, occasionally allowing his eyes to drift over me the way most guys do when they're wondering if I'm stupid enough to be wooed into fucking them.

"See something you like?" I ask.

"I do," he says. He displays off-white straight teeth, hoping I think, for me to reciprocate extracurricular interest.

"You reach for the jar, I'll rip off your hands," I say.

"Do I get 'I break, I buy' option?" He asks, his smile one of a man who thinks himself able to physically and mentally dominate me, a data point for me, and a huge mistake for him.

"Not for sale," I say.

"All woman for sale," Konstantin says. "Depends on price. Some command more than others."

"Who raised you? Cavemen?"

"What other kind of woman is there?" He laughs. "Even married woman sells herself for price."

"How un-refreshingly chauvinistic of you," I say. Although privately, I agree with him on that last part.

"Someday, you like me very much," He says.

"Keep dreaming… what is the name of this place, anyway?"

"The gentleman's club?" He asks, shifting his knees for more comfort and getting serious.

"If you want to call it that, sure…what is the name of this seedy strip joint?"

"It's nice place. Rick's Teahouse of the Dancing Lady," He says.

"Seriously? That is the cheesiest name for a strip club I've ever heard."

"Doesn't matter what is called. Your focus is target, Luca Harrington. He goes here. You make nice with shimmy and shake."

I imagine myself jiggling in front of stinky, sweaty fat guys hacking on stogies. It makes me want to puke. If this British Luca 'asshole' Harrington even thinks about putting his paws on me it will take everything I have not to jam my mom's red stiletto through his nut sack.

———

It takes my eyes a few seconds to adjust to the dimly lit bar, a stark contrast to the rare London sun loitering outside. I never paid much attention to the fact these sorts of places exist, strip clubs, where women build cottage empires on the firm foundations of bouncing breasts, and men are stupid enough to pay for this 'see but don't touch' bullshit.

"Hi K!" a dancer coos.

Konstantin hugs her hard, double pinches her exposed ass cheeks, and winks at me. I roll my eyes. Figures. He's a regular. "Harry Fairchild. He's owner. Everybody call him 'Slim'," Konstantin says, releasing the dancer who bounces off in another direction.

"Then why is this place called Rick's?" I ask.

"Rick takes bullet in head. Slim buys club and keeps name."

Boisterous laughter bubbles over to us from a nearby table, two strippers sitting with three expensively dressed men. One woman sits on a guy's lap, whispering in his ear. She tickles his lobe with the tip of her tongue and he pushes folded pounds into her garter. I slouch in a plushy chair and glance around at the lights, women, and sounds. Everything I've ever heard about strip clubs, and it isn't much, hasn't been positive. The scent of smoke and booze pushes me closer to memories of pool halls and taverns I'd sneak into as a minor back in Cleveland, using the fake ID Rosie gave me. These were places she sent me to cruise for drunk men, who's pockets might be rummaged for cash or drugs—except those places didn't have naked beggars walking around.

'DJ Platypus' calls someone named "Dasha" to the stage. He perches in a booth overlooking the crowd, cueing music, flipping switches on lights. With a look of mounting impatience, he tries again to summon his current 'no-show' to the stage. "Dasha, our gorgeous Ukrainian Queen, your subjects await the privilege of being knighted by your beauty…Dasha…hurry up…. *Dasha!* Get your arse to the stage. You're up!"

"*Dasha*" climbs the steps from the shadows near an exit of the club, and in slow, deliberate fashion, stretches one long frog-like leg into the spotlight. Head down, a thick robe of white hair covers her face. Her red sequined gown sets off a million twinkling sparkles when each gets caught in the footlights.

Wait.

One.

Second.

The stripper gracefully and slowly lifts her chin toward the rafters when a stream of lasers washes over her flawless frame. I lean forward for a closer look. *I'll be damned.* Jade Sokolov, the Russian spy lives…as 'Dasha' the Ukrainian stripper. I notice men sit a bit straighter and turn their chairs toward the stage. She's a damn near perfect sculpture in motion, and I am, as the British would say, '*gob smacked*' we'll be reacquainted, thanks to the testosterone laden business savvy of Harry 'Slim' Fairchild. I also find it hard to believe, given her chilly beauty, she's incapable of attracting a target like Sir Luca Harrington.

Jade teasingly peels away her gown and seductively gyrates in nothing but glitter-spackled nipples, high heels, and a thong. Her slender hips rotate shamelessly on a raised stage. She stares at her prey: a pudgy little man who leers at her from behind cinderblock-thick glasses. He's trapped in a 1960's brown and yellow plaid suit, too wide white tie, and stringy looking comb-over. If it weren't for Rick's Teahouse of the Dancing Lady, no goofy weasel of a man would stand a rat's chance in a viper pit of getting this close to Jade-slash-"*Dasha*" Sokolov in real life.

Jade swerves her taut ass around for the man's inspection. His cheek twitches as he fumbles with the five-pound note in his hand, crunch and release. A dreamy lust-alcohol smile wiggles across his lips. She playfully pushes the man away, drops to her knees in front of his crotch, turns around, and seductively cat-stretches forward until she lies on her stomach, her ass slightly lifted for a close-up. She rolls over and inserts the spike of her heel through her garter, stretching it open. Jade-*Dasha* slowly traces her fingers over a thin strip of floss covering her 'goody bag'. It's an offer too good to refuse. Under Jade's spell, the man places his contribution between her thighs. He is rewarded with fake fingernails tousling his hair. Man zero. Woman one—or in this case, five. Then I think, where else could a man like him get this sort of healing and attention for a few pounds? Jade was in charge every moment of her dance, something I never expected, and don't feel confident enough to replicate.

"I'm not doing that," I say to Konstantin.

"Not many women can," he says with an amused laugh. "Dasha is the best."

*Jade is the best shooter. Jade is the best dressed. Jade this and Jade that.* The memory train comes 'round again and my mind takes a quick trip to Plum Hook Bay where Jade was better at everything. She taught me how to grip my weapon. She also tried to drown Saratu, bullied Bennie, and called Tetana a 'faggot'. She put an arrow in Bennie's wolf. While confined at Plum Hook Bay, Jade and I engaged in almost weekly battles. I remember our fistfights, hair pulling, and name calling. I struggle to lay our 'mean girl' days to rest but hard feelings flit around a portion of my gut where immaturity, jealousy, and resentment still linger. I shellac my face with a counterfeit half-smile.

Jade flashes a toothy grin and approaches our table. "Sammy," she says whispering in my ear. "It's you, no? *YOU* are replacement? Ha! But you have teeny breast!" Jade speaks to Konstantin in Russian. "This mosquito is assigned to take my place?"

Konstantin pinches his lips against a bottle, slugs a sip, wipes his mouth with the back of his hand, and nods.

"Since you can't seem to close the deal, they sent in a real expert," I say to her in perfect Russian, which causes both her and Konstantin to raise their eyebrows toward one another before they look at me.

"Wait," Konstantin says. "You speak Russian? How you two know each other? Are you Russian agent too?"

"No," Jade says. "She is American, how you say, *white trash*?"

"You've been here how long and can't make your target?" I say. "You losing your touch, *Dasha?*"

Jade bolts up and reaches across the table but Konstantin grabs her forearm so fast it reminds me a little of Reggie. "Sit down," Konstantin says, impatient, I think, with both us. He looks directly at Jade. "This is not the sort of attention we want. You teach Sam to strip."

"*What?*" Jade and I both say, loudly, in unison.

"No way!" I say.

"Nee yet," she says, tightly folding her arms together and offering Konstantin a hateful frown that says she'd rather kill him than teach me anything.

"Woman gives me headache," Konstantin says. He shakes his head and cups his cheek with a palm. "Please. Very beautiful woman's, we have big job to do…bigger than dislike."

And just like that the hairs on my neck rise but not for the same reasons they do when Reggie loses his temper. I haven't forgotten these words, the ones Verity used to describe what she thought a Russian national said before he wiped the blood from her temple and left her propped against a wall. My hands rest under my chin. It's a pale effort to appear nonchalant in my scantily clad surroundings and to learn more about Mr. Konstantin Kurunov.

Strippers at the next table laugh at some guy who slowly slides out of his chair until he's a drunken puddle on the floor. The exotic dancers boldly fling their arms around other customers with loveable abandon. Oversized bouquets of currency, anchored to youthful thighs, make these ladies appear way more comfortable out of their clothes than I've ever felt in mine. And Jade too, seems at ease sitting around in nothing but a hot pink thong, which exposes ass cheeks as round and solid as a cue ball. She stands and bends over to retrieve another dancer's fallen wrap giving Konstantin and I a full moon view. She tongue-kisses the dancer, a show of shock, meant for me, I suppose, and the other stripper reciprocates, the two of them stabbing lappers for about ten seconds. "We begin now," Jade says, once their lips unlock. She motions for me to follow her.

"No, we can wait until tomorrow," I say, suddenly, really, very nervous. The loud music thumps through my chest and every muscle in my arms and legs shivers.

"Now is good," says Konstantin, a Cheshire grin creeping across his lips. "No dead waste, remember?"

I hate him.

I hate Jade too.

In fact, I hate everybody right now, including my bosses back at Langley who thought this was a great idea. *Idiots.* The thought of getting completely naked in front of a room full of strange men, who will judge my worth solely on how high my ass cheeks ride or what size bra cup I wear, is fundamentally fucked up. It also makes me want to pluck out everyone's eyeballs with a stir stick! Where's my sword? Don't these people have daughters?

Jade ambles over to the music booth to talk with DJ Platypus. They lean their heads close together, hair touching, and occasionally nod. Jade shakes her head, whispers some sort of negotiation, I think, as DJ Platypus peers and then squints at me over the top of thick, black-rimmed glasses. She hands him some pound notes and saunters away as he stares at her ass. "Got you audition!" She says. "You go on stage in few songs. I follow."

*Oh, shit.*

"Konstantin, my dear, dear comrade! You've returned to the fold!" A man's English voice booms through the bar between lulls in the music. "I swear if I were not straight I'd make a pass at you!" A robust figure, some guy who looks like a cross between the Planter's Peanut mascot and a male version of Lily Savage, strides toward us, arms out. He wears a top hat *and* an electric blue feather boa, and gingerly balances a champagne glass between his fingers. A fat cigar dangles from under a thick red mustache. Two supermodel Playboy types with puffy duck lips and fake boobs hang on each of his biceps—and here I am, unkindly judging all of them in a way I don't want to be judged.

"Good to see you too, my friend," Konstantin says, vigorously shaking the man's hand. "You headed out again?"

"Yes, flying to the Bahamas today."

"Slim has pilot's license and owns planes," Konstantin says to me.

"Planes as in plural?" I ask.

"Five of them," Slim says. "These ladies here have their pilot licenses too. They're flying me today. This is Mercedes and this is Chanel. And you are?"

"Oh, so sorry, forgive me. Please meet...um, what is your stripper name?" Konstantin asks.

"My stripper name?" I ask, trying to think fast. "I'm Peaches."

*God, from where in the rotten pit of my mind did I pull such a horrible and cliché stripper name?*

"Ah, my lovely," he says bending forward to kiss the back of my hand. "Sir Harry Slim Fairchild... at your service. But everybody calls me Slim, unless you prefer to call me Sir."

"Sir Harry? You're knighted?" I ask.

"By the Queen herself. She's quite progressive you know," he says.

I have my doubts the Queen of England would crown this clown with any title but go along anyway. "You fly your own planes?"

"Gulfstream jets," he says.

"And you teach them to fly too?" I nod at the scantily clad, blinged-out mannequins perched on each of Sir Slim's beefy arms.

"No, I don't personally, they graduated from flight school."

"Does every stripper here have a pilot's license?" I ask.

"Heaven's no, my inquisitive angel," Slim says. "Some of them attend medical or law school."

"Sir Slim pays for the college education or professional

training of any woman who works for him," Konstantin says. "He offers stock options to dancers too. They actually own piece of place."

"I keep 51%," Slim says. "You're American?"

"Yes."

"From Georgia, like the peaches?"

"From Cleveland, like the Great Lakes, but Perch isn't a good stage name," I say, remembering CIA *legends* always have some tidbits of truth in them. It adds sincerity to our cover story.

"Peaches!" He yells. "My sweet little American nectar. But you don't look like a peach."

"What do I look like?"

"I'd call you *Blaze,*" He says. "Your hair is a roaring fire. And you're skin! Why, you'd make freshwater pearls jealous!"

"Blaze it will be," I say, agreeing with him. It appears that Sir Harry-Slim Fairchild knows his stripping business.

"DJ Platypus tells me you're going to honor us with an audition," Sir Harry Slim says.

"Suzie! Pour this exquisite American torch some liquid courage!"

Suzie's sandy blonde Shirley Temple curls bounce, her beachball-sized frame waddling down the bar. She slaps three shots of whiskey on the ledge for me. "Meet my friend, Jack," she says. "He'll help you get acquainted with the place."

Normally, I don't drink much, but today? Today, I let the gasoline liquid race down my throat. I've previously jumped out of planes and witnessed more than my fair share of blood and guts... even speak seven languages and boast a doctorate in exobiology from Oxford...but getting naked in front of a room full of strangers requires all the distilled courage I can swallow.

I'm going to bitch-slap Agent Meadows when I get back to Langley, for suggesting this ridiculously sexist assignment. Fear consumes me when I consider Sir Slim might have hidden cameras.

"Follow me," says Jade.

The dressing room is cluttered with every imaginable vanity

enhancer a woman might use to cover over a multitude of insecurities. I thumb through a rack of costumes, if I can call them that—there's so little fabric to any of them. I select a royal purple number with shimmering gold plastic leaves. The alcohol kicks in.

"Oooh baby. You make good choice, Soopie know," An Asian lady says to me. She sits in a chair behind the door, the overseer of all things stripping.

"That's Su Penn, the 'house mom',"" says Jade. "She's from Thailand. She is attendant here. Soopie, what we call her, makes sure dancers have what they need. She sews costumes too."

I hold Su Penn's creation up to a light bulb. "Jesus," I say to Jade. "This outfit is only big enough to bandage a small cut. How do you wear this shit?"

"I have smaller ass," Jade says. "Try it on."

"Here? In front of everyone?" I ask.

"I don't care where," Jade says. "Use lady room, out there, but know, if you do, you have to walk across bar to come back."

A small swarm of strippers are too busy with their own costumes, make-up, hair, and personal dramas to pay me any attention. Some nod in my direction or look me up and down as if judging a farm animal at the fair. Nobody smiles or says hello. I quickly shed my street clothes and don Su Penn's outfit. "This barely fits," I say to Su Penn.

"You look soooo good," Soopie says. "Men throw you money *all* times." She leans forward from her chair, adjusts my bra strap, and unexpectedly plants a kiss on my ass. Her scarlet lipstick mark looks like a smeary flesh wound on my right butt cheek. She taps my rump with approval.

"Soopie's trademark for new girls," Jade says. "Fresh sushi…"

"*Fresh Sushi?* How empowering," I say.

"It's forty pounds for the costume," Su Penn says.

"Forty pounds for this piece of string?" I ask. "How can this floss cost forty pounds?"

"Cough it up or dance naked, I don't care," she says, flinging her multi-ringed hand as she regales me with an insulted stare that might make Reggie proud. She says something in Vietnamese, not a language I know, but I sense she's unhappy with me for complaining about the inflated price of her handkerchiefs passing as costumes.

I reach into my bag and pull out my red high heels as I hand her some cash.

"You got new ones." Jade says.

"My heels? No. They're the same ones I had before."

"They look new," she says.

"No. Same shoes."

"You fuck with me," Jade says. "These are new, but same, no?"

"Same shoes. I take care of my shit," I say. What I don't say is that my mom's red heels still look new because I stopped wearing them years ago and they were only pulled from Reggie's closet as a memory trigger for Avril when I visited her in the asylum. I was shocked Reggie packed them away until he said he didn't, his wife did, which surprised me even more.

"You do fine. You do just fine. Soopie know," Su Penn says, patting me again. Her black wavy hair reminds me of a waterfall the way it almost touches the floor when she stands up.

"Stripper is perfect cover," Jade says as we exit the dressing room. "Men too busy looking at tits, and most, how you say, *prudy* women outside of strip club, not think beyond 'sleazy job choice'."

I want to reach around and pull this thong out of my ass but there is no place for that annoying lisp of fabric to rest other than right where it is. My heart pounds in my ears next to the beat of the music but my head finally slides into a dreamy alcohol-induced fog.

"Ladies & Gentlemen, we have an exclusive treat for you today!" DJ Platypus screams into a microphone. "All the way across the pond joining our team from America, let us give a warm London welcome to our newest Teahouse tit-illator, the inferno of indecency, the flaming babe of the booby bonfire...*BLAAAAZE!*"

I stand.

On stage.

Facing an audience.

Exposed.

A spotlight shines down from somewhere in the rafters and the plastic gold leaves on this chintzy costume are the *only* thing shimmying other than my quivering knees.

"You must dance," Konstantin says as he plants two index fingers on each side of his lips and lifts. "And smile! Smile." He looks desperate and sorry for me but it's hard to tell because I now see two of him.

"Darling," Slim yells, "you have to move when you're on stage. Like this!" Slim rolls his hips and waves his arms. "Come on, dear, shake that groove thang…"

My legs feel heavy and it takes every bit of embarrassment bubbling beneath my phony exterior to half-heartedly kick my legs. A tingling sensation rises to my cheeks. People laugh. Lots of them. I wobble on my heels and stumble backward, into a silver pole, but don't fall. I grip the pole and try to look out into the audience but can't really see beyond glaring footlights.

"You have to at least look as if you're having fun," Sir Harry yells. "Take off your top. Show them your beautiful breasts!"

I turn my lips upward into a forced Joker-esque smile, barely crank my hips, and lock up my arms like a tin man around the pole—and it spins because it's got ball bearings at the base—sending me out of orbit from the stage. I clamor back up the small set of stairs by the curtains and crawl to the footlights. Shit. I lost a heel. Someone throws it back onstage and I sit there to put it on.

Jade falls forward from her chair into Konstantin's chest and belly laughs. I swear to God, when I finish this humiliation, I'm going to stomp off stage and punch everyone in the face.

"Take off your top!" Some guy yells.

I can't take off my top. I won't. I can barely stand up. My nipples are so stiff with fear they hurt and poke through the scant fabric covering them.

Konstantin walks up to the stage and roughly deposits a fifty-pound note into my garter, shaking his head. "Take off your top," he whispers. "Here, let me undo it for you."

I swivel my hips and squat down again, wobble, and land on my ass, my hands cupped over my breasts as he easily plucks the tightly drawn string out of its bow. It dangles down my back. He helps me to my feet and leaves me again without a male lead. I close my eyes and toss the top toward a table and lift my arms to the sky, slightly swaying but not dancing.

Once the song ends, and it couldn't happen fast enough, I exit the stage to wild applause. Slim helps me down the stairs and hands me one hundred pounds. "Honey, normally I'd say you should look for another line of work. But since you are Konstantin's friend, and he tells me you need the job, I'd going to give you a chance. I'm not sure what that was you did up there, but the gentlemen seem entertained."

"*You* must be desperate," Jade says to Slim.

"*Blaze* is a bit shy and uneducated about our industry," Slim says. "Some men find that refreshing."

Jade graces the stage again and it's no stretch to say she looks like a goddess, her iceberg hair and skin a stark contrast against hot pink lights. Men line up around the stage like velvet rope and she sexily extracts pound notes from every single one of them. And by the time she's finished, Konstantin has slipped away from me and out of the club.

# SIXTEEN

# MEETING LUCA

"DO YOU KNOW WHO THAT *IS?*" Mercedes asks.

"Everybody on the globe has heard of Sir Luca Harrington," I say. "He's the immensely rich hump who barricades himself from the real world behind 'weapons and defense' deals." With a flick of my hand, I toss his business card in the trash. I've been working here two months and he's taken his sweet time to arrive, but he's here—and my *real* job is to make myself memorable and score a place in his inner circle. From everything about him I've studied, he's smart and it won't be easy.

"He seems like a nice enough guy," she says. "He wants to see you in VIP. He specifically asked for Blaze." Chanel rummages through the waste can until she retrieves his card.

"No," I say. "You take my place. I'm busy."

Chanel gasps, standing behind me in the vanity mirror. "Girl, what you got goin' on 'round here that be takin' up so much 'o yo' time? He ain't never asked for anyone by name befo'. He's one rich motha' fucker," she says.

Mercedes practically leaves skid marks out of the dressing room, on her way, no doubt, to take my place in VIP, or to tell Slim.

"I've got five private dances lined up," I say. "Sir Harrington will have to wait."

"You one crazy-goofy bitch," Chanel says. "This guy changes lives with one click o' his finger and Princess Blaze here says she got five puny dances on her schedule. Girl, I'll bet just walkin' up to VIP once you been summon' nets yo' ass at least a thousan' pounds, maybe even two! You gonna tell me next you got tea with the Queen? He could buy her arse too."

"*Luca Harrington* change *my* life? Ha!" I say. "Men with money usually make up for shortfalls in other places. Why would any woman want to sacrifice herself to his shadow?"

"Because that's what we do," Chanel says. "And it ain't no sacrifice to be nice to a rich man. It's a sacrifice to fuck a poor one."

"You'd know," Jade purrs as she sits at a mirror and paints her lashes with mascara.

"And you wouldn't," I say. "All the men you take on, fall in... never to be heard from again. Except for Harrington...he just never called back."

She throws her hairbrush at me. I duck and it knocks over a perfume bottle.

"You bitches need to be stoppin' this shat right now," Chanel says. "Ya'll should be channelin' yo' inner Goddess and treatin' each other with respect."

"*BLAZE! BLAZE!*" Slim practically leaps into the dressing room. Tonight he sports a bright yellow silk smoking jacket with a purple derby plopped over his red curls, and oddly enough, it pairs nicely with his black lace-up combat boots and waxed mustache. If I didn't know any better, I'd think he was gay—but almost every lady who works for him has fucked him, they've said (something I find deeply disturbing), and claim he's awesome in the sack.

A few pebbles of sweat graze his upper lip and he dabs a pink handkerchief to absorb the dew. "Honey!" He says. He tugs on my arm to pull me up from a dressing room chair. "Luca Harrington is out there in VIP asking for you! Come on you sultry she-fox! Let's not keep him waiting! He said to give this to you."

He throws five hundred pounds on the vanity in front of me and Chanel's head swivels on her neck, her eyelids fluttering like bee wings.

"Why not keep him waiting?" I ask, yanking my arm back and applying a long blush brush to my cheeks. "Anticipation heightens intrigue, don't you think?" I stuff the money back into Slim's jacket. "And give this back to the man. Everybody wants his money. Poor guy. It must be hard not to have any *real* friends."

Slim blinks in shock, I think, touching the pound notes to be sure they're secure and won't fall on the floor or get gobbled up by women who probably, and unfortunately, need the money more than either he or Harrington does.

"Hell, honey, I'll take that man's pounds," Chanel says. "And shag 'im real good too."

"Get out, Chanel," Slim says looking at me. "I need to have a word with Blaze...privately. All of you, get out!"

Chanel throws down her paper dragon fan and rolls her head at both of us. "All this money flyin 'round here and the black girl gets dee-smissed," she says with a snap of her fingers. "I never seen so many crazy crackers in one place in all my life. Jeesh."

The rest of the ladies scatter hen-like from the dressing room as Slim tosses Chanel a fifty-pound note. "Go keep the man occupied for a moment," he says. "Tell him Blaze is on her way but wants to freshen up just for him." She flashes a bright smile and folds the money into her bra cup and saunters out to meet Harrington.

"Young lady," says Slim. "A very important man sits in VIP. Let's not be disrespectful of our guests... or your position here. He just used an expanded vocabulary to charmingly boot Mercedes' arse out of VIP. He's personally requested to meet you and you will go to him."

"Wait one second," I say. "You never force a lady around here to do anything she doesn't want to do. Why now? Because he's rich?" I wave the hairbrush at him. "We get wealthy and famous guys through here all the time."

"Harrington is different," Slim says, planting his hands against the top of my dressing chair, his mustache bending down a bit to match heavy creases in his forehead as I watch him from the mirror, his gaze shifting over my frame.

"He has a piece of this place, doesn't he? He *owns* you!" I say.

Slim doesn't say a word. He jerks his head back in surprise, a little pissed off I correctly guessed—but not really. I read it in his file back at Langley. Harrington gave Sir Fairchild a hefty leg up in the titty business with low-interest multi-million dollar loans, money Slim pays back *whenever* because his business is a shimmering front for backdoor weapons deals and intelligence operations.

"Of course," I say. "It makes so much sense now—he hangs out here every few months because he's your silent partner."

I lean back in the chair and press my head into Slim's soft belly. He yanks my chair around to face him and I now see a side of him I suspect other dancers rarely do—a commanding mean streak he uses to intimidate people when needed and I'm stunned by it. "Harrington and I served together in the Royal Navy. The man once saved my life. You *will* go to him."

---

My unemployed ass steps up to the food cart a few blocks from Rick's Teahouse of the Dancing Lady.

"I'll get that," a voice behind me says. "Keep the change."

A tailored sleeve reaches over my shoulder and hands twenty pounds to the vendor, gold 'eye of Horus' cufflinks gleaming under streetlights. His are different than the eye necklace I hide under my shirt.

"You have stock in the stalking business too?" I ask not looking behind me but knowing its Harrington. I feel him too close. "You touch my hair and I'll kick your ass."

"I'd never touch a woman without her permission," he says. "A simple and polite 'thank you' will do."

"Fuck off," I say. "I didn't ask you to buy me a sandwich. You muscled your way in." I walk off without looking at him and he follows.

"Wait," he says. "Why won't you even talk with me? I know you know who I am."

"A spoiled brat who wastes money throwing it around like scrap paper? I only offer curbside dances to the Prince of Wales," I say.

"Lucky guy," he says. "And I'll have you know I'm a self-made man. Nobody handed me, nor did I inherit, a dime. Right time, right place."

"Thanks to you, I've lost two jobs. I stay as far away from bad luck as I can get. Could you *please* back up a bit—like maybe to the Cotswold's'?"

"Two jobs?" He asks, letting out a short laugh.

I whirl on my heels to face him—to give him a piece of my mind for thinking another's loss of livelihood is so funny while he rides high on a privatized hog.

*Whoa.*

I didn't expect Sir Luca Harrington to be so handsome in person, and taller than me too. The butterflies in my stomach rapidly expand and collapse their wings all at once and my heart leaps over the moon. A whirl of electricity zips through my system. I've seen pictures of Harrington but they do little justice to the spell binding man now before me. If he were a magnet, he'd attract an entire scrap yard...but I recover. *He's just a man, Sam.*

"Yes, two jobs," I say. "Sir Harry fired me because I wanted to be polite to other guests and finish the private dances I committed *ahead* of you...and I was fired from your company too...for insubordination. But that's bullshit."

"Really? I can't imagine *you* being fired for such a thing," he says. "You've been *sooo* professional thus far."

"Piss off," I say.

"For which division of Harrington did you work?" He asks.

"Entry level nuclear systems engineer, on visa," I say.

"Impressive," he says. "How long have you been a case officer with the CIA?"

"I can't tell you that," I say. "Or I'd have to kill you."

Luca chuckles as we sync our stride along a nearly empty street.

"My former work as a case officer was part of the reason I lost my job with your company," I say, trying to think fast and cover my ass. A leaden lump of concern replaces the butterflies in my gut because Luca's given me no time to consider how he so quickly recognized I'm CIA, which likely means there's a mole back at Langley who told him. Maybe that's why he asked for me at the club. "I accompanied a small delegation to the Sheng Corporation in China. I was there to inspect some of the systems before a buyout by your subsidiary, but it was crap."

"The Orgon Collider is some of the highest quality technology ever built," he counters. "It's a good acquisition. I researched it myself. Small company but good stuff."

"That's what someone wants you to think," I say. "Your engineers didn't test the CP328-S carbon reactors and the Zanbar particles were shit. The three tests I ran were complete failures. I work up a report and your head of engineering changes it from fail to 'pass'. I'm fired as incompetent."

"Who fired you?"

"Ashley in HR. She got the order from Don in engineering."

"Ashley's loyal," he says. "She does her job. Don? Not so much."

We stroll in semi-awkward silence until we arrive at a cross walk and wait for the light. I can't help but steal little glances at his face, one I'm sure he uses to his advantage—a face that literally launches hundreds of war ships around the globe and probably breaks equally as many hearts. "Your mistake only cost you $40 million," I finally say. "It cost me *my* job and a good reference. So, here I am, busting my heels at a strip joint while you think everybody should come running to you because you throw money around and you're semi-handsome."

"You think I'm handsome?" He asks.

"You're okay for a multi-billionaire who thinks he can buy his way into a woman's heart with street cart grub," I say.

"Who says I'm after your heart? We could have some real fun if you don't take our relationship too seriously," he says.

"Oh, now we're in a *relationship*?" I ask. "Don't flatter yourself."

"Good sense of humor," he says. "I appreciate a woman who holds her own."

"Am I supposed to wag my tail now because my personal worth somehow rises to your approval?" His blond hair and electric blue eyes leave me knee-wobbly and I haven't had such a swoosh race across my hips since I met Genin years ago—and once, inexplicably, with Bennie, when we were kids.

"We could start this relationship with your honesty," he says.

"I *worked* for the CIA," I say, because I can tell by his extraordinarily calm and collected body language that he knows more about me than I do—although I'm not quite sure where or how he got his information and that concerns me. And I don't like it one bit he's tipped our game in his favor.

"I didn't go back to the U.S. because I can't" I say, which is a lie. "A woman accosted me in Trafalgar Square. She claimed Sheng would reinstate my job at Harrington, and pay me big bucks too, if I funneled trade secrets to them. I declined. Working at Rick's was the only job I could get 'off grid' until I figure out what to do because I can't compromise other case officers."

"Why didn't you tell anyone at my company about the Sheng approach?" He asks.

"You've got an infestation of moles at Harrington Technologies." I say. "Who would I trust? You've also hired too many chauvinists in the engineering department."

We cross the street, pass a park and get sandwiched between a row of buildings on a narrow avenue where the sound of pub revelers spills onto a nearby patio.

"Where are you going?" He asks.

"None of your business," I say, not really sure where I'm headed because his presence makes my head spin about as much as my worthless compass and I'm directionless, wandering aimlessly, caring more about being in his company than I do about building faux rapport.

"May I come too?"

"No."

"Why?"

"My husband might object," I say.

His cheeks flush slight pink and I can't tell if he's angry, surprised, or disappointed—perhaps *sagitated*. "I didn't know," he says. "Are you happy?"

"I don't cheat," I say.

"So, there's hope," he smiles.

There's *always* Hope, I think, wondering again about both my missing daughter and my Source Guide, our conversation rounding a difficult turnabout.

"Have you watched the movie *Indecent Proposal*?" He asks. "It came out last year."

"Did you write the misogyny portion of your employee manual?" I ask, shifting mental gears. "Yes. I saw the movie. I liked the ending. She chooses her husband."

"Yes, she wasn't a very good businesswoman either," he says. "In real life she'd pick the rich guy. And you strip. What sort of husband allows *that to* happen?"

"*Allows*?" I question. "A husband who trusts and recognizes I work on my feet and not my back. A husband who doesn't expect me to be the guardian of male morality and treats me as an equal partner, not a trophy. What sort of man patronizes a strip club?"

"A misunderstood one," he says. "I'm not buying you're married."

"You've got that right," I say. "You're not buying anything. I'm not for sale."

"Every person has a price," Luca says. "Got any kids?"

*Hope. I can't tell him.*

"No. Do you?"

"The DNA tests have, thus far, all come back negative," he says, twirling lightly around a street lamp. "Kiss me Blaze."

"No."

"Come back to work for me."

"Not a chance in hell," I say. "You're too dangerous."

"Don't you thrive on *danger?*" he asks. "Or do you prefer to wallow in overly sensitive seriousness?" Harrington puts his hands in his pockets, which tells me he's drawing into himself—but he did strike gold on my nerves. I let it go. Unbalancing him a little helps me.

Luca softly whistles and kicks a paper cup down the sidewalk. A Phantom Rolls Royce edges its way along the street behind us. The driver waits and watches for Sir Harrington's ring-less hand to summon a stop. He's been engaged twice but called off the impending nuptials both times. I read in his file that he's considered a rather low-key, private playboy. His former conquests rarely kiss and tell for tabloid dollars because he pays better for their silence.

"Hmm," he says.

"What?"

"I was just thinking. About all of us having a price. For most its money or status or fame but for some it's something else... revenge, pride, ego. What is your price? I know you have one. We all do."

"Don't you mean *vice* rather than *price?*" I ask. "What's yours?"

"I like redheads..." he says. "And yours is lovely. But I mean price...it's not always about vice." Luca snaps his finger. "I've got it. Sometimes the price isn't material...but *maternal.* I'll bet if you had a kid and I ransomed her for a price, you'd pay with your life to save her."

*Do.*

*Not.*

*React.*

"So hypothetically speaking," I say. "If I had a daughter, I'd pay any price to save her?"

"Precisely," he says. "You're a fast learner."

"And you're a cold prick," I say.

"Ouch!" He says, grabbing his chest and acting as if his mention of my daughter is no more serious to him than bartering for a bag of crisps. "Seriously, if I could figure out your price…I'd pay anything…to help you find her."

And the way he says this, with a micro-inflection of compassion, *almost* melts my façade enough to trust him, and sends my heart into a tailspin because I can't decide if he's bluffing and he has my daughter or knows she's missing. My mother's words flood my head: *'Perks come with high prices. Monsters need to be kept in cages.'*

"You help *me*? The return on investment isn't worth my price," I say.

"Ah, so you *do* have one!" He says. And I'm not sure if he means that he knows I have a daughter, or a price, but I don't ask because he's knocking *me* off balance now. "You've also zapped me again, this time in the ego." He rubs his ass cheek.

I offer him a bogus smile, hard for me to do, but I don't want him to know he's struck two major concerns of mine within minutes.

"Don't sell me short," he says. "The return on investment would be unforgettable," he winks.

*Gosh, what blue eyes you have. Stop it, Sam.* This man understands the art of intellectual check-mate all too well, which is both a thrill and an irritation for me, and leaves me on edge.

"Smells like rain," he says. "If you won't kiss me or work for me, will you at least allow me to give you a ride home?"

Luca runs a hand through his blonde hair. No wonder Jade didn't get anywhere with this guy. She's beautiful and smart but not Luca's sort of intelligent. He could have any woman he wants…and does…then it's over, she gets boxed up and returned to the moving van while he leaves no forwarding address. For me to think I'd be any different is a mistake most women make with men like him. He gets what he wants and he's gone.

Sir Luca Harrington, I'm convinced, views women as dispensable pieces of ass he can buy or trade, like commodities or gold cufflinks. Maybe he seeks something deeper in a woman, I think, something he's never found, but I'm not sure what that might be. I also sense a profound restlessness and discontent roaming through that body of his. I stop walking and look deeply into his eyes, feigning that he doesn't impress me a bit. "Tell you what," I say. "If you can pass a test, I'll let you kiss me."

"French kiss," he interjects. "With lots of tongue."

"Kiss on the cheek," I say.

"No deal," he says, staring at me. "It's not a good return on *my* investment."

"Take it or leave it," I say. "And by the way, I'm questioning your business savvy based on your lack of quality control. Who spends twenty pounds on a food cart sandwich?"

"Au contraire," he says. "The best deal may have walked away while I waited for change. I weighed the risk. God, you're just as beautiful as I remember, your hair, the perfect color."

"As you *remember?*"

"A dream," he says. "A long time ago."

"And my hair's the perfect color for what?" I ask. "Never mind! I don't want to know. But that's all you've *got?*" I exaggerate a yawn and stretch my arms up to the sky. "Boring."

"I could throw in a sunset cruise with champagne and caviar?"

"I'd rather eat fried bologna with my husband on our cracked balcony watching an empty parking lot," I say.

"You don't have a husband," he says. "It would take a special sort of man to handle a lady of your temperament. One kiss. Right here, right now. No one has to know," he says.

"I'd know."

"Damn woman, you're putting bees in my brain. What is this test of which you speak?"

"Kiss on the cheek?" I ask.

He shakes his head.

"Fine," I say. "French kiss."

He beams, happy for the win, I think.

"You ready?" I ask.

"Yes."

"Lick your elbow."

Luca plants his right palm on his shoulder and looks at his elbow. He stretches his chin, sticks out his tongue and then laughs so loud it echoes down an alley. Rain sprinkles crystal-drops that stick to our hair. I turn up the collar of my raincoat and leave him standing alone. "Good night, Sir Harrington," I say.

"I'm *Lord* Harrington now," he says. "I've been promoted."

I round a street corner too quickly for him to catch me. And just to ensure I won't go weak and change my mind, I fly low, back to my flat.

# SEVENTEEN

## THE INVITATION

ABAR AND MEADOWS WERE VERY curious to know everything I personally learned about Lord Luca Harrington. They ordered me into a briefing practically the moment I touch down on U.S. soil.

I didn't want to come back here so soon—not after our encounter and what he said about my daughter. Two months have gone by...not one word from Harrington and I'm still no closer to finding out who kidnapped Hope. I fired off answers to my superiors about him, mostly drawn from research, British gossip, the *Daily Mail,* and what I make up.

Like me, Jade got bounced out of the U.K. and landed another special ops detail infiltrating the *Brise de Mer,* a Corsican gang in the French Mediterranean allegedly expanding its drug and prostitution empire to include contract killing and human trafficking. She got reassigned someplace way cooler than my stuffy office just outside D.C. Konstantin is off grid too, gone before I could question him about any time spent in the states.

Would Lord Harrington help me find Hope? I've thought about reaching out to him but retract my fingers from the phone. *"Perks come with high prices,"* Mom said. I scratch the thought.

Abar stuck me back in the basement with Dr. Monica, researching the tribal murders. We're still meandering through a labyrinth of biological evidence, pieces of an oversized puzzle that lead us further into the abyss of dead ends.

"This is heaps bad," Dr. Monica says.

I'm trying to figure out how to get to Turkey to go spelunking so I can locate Verity's file, the one Seth left behind in a cave. It may hold a clue to these murders and give me time to do some digging around about my daughter. The trouble is, there are about 40,000 caves in that country and I can't come up with a solid reason to ask Abar to approve the travel without raising suspicion, let alone figure out how to get into and out of a cave system and smuggle an 'above top secret' Pentagon file out of a country falling into civil war.

"You received a special delivery," Abar says poking his head in our lab. "It came right to my office. Nice job keeping a low profile."

"Why didn't you send it back without response and stamp it *undeliverable* like we usually do?" I ask.

"Oh, we don't *always* do that," Abar says with a smirk. "Meet me in my office in ten…"

———

"You guys opened it," I say.

"Had to," Meadows answers with a shrug. "It's standard protocol to scan everything that comes through this building."

I remove the scroll from the small round container, untie the scarlet velvet ribbon, and unfurl a gold-embossed invitation set upon fine ivory-colored parchment.

*Dr. Samantha R. Blake, you and a guest are cordially invited to…*

"What's the Harrington Hunt Ball?" I ask.

"It's only the most coveted invitation of the entire United Kingdom social season," Meadows says. "The evening consists of a black-tie dinner and ballroom dancing, followed by a morning hunt."

"What kind of hunt?" I ask.

"A foxhunt," Abar says.

"A foxhunt?"

"The hounds are let loose ahead of the horses to locate a fox," Abar says.

"I know what a foxhunt is," I say, annoyed. "But why would Harrington send me an invitation, and how did he know to send it *here*?"

"We believe he's sending a message," Meadows says. "That he knows who you *really* are and to make us aware of that fact."

"I'll be damn," I say, scrutinizing the perfected gold-leaf calligraphy. *Does anyone really know who I am? I'm not sure if I know who—or what—I am.* Lord Harrington, as he calls himself, must have connections in pretty high places to learn my real name and the exact address where I work, which causes me heartburn over my own country's advanced security—or lack of.

"Sam, do you even know how to ride a horse?"

"Yes," I answer without thinking.

Both men look at one another then at me.

"You do?" Meadows asks.

*Shit.*

"You were raised as a Cleveland foster kid, where'd you learn to ride a horse?" Abar asks.

I can't tell them that one of my former foster parents had horses, because if they check, it won't be true. And I can't tell them the truth, that Reggie taught me how to ride wild horses bareback at NASA Plum Hook Bay, and I'm a natural, or I was—but that was a lot of years ago and I haven't been on a horse since. "I'd sneak onto the trains going to Chargrin Falls," I lie. "One of the stable boys taught me when I was a kid."

Thankfully, Chagrin Falls *does* have riding clubs.

"Oh?" Meadows says. "Which one?"

I shrug. "Can't remember. It was a long time ago."

"So how many years has it been since you've ridden a horse?" He asks.

"Does it matter? I'm not going. I want to get back to the tribal murders. May I go now, Sir?"

Abar puts a palm in the air to stop me from getting up. "You've made quite an impression on Lord Harrington," he says as he cups his suit sleeve with a hand and one leg dangles off of the edge of his desk. "You've provided him with a challenge, and that's much better than agent Sokolov could do."

Abar drops an old edition of the Daily Mail in front of me by the small accent table next to his guest chair. A picture of a smiling Luca Harrington looks back at me...a picture of him helping some woman wearing a lavender suit into a limousine, with a screaming headline he's *involved* with this Lady Olivia Ross, a British socialite who started a financial empire using daddy's money. I fight off the swooshy feeling that gallops across my hips and try to bury a flicker of jealousy, which is ridiculous because I don't even know this man.

"I'm not going," I say, folding my arms across my chest.

"You have to go," Meadows says. "This is as close as we've ever gotten to this guy. This event is exclusive—only one-hundred people receive an invitation and we can't just send somebody else. For whatever reason, he wants *you* there. We'd like to know why."

"That's not obvious?" I ask. "I didn't sleep with him. I blew off his attention. How did he figure out my cover, anyway?" I ask. "He knows my name and mentioned the CIA on the street when he accosted me. He made a joke about it."

"He works for the SIS," Meadows says.

"What?" I abruptly stand. "I thought he was a private defense and chemical contractor?"

"Oh, he is," Meadows says. "But he also served in the Royal Marines (a division of the Royal Navy) and earned the rank of Master Sergeant in 1985, before he retired from active duty."

SIS a.k.a. MI-6, conducts espionage operations in Europe, Latin America, and much of Asia. MI-6 is basically the reason the CIA even exists. During WWII, it helped create the CIA's precursor, OSS, and trained most of the CIA's original personnel. Our agencies often work together. Since it's against the law for the CIA to spy on U.S. citizens, MI-6 does it for us, then shares the intel—and vice-versa.

"I didn't see any reference to MI-6 in his file," I say, picking it up again and thumbing through it in case I might have missed that important detail. "I didn't because it's not in here."

"Professional courtesy," Abar says. "We were specifically asked by MI-6 to keep his clandestine service to the U.K. out of his file."

For a brief moment, I remember how Dr. Evelyn and Reggie built a new case file for me with Septum Oculi's help, so I know this is possible. Not even my bosses at Langley know that I work for Septum Oculi, which Bennie once told me, "flies *above* the law".

"How did he score a royal title?" I ask. "He mentioned he's a Lord now. Is he descended from British royalty?"

"He isn't royalty," Meadows says. "The prime minister, under the blessing of Parliament, appointed him a 'life peerage' with the Queen's approval. Evidently, the Queen thinks a great deal of him and occasionally invites him to tea."

"Are you telling me that this guy *bought* himself a royal title?" I ask. "And that he really shares tea with the Queen—the Queen of England?"

Meadows nods, one finger across his lip and his thumb cupped under his chin, which means he's thinking. "He's helped a lot of people, built schools, provided thousands of jobs…"

"Yes, at the expense of others the world over," I say. "People who might be too poor or less equipped to fight back against his advanced weapons systems."

Abar taps a pen on his chin, one he's pulled from a holder from atop his grand wooden desk. He stands up and walks around it to look out the window. "I'm surprised to hear that coming from you," he says.

"I don't kill people for sport," I say.

"Neither does Harrington," Abar finally says. "Insofar as this agency is aware, Lord Harrington is squeaky clean…"

"I hear a 'but' in your voice," I say.

"But...he's up to something," Abar says.

"What do you think it might be?" I ask.

"Three days ago, he rented out the entire Randolph Hotel in Oxford and he's been there ever since," Meadows says.

"So? Maybe he needs a vacation," I say. Although I'm curious as to why he chose Oxford. I look at the map on Abar's wall. Oxford is practically a straight line 150 miles due South of Harrington's estate.

"He visits a pasture outside the city near Jericho around sunset," Meadows says.

My ears practically catch fire when Meadows brings up Jericho. *"Avril preferred isolated pursuits, walking in the woods outside of Jericho, or reading for hours about plants among the stacks at Blackwell's,"* Dr. Evelyn told me. "Is he meeting someone?" I ask.

"No," Abar says, pointing to Jericho on the map, located a couple of miles outside the University of Oxford, a place I've never been, but have a degree, one bought for me by Dr.'s Dennison. Then a thought occurs to me. I really don't have much room to look down on Lord Harrington for his purchased peerage and maybe we share more in common than I thought, which is grudgingly hard to admit and irksome.

"Harrington walks to a certain spot in the field and spends about two hours staring up at the sky while pasture horses shit around him," Abar says.

"Why?" I ask.

"We have no idea why," Meadows shrugs. "There's *nothing* out there except grass and pasture horses. The Thames wraps around it on one side. It runs along a wood line where some houseboats are permanently moored, near a pub called *The Perch,* but he doesn't visit. We've combed that entire area. NSA monitors space traffic too. No planes, satellites, or spaceships coming through."

"He's looking for something," Abar says. "We'd like for you to gain his trust, find out what it might be."

"And how am I supposed to do that during a dance and foxhunt located one-hundred-fifty miles away?" I ask. 'Everybody there will be scrambling for his attention. I can't build that sort of trust in a day or two."

"Tell him about the tribal murders," Meadows says.

"That's classified!" I protest. "Above top-secret, remember?"

"Tell him," Abar says. "You have agency permission. I'll sign the order. He already knows about the tribal murders—but let's see how he reacts when you confide in him."

If two of my superiors order me to share sensitive case information with Lord Luca Harrington, it means they know that he knows something we don't. And secretly, a part of me feels excited about returning to the U.K. to see him again, to ask more questions, and gauge how much information he has about Hope.

"May I go now?" I ask as I move toward the door.

"Just one more thing…" Abar says. "You have two months before the Harrington Ball. Your job every day for the next eight hours, five days a week, will be learning ballroom dancing and fox hunting. You'll also need a gown and the agency will provide your plus one."

"May I put in a request for my plus one?" I ask.

Both men look at one another and then at me.

"Genin Paranos," I say. "Physically, he's every bit Harrington's equal."

"But they don't look anything alike," Meadows says, confused.

"That's not what she means," Abar says with a laugh. "I think you're onto something, Dr. Blake. I'll contact our new Office of Military Affairs so Genin can report to the U.K. for this detail. Likely do him some good, anyway, to get out of that sand pit he's been in for a while."

# EIGHTEEN

# HARRINGTON HOUSE

I EXTEND my limbs and stretch myself over Genin's lap in the back of a limousine, watching autumn scenery rush by through an open sunroof, a pallet of green, gold, crimson, and soft yellow leaves floating beneath a cloudless azure sky. It's late September and much of the United Kingdom is blessed with gloriously crisp and mostly sunny weather, perfect for a party.

I read that *Harrington House* resembles a five-star hotel more than a private mansion boasting three hundred plus rooms. It's twice the size of Buckingham Palace and employs well over five-hundred staff members to run the grounds, manage security, and handle the village's thousands of acres of farmland. Not too shabby for a man in his mid-thirties who has an estimated net worth of almost twelve *billion* dollars.

Lord Harrington's uncommon hyper-success is also cause for concern at Langley. Some think he's an international security threat, potentially earning grand sums of money selling advanced weaponry and chemicals *off-book* to enemy nations. Others consider him cleaner than a bottle of bleach. I'm not yet sure what to think. Maybe he uses the bleach to disinfect himself against any criminal dirt we might excavate. He seems to have risen from relative obscurity, the illegitimate son of a Cotswold woman, who refused to name the father of her baby. She died years ago in a house fire.

*Lord* Harrington purchased his home about three years ago, one in serious disrepair, from the Iiliam Dhone family. Their patriarch, Baron Illiam Christian Dhone, commissioned the place in the 1500's but was executed on the Isle of Man for treason against the crown shortly after its construction. He was posthumously pardoned by King Edward VI.

Harrington House, as its now renamed, much to the consternation of the region's nobility, has hosted important figures through the centuries including royalty, most notably, Queen Victoria and Prince Albert. But it is the countless scandals and alleged curse for which this estate is known; the mysterious deaths of two nobles in the early 1700's, an illegal gambling house and brothel during WWII, and the secret meeting place of two international celebrities carrying on a torrid affair, who died together in a never fully explained horse-riding incident.

It is also rumored that a maidservant named Alyce Hastmier cast a curse over the grounds centuries ago, when her betrothed was disemboweled, she claimed, by strange creatures hiding 'under hill'. She was hanged from a tree that still stands in the garden, put on trial for practicing witchcraft and convicted of her lover's murder. Given what I witnessed at Plum Hook Bay, and the mysterious death of its maid Gladys, after she allegedly witnessed White Bigfoot, I can't help but think Alyce was wrongly accused.

Genin rests a large hand on my thigh, affectionately cups his other palm over my ear, and kisses my forehead. Our relationship, if I can call it that, is unconventional. We're close friends for sure, and we click in the sack, but we mutually decided our lives are too complicated for monogamy. I love him but neither of us is "in love" with the other. I've never been *in love* and assume that once the flares subside, people get left with cinders, boredom, and enough emotional debris to load up a landfill. But then again, I consider Barbara and Reggie, and Rakito and Priyanka—two couples who seem rather fond of their spouses, years into their marriages. I'm not sure how each manages that sort of commitment. I wonder if a happy union is a gift only granted to a select few…or perhaps a curse-in-waiting, as change comes to us all in the form of sickness, accidents, infidelities, or death.

My brown leather Louis Vuitton occasionally bumps my leg, the same one Drs. Dennison bought me seven years ago. I was sixteen and newly arrested by 'Cameron the Cop' for stealing lipstick. I think about that day, how defiant and mouthy I was— still am. At the time, this tote held only a few pairs of ugly over-washed-gray-tinged granny panties and a toothbrush, compliments of Cuyahoga County Social Services. Today it carries my compass, the buckeye Mokonen gave me, and expensive toiletries. I keep the portal key on my person—collapsed and concealed on a sturdy gold chain, hidden beneath a blouse and below my eye necklace, where it hangs just above my belly button.

Clusters of winding pines give way to rippling slopes of perfectly manicured grass. We enter the grounds through wrought-iron gates and glide past a stable building so grand I mistake it for the castle. Groomers brush, massage, and trot fine horses around. A motto, carved into the building above the stable door, reads: "Y Gwir Yn Erbyn Y Byd", meaning, 'The Truth Against the World', often cited, Verity once told me, as a rough interpretation of Pontius Pilate's words to Jesus, "What is Truth?"

*Verity.*

The thought of her pulls a tight cloak of sadness around my heart. She lost her life just when it was taking off. I struggle to rearrange the hurt of her death, to keep my mood light. The Gaelic words written on this particular stable stone is actually an ancient Druidic motto Christians borrowed, a sort of password for a portal into enigmatic wisdom.

"Dr. Blake," a man says taking my hand as he helps me out of the car. "I am Sir Robert Winchell, Harrington House Comptroller. But you may call me Bob."

"How do you know who I am?" I ask.

"The entire staff is aware of your arrival," he says smiling. "It's your hair. And frankly, Lord Harrington is right, its lovely. He said I couldn't miss you and I see this to be true."

Bob looks about seventy-years-old, mostly bald, his manner jovial and gentle. His eyes resonate with all the warmth of a neutral plush throw, the kind that gets on well with almost anything.

Genin defensively folds his arms as he steps out of our limo, eyes darting around with suspicion to memorize who is who and what is where. It's still hard for me to envision Genin not slurping K-rations from a rucksack or threatening to kill everything in his path. Even in civies, a button-down shirt and slacks, Genin can't conceal the special ops man conducting "recon" beneath his buff exterior. He debates with one of the attendants over his suitcase. Each man locks hands around its handle in a pride loaded tug-of-war. I eye him disapprovingly to 'give it up.' He smirks and abruptly "let's go" of his luggage. The much smaller valet struggles to keep from falling backward.

"Hello, Bob," I say. "It's wonderful to make your acquaintance."

Sir Bob extends his elbow and I thrust my arm through his. He escorts me up ultra-smooth wide limestone steps and we breeze through a super-sized foyer. "Wow," I whisper, craning my neck to see the gold leaf details and angel carvings on the ceiling. "How big is this place?"

"I'm not sure about the exact number of rooms," Sir Bob says. "It would it take a lot of time to try to count them all, but it is hard to classify what is a "room" given that there are anterooms, storage spaces, and cupboards bigger than bedrooms, giant corridors filled with furniture and artwork, and the like."

"I read that Princess Victoria used small strips of paper to find her way back from the dining room to her guest room," I say, the coolness of marble and shadow settling over my skin.

Sir Bob lightly pats my forearm with a white-gloved hand.

"You've been studying this place. Good. Try not to get lost. I can supply you with birdseed if you'd like?"

I toss back my head and laugh—something I haven't done in a long time. Sir Bob leads us through a confusing and gloriously decorated series of rooms, where it's easy to see how guests get lost and I think about Bennie's bullet ant farm—how it hung so large and imposing on the rafters of his lab, the fifty-cent sized insects trapped between two gigantic panes of tempered glass where he and I had a full view into every chamber. People stream past us, some in uniform, some not, their faces proud and solemn, focused on this or that duty. Bob points out the direction of Column Hall, Whistlewolf Saloon, Sky Dancer Room, and a sealed chapel, which I find both curious and unusual. Each hall leads to another room or hall, some with thick cut windows permitting light to enter, and other halls deprived of sunlight to protect priceless works of art.

The decorative and architectural styles, as Genin, Sir Bob, and I meander through this labyrinth, run a seamless blend from Rococo to neoclassical, which houses works by Reuben and Raphael, hanging among life-sized bronze and stone statues of important men and women like Harriet Tubman, Ghandi, Martin Luther King Jr., Sir Winston Churchill, Queen Victoria, Queen Elizabeth I, Cleopatra, even Nikola Tesla and Mark Twain, standing beside Sir Isaac Newton and Charles Darwin.

The Equine Room boasts paintings of the property's prize horses, English Foxhounds, and too many stuffed red foxes to make me feel comfortable, so I look straight ahead, moving myself beyond the space, my head and body forging onward to the most famous room, Sky Dancer. It's a grand plasterwork and multi-colored marble floor wonder, completely surrounded by surreal statues of mythical creatures, nymphs, fairies, bulls, angels and Gods, their sculpted faces and folds so life-like I wonder if they wake up to socialize when humans and hybrids go to sleep.

"This is where the ball will be held tomorrow evening," Sir Bob tells us.

"Where is the library?" I ask.

"This way…"

The study connects to the library, which leads out to a corner tower overlooking a gatehouse, a courtyard, and a moat. Except for the gun ports and armed bodyguards walking about, Harrington House is a non-standard run-of-the-mill overstatement of luxury. My eyes scan detail after detail. An autographed collection of Mark Twain, one of my favorite authors, a gold astro-globe, leatherbound books, maps on the walls—weird maps, some places I can't pronounce or have never heard of. I touch the bust of a face I don't recognize.

"Let me show you to your rooms," Sir Bob says.

"Rooms?" Genin asks.

"Yes sir," Bob says. "You must be tired and might appreciate a few hours to yourselves to freshen up."

"We room together," Genin says.

"I'm afraid not sir," Sir Bob says. "It is not customary for unmarried couples to share a bed chamber at Harrington House."

"Why?" Genin says, fixing his eyes on the comptroller.

"In part, because it's a tradition among the British upper class," Sir Bob says. "And in part because it's a more practical arrangement than trying to sleep in the same small bed. I wouldn't want you bothered with snoring or the flinging about of a leg."

"I could use some rest," I say. "And I'm sure that *Don Paranos* appreciates your thoughtfulness."

What I don't say is that I imagine Lord Harrington coming to my room later and experience a brief 'flash fantasy' of what it might be like to writhe beneath him, staring into his blue eyes. The thought brings a slight blush to my cheeks as I avert Genin's glare, which I feel boring into me like black daggers.

"Right this way," Sir Bob says.

"What time should we be dressed for dinner?" I ask.

"Dinner will be a casual affair this evening," Sir Bob says. "Since other guests are still arriving, dinner will be served in your rooms around eight o'clock."

"Oh? Where is Lord Harrington?" I ask.

"He is away at the moment," Sir Bob says, to my

disappointment. "He sends his regrets but will join all of you tomorrow evening for the ball."

Sir Bob leads us two steps ahead toward our separate quarters. Genin leans over and whispers in my ear using a fake British accent, "Your despondent expression over Lord Harrington's absence was most evident on your face, Lady Blake…"

---

Night creeps into the tower, crosses the lawn, and slides into to my guest quarters. It slowly unfurls a gray cast over a list of fox hunting rules and a first edition 1889 copy of, *A Yankee at the Court of King Arthur*, by Mark Twain, one Sir Bob sent over from the library.

I tug a small chain on the lamp, stand up to stretch, and consider ringing for more tea. Stars and distant streetlamps glimmer from nearby villages. My eyes adjust on the serene landscape from an oversized screenless window. It's close to midnight but still pleasantly warm, and thankfully, no mosquitos. I push the glass wider to welcome more fresh air.

*Hope.*

My daughter would be almost four-months old now, if she's still alive. I've desperately tried these past few weeks to 'remote view' for both Hope and my fox, to seek out their respective locations in my mind's eye—without success. I'm still grieving over, and angry, with Verity. Bilocating is nearly impossible if one is psychically off balance.

I can't help but feel that Verity's maternal clock overrode logic —and I'm still upset she, my best friend, didn't tell me about this offer—nondisclosure agreement with Dr. Evelyn or not.

Humans and hybrids in our line of work shouldn't have children. It's too risky. I suppose if Verity hadn't agreed to carry and give birth to Hope, Dr. Evelyn would have chosen a stranger instead. I ache over the fate of my Hopes' and wonder if Lord Harrington's comments about paying any ransom to retrieve my daughter was sincere.

What surprises me most, is how much I *feel* for this child, having never carried her, felt her kick, birthed her, or met her. It's new—this unbound maternal worry and helplessness deeply entangled with instinctual affection. How can such a fragile being, incapable of lifting her head or caring for herself, live without a mother? The anguish expands through my heart, settles into every fiber of my body, leaks out of my pores, and stretches an invisible tentacle, searching for her...loving her... and praying, yes, praying to the Source that she's safe.

*Turn it off, Sam. Turn it off like a faucet.*

Such childish days of pretending to be pain free fall away like dead leaves and I'm forced to embrace my agony in eerie silence, gazing out over the distant fields of a foreign country, not knowing if I'm closer or further from Hope, and for the first time, not being able to *turn it off* and not wanting to. I clench my fists, set my jaw, and turn away from the window.

It's no use.

As hard as I try to hold them back, tears for my daughter and my fox freely tumble and splash on the marble floor, a sea's worth of pain capsizing the heart in my chest. I heave sobs of despair, unable to stuff any extra sorrow into the pit of my plexus, or block grief's blows with my sword, a blade I haven't wielded in years, a different sort of pain I think I might prefer to that of a missing daughter. When the dam of my tears runs dry, I rise to my senses.

For both Hopes' I must remain clear and reexamine everything. Silence spreads over me and there's no better listener. I join together with nothingness, not to still my tears but to hear them. And in doing so, I realize, I must trust the observance of my enemies more so than their words, and my instincts too. Natural abilities...that's what Reggie, Dr. Evelyn, my mom, and Dr. Awoudi called them...*potential wunderkind*...is written in my old file, the real one Dr. Awoudi has, somewhere.

The moon casts a welcoming half ray over the books in my room. So many years I've wasted sifting over the faces of authority, looking to them for answers, consumed by fear of failure, disapproval, or second-guessing, cognitively efficient, emotionally numb. No more.

It's a great evening for star gazing, I think—dark enough to see pearlescent curly ribbons of faraway places. Small meteors zip by, their cosmic tales but a blip on the pages of time. A satellite or two. A shooting star.

Then...

...*it* appears.

Approximately one-hundred yards to the right of the stable just beyond the wood line, an extra-large animal bi-pedals—too big to be a coyote or a fox. It gallops parallel to the mansion until it disappears somewhere near the garden on the back side of the estate. If I wind my way through the vast passages of Harrington House it will take too long to get outside. Plus, I risk bumping into night watchmen or maids who will ask what I need or how they may help—and what would I say? That I thought I saw a dinosaur walking under my window?

I tuck the gun Reggie gave me into my waistband and hoist myself onto the ledge of the castle, leaning against air-chilled blocks of stone. Arms, outstretched, palms up, I launch. If cameras are trained on this part of the house, I've likely just provided the evening's entertainment, alarm, and/or confusion, but probably not any more so than what I *thought* I saw.

I connect with solid ground, a gentle *thud,* tuck and roll. I wish I could figure out how to fly longer than a couple of minutes but it's the bane of my contemporary humanness. Gravity and matter keep me mostly grounded. It is only due to my father's blood, mom said, that I'm able to liftoff. But I haven't been able to really fly, to glide over the trees and soar to the clouds, since I lived at Plum Hook Bay.

...Advancing to the back of the property, I conduct a systematic eye sweep of my surroundings. Nothing unusual. The garden gate is slightly ajar and it makes a *creak creak* noise every time the wind whispers between its bars. Mist hovers near the fountains, and a midnight chill tap dances with the sweaty dampness on my shoulders. I silently slip through the gate…and there it is!

An ominous shadow of hugeness blackens the trunk of tree where Alyce Hastmier was hanged. Ducking behind a hedge, I belly-crawl the way Reggie taught me, across a short expanse of manicured lawn so perfect I smell its heavenly sweet grassy scent and briefly wonder if it was trimmed blade by blade with hand clippers.

A small 'hissssss' steam sound escapes the creature's mouth. It abruptly twists its head, glowing ember eyes searching, nostrils flaring. This thing resembles an oversized reptile, but it isn't a dinosaur, at least not any sort I've ever seen in books. Thankfully, deep shadows of mansion stone and a thick parade of rich roses, their scent picked up every now and then by a gust of wind, stretch far enough over the grass to cover me—but can this thing *smell* me?

The creature's thick tail is outfitted in armor-like silver scales, which makes a *clink zssst* sound. The tail periodically shimmers firefly green when its captured under a sliver of moonlight. The beast rears up on two hind legs, wraps bowie-knife-sized front claws around the fountain's pool rim, propels its hindquarters over the edge, and disappears without a ripple.

"That's not possible," I whisper to no one.

I creep toward the water feature on my tip-toes and hesitantly, slowly, peer over. This thing, whatever it is, seems capable of holding its breath for an inordinate amount of time, the way Pa Ling could do at Plum Hook Bay when he swam in the river. But the water in this fountain is calm and shallow, casting only my reflection. I see no monsters swimming beneath.

The monolith perpendicular rock centered in the fountain—an obelisk that bears odd hieroglyphics carved upon its base, is similar to the boulder at Plum Hook Bay but different because the markings aren't exactly Egyptian or Native American or like anything else Verity and I studied. A light rumble vibrates under my feet and then…nothing. Not even crickets or frogs.

*Thunk!* I'm snatched me from behind, a surprise attack, which locks my arms at my sides, and I'm lifted as weightlessly as a ballerina. We tumble into the frigid water and make a *huge* splash, dragged under by a current so strong it slaps the edges of the retention pool like whitecaps in a pissed off ocean. Whatever has hold of me releases its grip. I hold my breath, tasting salty wetness on my lips until my face is out of the water and I'm dumped with a hard *thwack* onto solid ground, the sound echoing down a dark corridor until it fades away.

"Christ, Genin, you scared the living shit out of me!" I hiss at him, annoyed that he crept up behind me and I failed to notice. I kick him off and we untangle our soaked selves from dangling tree roots.

"I was concerned," he says, jumping to his feet as he holds out a hand to help me up. "I went to your room and you were gone. I figured you took a leap out your window to check on something. I followed your tracks."

"Did you see what I saw?" I involuntarily shiver against the cold, my body heat pressed out of me as my clothes cling to arms and legs, dripping a trail of cold water. Every step I take is a *squinch, squinch* noise of liquid-logged sneakers pushing fluid through the laces.

"Yes."

We each check our respective weapons for damage and thrust them back in our waistbands. "I've never seen anything like it," I say. "And we've both seen a lot of weird shit. Where are we?"

"Cave system," Genin says. "Under the fountain," He swipes his hand through slick, glistening hair. "I'm not sure I like hanging out with you. I remember what happened last time we fell into a cave together."

Unlike the extraordinarily large quartz crystal and black granite cavern full of ancient relics we once tumbled into at Plum Hook Bay, this one is rough-hewn, barren, wide, and low. We're forced to stoop but it widens about twenty feet away. "This way," I say.

We straighten ourselves when we reach the clearing. From here, the cave reaches back another one-hundred yards before it bends right, which I assume leads under the house or perhaps beyond. But the funny thing is, we're able to 'see' because a 'glow', a magnetically induced phosphorescent illumination system lights up the stone walls as we walk, even though we can't locate its source.

"You ever see this type of lighting system?" Genin asks.

"Never," I say, my teeth chattering. "You?"

"No."

The floor slopes slightly downward, so we follow it to the bend, where again, we're able to see a long way ahead and down. Slabs of rock, at least a few tons each, hang on hinges we can't see. Genin takes hold of a small stone latch, and the door releases using a counterweight measure as easily as a toddler pushes a toy car.

"Look at the walls," he says. "And the floor."

The cavern this far in is smooth and worn, as if it's been used for centuries as a secret passageway. Gun-metal gray walls seamlessly melt into the same type of floor. A baseboard of neatly carved hieroglyphic symbols lead as far down the tunnel as we can see.

"It's wide enough for a decent pilot to fly a Boeing 747 through without much trouble," Genin says.

"Do you know what the symbols say?" I ask.

"Not really," he says. "Maybe some cross between Egyptian, Mayan, and something else. Can you recognize or translate any of this?"

"Part of it is a curse I think, a warning here and there, mixed in with a splash of death threats, but that's all I recognize," I say. "How is this cave different from the one you guarded in Istanbul?"

"Nothing this elaborate," He answers, running the flat of his palm along a smooth wall. "It's like comparing the subway system of New York City against Moscow's Metro, a damn ballroom compared to ours. This cave was constructed by mechanical or chemical means, using a super amount of heat. The odor is clean too."

I draw some air into my nostrils and it smells like ozone and ions. "It reminds me of the non-rotting corpse odor on the

Sentinelese," I say. "Very strange. What were you guarding near Istanbul?"

"You know I can't tell you that," he says. "I have UMBRA Clearance and it will be fifty years or more before the project gets declassified, if ever."

"Don't you ever get tire of it?" I ask, taking note of his UMBRA clearance, which means he has first account raw intelligence, the innermost and darkest part of a shadow project.

"Get tired of what?" He asks.

"All the secrecy," I say as we push deeper into the cave.

Genin shrugs but doesn't look at me. "I suppose it keeps us from being compromised."

"Like it did Tetana, Verity, Pa Ling, and Fensig?" I ask.

Genin seems annoyed that I brought the death of our friends into this conversation, a painful subject for both of us. "They honored the oaths they took and understood the sacrifice," he says, adding enough terse to his words to make them extra heavy and meaningful.

"Did you know Verity's husband, Master Sergeant Seth Sahin?" I ask.

"Special Ops is a small world," Genin says. "Yes, I knew him. He was stationed near Seluk on Mount Pion."

"The Caves of the Seven Sleepers," I say.

"Which one?" He asks.

"What do you mean, which one?"

"Four locations make up the Caves of the Seven Sleepers, none proven to be 'Thee One'. He toured all of them."

"Where are they?" I ask.

"Afsin and Tarsus, in Turkey," he says. "Tarsus was once a Hittite temple. The Seljuks used it until most of them were wiped out in the tenth century and fled to Anatolia."

"Seljuks?"

"Sunni muslims…but they converted from Buddhism before they were Muslims."

"Oh, right, the opposite of Shiites," I say.

"No," says Genin. "Shiites are a subset of Sunnis."

"Oh," I say. "Then why do they fight each other?"

"Dogma," he answers flatly, as if he's disgusted wars are fought over paltry faith, the kind men and women forget when power or bloodshed trespasses beyond their personal convictions and they fall prey to groupthink.

"You said there were four potential sites for the Caves of Seven Sleepers. What's the other?"

"A cave near Amman, Jordan, which has seven graves. Sam?" Genin says, thin beads of sweat condensing on his forehead as the cave gets warmer and we dry off a bit. "I *can* tell you there's something sinister about the Caves of the Seven Sleepers."

"What?" I ask, perking up my ears so I don't miss a syllable of what might come out of his mouth, anything I might use to locate Verity's file.

"I'm not sure if it's the cave or just that area of the desert," he says. "But something happens to the minds of Marines who spend too much time there."

"Such as?"

"Entire units disintegrate to the point we try to kill each other."

"What happens?"

"I'm not sure," Genin says. "The NSA finally ordered the CIA to recycle special ops every four-weeks instead of every eighteen months after chaos between units broke out."

"The NSA? Why would the Department of Defense's Communications and Encryptions arm interfere with the CIA's cave guarding?"

Genin squats to inspect the hieroglyphics. "Yea, that didn't make much sense to us either," he says. "I figure a weird experimental SIGNIT technology is in play through that area, maybe our government experimenting on active duty members with some sort of electronic or microwave psyops technology. It got pretty crazy. I was happy Abar made the call to pull me out for a while."

"You hurt anybody?" I ask.

"I did."

"Who?"

"I caught a guy in the act of raping a little girl from a nearby village. I slit his throat."

I squat beside him and gently cover his forearm with my palm. He covers my hand with his free one. "I saved her life," he says, his expression intense. "Everything got 'covered up' but I was beyond pissed when the locals didn't care. They told my commander I ruined their sacrifice, said she needed to be 'deflowered' and sealed in the cave."

Tears bubble up in my eyes but I don't cry the way I want to cry in front of Genin but can't. Inside I hold in this new bank of tears, all the pain, terror, and anger I feel anew, or perhaps haven't completely processed—an eye for an eye—but not tonight. "How could they be so ignorant and cruel?" I ask.

*"If thou hadst come up on to them, thou wouldst have certainly turned back from them in flight, and wouldst certainly have been filled with terror of them',"* Genin says.

"I've never heard you talk like that," I say.

"It isn't me," he says. "It's in the Qur'an, Surah al-Kahf, Chapter eighteen. Just something I heard one of the Arab soldiers say when they refused to enter the cave. Locals claim they need sacrifices to keep beasts at bay, real wonky-crazy shit." Genin twirls his index finger in a circle next to his ear. "They insisted this little girl would keep beasts from hurting humans."

"God, that's awful," I say as we both stand, me trying not to think about the fate of this little girl and hoping against hell I find mine.

"Yea, it was sick," he continues. "I'm not sure what the hell was going on when some of our unit dragged that girl back into the cave, except maybe our superiors agreed her death was a nominal sacrifice to prevent us all from being killed. As for the legend of the caves, some boys hid in them centuries ago and reemerged about three-hundred years later not looking a day older."

We continue into the depths another fifty meters. A frosty wind blows when we encounter a narrow staircase, which leads deeper still, into the Earth. At the foot of the steps, another bend, and more stairs. I count one-hundred fifty as we reach bottom, where it's suddenly a lot warmer. I fall silent thinking about the little girl Genin saved and then didn't—the pain and terror she must have felt when her rescue was short-lived. Why this particular girl? Maybe she didn't have a mom. Maybe she did have a mom but the mom was too weak, or frail, to save her daughter. Maybe the mom was already dead…"Will we ever eliminate the world of terrorists?" I ask.

"The goal is not to eliminate terrorists," Genin says. "The goal is to minimize the risk of most humans meeting them. It's better to send a strong message of zero tolerance for those who purposely cross our national security lines than it is to wake up one day owned by the enemy."

"Do you think this planet will ever stop fighting wars?"

"You mess up your wiring when we took that fountain fall?" Genin asks. "I don't believe humans will ever stop killing each other until some depraved asshole is the last man or woman standing."

"Then why do you do this?" I ask. "Why do you even try to make the world safer if you know war and terror never ends?"

"What happens if the garbage man doesn't pick up the trash every week?" Genin asks.

"The garbage piles up," I answer.

"Exactly," he says. "That's why I do what I do…"

Genin and I confront a large tangle of corridors that branch off in several directions. On a wall above one archway is carved an Egyptian eye symbol, not like the one I wear around my neck, but similar to the design on the cufflinks Lord Harrington wore the night he reached over my shoulder at the food truck in London. Ahead is a pale but steady light and the rumble of what sounds like large machinery.

I tug Genin's damp sleeve to direct him toward the archway with the carved eye but he doesn't budge. His aura goes gray as we're accosted by a glowing sphere that instantly materializes into a shadowy hooded figure, its form a soft chalk-lined glow. It points a plasma loaded fluorescent tube at us.

"This isn't the dragon creature we saw jump into the fountain," I whisper to Genin. "It's too small."

"*SSSSSSS!*" The thing hisses at us.

"What the fuck is it then?" Genin asks.

"I'm not sure," I say. "But I think its pissed off."

The hairs on my neck stand at attention. Genin steps in front of me, a tactical move born of his military training, combined with a biologically-driven 'protect' gene inherent in males of his ilk. I don't hold his chivalry against him, he can't help it. Reggie explained that it's a sought-after planetary trait, where *real men*, he says, stand in harm's way and are willing to die for a brother or sister in arms, an instinctive gesture, which affirms my hope humans are still worth saving.

Our weapons are invisibly lifted from our respective waistbands and replanted against rock walls.

*Damn it!*

"We're screwed," I whisper.

This thing aims its light baton at the wall where it's stuck our weapons like magnets.

*Drip-sizzle-drip...*

...Gray blobs, where our guns were, ooze drops of metal to the ground.

"Did Lord Harrington design this creature's weapon?" Genin asks.

"Forget that," I say. "Did he make this creature?"

"Humans do not enter unless brought by another Kindred, they have not the appropriate consciousness to be here," The creature hisses.

I shove Genin out of the way when it points its crystal baton at his chest.

"Take me," I say, facing the creature and its weapon. "Let him go."

The phantom tilts its head in what I think is surprise and retrains its weapon. A bolt of plasma races toward my throat but...

....nothing happens.

I touch my eye necklace and look down to see if I still have legs. Genin, thank God, isn't a gooey puddle on the floor, either, but locked up against the wall catching his breath. The hooded creature quizzically inspects the end of its wand, taps it, then looks at each of us.

"We're just as confused as you are," I say, trying not to puke.

A faint glow emanates from my eye necklace, first a dot, then a beam, until it forms a very small blue-green orb that floats directly between the creature and me, at eye level, before it almost but not quite divides into two globes, and slowly rotates between us, a three-D infinity of a sideways Figure 8.

The creature unexpectedly bows and lays aside its weapon. "Zumar, suna de Scathatch," it says. "Unk izi zen."

"What did this thing say? Do you know?" Genin asks.

"It called me 'your highness' and said that its lived hundreds of years but never did it believe it would live long enough to see my return. It also wants me to spare its life for trying to kill you."

Genin nervously chuckles. "You? Her *highness*? This thing said all of that with so few words?"

"They're packaged concepts," I explain. "It's Enochian, a constantly mutating language with origins that predate Sumerians."

"Did you hit your head when we fell into this hole?" Genin asks. "What is this thing?"

"Kedu zura kan paia," I say to the creature, asking it to remove its head covering and asking what it is. "I'm not sure what it is, but I think it mistakes me for someone else."

The creature peels back its bulky hood to reveal a head with scales the texture and color of crocodile skin. It has lobeless slits for ears and gill-like cheeks, and stands at least seven feet tall.

"Ak-shun doble nom," the creature says. "Eresh."

"Whoa," Genin says as he leans back against the wall and looks around for a place to take cover. "What the fuck? Should we kill him?"

The creature loudly hisses again.

"Genin, this is an Usta, a biologically engineered *female* terrestrial named Eresh, and she just said, she makes no mistakes.

She also told me that her kind once guarded the Musovii's, the first Earther's that helped Ebians seed races among galaxies" I say. "The Musovii's are about as ancient as Earth itself, a beautiful people of gold tinted skin a lot like yours."

"I'll buy the bio-engineering crap but this outer planet Panspermia E.T. seeding shit—that's pretty goddamn looney," Genin says.

"She's launching telepathic memories into my brain," I say. "The legend of the Usta appears true and stands before us."

The Usta extends three long claw-like digits toward Genin, and speaks, robotic-like. "You are born of a blood bred on these lands for untold thousands of years. Your ancestors living in all of the mountains and prairies of Earth for numberless generations, have seen us, and passed down our history in the unwritten legends of your people."

"I think Lord Luca Harrington graduated from advanced weaponry and chemicals engineering to something far more advanced," I say.

"You think he *made* this thing?" Genin asks.

The creature hisses at him a third time and takes a step forward. Genin meets her half way, although I can tell he's confused and hesitant to engage in what I'm sure he understands will be a losing battle—for him.

"Please don't blame Genin for being blind to you," I interject. "Raga makes humans forgetful—turns their eyes and ears inside out. And speaking of Raga, do you know where I might find her?"

"Who the hell is Raga?" Genin asks.

"Shh," I say. "Let her speak."

"Humans and their scornful disbelief close our lips in bitterness against the outward flow of such knowledge," Eresh says, looking disdainfully at Genin. "Your highness, I beg, Raga has taken form...but not in the way you might think. Beware of chimeras. To mention or think of her invites curse."

She spits a slimy green gel saliva on the ground, where I look to see if it will burn a hole. It doesn't.

"She's already cursed the upper world," I say. "Humans are unaware of the danger they face."

"I care not for the plight of cruel and violent humans," Eresh says. "They deserve the consequences of their decisions."

"Most of them don't," I say. "A few humans wrongly decided for the majority they'd hoard celestial gifts. Most humans know nothing of this war."

"War? What war? The Gulf War? What is going on?" Genin asks. He places both hands on his hips and looks between Eresh and me. "What in the hell *are* you, anyway?" He waves his hand up and down in front of the creature. "This isn't possible," he says, looking at me with confusion galloping across his brow. "We haven't taken any drugs this time...*have we*?" "No," I say. "We did not consume psychedelics tonight."

Eresh plants her three-digit claw on the cave ceiling. "We do not tolerate subterranean war. We will not risk harm to this planet's heart. The one called Saratu says you must go. Take this path..."

"Saratu?" Genin asks.

"Now I get it," I say. "Remember how Saratu once saved Pa Ling from drowning at Plum Hook Bay?"

"Yea," Genin says. "She tapped her feet on the riverbank and pointed to the water. We all thought she was nuts."

"Saratu is a bit of a dowser," I say. "Her tribe could locate water in the Sahara, using their feet."

"So?" Genin says. "I mean, that's cool and all, but how does it tie in with this thing?"

"Saratu is able to divine more than water below ground," I say. "She must be guarding 'under worlds' all over the globe from her monastic perch in Nepal. She communicates with hidden worlds..."

"You wear the Eye of Sakhet," Eresh says. "The one before whom evil trembles."

"Wha..."

The Usta shoves Genin and me under the Eye of Horus arch so fast we have no time to react. She summons her magic plasma death ray with a command and promptly seals us in darkness. Before we're able to protest, a door opens, and we tumble out of a pantry and into the kitchen at Harrington House.

A nonplussed Sir Bob sits at a table with Reggie and...

"Miss Barbara?" Genin and I say in surprised unison.

Reggie grins and takes a sip from his mug as the three of them watch logs burn in a small fireplace.

"Cuppa tea?" Sir Bob asks.

# NINETEEN

# THE BALL

STANDING BACK from the looking glass, I hardly believe this is me, a gilded veneer of expertly applied makeup, poured into exquisite pale blue and gold fabric, designed to accentuate both my figure, and the hollow underbelly of class hierarchy in which I'm about to poke my hesitant heel-clad foot.

As an Ohio foster kid, I only dreamed of attending lavish parties such as this, thinking the *upper echelon* of society somehow superior, having *arrived*—although arrived to where I've never been sure. But starchy celebrations now make me edgy and restless. It isn't that I can't *hold my own*. I've had etiquette lessons thanks to Dr. Evelyn's insistence, while matriculating at Plum Hook Bay, and again upon orders from Langley, but I've never pranced around polo fields or been presented at a debutante ball. But these blistering omissions on my ramshackle pedigree seem trivial compared to finding my daughter. Can I bear faux grinning my way through an evening of civilized "Me, Me, Me, I, I, I" one-upmanship passing as repartee?

Why on Earth would Lord Luca Harrington waste such a coveted invitation? I can't imagine he'd go to such lengths for a conquest—to bed me—but he is a guy, so maybe. I shouldn't discount such a stupid plan. But he isn't stupid. Maybe he thinks my awkwardness will provide comic relief or I'll look to him for rescue from the complete banality of it all. Ha! No, thank you. Or maybe he…

"Perk up, child. You, look absolutely stunning," Barbara says as if reading my mind.

She gives the hem of my dress a light tug and straighten, focused on fixing a stray gold thread. I offer her a half-smile. It's true. I certainly look different—maybe even beautiful.

I toss back my shoulders and elongate my neck to gaze confidently forward, into the mirror, my normally savage red hair perfectly coiffed, a few loose ringlets trailing into my cleavage. I refuse to remove my eye necklace but Barbara agrees it adds a 'demure and mysterious touch', this Eye of Sakhet. I haven't yet had time to look up its meaning in the library or why it might have glowed in the cave. The portal key, which really looks more like a flat gold map of the Pleiades star system when I compress it, hangs secure near my navel, guarded under a girdle that uncomfortably chokes my waistline.

"May I please have another sip of champagne?" I ask.

"Not too much dear," Barbara says, standing up and handing me the crystal flute. "I understand you're butterflies but the worst thing you can do is wind up half in the bag before the party even begins. And remember, Jesus doesn't encourage drunkenness."

"Then why did he turn the water into wine at a Cana wedding?" I snark, which earns me a brief sanctimonious stare before we collapse into giggles and hug.

It's good to see Barbara again after all these years. Reggie flew her 'across the pond' for a temporary role as a sort of 'lady-in-waiting' to ensure, I suppose, I didn't decide to leave the fancy gown on the bed and slip into camo instead. I was initially surprised Barbara knows so much about this sort of pomp and circumstance, a skill set, I think, that resides more in Dr. Evelyn's wheelhouse.

Reggie said Barbara studied every English high society detail to help me dress because he doesn't want to take a chance with strangers attending me. It was a hard sell for my bosses back at Langley until Septum Oculi slipped pristine credentials into Barbara's profile. She thrives on being 'in the know' and helping others—and there aren't too many like her. As I age, I see why Reggie is so crazy about his wife. What she lacks in secret clearance she makes up for with altruism—and enough Christian sermons, I'm sure, to rally "God's" angels from even the most remote reaches of the universe.

"I'm so glad to be out of that missile silo and away from Ike, the heathen..." she said last night. It seems that Ike, according to Barbara, lived beyond the clutches of Jesus Christ, incapable of being "saved". Things fell apart between them when Ike shared that God had better fear *him* if the whiskey ran dry. Barbara was insulted for God and that was that...although I have no idea why Reggie felt it necessary to keep her hidden at his friend's nuclear missile silo, which runs 'canon' experiments for the Pentagon. Genin and I also learned that Sir Bob and Reggie served together on some secret Septum Oculi task force, similar to what Genin and I now do. Special Ops, as Genin says, *is* a small world.

There's a light tap on the door.

"Come in," I say.

"Holy...wow," Genin says when he steps into the room.

"What?" I turn from the mirror to face him. "Is something wrong?"

"Nothing," he gulps. "It's just that...I've never seen you...you look gorgeous, Sam. I mean, like a princess or something."

"Glad that my looks have value as your arm candy," I say with an eye roll and a glance back at the mirror, just to be sure he means what he says.

"Sam," Barbara scolds. "The man is paying you a compliment."

"That's not what I mean," Genin says. "You fit the look—like you've been born into this sort of thing all of your life."

"Born into what?" I ask. "The lavish scene that propels Lord Luca Harrington into unexplainable, extraordinary, and likely unscrupulous wealth?"

"Come on, Sam. *Damn.* Do you have to be so difficult? A

simple thank you will do." He says softly...and it makes me feel slightly bad for so easily falling prey to my physical insecurities and distrusting his sense of beauty.

"You're right," I say. "I'm sorry. You look stunning too, very handsome."

Genin gives me an impish smile and I melt faster than toasted marshmallows. His black tie and clean shave elevate him to Greek God status, which couples nicely this evening with his Alpha magnetism. His aura too, is relaxed, a soft-white incandescent glow of quiet James Bond-like confidence. He's grown up some since our time together at Plum Hook Bay and carries it well... when he puts his mind to it.

I sometimes forget Genin deals with a lot of high weirdness, especially in my company, and falls more deeply each day into the fray that is supernatural phenomena—stuff that most humans never experience, notice, or believe. He's forced to come to terms with everything he's ever been taught as a special forces kind of guy, where things in the U.S. military appear much more black-and-white than the foggy-misty 'other worlds' I know.

But Genin required more than tea to calm down last night. I can't blame him. Who wouldn't be freaked out after meeting an Usta? He's still baffled that his weapon is useless against a highly advanced underground lizard-looking terrestrial able to disarm us with "crystal twigs". Reggie gave him some weed and offered to teach Genin more about his Amazonian ancestors, a remote tribe of nearly extinct Chachapoya, otherwise known as Cloud Musovii's, who once worked alongside Usta.

We all agree it's a bit too convenient that a hidden Usta doorway to the underworld just happens to be built under Lord Harrington's garden fountain. If Harrington knows about these creatures, and I'm sure he does, did he somehow discover their DNA lying dormant somewhere and recreate them? Or were Usta always lurking around, in hiding, and then made themselves known to Harrington? Do they possess something he wants? Or does he have something *they* need? Genin absorbed it all in bullet point fashion.

"You two need to get going," Barbara says as she looks at her watch. "It's almost time. Now remember, don't descend the stairs until you're *both* announced."

Genin holds out his elbow and I slip my arm through and we practically float along the supersized hallway. It's my understanding during high society *'Descension'* events, the *least* important people are introduced first, having to wait at the bottom of the stairs to greet each descending couple of higher social status—unless it's the host—if that's the case, he or she descends last as a show of 'respect' from the guests regardless of status. The older the title, the more senior the title-bearer and the further he or she is at the back of the line. As American outsiders, Genin and my intro will likely be first and basal, to the applause of hired help, but no matter. This isn't our party.

Genin leans over and lightly kisses the nape of my neck, which causes my cheeks to flush. A zap of passion zig-zags through my veins, almost like the first time we met but tempered with familiarity.

Rounding a stately column, we confront a hoard of people ensconced in glittering finery, a rising cacophony of conversation, air kisses, and robust greetings. Wars have been fought, neutrino's split, and technology advanced, but I notice right away that upper English society remains time warped, stuck in strict adherence to uncompromising rules of behavior and the overripe air of old money. Despite this, Harrington's Ball has become, according to the *Daily Mail*, the most coveted invitation in English history.

The crowd hushes as we *Yanks* enter their ranks, grudgingly acknowledged but never fully accepted. Americans, I learned from Dr. Evelyn, are considered boorish, loud-mouthed, and gluttonous —but Brits also appreciate our ambition, generosity, and 'straight-line' talk, so it isn't all bad. They resume their positions, slightly raising eyes and glasses in not so subtle scrutiny as we pass.

Genin suddenly stops and I almost trip over my heels.

I scan the crowd to see what has seized his attention—and there she is, Lady Olivia Ross, the belle of U.K. society, today's "it" girl, and Lord Luca Harrington's latest conquest.

Olivia is deep in conversation with my not-so-dear aunt, Dr. Evelyn Dennison, and seeing *her* again causes my blood to simmer. I should have known Evelyn would be here given her self-proclaimed U.K. pedigree. She always has a way of inserting herself into only the most luxurious work assignments. God forbid she'd ever stomp around on a remote island with Dr. Monica bagging murder victims. As I remember it, the corpses come to Evelyn.

Genin's eyes are fixed on Lady Olivia. I feel his immediate desire for her leaking through his pores, uncontained electrical sparks that singe my soul. A cold shower of jealousy snakes its way through my heart.

Lady Olivia Ross stands in the corridor framed by an oversized doorway, amber light emerging behind her, setting off a perfectly proportioned woman of elevated style, cut from the finest upper society silk, where she perfected, I see, the art of muted grace. She is dressed in a sleek low cut black sequined halter dress with sparkling upswept vanilla blonde hair. Around her throat, a jaw dropping Garrard & Company diamond necklace, too cold and big for her, almost strangling an otherwise perfect presentation. Her chic thinness has a tennis-like quality and it pairs perfectly with her slightly upturned nose and flawless milky way skin.

Genin is gone.

Game. Set. Match.

And I feel forfeited.

Lady Olivia glances in our direction, and she too, appears equally transfixed by Genin.

I love Genin—my close friend and confidant, and in many ways, consider him "*mine*". I know this is wrong—to think of a human being as property, but the thought of potentially losing his friendship to another woman, after losing so many other people in my life, is a lot to bear. It isn't that I'm '*in love*' with Genin the way Priyanka flipped for Rakito (and he for her). But I do cherish our intimacy, even if it is infrequent and noncommittal.

Lady Olivia smoothly approaches alongside Dr. Evelyn.

"Don Genin Paranos, please permit me to introduce you to Lady Olivia Ross," Dr. Evelyn says.

Genin deftly loses my arm to take Lady Olivia's. He bows before kissing the dorsal side of her sapphire clad right hand, staring deeply into shiny speckled violet eyes—eyes that appear in need of rescue, taunting the beholder to simultaneously treat her with both awe and pity, the way one might be emotionally struck when confronted by a wounded baby animal. She lightly blushes, looking up at him, the intensity of their mutual attraction crackling on the air strong enough for even Dr. Evelyn to notice. Evelyn tilts her chin in my direction and gives me a knowing eyebrow raise. I remain as cool as a poker player bluffing a low suit hand. And Lord Harrington has perfectly played *his* royal flush. I don't like to be so easily outwitted. Where is he, anyway?

"It's such a pleasure to make your acquaintance," Lady Olivia says to Genin before she turns to me. "And you must be Sammy."

*Grrrr. Nobody calls me Sammy.*

Men like Genin find women like Lady Olivia irresistible—but what he fails to notice, as most men do, is that she possesses an underhanded streak, evidenced by her charmingly informal, not so innocent reference to me as *Sammy*. It takes everything in me not to bristle or correct her. Human females are notorious for circling around their competitive targets rather than lunging in for a kill. It's not entirely their fault. They're taught from the cradle to *play nice* and to 'keep the playing field level', so they learn instead, to softly attack their opponents with a gazillion needle pricks—much less efficient, I think, than a swift swipe of the blade through one's throat.

Lady Olivia beams and leans into me for a two-cheek air kiss. She smells of Chanel perfume and quality caviar, possessed of a falseness and abstract sensuality, Genin, I conclude, finds intoxicating and mysterious. I'll have to wait for their respective rose-colored glasses to crack. I can tell by the look on her face she's already made the decision to fuck him. It doesn't even register in her mind that I might care about that, or if it does, she doesn't care.

"I apologize," Genin smoothly says, trying to contain his enthusiasm. "Lady Ross, allow me to introduce my friend, Dr. Samantha Blake."

*Friend?*

"Oh? Another doctor?," Lady Olivia asks raising her hand to me in light surprise and acknowledging Dr. Evelyn, as if *doctors* come in jumbo packs. "You will have to share your thoughts with me later on the evening's collective diagnosis."

Lady Olivia impersonally drops my hand to grant her ear and eyes to Genin, her pale arm now comfortably cradled in his, having moved to his other side. I regain his opposite arm in a light attempt to remind him that I was the one who invited him to the party, requested his escort—got him out of that desert hell hole for a while and into this assignment.

"Aren't you a lucky guy," Sir Bob says to Genin as he and another staff member compare notes on their descension line-up.

My eyes roam England's finest, who appear reservedly excited and who talk with low, staid, proper accents. They're extraordinarily aware of the ease with which wealth and lavishness hover around them, ripe for plundering if they learn what investments Lord Harrington might throw his heavy pounds toward. I still do not see this man of no honor or hour.

An older couple, the Duke and Duchess of Gatsford eye the décor like disenchanted tourists and wear their compelled wonder not nearly as loudly as their extravagant clothes.

A short distance away stands Dr. Maxine Kanumba, a renowned Tanzanian epidemiologist, with her partner, Dr. Nadia Kimathi, equally worth her own as an archeologist and best-selling author from Kenya. I've read all of her books about the stone circles of Senegal and Gambia. Dr. Kanumba's light teal silk turban and exquisite mermaid print gown lend her an ease of elegance and approachability. She lightly smiles at me and her aura is one of a sage woman, a shaman of great inner power and pristine outer beauty. Unlike me or Lady Olivia, she doesn't have to "try".

And just behind us? Gigi Rothschild leans slightly forward with a meticulous and intent expression. She sprinkles a pleasing small-scale laugh over a joke being told by a McManus twin, Scottish siblings in the export business. The other twin, Sir Oliver, seizes a cocktail off a silver tray when it floats by and he winks at me.

*"The media circus stretches from here to the Cotswold's..."* is part of what I hear.

In this mild confusion, I spot Sir Harry "Slim" Fairchild, too far away to greet but he nods in my direction, looking more 'normal' than I've ever seen—until I notice his banana bright patent leather shoes peeking out from tailored tuxedo trousers and his black-and-white checkered cummerbund and tie. Leave it to him to dress like a New York City taxi. He lines up half way down the descension line with some gorgeous lady wearing a peacock feather dress. It appears he really *was* knighted.

"It seems my escort is behind schedule," Lady Olivia says, casting a nervous glance. Everyone here is keenly aware of her lofty position. She could slide down Harrington's banister naked if she were so inclined, and this crowd would still applaud and kiss her lavender powdered 'arse'.

"Let Genin escort Lady Olivia during Descension," Dr. Evelyn whispers to me.

"What? No way," I whisper back. "It's not my problem if her date is late. She needs to find her own man."

"Seems she already has," Dr. Evelyn replies with a Cheshire grin, peering over at the new coupling.

"Go to hell," I whisper. "And where have you been hiding? We need to talk."

"Lady Ross has not had your special training, nor is she, much to her chagrin, I'm sure, able to capture Harrington's heart," Evelyn says, adjusting her stunning gold, diamond, and pearl necklace. "If you want to talk with me, stand down. Allow Genin to serve as her escort until Lord Harrington arrives."

"Piss off," I hiss. "Who are you to order *me* to stand down after the bilge you brewed with Verity?"

Genin and Lady Olivia glance over, curiously aware, I think, of the rising contempt I just slung at Dr. Evelyn. They quickly resume their engrossed conversation, no doubt content to cast away from us if they could.

"Verity knew the risk," Evelyn says quietly. "There's more to this story than what she confessed on her deathbed."

I shift my body toward her, a small look of surprise on my face that I fail to conceal fast enough.

"Yes, I know about that," she says. "Who do you think intervened to ensure Abar and Meadows didn't receive your blood sample back at that D.C. hospital? If you step aside, I'll share with you, in private, why I created a child between you and Bennie."

I wasn't expecting that, for her to be so forthcoming.

"What you did is violate our bodies without our knowledge or consent," I say, trying to contain my rising anger by lowering my voice. "You mixed our hybrid DNA, then lied to Verity about her inability to conceive. What you did is criminal. We were kids. How could you? And now, you've taken my daughter. I *will* find her, even if it kills *you*."

The lights in the corridor flicker before they regain composure.

Dr. Evelyn drops her eyes as the Duke of Avondale approaches. "I don't have your daughter," she says before he gets to us.

"My dear cousin," he says, with a happy-hour silver-eyed twinkle that draws attention to thinning tin-shiny hair. "It's almost our time. And this must be your niece?"

I'm astonished that Dr. Evelyn would mention her bourgeoisie American niece to anyone of substance in the U.K. "How do you do?" I lift my hand and curtsy to accept the Duke's formal greeting. As an American and a hybrid of noble blood, I'm not required to curtsy before any sentient being, but do so as a show of respect rather than prostration.

"George, please meet my niece, Dr. Samantha Blake."

"Pleasure, pleasure. *Lady* Blake?" He asks.

"No," Dr. Evelyn replies. "She's American. She has no peerage, royal, or otherwise. But she is an exobiologist."

"Pity," he says. "She's angelic. We should marry her well so she may gain title."

"Some do refer to me as Princess Scathatch," I say, thinking he surely has zero clue about that old story.

Dr. Evelyn darts a look in my direction to say no more.

The Duke chuckles. "How utterly clever. It's rare to find anyone, let alone a yank, who's learned *that* novel Scottish fable. You must be well schooled."

"I had a beast of a tutor," I quip, looking at Dr. Evelyn and patting his hand, pleasantly surprised by his level of knowledge.

"Careful," he says with another wink. "I'm much older than you, but I'm a widower and could use a good wife. If you're a Scottish half-goddess, I'd wager I would not pass your tests of rigor. But I do like my tea served with milk."

I toss my head back and laugh. "My tea serving skills need work," I say. "I fear I'd leave you irreparably scalded, Duke Avondale."

"Oh, how delightful she is," the Duke says, clapping both hands together. And I feel the same about him. "Countess, where on Earth have you been hiding this precocious jewel?"

"*Countess? You*...have a title?" I ask Dr. Evelyn.

"Yes," the Duke says. "You don't know? Your aunt is Viscountess of Teviot. *She* married well. Why she prefers to be addressed as 'doctor' instead of Lady, is beyond our ilk."

"Dr. Sterling is a nobleman?" I ask, sweeping accusatory eyes over Evelyn.

*Gold digger.*

She softly nods with a smile. "I'm not a gold digger."

"True. The Countess doesn't dig for gold. She uses a trencher!" Duke George chortles. "Smart woman your aunt. It seems she has kept much from you."

"You've got that right," I say, remembering how she used to sometimes read my thoughts at Plum Hook Bay and examine dead people in yellow body bags. Seems she hasn't lost her telepathic capabilities either and it's a reminder for me to tread carefully. Dr. Evelyn is not a hybrid—she uses drugs and heavy meditation to upgrade her biology beyond that of most humans, skills that a special sect in MI6 taught her—and I already know she's able to kill without compunction because she told me so back at Plum Hook.

"Where is the old chap?" The Duke asks.

"Away on business," Dr. Evelyn says without elaboration—a perfect answer to dodge the question.

"Again?" The Duke asks. He nods at me. "I fear that your aunt and uncle rather *like* keeping me in the dark."

I empathize with his comment. Yet my reality remains... without a title I'm considered a commoner here and cannot participate in Descension unless accompanied by an escort of my equal or greater. Asking Genin to escort Lady Olivia is a small concession to make in order to gather information about Hope from Dr. Evelyn. Besides, I'd just be staring at the back of Genin's head all night anyway while he pines for Lady Olivia. Why put us both through him struggling to find a believable 'ditch tactic' to spare my feelings? "Genin," I say. "Since Lady Ross' escort seems otherwise disposed, I insist you accompany her this evening, at least until he arrives."

Genin's integrity steps up and he manages a very convincing, "I can't do that Sam, I'm here with you. You're supposed to dance with the person who brought you to the party, remember?"

Lady Olivia's face slightly droops, crestfallen by Genin's sense of duty. She rapidly switches to brave face so I won't notice. It must suck to be left standing at the proverbial upper echelon altar, and for a moment, I feel sort of sorry for her. According to the papers, Lord Harrington makes an annoying habit of keeping all of his ladies in waiting.

"What wouldn't be right is allowing a noble woman to forgo a proper introduction," I say. "This is her turf—make her look better than everyone in the room."

"She doesn't need my help to do that," Genin says, looking at her warmly.

Lady Olivia tilts a coquettish grin toward him, a blush cresting her well-etched cheekbones and it makes my heart hurt.

"Do this for me," I whisper to him. I softly kiss Genin's right cheek.

Sir Bob winks at me and Dr. Evelyn sighs in relief as couples descend the staircase, two-by two. Lady Olivia looks as if she just won the lottery, although come to think of it, that would be pocket change for her. The new couple is relocated to the very back of the line, just in front of Dr. Evelyn and the Duke of Avondale. I have to hand it to Genin for so swiftly and successfully mounting the British social ladder, and later, likely Lady Olivia too.

I duck out of the way, near the door where Lady Olivia once stood, waiting for Sir Bob and his staff to finish their duties, my heart feeling burdened by a myriad of concerns.

"*Lady Olivia Ross, escorted by Don Genin Paranos,*" the announcer says to rousing applause and a few *oohs*. I feel the collective energy of the ladies on the lower floor, and a couple of men too, as they swoon over Genin. He's as lost to them as he is to me now, overthrown by Lady Olivia.

"*Ladies & Gentlemen, presenting the Duke of Avondale and the Viscountess of Teviot, Dr. Evelyn Dennison...*"

And so it concludes.

Everyone below gazes expectantly up the staircase for Lord Harrington, their host. I retreat a couple of steps backward, into the shadows.

Miss Barbara stands down corridor with Reggie, her eyes tear-glistened, watching me, as he protectively settles a solid palm over one of her shoulders. She dabs a kerchief to her face to soak up our mutual disappointment. I feel badly about her hard work gone to waste. I haven't yet confided in Barbara and Reggie about my daughter Hope or what Evelyn did to create this child. It's time.

"I'll be fine," I say to myself. "Chin up, shoulders back." It's a hard act for me so I bite my bottom lip to keep from crying too.

"Hello, sad eyes," he whispers as he steps out from behind an oversized bronze statue of the Egyptian God Osiris. I feel his breath upon my neck and the heat from his slow exhale sends my heart into a tailspin and forces my back ramrod straight. "You seem in desperate need of an escort."

"Where have you been? How did you..."

Lord Luca Harrington steals my air and makes me feel dizzy with excitement. He circles me, and when our eyes meet, I avert my gaze, a pale effort to quell his azure stare, as if he's trained a spotlight on the darkest corridors of my heart. A swoosh fires across my hips and almost knocks me off my feet—but I make no show of his effect on me.

"You left Lady Olivia in the lurch," I say. "Shame on you."

"Outside of her contacts, I'm not all that interested in Lady Oliva," he says.

"She's your *date*," I say.

He glances over the railing. "Correction. She *was* my date until she thought I wouldn't arrive. Fickle woman. She's found a rather striking replacement, though, don't you think?"

I push my brows together and then undo them, pretending this doesn't bother me.

"You're *jealous*," he says.

I shake my head. "No, you pompous ass, I am *not* jealous."

"*Ouch*. Me? Pompous arse? I'm afraid you've been misinformed." He chuckles. "Lady Olivia is very beautiful, don't you think? She's skilled, smart, and easy to gaze upon."

"Trying to make me feel better?" I ask.

"You, my warrior princess, put goddesses to shame," he says. "Lady Olivia is rather stale and predictable, like most human females. I prefer to cavort with hybrids. Shall we?" He thrusts his elbow at me.

"You're a creep," I say, completely caught off guard by his insolence and the fact he knows I'm hybrid, although I don't know how he knows. "I will not Descend with you. You left Lady Olivia dangling. Genin was man enough to stand in for you."

"Lady Olivia is deviously resourceful. She found an acceptable solution at your expense. So, you think I'm a creep for noticing this?" Luca asks. "Come on, now—let's give them an unforgettable show."

"I will not."

I turn on my heels but Luca wraps both hands around my waist and spins me around so fast I stare into a couple of hundred faces gazing up at us from the ballroom. "Trust me on this one," he says.

Sir Bob nods at me to proceed.

My heart thunders in my ears. I grudgingly slip my arm through Lord Harrington's elbow to descend.

*"Ladies & Gentlemen, may we present your hosts for the evening, Lord Luca Harrington and Lady Samantha Blake, Countess of Skye."*

I stop descending. *"COUNTESS?! Of Skye?"* I ask, glaring at him. "What are you up to?"

"Um, Samantha, we're supposed to keep descending. Or would you prefer I call you *Blaze?*" he says with a laugh, patting my hand and turning over my wrist where my prong scars are now exposed for his viewing pleasure.

He knows, I can tell, what these prongs mean because a micro reptilian eye flicker betrays Lord Harrington's cool exterior when he looks at me. Suddenly, I realize,—Luca is not pure human, but high hybrid. Bennie's eyes once flashed the same way when he confided our progenitors. And then I'm struck by something enchantingly familiar about Luca too, something beyond the reaches of my mental cache—a shroud pulled over my recollections, even though my mom restored my memories. But now I wonder, if she held any back from me, the way she did with Reggie—maybe shaved off the most painful stuff.

Guests gasp, which snaps me back to the moment, and I ogle Lady Olivia to gauge her reaction, which registers as shock and anger. Claps slowly gain crescendo to respectable applause. Luca and I reach the bottom of the stairs, turn to one another, and he bows as I curtsy. With his free hand, he snatches a flute of champagne from a waiting tray and passes it to me.

"Welcome friends! You honor me with your presence this evening," He says. "As you're aware, I'm not known for adhering to convention, which makes this party the best of the social season. (Everyone laughs except Olivia.) Tonight's ball is in honor of women—our sisters, daughters, cousins, aunts, friends, lovers, wives, and mothers... I raise a toast. Without ado, let the games begin!"

"Here, here!" A man yells. Another whistles. Everyone raises their glass to sip, smile, and nod agreement. Lady Olivia, Genin, and Dr. Evelyn stand by dumbfounded. The remaining ninety-five people and a myriad of staff in the room are blindingly attentive, to an excessive or servile degree, with their politeness. How glaringly simple it is, I think, for hybrids and other worldly beings, to purchase the mercurial loyalty of humans.

"But..." Lord Harrington says, as he walks me toward the front doors. "We have a temporary conflict. I humbly request the Duke of Avondale and the Viscountess of Teviot act as your hosts until my *fiancée* and I are able to remedy our small dilemma."

"*What?*" Lady Olivia yells in shock, dropping her flute. Murmurs and gasps and then resounding applause so thunderous I wonder if it will shake the foundation of Harrington House.

"*Me?*" I ask, as I poke an index finger between my cleavage and cradle my glass.

"Yes," he says. "You."

"*Fiancée?!*" I yell. "*No!* Ladies & Gentlemen, This. Is not true." I vigorously shake my head for effect. "We are *not* **betrothed!**"

I plunk the champagne down so hard on a tray that a poor server is forced to balance it or drop them all. The glasses shatter on the marble floor, prisms of crystal sparkling under fizzy bubbles and chandeliers. People laugh but I don't find this a bit funny.

Genin takes a step forward to intervene but Lady Olivia tugs his jacket sleeve. "No," she says to him and shakes her head. Genin glances up at Barbara, Reggie, and Sir Bob who lean over the mezzanine, Barbara's kerchief now covering her mouth, eyes wide. Reggie curiously signals Genin to stand down.

Luca firmly wraps a large hand around my bicep and I fight the urge to drop kick a heel to his wrinkly twins and flip him to the ground. He effortlessly pulls me toward the threshold of the main doors of Harrington House.

"And that, ladies and gentlemen," Luca says as I struggle to break free, "is our dilemma. Please enjoy the party. We'll soon return."

Outside in the cool night air, a million flashbulbs go off, each accompanied by nosy zoom lenses propped up on the stone fence that runs for miles along the road. The media, I fear, will confetti my likeness all over the globe—and Abar will be completely pissed my cover is blown. I clamor-stumble down the outdoor steps in a ballgown, pulled along by Luca.

"Are you out of your fucking mind?" I yell, finally yanking free from his grasp. "*Fiancée?!* Why on Earth would you tell your guests and staff we're *engaged?* You give me this big talk about honesty at the top of the stairs only to throw it in the trash by the time you reach the last step! Are you *insane?*"

"I *WAS* honest," he said. "And you look stunning, by the way."

"We are *NOT* engaged, and I most certainly am *not* a Countess…but thank you."

"True. You got me on that one—you're actually a princess, but you *were* a countess once, when we first met. Remember?"

"What?! No! I do not! Are you off your fucking meds or something?"

"Tsk Tsk. Such a mouth. And that temper? Egad!" Luca says, tilting his head and looking up at the night sky.

"Egad? *Egad!* What is wrong with you? My face is going to be plastered on every damn newspaper from here to Singapore! You just announced to England's finest that we're *ENGAGED!* I shouldn't be upset?"

"A fine move on my part, don't you think?" He asks.

"*No!* Not a fine move."

Luca shovels a palm through his thick blonde hair. "Oh. Yes. The CIA. They won't dare interfere now. Too much risk. They'll stick to what they do best—plausible deniability. Amateurs. Frankly, you could use a break from that outfit. Also, I know you aren't married, so I'll snatch you up now to eliminate any competition."

"I get no say in this? You're out of your mind!"

"No," he corrects me. "I'm out of my world. Get in…"

"Get into what? I don't see anything." I say, looking around for a car.

"Oh. Right. I forgot to remove the cloaking device. My bad." Luca says.

*Cloaking device?*

Vigo barks incessantly from the stable. A man yells for Reggie's dog to quiet down as the horses kick their doors. "Hey! Somebody grab that dog!"

Lord Luca waves at the media perched atop the wall, which sends up a wail of cheers and flashes so bright I barely see Vigo closing in...

...Luca twists a gold ring he wears on his right hand and a ripple-like shimmer appears, a sort of curtain between us and the crowd on the other side of the wall.

The cloaking device reveals a...I don't know what this thing is...a flying craft, I think.

Vigo breaks through the shimmer...but doesn't attack Lord Harrington. Instead, Reggie's Source Guide runs around Lord Harrington and jumps into the...whatever it is...

"*Grr.* Some watchdog you aren't!" I yell at the dog.

Vigo swishes his tail back and forth like a fan switched to high.

The key device under my girdle uncomfortably sucks me toward the vehicle as I repel against it and almost lose my balance.

"Get in quick," Luca says. "I solved your dilemma."

"Did you telepathically let the world know we aren't a *thing?*"

"No. I ruined their film. Every roll. It will process nothing but a black blob for your likeness. Now, get in..."

"No," I say.

Vigo barks at me, jumps out of the craft, and nudges me toward it with his muzzle.

"What is wrong with you, Vigo?" I ask, yanking a piece of my gown out of his mouth. "Didn't Reggie teach you not to ride with strangers?"

It takes two seconds or less to see there are no rivets or metal seams inside this thing. It's practically noiseless too, except for a barely audible hum, an occasional low '*om*' sound. The craft possesses a flat copper-colored bottom with a front curved up like a toboggan. I don't see a driver's seat. In fact, I don't see much of anything except cloudy glass, as if we've climbed into an igloo made of crystal. There exist no conventional electronic controls other than two horse-shoe shaped objects that face one another and have easy-to-remember yet strange markings, of which I have no idea what they mean.

"What is this thing?" I ask.

"Something I designed from one of Nikola Tesla's classified patents," Luca says. "Advanced magnetics with a plasma illumination system. It will get us from here to Oxford in less than two minutes—unless we run into a hiccup. Cute mutt. What's his name?"

Vigo licks Luca's cheek and settles between us. Never saw this dog do that before—like Reggie, Vigo hates almost everybody.

"Vigo," I say. "What sort of hiccup?"

"I haven't quite worked out the glitches," he says. "There's a possibility that this thing might explode. It requires more testing. Is Vigo your Source Guide? "

Vigo lets loose with a series of howls and looks at Luca, then me, before he launches across my lap and paddles his front paws on the window to escape.

"What?! No. Vigo, stop! This is Reggie's soul guide. Vigo, stop! You're the damn mutt that wanted to go for a ride and pushed me in here too," I say. I reach for a handle but there is none.

"Where is *your* Source Guide?" Luca asks.

"I, um…she's in hiding," I say.

"One should never misplace their Source Guide," he says.

"So I've been told," I huff. "Now let us out of here, we're not going with you," I say. But I can't move. The portal key acts like a weight, pinning me to my seat.

"You should both reconsider," he says.

Vigo whimpers and his dark brown eyes guiltily plead with me for help.

"Reconsider getting blown up? Okay…um, no," I say. "Let Vigo and me out of this thing."

"That's not what I meant. You should reconsider trusting me," he says.

"Why? You don't exactly have a great track record."

"You're trying to find your daughter and I'm trying to locate my siblings," Luca says.

"Siblings?" I sit up straighter. Vigo plants himself firmly between us and growls at Luca.

"Yes," Luca says. "I'm convinced you know them, that you met at a place called NASA Plum Hook Bay."

"What are their names?"

"Benjamin and Brigdhe Bathurst," Luca says. " They went missing years ago."

Luca firmly smacks his palm on the crystal console, Vigo howls, *"arrrrooooooohhhh,"* and we hang on for the ride of our lives...

# TWENTY

# X POINT

WE CONTINUE our mad journey in Luca's weird conveyance, having rounded the house and plunged into the garden fountain to ride through the caves. It's long enough for Vigo and me to get used to the terrific speed but just at the point where I overcome fear of a wreck, we clip some rock, throw off sparks, and skate along a cave wall, before we crash—upside down—Vigo's tail stuck in my face. We climb out of the overturned, now inoperable craft, which thankfully hasn't exploded...yet...and so far, appear unscathed.

The key device hidden under my dress vibrates and casts a fluorescent green light through my gown. It's something I can't hide. Vigo licks my face and I push him off of me, where he quickly disappears up some stairs.

"Vigo!" I yell. "That damn dog never listens."

"That's because he's not *your* soul guide," Luca says as he helps me to my feet. "Whoa. What do you have there?" He points to my belly.

"None of your business." I readjust my half-undone hair and smack cave dust off my ballgown. "This thing, your whatever-it-is, it won't blow up, right?"

"It's called an Ether V and has a backup nuclear propulsion system in case we need to go air born fast, so technically, yes, it could blow. But don't worry, I disengaged and powered down the small reactor. You're not going to give birth to an alien are you?" He asks, staring again at my abdomen.

"No," I say. "How do you drive this thing? I see no controls."

"There are 3 amplifiers on the Ether V. It can lift off with a single one but requires a melding of bio-electromagnetic energy to maneuver," Luca says. "My energy must connect with the craft, in simple terms."

I scrunch my brows in doubt.

"There are two different avenues for propulsion," he says. "The Ocron configuration or the Alta configuration, the latter meant for interstellar travel. It works best when the craft tilts sideways, contrary to sci-fi movies that show UFO's as flat flying disks. Moving around a source of gravity is a problem of interference on this planet. But I use interference and my DNA as a benefit."

"You failed," I say. "We crashed."

"We didn't exactly *crash,*" he says, a pinch of irritation seeping into his voice and across his brow. "The Ether V creates distortion. Instead of propulsion,..." he struggles to describe the concept in a way I might understand, "...this craft rolls down the slope of a perfect right triangle and chases distortion."

"But it's unstable," I say.

"Problems occur anytime the Ether V flies over Earth's gravity field," he says. "It depends on the minerals and density in the ground underneath it, which sometimes causes handling problems in low speed."

To his credit, Luca's craft managed to cover approximately 150 miles in less than two minutes through what looked like an underground railway without any rails. If this is his idea of 'low speed', I wonder what this craft can do at high speed?

"Unfortunately, your accident left us without a quick ride back to Harrington House," I say. "We'll miss dinner."

"I don't consider that a misfortune," he says.

Luca presses his fingers into an engraving on the underside of his vehicle. I'm desperate to speak with Dr. Evelyn about why she created a child between Bennie and me but now our conversation must wait. An unexpected shiver rolls over my skin and the hair on my forearms rise when my key device gently pulls me toward the stairs, a tug I struggle to resist.

"Bennie was your *brother?*" I ask, still reeling from the bombshell Luca dropped before we zoomed away from Harrington House. "You don't have any resemblance to one another, except for maybe your arrogance and a penchant for glitchy inventions."

Luca's azure irises and flaxen wavy hair are completely dichotomous to Bennie's dark ringlets and black-granite eyes. They *do* share the same luminescent gold skin and good looks. And like Bennie, Luca completely ignores me when he zones out to focus on his weird craft.

"There was no mention of another sibling in Bennie or Brigdhe's files either," I say, watching Luca balance a leg on the underside of the craft, as if lost in some sort of mental engineering journey he forgot to calculate into his flight plan.

"Where are those files?" Luca finally asks rubbing his hands together and looking at me.

"Dr. Evelyn confiscated them from me when I was sixteen," I say.

"Evelyn deserves death," he says.

A chill trickles through my center as I consider how to tell Luca, if he doesn't already know, about what happened to his siblings. "Dr. Evelyn is my *aunt,*" I remind him, thinking about the yellow body bags she used to bring into NASA and not exactly disagreeing with him. "How did you find out about NASA Plum Hook Bay? Dr. Evelyn?"

"Indirectly...I learned about it a few years ago," he says. "Ni uko purtu Camaeliphim. Izan-zen."

"I'm not so sure I'm a daughter of the heavens," I respond. "And yes, I've been harmed, but a death warrant is extreme. You speak fluent Enochian, like Bennie and me. You're Camaeliphim."

"Yes."

What I don't mention is that I also feel something different in

Luca, something I can't quite put into words because it's about as clear to me as heavy smoke. His aura feels *off*, a bit sad, oppressive, and dangerous too. "I have problems with my memories," I say.

"I realized such when you didn't recognize me." Luca picks up a small branch and pokes it in the ground before he boomerangs it up the stairs. "You will fully restore. It takes time."

"How long?"

"It depends," he answers. "Implants and plasma drains weaken your memories. Thankfully, our blood makes us difficult to decode or control. This is why Dream Stealers don't work well on us."

"I suppose that's some good news," I say, examining my scar.

"The bane of Earthly bureaucracies is that they spend an incomprehensible amount of this planet's gold repeating mistakes," Luca says. "Black agencies require enemies to fight in order to thrive and sometimes, unfortunately, they target potential allies as enemies."

"Isn't that what you do as a defense and weapons contractor?" I ask.

"I fight fire with fire," Luca says, glancing at his own wrist. "An eye for an eye."

I reach over and pull down the cuff of his shirt with my forefinger. "You too?" I trace my finger around his scar.

Luca doesn't say anything but slightly nods and re-covers his skin. "Do you know what happened to Brigdhe and Bennie?" He asks.

"Brigdhe…" I swallow hard to get past the expanding lump in my throat and push a mental compress on deep emotional wounds in my head.

"My sister is dead," Luca says, sparing me from having to stumble over difficult words.

"Yes," I say.

"How?" He asks.

"She pulled a Nephilim into an abyss under the nuclear reactor at Plum Hook Bay," I say. "She sacrificed herself for the rest of us."

Luca turns away from me and pretends, I think, to scan his

injured craft again but I notice the dents are no longer there, as if the craft magically healed itself like new. "And Bennie?" He asks.

"He never made it out of the caves," I say. "At least that's what I was told."

Luca smashes his fist into the rock and the force of it sends cracks scrambling, followed by a long silence. He swipes a tear from his cheek with a finger. "Bennie was different from us," he finally says.

"I know," I say, trying to tap down an uncomfortable ache in my gut. "I sensed this, even though I never fully understood why."

"Bennie's an ancient prodigy of the Source—a favored one, what mortals might consider an archangel," he says. "Bennie also had a soul and could die."

"I'm not so sure he's dead," I say.

"You think my brother is *alive*?" Luca asks, his eyes shining like the turquoise ocean off the coast of the Sentinelese Islands.

"When Dr. Sterling Dennison, Evelyn's husband, accidentally split neutrinos at NASA Plum Hook Bay, Bennie told me this tore holes in the universe," I say.

"And?"

"My mom was a patient in a military asylum until recently," I say. "Her nurse told me another patient always stood outside her door. The kid matches Bennie's description, except officials didn't give him a name, only a number. Then, while I attended a funeral in Nepal, someone hand delivered my mom's custom-rolled poison cigarettes to a monk, which I initially thought were meant as a warning for me."

"I'm not making the connection," Luca says. "Hand-rolled poison cigarettes?"

"The cigarettes were a message," I say. "It's probably wishful thinking, but maybe there's a solid reason Bennie can't make direct contact with us. The cigarettes were in an envelope, along with a picture my mom drew, the eye of Horus, like the one you wear as cufflinks."

"What number was this male patient given?"

"611."

"The NORAD of the Antarctic..." Luca trails off.

"What?"

"611 NORAD is a covert military base responsible for the execution of aerospace scans, conducted twenty-four hours a day, seven days a week. It looks for national security threats," he says. "High value assets like Bennie receive numerical names, like zip codes, for clandestine transport. 611 was sent to the Antarctic."

"Why?" I ask, wondering where my number, 001, leads.

"The Antarctic is home to an unfortunate nuclear accident that blasted the largest dimensional hole on the globe. It allowed a few Bezaliels through, but they haven't yet been able to take form. Nephilim destroy indigenous tribes..."

"...To increase Bezaliel density on Earth," I interrupt. "For the ones that did squeeze through."

I make a mental note to tell Reggie and I think Dr. Monica should probably be 'read into' this if she hasn't already. "Bezaliels or Nephilim could scan humans or hybrids for special blood and conduct covert draws. Why so much violence when they strike tribes?"

"Bezaliels require fear-infused plasma, a Raga offering, where each feeds on the negative energy," Luca says. "Reggie told me you'd been relocated to a U.S. facility more heavily guarded than Area 39. You had a plasma drip. Someone was taking *your* blood. How did you escape?"

"Not Who," I say.

Luca let's out a low whistle and plants a palm to his chest. "Fascinating... It *helped* you?"

"What is Not Who?" I ask.

"Celestial mercenary energy, created by Tall Whites, or Ebians as we know them. It's highly unusual for them to alter time patterns for hybrids."

"I accepted an offer..."

"What sort of offer?"

"I have to throw Raga into the Source Vortex," I say.

"Sweet deal if you're into certain death," Luca says, tilting his head back to look up at the cave ceiling. "You do realize what this means, right?"

"No."

"Success is damn near impossible," he answers, meeting my eyes. "Raga is too strong for a single-mind."

I shake off a shiver of doubt about my ability to independently do the job. The key pendant beneath my gown pulls me forward two steps. I regain balance and hold ground. "The warrior-minded ideology of Camaeliphim seems counter to defeating Bezaliels." I say. "Wouldn't our fighting play right into Bezaliel plans for achieving density faster?"

"All worlds, regardless of size, make-up, or location, utilize balance between chaos and coherence." Luca says. "A return to randomness is the purpose of the Source. This interplay lends *everything* meaning. Camaeliphim serve as intercessors between the two, which the Source does not recognize as good or evil, only necessary, and sometimes that requires blood-letting."

"And sometimes it requires compassion," I say.

"Agreed."

An edgy reticence creeps over us until I fidget with my eye necklace, wishing I could command it to return me to happier times, like maybe when I lived with my grandma and all I had to worry about was licking a spoon loaded with cake batter. "Death seems a steep price for Dr. Evelyn to pay," I say. "I mean, she's self-serving, yes, but death?"

"Dr. Evelyn Dennison stole and sold Bennie and Brigdhe to the highest bidder after our parents were murdered."

A mask of *sadgitation* leaps between Luca's eyes and his etched cheekbones turn stone gray. He calmly stares at me without a flicker of alarm or possession over the horrible circumstances that force us to collide, having I think, processed this shocking news years ago—news that newly disorients me as if suddenly being trampled by a stampede of elephants.

"I thought your parents were killed in a car accident."

"Wrong," he says. "Evelyn did not personally wield the blade that slit their throats but provided a path for Nephilim to find them."

"Evelyn *adopted* Bennie," I say. "I saw the paperwork."

"Dr. Evelyn is addicted to self-interest," Luca says, staring off in the distance at nothing in particular. "Your aunt arranged to closely study my brother alongside a dark faction within your government. She *forged* his adoption papers."

"Why didn't Bennie kill her and escape?"

"It wasn't that easy," Luca says. "He wouldn't leave the captives."

I'm not sure what to say as I teeter between anger and despair, thinking about how my aunt is not much different than Rosie was when it comes to her lack of caring for people, yet I'm troubled by something. "Why would you invite Evelyn to Harrington House?"

"She does not know Bennie is my brother," Luca says. "I have a different mother. Reggie ensured my true nature and identity never showed up in any clandestine files, including the ones Evelyn requested in her effort to win my trust."

Tears spill over the rims of his eyes and I'm unsure what to do when he turns away and walks up the stairs. I'm more of a prickly than fuzzy-feely sort of hybrid, one who, like the Sentinelese, prefers to cocoon my vulnerabilities within a cage of spears, and I'd thought the same about Luca. My throat closes and profound grief suddenly triggers an oppressive ache in my heart. "Why haven't you killed Dr. Evelyn?" I ask, following him.

"Why haven't you?" He asks.

"I-I-I don't know…" I say. "She has information."

"We need her," he says.

"We *need* her?"

"She has important information about the Code."

"What about Dr. Sterling?" I ask. "Is he helping her?"

"Dr. Sterling is innocent," Luca says to my huge relief.

"Do you think Evelyn killed him?" I ask. "He's missing."

"No," Luca says. "Would you agree that the best way to learn about your enemy is to get into their camp?"

"I suppose," I say.

"That's what we've done."

"You mean by becoming a defense contractor?"

"I'm tri-bred," he says, making it sound as if anybody listening should know what this means.

"Tri-bred?"

"Dr. Sterling inserted Bezaliel mist into my DNA," Luca says.

"Oh. My. God." I back away from him, fighting an urge to run. The strong scent of peat moss bubbles up from grass beneath out feet. "Dr. Sterling? Why would Dr. Sterling do such a thing?"

"We wanted to learn how Bezaliels think," Luca says. "Unfortunately, I haven't worked out all the glitches."

"Dr. Evelyn thinks he's missing—we all thought Dr. Sterling was missing. Oh my god, wait. He's your silent partner."

"He's my reliable source, working underground, and how I learned everything I could about NASA Plum Hook Bay. He wooed and seduced Dr. Evelyn to get closer to Bennie. It wasn't difficult. When the Viscount of Teviot offered her marriage, old money, and a royal title, she acted as if she'd settled. The poor chap was quite broken up about Bennie's disappearance, loves him like a father should."

"You're both certifiable," I say, unable to wrap Luca's words around my head. "Nobody has ever purposely deposited Bezaliel mist into their bloodline! It's got to be some sort of universal violation."

"Probably so," Luca says.

Luca's words worm through me looking for a place to settle, but my mind follows it along the shadows of my head until brought into focus, a realization that Dr. Sterling loved and protected us, like Reggie, the best he could. I remember how Dr. Sterling's blue eyes would tap dance with wonder, revealing all that might be good in this world, until the moment he looked at Dr. Evelyn in the car, on our way through the gates at NASA Plum Hook Bay that first day, when his warmth suddenly faded, glazed over by what I now recognize as contempt.

"We need to keep Dr. Sterling Dennison MIA," Luca says. "He's the only nuclear engineer who reasonably understands

Bennie's work but he has a price on his head, compliments of your aunt."

"Why?"

"Bennie is missing," he says. "Dr. Sterling is worth a lot of money. If he's dead, I get an unwanted and greedy partner with practically zero skill sets where it counts, in addition to someone who'd sell her soul, my business, and Earth's security to Nephilim."

I cradle my elbows, chew my lower lip, and consider telling Luca that his brother is Hope's father. Dr. Sterling wouldn't know this because Verity said Dr. Evelyn compartmentalized her egg snatching and went 'off-grid'. I can't help but feel for Luca, this lonely and uniquely designed creature surrounded by every comfort known to man or hybrid, yet lacking two things more valuable than money: love and family—and perhaps too, common sense. But I'm overjoyed to hear Dr. Sterling is alive, except now I have another worry to add to my already overloaded mental landfill. Given Luca's adulterated DNA, is it possible for Luca to *love*? Maybe he doesn't feel anything at all and uses hybrids and humans without compunction—maybe his Bezaliel mist renders him a complete sociopath, and therefore, incapable of earning my trust, or worse, falling prey to Bezaliels and becoming one of them.

"As far as I know, no other tri-bred exists," I say.

"This would be true," he says. "But humans and Nephilim are close to finding the Word. "A few of them have already reverse engineered celestial technologies."

"Such as?" I ask.

"Moving large boulders and their bodies using levitation, harnessing the astral power of crystals, tapping free energy derived from the Earth itself, fed to it from space."

I'm a bit surprised a few humans figured out how to decipher particular aspects of celestial technology, knowledge my Camaeliphim ancestors were forced to destroy, Bennie said, when both Lemuria and Atlantis once created and enslaved unnatural creatures.

"It was agreed by the Ormian Council, to never share this

knowledge with humans again, until they spiritually evolved—yet according to my calculations, their collective consciousness has failed to register even a blip of enlightenment on the intergalactic spectrometer," Luca says. "And the Ormian Council is now in session."

"To order you back?" I ask. "For being so reckless with your DNA?"

"No," he says. "To decide if universes can remain synchronized without humans."

"If the Ormian Council votes for genocide, it perfectly sets up the Bezaliels for complete victory," I say, leaning my torso against a tree, every smudge on my face, I'm sure, visible under a large moon.

"How?" He asks.

"Widespread chaos," I say. "It would kill humans, as intended, but it would also annihilate plants, water, oxygen, fungi, bacteria, and animals too. Balance. Gone. And as your brother once told me, the Source would then suffer extensive multiverse collapse. Nobody wins. Game. Over. This tiny marble of a planet keeps everything in order because it serves as a repository, a seed bank, for every bit of life in the cosmos, and that's what he's trying to protect."

"I wasn't aware of this," Luca says.

"Your brother was," I say. "He told me about it when we were fostered at Plum Hook Bay."

Hundreds of purple and white orchids dangle around us, their roots straining to meet the grass from low hanging branches. In the distance, shadowed silhouettes of grazing pasture horses roam. Two white swans float by in a river steps away, one that runs thick along a verdant tree line. Sucking in fresh air, I realize why poets and novelists based fairytales here. Luca spends hours scanning the sky, searching for something. No wonder the CIA, DIA, or NSA couldn't track him until he arrived. Luca uses *underground* bio-electro-magnetic transportation, which scrambles their radar and makes him invisible until he's here or takes up residence at the Randolph Hotel in Oxford. Wait a second. The Randolph Hotel.

Bennie named his Source Guide, Randolph. He told me it meant 'shield wolf'. I don't know much about the hotel but it seems too convenient to be coincidence.

"What is this place?" I ask.

"Port Meadow," Luca replies. "Just outside of Oxford—close to a town called Jericho. It's history stretches back thousands of years."

Port Meadow cradles the River Thames, this I do know. I read back at Langley that Lewis Carroll rowed Alice Liddell here and related *Alice in Wonderland* to her on this river. And Gerard Manley Hopkins wrote, *Binsey Poplars*, a Victorian ode against the felling of trees for a railway line. It is a place too, where my mother spent countless hours walking and reading when she attended Exeter College.

"Why did you bring me here?" I ask.

"I brought you here because in the early 1940s, a man named Arthur Matthews wrote a book called, *The Wall of Light*."

"Never heard of it," I say. A small gust of wind sweeps over us.

"Matthews was Nikola Tesla's secret son and apprentice," Luca says. "The first part of the *Wall of Light* is Tesla's autobiography, a reflection of experiences, feelings, research, and his strange life among humans—but the latter part was a global warning to beware of false prophets who pedal accords through weaponry."

"Are you saying Tesla was extraterrestrial?"

"Fully." Luca says without hesitation. "Tesla came from a dimension well outside anything we know. He was an otherworldly biological diverted here on July 10, 1856."

"How did he get here?" I ask.

"It was a double leap year for Earth's Gregorian and Julian calendars," he says.

"So," I say.

"Leap years keep celestial calendars in sync for humans," he says. "But for extraterrestrials, these leap years illuminate X points."

"X points?"

"X-points are where realms crisscross. When magnetic fields

join, they propel charged particles to create an 'electron diffusion region' or what you might know as a *portal gate*. Tesla's craft landed in Croatia. Thankfully, he was saved by a Camaeliphim—whisked to safety on a remote farm. The couple that raised him, a pastor and an engineer, swore secrecy to Tesla's true origins."

"Tesla died in the United States in a New York Hotel," I say. "The Office of Alien Property confiscated his papers and patents on behalf of the FBI."

"No. He didn't," Luca says. "He fled to another realm. Most of his papers were confiscated but not on behalf of your FBI. His most valuable contributions were labeled 'Top Secret', hidden away, and remain so."

"Tesla was involved with national security work such as the Philadelphia Project," I say. "It's not unusual for his papers, like that of German scientists after World War II, under *Operation Paper Clip*, to be classified."

"We the '*people*' were told Tesla died of 'coronary' complications, but it wasn't so," Luca says. "His papers were inventions and maps to locate every part of the Word, piece it back together, and get it the hell out of here using an X Point. He was intercepted in New York by someone who made him an offer to perfect his invention for Bezaliels to cross over. Tesla declined and to avoid being compromised, he was taken up by Ebians."

"What happened to his papers?" I ask.

"Just after World War II, there was renewed interest in Tesla's work. Classified copies of his papers on particle beam weaponry were sent to Wright-Patterson Air Force Base in Dayton, Ohio. An operation code-named 'Project Nick' was heavily funded and placed under the command of a Brigadier General to test feasibility. Details of the experiment were never published and the project was allegedly discontinued, except it wasn't. After that, Tesla's papers disappeared and nobody knows what happened to them."

Vigo runs past us barking at a swan. "Vigo! Stop!" I yell.

The dog briefly pauses before he gives up chase and begins sniffing the ground around us while I feel taken away from here, thinking of Verity, an accomplished woman, no longer skittish or lost in voodoo prayer chants, but a mother to my child, one filled with enough courage to steal and hide Tesla's papers, once she realized what she had, and send them far away, into a Cave of Seven Sleepers. "The file was hidden," I say. "I suspect it may have gone *underground*, literally."

My pendant glows so brightly it makes me look like an oversized firefly.

"Tesla worked with a colleague, a man named Ian Windsor," Luca answers. "What is up with that stomach of yours?"

"Ian Windsor was my grandfather but we never met," I say, covering my abdomen with a palm. Evelyn told me back in the states that he worked with Tesla."

"Your grandfather not only worked with him," Luca says. "Ian hid one piece of an X Point locator device they built together, somewhere here in the U.K. and Tesla hid the other part somewhere in the U.S."

"You think my grandfather's piece is somewhere here?" I ask.

"I do," Luca says. "Do you understand how boat locks are used to make a river navigable, or to allow a canal to cross land that is not level?"

"Yes."

"Your grandfather and Tesla were inventors," Luca says. "They built an advanced lock and key device, one that would have enabled Tesla and your grandfather to leave Earth with the Code of Everything using beam technology—a 'relocation' plan if this planet collapsed, but they were forced off this planet early, leaving their invention and the Code of Everything behind."

I scour the meadow as Vigo wanders further afield. A couple of horses snort and trot. Reggie's dog furiously digs and I barely make out his wagging tail and flying clumps of soil in the husky darkness. "Reggie really needs to get his Source Guide into remedial training," I say. My eye necklace launches me forward another few steps and I stagger backward to keep my balance when Luca catches me.

"What's happening?" He asks.

"I'm not sure," I say. "My necklace is 'pulling me'. Is there a heavy magnet somewhere near?"

"You wear the Eye of Sakhet," Luca says. "Your necklace is not the issue. It's composed of silver, crystal quartz, and your ancestral DNA, mixed with a trace element of Astatine. It wouldn't act against you, but with you, and for you."

"What's the Eye of Sakhet?" I ask, changing the subject, not wanting to tell him about the collapsible cube I made into a pendant and now hide under my gown, a cube Bennie was convinced held part of a key to other realms.

"You don't remember?" Luca asks.

"No," I say.

"Sakhet is a warrior goddess and healer to Earth's people," he says.

"Bennie called me Scathach once," I say, trying to block out the memory of my celestial name carved on Pa Ling and Fensig's corpses.

"You have many names," he says. "Scathach, Sekhmet, Skadi, Skaoi and sometimes, Anahit, or Inanna depending on where you do battle. Your abdomen is glowing blue-green. I've heard of lady troubles but I've never seen..."

Crisp leaves flutter to the ground when a cold chill sweeps through. The occasional gusts merge into increasing winds and the terrain becomes damp with a steady mist that clings to my skin. The sudden gale snaps and lashes our legs, whipping my hair like fan blades.

"Vigo!" I yell above the howling wind. "Vigo! Come here boy!"

Chattering voices above our heads speak a strange crackling, scratchy language, loaded with the same dread and evil I felt when I was at Plum Hook Bay.

"Bezaliels," Luca says.

"Here?" I ask.

"Sort of..." he says. "They're veiled in a dimension next to ours, unable to press through."

A figure of blue light watches us about twenty yards away, a soft-glowing silhouette of a nonhuman entity, void of gender, eyes, or hair, its outstretched arms emitting a series of symbols and numbers, packages of photonic concepts pushed toward us to fade away and a gust of wind rattles some houseboats. Luca and I tumble backward together when the wind suddenly ceases.

"What in bloody hell was that?" Luca asks.

"I've seen this before...once years ago in my room at Plum Hook Bay. It's here to help. I think." Oh, boy, do I hope it's here to help.

The depths of Earth decide to exhale, Gaia's breath a squall of fury. I grab hold of Luca to keep from being windswept again. He holds firm to my arms when my feet get tugged out from under me. "Let me go!" I say, realizing we're in the direct path of an impromptu tornado. "We can't both be sacrificed."

"Hell. No." Luca softly says, almost whisper-like, his vice-like grip plastered around my biceps. "I will not let you go again. But this might be a good time to kiss me."

"*What?!* Are you insane?"

"Yes," he says. "For coming to this planet to find you. I think you want to kiss me and this may be our last opportunity."

I'm dragged full tilt, yanked from his grasp by some unseen force rushing through the pasture...

# TWENTY-ONE

# LUCA'S PORTAL

"SAMANTHA!" Luca yells.

Every rock, twig, and clump of dirt rips apart or clings to this once beautiful ballgown, my hair a wild tangle of disheveled copper. I'll bet that hybrid doesn't want to kiss me now, I think. I I fall with a thud into a hole where bony legs wrap themselves around me. I raise my fists and take a swing...at a skeleton.

Vigo is down here too, having dug his hole too damn deep. He tongue swipes my cheek and his sweaty fur smells like a cross between musk and cow dung. "Get off of me!" I yell. "Stupid dog. Yours wasn't the sort of kiss I expected."

"Grrrwooof!" Vigo barks in protest, planting muddy paws on my chest and wagging his tail.

I clamp my fingers around his collar but can't move. Lord Harrington's head pops over the side of the hole and he laughs...hysterically.

"I don't think this is one damn bit funny," I say.

"You're covered in horse shat!" He laughs. "Of course, it's funny."

"Fuck off," I say, having lost all my patience. "Get us out of here!"

"Oh, that naughty mouth of yours. Hold on." Luca removes his dinner jacket, loosens his tie, and snaps off his suspenders. He tries to lower his jacket sleeve for me to grab but I can't budge.

"Vigo," Luca says. "Bite the end of my suspenders and hoist yourself up with your paws."

"That's all you've got?" I ask. "Good god...you're considered the most brilliant defense contractor on Earth. Don't you carry around some sort of wizard weapon for moments like this?"

Vigo actually listens to Luca and is free within moments, his hind quarters pitching rich soil over my face. "Blech!" I spit. "Vigo!"

A dog and a hybrid stare down at me, stuck in this tumulus, covered in horse crap, holding court with a skeleton, and I still can't move.

"You can't move a finger?" Luca asks.

"No," I say. "Why might that be?"

"It's a forcefield!" he says. "Sam! Vigo found it!"

Luca scratches Reggie's Source Guide between the ears, fluffing up the fur, and curling over an ear that Vigo doesn't even bother to reset. Vigo then struts around the perimeter of the hole, snout raised high, his chest stuck out like a proud toddler playing soldier.

"Vigo, you should have been born a rooster," I say. "What did he find?"

"Shat," Luca says. "Don't move."

"Grrr. I can't move—but why should I not move, you know, just in case?"

"You could be vaporized."

"*What?!*"

"I think you're stuck in a plasma field."

"I don't know what that is," I say. "But it doesn't sound good."

"I've always looked above ground for this. I neglected to under," he says. "I didn't consider plasma fields could be buried. " Luca paces back and forth above the hole, talking to himself.

*"Instead of looking up, try looking under..."* *The lady in blue*

*robes taps a long finger to her neck, tilts back her head, and fades away...*

"Hello! Earth to Luca! You going to get me out of here?"

"Remarkable," He says. "They did it..."

"Who? Did what? Damn it, Luca, don't just leave me in a hole covered in horseshit! Find a way to break the forcefield without annihilating me!"

"That's it!" He says. "You can't move because you're the conduit! Whoa. What's happening to you?"

"It's my pendant hidden beneath my dress," I finally admit. "I found it in some tree roots a few years ago, in a cave under a river in Ohio."

Luca jumps into the hole and straddles a knee on each side of my waist.

"What the fuck are you doing?" I protest. "You'll get us both killed!"

"I could kiss you right now," he says. "And you would be completely helpless to do anything about it..."

"Really? Without consent? You're going to assault me at a time like this," I say, willing my body to move but it won't. I'd kick him off of me if I could.

"Not my style," he says laughing, looking into my eyes with a mischievous smile. "I don't find the Ode du horse crap you wear this evening particularly enticing."

"What...are you...?"

*Cuuuuusht...* Luca effortlessly tears the front of my dress to my waist where he's met by a girdle and he gives me a funny look... "Pardon me," he says.

"Get off of me!"

He plunges his arm between my breasts and slides his beastly appendage along my abdomen until he reaches the portal key device.

*Bzzzzt!*

Luca is catapulted against the dirt wall where soil rains over his head, but I remain, thankfully, unscathed. "Ha!" I say, still unable to move, but my pendant intact. "You deserve that!"

He brushes some of the grime crumbles from his scalp and crawls back to me. He moves aside a portion of skeleton beneath me and uses an arm bone as a makeshift spade to claw into the dirt under my body.

"Hold very still," he says.

"Um, yea, okay…since I can't move that shouldn't be too hard. Some weapons expert you are. *NOT!*"

"Got it!"

Luca holds up a shiny strange copper tube-like object of what resembles an inflated round multi-tiered gold piece at one end and a weird blue-green glowing silver square box at the other and I float up off the floor of this hole with it. When he taps its underside, I'm dislodged from its hold and slam back to the ground. "Damn it, Luca! Stop fucking around!" The object, it glows, and I sit up beside him, staring. "What is it?" I ask, tucking the folds of my gown under my legs, staring at rings of copper among a host of other materials I don't understand.

"It's a Tesla coil, sort of…wow."

"What do you mean…sort of?"

"Tesla coils were used to carry currents through electrical charges. Unfortunately, they produced unpredictable lightening too, which we both know, can be lethal. It's similar to a device invented by Nikola Tesla in the early 1900's, which enabled humans to safely use alternating currents for electricity." Luca studies the object, carefully using the glow from my pendant to scrutinize its components.

"Samantha—Tesla and your grandfather," he says, "they had 'otherworldly' help for this…wow. What these two accomplished is incredible."

"What did they do?" I ask.

"They successfully utilized force fields to control matter in both biological and artificial systems," he says. "This little device, constructed with iridium, silver, and gold, generates a tractor beam effect using nanoparticles that assemble themselves into conduits, which form a naturally occurring circuit. It absorbs energy to create X points or…"

"Or what?"

"The sphere that floats over the top is missing," he says, momentarily distracted. "This marvelous gadget has a host of practical applications."

"Such as…?"

"For starters it can wirelessly create a powerful force field at distances far greater than any of us could ever imagine. It's Arthur Matthews *Wall of Light* made manifest, used to cloak entire continents or maybe even planets. This thing might enable humans and other sentients to astral travel faster than thought, or to communicate with interdimensional beings. Alternatively, it could kill—or produce Ozone, and save Earth from environmental degradation."

"Can it bring people back from the dead?" I ask, hopeful—thinking about Verity, Bennie, Katie, and the others.

Luca shakes his head. "As powerful as this is, we can't manipulate life forces without putting others at risk or throwing the Source out of balance." He pauses and looks up for a moment, adrift in thought. "I wonder if the sphere is buried here too." He pitches his hands into the dirt, digging away from reason and further into Tesla mania, centuries of compressed sediment holding firm.

"I think I know where the sphere is," I say.

Luca's head pops up and a gush of potent air charges forth. "Do you think the DOE already found it?" His eyes narrow over my face and he tightens his jaw. He releases the tension and smooths creases that scuttle across his forehead. "Forgive me," he says. "I've forgotten myself. Where is the sphere?"

"It's guarded back at Plum Hook Bay, under a river in a cave."

"By the DOE?" He asks.

"No," I say. "It's far underground beneath a cave system of black granite. Six Astral Weavers sit in a circle, eyes fixed on a suspended sphere above a holographic pyramid. It's covered in spider webs sharper than razor wire. I fell into them once and cut my arm pretty badly but not as badly as Genin did."

"The pendant you wear opens the heart of this device," Luca

says. "The combination of your 'golden blood' and this gadget renders you a sort of beacon." He holds up the coil so I can view its underside—and there it is—a shallow etching where I recognize my pendant will perfectly fit if I expand it from collapsed Pleiades' map to cube.

"I'm not a walking weapon?" I ask.

"You're more like a lighthouse," Luca says. "For interdimensional reinforcements to find us—and I'll bet those Astral Weavers are waiting for the right sources to come together before they hand over that sphere."

"Project Looking Glass," I say.

"Project Looking Glass?"

"A friend told me about a clandestine CIA project that tries to see into the future or the past. It involves a collapsible cube, a laser, and timeline wars. Humans need the real cube to manipulate the timelines...and I'll bet they're scanning time, like combing through book pages, to find the cube, so they can grab that sphere."

"And you wear the cube that won't screw up probabilities or rearrange nature's natural patterns," Luca says.

"Yes. How does this device work?" I ask.

"The pieces of this device, the key, this coil, and the sphere, must be put together," Luca says. "Once that happens, we're able to control timelines to our advantage because probabilities will not randomly change even if human influence is injected."

"I wonder why my grandfather decided to hide the coil here," I say. "Seems like a risky venture in a place so open to the public."

"Your grandfather, I suspect, knew Port Meadow is in perpetual trust and cannot be ploughed. It must remain free for use 'by the people'," Luca says. "His preservation of this device at Port Meadow is symbolic. Tesla probably traveled from New York to Ohio, and buried the piece you carry around your neck. Each can communicate great distances but need your ancestral DNA to work, much like the Ether V requires mine to operate. I'll bet Thomas Edison was onto Nikola Tesla and Ian Windsor."

"What does Edison have to do with this?" I ask.

"Thomas Edison was born in Milan, Ohio—just steps from where NASA Plum Hook Bay was later built. He was always thwarting Tesla's progress. The public just thought of it as friendly competition, but Tesla once worked for Edison. Tesla walked off the job after Edison took credit for one of his inventions and made a great profit."

"The U.S. government exercised eminent domain on Plum Hook Bay," I say. "Tesla likely hid the portal key under Edison's nose, with the *Firelanders*. I'll bet Edison worked with the Atomic Energy Commission to try and locate the sphere and cube but he died before it was found."

"Firelanders?"

"During the American Revolution, British troops burned several Connecticut towns to the ground," I say. "Residents lost everything and were given land in the state of Ohio after the War of 1812, to start over again. The Firelanders were displaced British nationals, mostly ancestors of ancient Celtic tribes. They moved to Ohio and became U.S. citizens."

"Do you think the Atomic Energy Commission located Tesla's sphere?" Luca asks.

"The problem they have is extraction," I say. "The U.S. government, on behalf of the DOE took land back from the Firelanders. Why else would they eminent domain that land? Druids helped Astral Weavers protect the sphere and cube on Earth. It would make sense for that tradition to carry forward with the Firelanders. Since Druids kept no written records, their history was probably lost and their ancestors pushed from the land. The DOE experiments with Project Looking Glass but it fails because they don't have the coil or the key."

Vigo's head pops over the edge of the hole. "*Woof.*" He prances in a circle again, the shadow of his wagging tail dancing on dirt walls.

"Should we put these pieces together?" I ask.

"We can't," Luca says. "We need Tesla's papers to locate the codes strewn all over this planet so we can learn the password."

"Password?"

"The Astral Weavers require a password from a chosen Camaeliphim, a balancer, before they'll hand over the sphere."

"I don't remember the password," I say. "Shh. I hear something…"

Luca tilts his ear toward the sound. "One of my helicopters," he says. "The beacon on my craft sent a signal to my office. Let's get back to the party. But first…"

Lord Harrington reaches into his pants pocket, retrieves a small silver box, and opens the lid. A golden 'Eye of Horus' ring stares back at me, its 'pupil' a large red sparkling stone surrounded by canary diamonds.

"It's beautiful," I say. "Probably the most stunning ruby I've ever seen."

"It's a flawless red diamond," Luca says. "It's a symbol of our promise to wed chaos and order—plus our *engagement* ties a huge knot into Dr. Evelyn's plans." He slips the ring over my left finger. "And with this ring, the Viking holds the Isle…"

…And my mother's words thunder through my head, "*Engross a blood diamond as cleanly as a wolf passes through the needle of a compass…*"

---

It's almost midnight when we're met on the rooftop of Harrington House near the helio-pad by a perplexed looking Reggie and Sir Bob, their micro-expressions quickly covered over with decorum.

Below our feet, the band plays and boisterous laughter fans out through echoing halls. People swept away with too much alcohol roam the corridors. Bezaliels lurk, I suspect, their ears bent toward us just on the other side of this earthly dimension, longing to take form in new hosts, yet only able to fire their mental interference between a murky plane of existence. We wind our way through the upper labyrinth of Harrington House. Humans lead one another into darkened rooms and I wonder if Genin has taken Lady Olivia to his.

A small group of half-drunken debutantes stand together and

adopt borrowed poses and opinions as we pass, whispering about my god-awful appearance as they fan their faces from my stink. Another woman, somewhere, sings in a booming voice. She exaggerates each word as loud as a car horn, her futile attempt, I think, for attention. A group of men laugh, their voices low and deep. Some people wander and wonder, arm in arm, admiring architecture or paintings. One man is nearly passed out on a plush chair, chin to chest, ice tinkling in his scotch drained crystal glass as it falters in loose hand.

Every guest appears to exert their will on another, until each privately gives in to Raga's virus in a unique and personal way. I observe them, study their auras, their universal illusions, their common dreams. They'd be instant casualties on the front lines of a galactic war, I think, these soft, undisciplined, semi-sleeping fools. And yet, I envy them too, their ability to temporarily take leave of their strict codes, to live oblivious of the intangible danger that stalks their realm, and to fully embrace the folly of being human. Carried along these drawn out corridors, on the alcoholic breath of semi-rose-colored truths and into ever changing alliances, fantasies rise and fall. The ultimate pretenders, these lonely but together humans.

"Vigo," Reggie says, looking at Luca and me as if we're from another planet, which is half true. "Come on boy, we're going to bed."

My dress in tatters and Luca's dinner jacket draped over my shoulders, Lord Harrington lightly and platonically kisses my mud and horseshit covered cheek.

Sir Bob clears his throat and leads Luca and me to separate baths and glass of port. He looks at my ring finger. "Good to see the two of you have solved...your, ahem, *'small dilemma'.*"

# TWENTY-TWO

# HOPE

AT THE SOUND of an eight-inch long copper tube that produces two notes of great carry and penetrating quality, a pack of English foxhounds will charge forth from their cages.

Sir Bob, the *Huntsman*, is the person who actually *hunts* the hounds with the *whippers-in*, staff that act as his eyes and ears. Genin and are invited by Lord Harrington, the *hunt master*, to join 'first flight'. Fifty people line up. We steer our mounts around mild brush and take up our position as morning birds unleash winsome songs. Sir Bob makes announcements soon after sunrise.

The entire scene makes me feel ready to hurl my breakfast into nearby bushes because a helpless and terrified animal will run for its life until captured. I understand hunting animals for food, I've done so, but not for sport. Oscar Wilde once called fox hunting, *"the unspeakable in full pursuit of the uneatable."* I agree with him.

I wonder how many people would join *any* hunt if the target was instead, an armed Skalor, a nasty sort of intergalactic cyborg, which to me, would make this a fairer event. I reap some solace imagining people thrown from their horses, screaming for cover as alien beasts tear through bushes going after them. Human fear, I've learned, is no different than what a fox experiences being chased by dogs trained to kill.

A cry of the hounds, notes of the horn.

Using voice and trumpet, Sir Bob controls his animals, moving them from scent to covert as we ride near a field edge. We remain mostly silent and face forward toward the sound of the pack. The dogs bay and move off searching woodlands for the elusive fox. My stomach twists itself into a pretzel. The screech of a peregrine falcon, a bird of prey also known to hunt foxes, glides over meadowland, circling our party—then follows the pack into a thick, swooping now and then, his flesh-tearing claws grazing tall field grass.

Harrington's hounds, Sir Bob told me at breakfast, "consist of bloodlines selected to produce good scenting ability, voice, obedience, stamina, drive and desire." I don't doubt him. It's their prowess that concerns me. He's very proud of his pack—and he should be—they're just as efficient and beautiful as the horses we ride, mine given the name Neper, a pale golden cross between an Irish Draught and English male thoroughbred, "with stable feet and a love of good grain."

I plod alongside Lord Harrington, trying not to look at him. I'm troubled by our sudden *engagement*, a ruse born of mutual duty and a secret alliance, but I don't blame Luca for pushing into my world, or for the choice we made to combine our skills and resources. I just hope no one gets irretrievably wounded.

Genin and Lady Olivia follow close behind. Dr. Evelyn and the Duke of Avondale bring up the rear of our party of six. Rules dictate we remain relatively quiet, which normally wouldn't bother me, except for the fact I need to speak with Dr. Evelyn about my daughter and I won't have an opportunity here.

Lady Olivia's nervous energy bounces off of her aura, flinging mini-lightning bolts into my back. I think she wonders how Lord Harrington so easily slipped her grasp and grabbed my attention. She's too polite and proud to ask me personally. She tried, tacitly, to speak with Luca at the stable this morning. Luca dryly told her that whatever she needed to say, she could share with the group. Her cheeks turned multiple hues of crimson and I suspect it's a first for her, being summarily and coldly dismissed by man or hybrid. Olivia's bottled up hostility tap dances through violet orbs whenever we exchange brief glances and I pity her. Luca can be an *arse*.

Genin is upset too but he hasn't kept so quiet. He believes I maliciously and meticulously planned my newly engaged status and was "fucking Luca on the side" while working at Harrington Technologies and told Olivia as much. Reggie broke up our fight in my chamber this morning after Genin charged in, lost his temper, and accused me of treason.

Barbara spent the morning praising God for my newly engaged status and is convinced my impending union to a *Lord* is the result of 'divine intervention'. She's already planning our wedding and took off to London with a few of Harrington's staff for party ideas.

Dr. Evelyn—or should I say, my aunt, the Countess of Teviot, registers only tepid enthusiasm—as if she'll believe my marriage to Lord Harrington when it happens. Her chilly repose reminds me to tread carefully. I may think little of my aunt, but one thing she isn't, is stupid.Reggie and I privately discussed the Bezaliel mist coursing through Luca's DNA after I ordered Genin out of my room. Reggie says Luca's bio-tweaking handicaps any hope we should have for Lord Harrington's loyalty. "He could prove dangerous for the mission and you," Reggie said.

Morning papers show a black blob of my likeness, just as Luca promised, and my picture did not make it around the globe. The downside is that everyone on the planet now knows my name because it was announced during Descension at the Harrington Ball.

Scholars and historians engage in verbal 'telly' babble about the *Countess of Skye*, sending British tongues wagging, and some members of Parliament call my title "utterly preposterous!" "An American woman with even a drop of Scottish blood cannot hold title in her own right," '*they*' say. The Queen hasn't yet weighed in, but Barbara said her royal highness rang the estate this morning, to offer Luca congratulations. Others call for the Queen to strip Luca of his Lordship. And in America, its pandemonium, because on paper, I don't exist. People on both sides of the pond ask if I've fallen from the sky.

The *National Enquirer,* Barbara showed me, posted a photo of some hazy looking *angel* hovering over the D.C. Tidal Basin months ago, given to them by a tourist. Thus far, nobody believes the tourist, except for people who were there—witnesses who now claim they're visited by Men in Black, who strongly suggest silence on the '*never happened*' matter. Reggie is in crisis mode, working with a special ops team to ensure photogs don't break the perimeter of Harrington House and snap more pictures. Abar repeatedly tags my beeper. I shoved the blasted thing under a pillow last night and have yet to return his call. What would I say?

"Tally-ho" someone shouts.

"That didn't take long," Lady Olivia says as we break into a trot across the field.

Flaming orange flurry darts from den to woods. "Holloa!" Lady Olivia shouts, which means she too, has viewed the fox.

We slow our pace into the woods and anxiety expands in my throat, making it difficult to swallow. Lady Olivia pokes her thin riding crop into a thick fern patch. Thankfully, no fox. We back up and allow the dogs and the 'whippers-in' to pass, per the rules. Lady Olivia's cheeks flush with excitement and her horse rears back. "Isn't this lovely? I believe a mask is in my cards today," she gushes. "Tally-Ho!"

A terrified fox bursts forth from the underbrush.

Lady Olivia smacks her horse's *arse* with a riding crop and the beautiful beast canters away, its nostrils flaring as it gains warp speed on the flurry red fluff of fur trying to outrun it. I veil my grave concern for the fox, thinking about its head, or *mask,* as the Brits call it, being torn from its body and paraded around with pride as a macabre trophy. Olivia flawlessly jumps log and bough and it reminds me of Jade. Despite weeks of riding lessons, and building thighs stronger than concrete block, my equine skills are still beneath Lady Olivia's and I barely keep up. "She's been riding ponies since she was two," someone said over breakfast.

"Hold up," Luca says, putting an arm out in front of my staid.

"This is a no-kill foxhunt, right?" I ask.

Luca doesn't answer.

Lady Evelyn trots up beside me, "Is there a problem?" She asks.

"Lord Harrington, I was told by your staff that this is a 'no-kill' hunt, a capture and release, or a 'let go' if the fox burrows. Is this true?" I ask.

"Sam, Lord Harrington is *Hunt Master*. He decides the fate of the fox," she says, leaning over and laying her hand on mine. "Foxhunts typically end when we're outsmarted by the animal or the hounds make a kill, which is usually quick."

I yank my hand out from under her. "Usually?"

"Yes," the Duke of Avondale says as he clears his throat. "Virtually instantaneous death for the vermin. It's been a noble tradition of ours since the fifteenth century."

Traditions need to change, I think, but don't say so out loud. "Luca?"

The sounds of the hounds running across the field fade.

"Tally-Ho!" Lady Olivia screams.

"Tally-Ho!" Someone else shouts, and it echoes through the hills.

The fox appears to lead the hunters in a circle but they close in on her. I silently pray she outsmarts them all. Twenty riders pull back to let the hounds and *whippers-in* pass again into another field. The fox zips into the woods on the southside of the property, a frightened orange blaze that pings my nerves.

A very hung over Sir Oliver lets out another yell, pulls off his cap, and uses it to point out the direction the fox runs, then vomits *his* breakfast into the grass. "That's better," he says, galloping past us with a tip of his hat.

"Lord Harrington? Is this a kill hunt?" I ask.

Ours is an awkwardly long silence, designed to test my patience, I think, of which I haven't much, particularly when it comes to the life or death of an underdog—or in this case, a fox. I sense a contest of wills here and it pisses me off. "Look at me," I say. "Or haven't you the courage?"

"Samantha!" Dr. Evelyn yells.

"It's Countess to you," I say to my aunt, who's face turns to stone and if I had a hammer I'd chisel her to pieces. "Luca!" I scream. "What will happen to this fox?"

"Whatever she decides," Luca says, finally and coldly. "If she saves herself, she shall live. If she cannot, her brush, mask, and pads will be given as trophies among the hunting party. The body of the fox will then be thrown to the hounds."

"This is a fucking stupid sport," I say. "I forgo the rules of this horrible game until you get your *mist* under control." I kick my boot heels into the side of my steed and tear across the field, reentering the woods on the other side.

"Samantha!"

Two or three whippers-in assist in reconnaissance and keep their hounds together as a pack, searching den and ditch for the fox when I come up behind them. "L-l-l-ady Blake," one of them says. He swallows a heavy gulp, unsure of how to address me, then clears his throat. Everyone else rises to attention and half-heartedly bows refusing to meet my eyes. Last night I was a Yankee commoner...but today? I'm betrothed to a hybrid-human with a well-funded *courtesy* title. This confusion is bound to impact everyone I meet until they get used to the idea—or not. I don't blame them a bit because this non-Empress wears borrowed clothes.

"Madame, whippers-in take precedence over all other riders to hounds," a man says, removing his hat and nervously eyeing my horse's snout. "Under the rules, you are not permitted to pass."

'*Earth stoppers*' close up a den using dirt and brush, which prevents the fox from burrowing to safety, pretty much guaranteeing a sure kill, and in my mind, constitutes cheating. A more unfair fight there's never been, I think. Another groomsman holds a kit in each hand and stares at me with wide-eyed fear. This fox, I realize, is a mother of two.

"What are you doing there?" I ask, pointing my riding crop at the groomsman.

"Countess," he stammers, "we use these here wee ones to train our hound pups to hunt."

"Not today, you don't," I say. "Give them to me."

He looks at a whippers-in for guidance and then back at me, unsure of what to do. I see his struggle. In his eyes, I'm a "Yank", on his turf, a sophomoric intruder upon a centuries old tradition in which the British upper class take great pride and enjoyment.

"Give. Them. To. Me." I say, swishing my crop at them.

"But…"

"Jeffrey," Luca says as he rides up and pulls back on his horse's reigns. "It seems my future bride finds our tradition a bit too brutal for her delicate American senses. Please ensure no harm becomes these kits. Take them to the stable. If their mother becomes game today, Lady Blake may raise these two as pets, so she choose."

"How dare you!" I yell, because I'm so angry I could spit staples into Luca's head and can't think of anything else cleverer to scream at him.

"How dare you, Lady Blake," Luca gently says…and the hair on my forearms rise, but not because I'm scared. "You've overstepped your bounds."

"Why? Because I have respect for life?" I ask, the fire in my cheeks making me feverish with anger. "Why should you, or they, get to decide a fox's fate?"

"I told you she would decide her own fate," he says.

"Your words are a shallow and senseless distribution of cruelty." I steer my mount around him but the hounds surround Neper. "Whoa, boy," I say, grasping my horse's mane when he rears up on hindquarters. His muscles shiver under saddle. The pack nips at his hooves, teeth gnashing, low growls. Neper spins and stomps at the dogs, kicking one away, and it squeals but stands down. "Please control your damn hounds," I yell, "before this horse tramples them to death!"

The whippers-in command their charges to heel, which they do, after some effort. "*AAAARRRRROOOOOOH!*" Another dog howls, one off in the distance.

"It's okay boy," I say. I stroke Neper's glistening neck with a gloved hand, wondering why the hounds went after my horse.

"Did one of the dogs leave the pack?" Someone asks.

"All dogs accounted for sir."

"What in bloody hell is...*that?*" someone asks. All of us squint toward the field.

A peregrine falcon circles overhead. We trot our horses over a wheat-colored ridge for a better view. The Duke of Avondale nods in the direction of the fox, looking puzzled. "That's the most peculiar thing I've ever seen," he says. "Wolf?"

"Hardly," Dr. Evelyn says with a roll of her eyes.

From a hundred yards away Vigo gracefully lopes in a series of figure-eight turns. He barks at the fox and she chirps and chatters back at him, running *toward* him, and then hides *behind* him. *Smart girl*, I think.

The fox nervously peeks back at us, her eyes a shocking shade of brilliant yellow, which stabs my heart and unleashes a flood of dread. "Hope?" I whisper under my breath. This very fox Bennie gave me for my re-birthday when she was a kit, in America, more than six years ago.

The falcon does a death dive into tall grass behind Vigo but Reggie's Soul Guide stands firm, looking at us, ignorant of the battle behind him. A wing appears then disappears. A black-and-white tipped red tail fans out, before it too, vanishes. A dizzying array of red, black, and blue feathers spin, a bundle of orange and white fur arches and twists. The Peregrine falcon lifts off...with Hope firmly embraced in its talons!

"No!" I scream, jumping off my mount.

"Woo! Look at that," Evelyn yells with a laugh and single clap of her leather gloves.

And its then I know, it was she who ordered my fox shipped out of the states and sent here. The smug look on her face dares me to challenge her but I won't dare. Not here. Not in front of all these unwitting humans. She knows this too. *Bitch*.

Vigo sprints after the pair jumping at the falcon without success and the three of them disappear behind a beefy wood line. I madly dash after them but Luca blocks my path with his horse. My feet hover an inch off the ground. "She's gone," he whispers, gritting his teeth and staring me down. "***Do not*** fly in front of these humans."

I burst into tears and come down to Earth.

"Sir Bob, continue the hunt," Luca says, placing the Duke of Avondale as hunt master. Luca calls for groomsmen to relieve him and me of our horses. "Leave us," he says to his staff and our party. "We'll walk back to the house. It will give us time to discuss the nuances of a fox hunt in greater detail."

"As you wish," Sir Bob says, not looking at me. Nor does anyone else in our party, which I've ruined, and don't care.

"I won't be able to finish my mission," I say to him, my eyes streaming with tears. "I will soon be dead."

"Is that so?" He acts so nonchalant and unconcerned it makes me want to punch him in the nose. "Would you like a ride back to the house to phone a barrister?"

"That fox was *my* Soul Guide," I say. "Her name was Hope." I press my forearm into a tree, lean into it, and sob, snot and tears comingling on my shirt cuff.

"You want to tell me about your daughter before you depart this world?" Luca asks.

"How do you even know I have a daughter?" I ask, blinking my eyes dry, pulling away from the tree with renewed suspicion. "You mentioned her the night you bought me a sandwich back in London but I wasn't sure how to respond."

Luca peers through the trees behind me, hands on hips. "Dr.

Evelyn sought my help to find her a few months ago," he says. "It's why I asked Sir Harry Fairchild to somehow get you here where we could safely speak, because I knew there was more to her story."

"What?!" My voice cracks and I feel alone, a sudden realization that I've always existed within a personal vortex of fucked up reality and despair, especially where Dr. Evelyn is concerned. But this time she told me the truth; she doesn't have my daughter.

"The Countess of Teviot has a keen interest in this child," Luca says. "I'd like to know why. Lady Evelyn rarely does anything out of the goodness of her heart."

"She didn't tell you?" I ask.

"She told me you used a surrogate—that the baby was *enhanced* in vitro but she didn't know how or who her father might be."

"Enhanced how?" I ask.

"She didn't say," Luca answers. "I thought you knew. I told her if she didn't get me the details I wouldn't help her—but I would help you. Why would you use a surrogate?"

"That surrogate was my best friend," I say, wiping away tears. "She's dead. The Countess of Teviot lied to you. She knows *exactly* who Hope's father is…"

"I'm sorry," Luca says. "Did your best friend die giving birth?"

"No," I say. "Head trauma. Verity fought off her attackers and tried to protect my child as if Hope were her own," I say.

"Verity Lane?" Luca asks.

"Yes," I say, surprised he'd know this name, but then again, perhaps he learned about every missing kid sent to Plum Hook Bay while searching for his siblings. "You knew her?"

"She worked for Nephilim," he says. "She's dead?"

A chilly sweat trickles down my back and slithers into my heart. I pace among thorny brambles and dying vegetation, consistently shadowed by this shiny new heartache and the rusty colored tree canopy above our heads.

"My mother promised L. Smooter and me she wouldn't kill Verity," I say.

"I don't think your mother broke her promise," he says.

*"Relax Louie,"* Mom had said. *"I promise I won't kill her. She'll do that on her own…"* "Verity got trapped by an offer she couldn't break," I say. "Confessing to me about Hope and Tesla's file were small consolations she likely prayed I could make right, a last ditch effort to right her wrongs."

Luca lifts my chin with his finger but doesn't say a word.

On the inside, Verity hadn't much changed after all, I think. She was still a frightened and easily led child, caught in a noose, one impossible to escape, her fate sealed when Dr. Evelyn kicked the proverbial stool out from under her. I struggle to reorient my plummeting disappointment, to breathe and consider Verity's naïve betrayal. "It makes sense," I say. "Verity and Dr. Evelyn working together to steal what Bennie and I were determined Nephilim would never take."

"And that might be?"

"Earth," I say. "Everything green and good that's left of it anyway, for Bezaliels to descend upon like locusts—until this planet is scrubbed of Life and weakens enough to open countless portals to endless free buffets of gluttony and waste."

"It isn't too late," Luca says.

"You don't understand," I say. "Verity was the CIA source who told me about Project Looking Glass and *she'd* found Tesla's files. She sent them off to Turkey with Seth Sahin, her husband, who buried them in his rucksack and was supposed to hide them in the Caves of the Seven Sleepers, but Jack Meadows told me Seth was killed by a sni…oh my God!"

"What?"

"Genin," I say, thinking about how much alliances and relationships remind me of sand dunes. "He said special ops is a small world when I asked if he knew Verity's husband…"

"Who is the father of your child?" Luca asks.

Lord Harrington comes up behind me so fast when I turn away from him that I have little time to react, his breath on my neck. He spins me around and pushes me hard against a tree, flattening my fingers against the bark. His body presses into mine.

He unleashes my hair from its riding cap and his eyes turn ink black. It takes every membrane of my body to disconnect from the charge of adrenaline bolting through my spiraling blood like an overloaded circuit. I scan the area looking for a hefty limb or rock, anything I might gather up or telepathically summon for a weapon.

"Tell. Me. Who is the father of your child?" His voice thunder-whispers against my beating ears, chest to chest, an otherworldly fire I've never experienced. Each push against him is met with his squeezing closer. I'm not sure if its protection, desire, or danger I feel. Maybe a combination of all three.

"Your brother," I finally say, feeling potent shame and guilt over an intimate act that never happened and a birth in which I had no knowledge. "Bennie is my daughter's father and she is your niece."

Luca smashes his forearm into the tree above my head, which wobbles before it cracks and tumbles to the forest floor with a thunderous crash that echoes through the fields and shakes the ground beneath our feet. "Your daughter is only a few months old. You said Bennie went missing in a cave under Plum Hook Bay. You *LIED* to me?"

"I did no such thing!" I say, meeting his intense stare. "Think, Luca! This child was *not* the product of a natural seduction. Dr. Evelyn created this baby without our knowledge—in a fucking lab! She combined Bennie and my DNA and made this embryo when we were kids. *Kids!* Get off of me before I do something I might regret."

Luca backs up and paces back and forth before he stops and looks at me, gripping a low branch. "A hybrid Cultivar," he says.

"A what?" I ask.

"Hybrids are not always a blending between parents," he says. "Sometimes they're stronger or perform better than either parental lineage, a phenomenon called a hybrid Vigour, but in this case, Dr. Evelyn Dennison enhanced the most desirable characteristics of your child while extracting what she didn't want. She created your daughter as insurance."

"Against what?" I ask.

"You," Luca says. "She removed the wild stock, the *human* DNA."

"To create a fully-fledged Camaeliphim, here on Earth."

"Not a Camaeliphim," he says. "A Bezaliel stripped of human or hybrid genetics—a portal for Raga to enter. Camaeliphim DNA was her springboard."

"No!" I try to imagine something else, anything that might give Evelyn some heart and reprieve, perhaps be a mistake. I close my eyes but only see a memory of Verity and Evelyn in my room at Plum Hook Bay the day I discovered Katie was murdered...

*...Verity is ushered to the door of my room by Dr. Evelyn, who gives her a trinket, as if Verity's a lab mouse getting a pellet for doing something good. "Dis' 'ting you do, does not feel right," Verity says. "Don't worry," Evelyn replies. "You'll do your friend and your new country a great service...I'll be with you every step of the way."*

*Verity tells me in the library at Plum Hook Bay, "...an old beam in the church gave way, bringing down half the concrete ceiling... people died...thought I was possessed. The priests held a meeting...best if I never came back...I felt something inside when that Holy water hit me...a good spirit passing through...evil was chasing it..."*

I scarcely move or breathe for fear my heart may shatter into shards of steal that crush my stomach and leave my compassion dangling by a venomous thread in a hollow plexus. I tightly recoil my mind, to convince myself this is some grand mistake, that Verity was my best friend and Dr. Evelyn my aunt—but the essential truth, one impossible to deny, is that the blood or bonds created between friends or family are sometimes chimeric illusions, just as the Usta said.

"Dr. Evelyn Dennison is in the business of human and hybrid trafficking, gliding under a ruse of upper echelon respectability," Luca says. "She created a being between you and my brother but someone stole her golden child. This is celestial strike two against the Countess of Teviot."

I shift uncomfortably, feeling defeated and small, thinking Luca is right—this mission is too big for a single Camaeliphim and wondering why I'm not stronger, braver, or getting anything right—and what in the hell was I thinking accepting an offer from Not Who to toss Raga into the Source Vortex, only to discover she will be living in my *daughter?*

"We've got to find Tesla's hidden papers," Luca says.

"Take me to Genin," I say. "I need to speak with him."

"We've no time for that," he says.

"If you do not, I will fly to him," I say. "In front of everyone. Seth was targeted precisely for that file or maybe he hand-delivered it to Nephilim and they killed him for his service, but it's not what I suspect."

"What do you suspect?"

"We've been played," I say. "Again by Dr. Evelyn, but this time she's brought in an accomplice in Lady Olivia."

"Lady Olivia? She's a spoiled child," he says.

"Correction," I say. "She's a clever, wealthy, and beautiful strategist who took lessons from Dr. Evelyn and, like her, covers every horse in a race, including Genin."

"I'll drain the life from both of them," he says.

"Not yet," I say. "Like Verity, I'm sure Lady Olivia is a pawn for my aunt. And you yourself said we need Lady Evelyn because she has some piece of the code. Luca, have you ever heard about the Book of Enoch?"

"Of course," he says.

"Ever heard the name Basaseal?"

"No."

"Bennie told Reggie that Basaseal is rarely recorded among sacred texts, a fact Bezaliels count upon to keep their kind hidden among humans and hybrids," I say. "We don't know much about Basaseal except he's allegedly beyond redemption. But Bennie said chaos cringes when Basaseal is near, which tells me he's a potential *ally,* maybe somewhere on Earth, perhaps an extraterrestrial in exile?"

"Where?"

"I'm not sure but we might ask the Usta."

"You know about Usta?"

"Um, yea, Genin and I met one night before last when we accidentally fell into your garden fountain."

"I'm surprised either of you still stand," he says.

"She recognized me as a Princess," I say. "Why would she call me that?"

"I can't tell you," he says, a look of surprise crossing his face before he recovers. "You must regain your memories. It will unbalance your work if I tell you, and that is *my* curse."

I'm not sure what Luca means by that but let it go…for the moment. "Verity once told me Enoch was allegedly given secret sacred knowledge straight from God. She warned me when we were kids, the Book of Enoch is apocryphal. But Bennie disagreed. He said humans didn't have the clearance to know Enoch's canons, but what if Camaeliphim do?"

"We could decipher the code," Luca says. "to find the password, earn the sphere, and move through an X Point, to deliver the Word back to the Source."

"Angels of God," I say. "That's what Reggie called us. Fragments of the Book of Enoch were found in a Qumran cave about 1948 and are in the custody of the Israel Antiquities Authority, but the rest…"

"…is scattered all over the globe," Luca says, finishing my sentence. "Damn near impossible to find—but must be done—or this planet is shagged."

"Why can't the Source reach into Earth and take back the code?" I ask.

"The Source is beyond human or hybrid conscious horizons," Luca says. "If the Source reached directly into Earth, without benefit of intercessors, the result is multiverse collapse."

"We'll need a team to search the Caves of Seven Sleepers," I say. "A forensic doctor, an archeologist, a nuclear engineer, a religious scholar, a geologist, a few private contractors, weapons, supplies, and a shitload of funding. But first, we retrieve Bennie from the Antarctic."

"We'll also need something else," Luca says.

"What?"

"A kiss…"

Without warning, he presses his lips to mine. His large hands wrap around my head to clasp me in place. I raise my fists to his chest, a futile and phony attempt to push him away. A heat spreads through me, tethering my hips to his. His tongue searches me, our eyes closed, and his touch as he pulls me into his arms, defrosts my heart. I return this soulful kiss. And, oh, it is, without a doubt, the best kiss I've ever shared, bar none.

"We'll require a spelunker too," he whispers, pulling back, smiling into my eyes. "But Bennie isn't in the Antarctic. As soon as you mentioned patient 611 I contacted sources to learn more. He wasn't there."

"Oh," I say, disappointed. "It wasn't him then."

"It was him," Luca says. "He escaped."

I do nothing but breathe for a moment, hearing Luca's words, a panic clamoring up my throat. "Bennie's really *alive*?" I ask, hoping, praying for it to be so, a single blessing of fortune among too many curses.

"He's in hiding, I'm not sure where," Luca says. "He can't be tracked…but a curious thing I heard."

"What?"

"It's rumored he fled 611 NORAD with nothing but a small bundle strapped to his chest."

"Hope?"

"Yes, if I have to guess," Luca says. "He may have been onto Evelyn's scam all along and remained in those caves back at Plum Hook Bay to wait her out, to take back what he knew she'd someday create…"

"…To spare me the pain," I say. "And to find a cure for our daughter."

"That would be my guess," Luca softly says.

"The falcon killed my Soul Guide," I say. "My time is limited and I'll be of little use since my fox, likely the best spelunker on the planet, can't guide you through Earth's labyrinth of caves."

"Vidar, the falcon, is *my* Soul Guide," he says. "Your Soul Guide is safe and rests with Vigo…"

—————————

…And by the time we return to the house to confront Dr. Evelyn Dennison, the Countess of Teviot, she is gone, fled to parts unknown along with Lady Olivia and Genin…

## TWENTY-THREE

## CAVE OF BEASTS

WE'VE REACHED the Wadi Sura—also known as the Cave of Beasts and Swimmers, along the western edge of the Gilf Kebir plateau, a remote corner of Southwest Egypt, butt up against the Libyan border. It's a 'backdoor' to one of the Caves of Seven Sleepers almost 1,600 miles away. We'll travel via tunnel systems *under* the Mediterranean Sea searching for Tesla's file, and more importantly, looking for missing humans who've disappeared all over the globe, lost ones who occasionally resurface in the Middle East as slaves, far from their homelands.

Each suffering I encounter is personal and tragic. Kidnapped tribal members often become sacrifices, their organs and blood a pointless feast, remnants of human flesh and bones left to bake under desert sun. This crime scene is compliments of subversives who believe unspeakable horror conveys the power of gods. It's easier for me to buffer this 'holy' terror around words like *some, many, all, a few...bodies, cadavers, remains...*I suppose it insulates and temporarily separates me from the unspeakable 'collateral damage' and makes it, somehow, easier to do my job—to catalogue the dead and rebalance the scales of justice through compassion and sometimes, vengeance. Balance between chaos and order requires both from me.

We confront another abandoned camp of dehumanized carcasses. I turn away to soften my eyes and the mental blows over the senselessness of it all. I think about the little girl Genin couldn't save, the one who got sealed in the cave miles away and realize, I bear de facto witness to very personal final moments. So I stop. I take time to make note of the grisly details—empty sockets, strips of leathery skin, smeared blood turning black against the rocks, people stripped of their clothes, jewelry, lives, and dignity. I mostly guess, sometimes imagine, what this or that person was like pre-corpse, when life roamed freely in them, from where they came, what they did, their passions, and who misses them, my small touch of last respects. Everyone on our team falls silent when we discover new bodies, a solemn sadness surrounds us, and there is nothing to do but surrender this collective bottled up mourning. We tag and slip each corpse, or what's left, into body bags.

Disaster, illness, torture, and death are things that happen to *others*, those less fortunate in faraway places, the *fallen*. But we are all fallen on some level, I think, our stories not particularly special or extraordinary, the depths of our souls, never truly explored or known. And here I am, not far away, but in the thick of death, where white Egyptian vultures scavenge on the remains. Soldiers call the birds *Pharaoh's chickens* and shoo them but don't shoot them. Macabre jokes bring levity to a leaden situation.

Once we close the book on another's existence, we tend to ease our attention toward death and resume our comfortable but fleeting earthly fables, tall tales we tell ourselves to raise our sense of importance high enough that maybe death will pass us over. But time eventually grows late for us all and our story ends, no matter how hard any of us might bargain, beg, or choose to ignore the inescapable.

Reggie feels otherwise. He says all sentient beings are created as an extension of the Source, and therefore, exceptional universal miracles—our lives and personalities as unique and beautiful as snowflakes but part of a conscious and intelligent collective where some who die before their time may choose to return again. He says humans are capable of great feats and even greater acts of love, that peace is possible even if war is inevitable. Sometimes I feel his optimism, especially if I'm able to pluck survivors from a deadly pile, study their hearts, see their fading aura's, take time to listen to their stories and connect with their souls—like gazing at a single snowflake that's landed on my fingertip before it melts away to take a different form.

Gilf Kebir translates as "the Great Barrier", a thousand foot high sandstone plateau about the size of Cuba, its name bestowed by a local prince more than a century ago because it had no name. It's a strange place known locally as a blockade between worlds, its rugged beauty, bizarre geology, and dramatic petroglyphs depict, scientists argue, either a lost era or a mythical landscape.

Glimpsing over the ancient underground maps and charts sprawled out in front of me, I've had enough for one day. I churn my wrists, the maps roll up like coiled scrolls, and I safely re-tuck them into my camel saddle.

We've set up camp near the Cave of Beasts, where drawings show disfigured long-tailed, three-footed creatures surrounded by headless humans. Handprints left on the walls aren't human either, but massive lizard-like impressions, bigger than Usta, as of yet, unknown and unmet. If these beasts actually exist on or under Earth, I don't care to meet them.

The Cave of Swimmers on the opposite side, which I find decidedly more peaceful, contains ten-thousand year-old images of floating beings, many with wings. Some claim the beings are swimming humans, that this area was once significantly greener and wetter than it is today. Others contend this part of the Sahara is the most arid on Earth, has been for millennia, and the 'beings' portrayed, not human, but nonexistent, unexplained myths. I push my fingers into the etchings, feeling war and loss, but also hope. Things, I think, are only nonexistent or unexplainable until they aren't.

Hundreds of sacred birds carved on the ceilings of both caves, Luca told me, signify celestial wisdom. Ancient Egyptians believed the *Ba*, or soul, leaves the body during death and one day returns, a process of resurrection. Western Christians only recognize one resurrection, that of Jesus Christ, and this is how I was raised in Ohio, but it makes me wonder: If the Christian God made man, woman, and others in *His* image, like Barbara firmly believes, then isn't it plausible this includes the potential for reincarnation too? She smacked me with a resounding "NO!" when I asked and said I had to take it on faith. I'm more of a 'just the facts' sort of lady, infused with a healthy dose of adapt or perish. Either way, we all meet death just the same, faith or no faith, and if there's no resurrection, how can there exist a heaven…or a hell?

I suppose Christianity is one vantage point humans might use to gauge their world, like other religions, but unfortunately, I think practicing only one limits our vistas. It's like a fighter who makes the mistake of mastering a single weapon, and then proclaims herself an expert on war. Then again, maybe the nostalgia and comfort of religious rituals are requirements for humans, a way to gain advanced spirituality and raise faith, needed as much as food or water or hope.

Luca tells me, according to his calculations, there's a few undiscovered ancient freshwater mega lakes under these sands. "We'll need them to stay hydrated," I say. I stare off into the horizon at nothing in particular. It's rocks and sand as far as my eyes can see, a desolate landscape hiding secrets, shimmering sands rolling away with the sun.

Seth Sahin may have hidden or handed off Tesla's file anywhere along this deep black trail—or maybe it was taken from him, or it isn't in the caves at all and our mission a fruitless tail chase. I don't believe the latter. I'm taking it on *faith* the file is still 'out there', lost in a literal 'no man's' land. Seth's unit initially thought he'd been kidnapped or gone AWOL. It happens all the time, people convinced by 'the enemy' to lay down their weapons and deepest held convictions, to adopt a culture or ideology so foreign from their upbringing or sense of duty it doesn't seem possible. But that's not what happened.

According to a Defense Intelligence Agency report given to the

CIA and Septum Oculi, Seth's rucksack was empty when he was killed by Genin, having finally come out of the caves without permission or clearance. It was a case of *friendly fire* according to the military, an unfortunate accident. Witnesses couldn't understand why a Master Sargent would even take his rucksack into a cursed cave unless he planned to stay a while. Either way, it was empty, and Genin too, empty-handed.

Dr. Evelyn and Genin formed their own search team with the help of Lady Olivia, and got a head start into the caves through Jordan. I heard Olivia insisted on going along or wouldn't fund the venture, then got word to her father she'd been kidnapped. Newspapers around the world scream about the missing UK heiress. Luca faced a barrage of search warrants at Harrington House, a tactical delay on Dr. Evelyn's part, one he pristinely and quickly cleared, because on paper, he's cleaner than bleach.

Gossip columnists speculate Lady Olivia committed suicide over Lord Harrington's surprise engagement to a common *nobody* or Luca killed her and the body is buried on the grounds at his estate. Conspiracy theorists grab unrelated bits and pieces and bang them into a mishmash of theories about how Lady Olivia hung herself from a tree in Harrington's garden the night of the ball and it was all covered up by *reptilian* creatures sent here to destroy Earth or she was abducted by aliens. Come to think of it, the latter may be closer to the truth than the rest. Con artists continue to send phony ransom notes to police seeking glorious sums of money and all sorts of questionable head cases call in useless tips to Scotland Yard.

As for Genin, it still stings that his sense of duty and loyalty wasn't with me but with Dr. Evelyn.

It's evening and a warmer than average November night for this part of the desert but an odor of chill edges over the plateau.

Genin's grooming, I'm convinced, began at Plum Hook Bay when we were sixteen.

I pull a stick from the fire and prod its dull orange tip into the rocks. I stare up into a vast sky, my teeth sinking into my bottom lip and hold tight to my thoughts. Gone are the red buses and black taxis of London, along with the rolling green fields of Harrington House and its countryside. The USA, with its 'taken for granted' amenities and Plum Hook Bay too, feel an entire universe away.

Genin too, our friendship, or what I thought was friendship, a farce, and gone too. I toss the stick into the fire. The Usta warned me things, or people, aren't always as they seem. Genin's wound is fresh and deep and memorable, a laceration of the heart. Reggie and I trusted him, invited him into the inner sanctum of Septum Oculi. Our mistake. I can't decide if Genin's a rat, a mole, or a sellout. Maybe he's all three.

A team of hired hands, twenty of them, undo and redo thick black straps or check handles on instruments and weaponry. They hastily toss the day's riding robes and garments aside to sit together on a ridge, away from us, and share whatever tales Tibetan Sherpas share. Luca says the Sherpas are cosmically blessed as the best guides for inhospitable terrain, that they understand Earth's topography and its secret underground about as well as they know the Himalayas. We'll wear Luca's patented technology, pulsating electro-magnetic frequency suits, to ensure our cells retain optimum oxygen and we can communicate underground.

I pull out my compass, it's dial serenely complacent, hovering Northeast with only a slight bob and wobble—about time it finally works. I wonder if life on Earth is illusory, our trials, and tribulations, momentary joys, adventures and dangers, merely a three-dimensional simulation of cosmic imagination—a test—or maybe worse, an aimless exercise in futility, with no goal in mind except birth, existence, and death.

During the third millennium BC, twenty-thousand people shouted, quarried, or dragged stone where I stand, most against their will—and for what? Tonight, the cacophony where large blocks were once pounded and people whipped until they bled, is only a melody of dusty wind and the attractive song of Nightjars, medium-sized nocturnal birds that primarily nest on the ground.

Ah, such rare and temporary serenity, I think. I'm not sure how much of it I can stand.

I suppose I should be grateful for this moment of peace, something to carry me forward through the caves, where we'll be completely on our own, hidden from the roving eye of the sun, unfriendly governments, or fresh air, for weeks—potential game for anything lurking in the subterranean abyss. Sometimes the thought of winding up monster food makes my stomach crater with fear. Worse than the prickly neck fear back at Plum Hook Bay but not as scary as facing a Bezaliel.

A heady scent of cinnamon, cloves, and coriander simmer lamb into tender acquiescence, a soft bubble of comfort wafting over me from a nearby worn black cauldron. A pale moon finally shows her quarter face, surrounded by a court of brightening stars. I place a buckeye seed on a rock, a tiny testament to the world we are here but the world doesn't hear, know, or care. Barbara gave me a small sack of *hetuk* seeds, thinks they may come in handy on our journey, although I don't see how. I didn't argue but found room for them and her Bible, on my camel. I didn't know until Reggie told me, that camels are actually the best animals to take underground because they can carry triple their weight, last for weeks without food or water, provide milk rich in nutrients, and we can eat them, if necessary.

Dr. Nadia Kimathi, archeologist, sits beside me on a toppled boulder where I've settled. She hums a pleasant tune I do not recognize and makes notes in a leather bound journal. Her honey-like voice oozes over the holes in my psyche, a multitude of scars, mostly healed, but personal reminders and medals of honor—and sometimes dishonor—I'll always carry.

Dr. Monica whittles next to Nimbu, our lead guide from Africa. This is his stopping point he says, believing the caves belong to his ancestors for eternal reflection and meditation, that to enter them, invites curse. Dr. Monica examines one of her weapons, checking its slide and barrel and shows Nimbu how to grip the semi-auto .45 without a flinch. Dr. Monica joined our mission thanks to Reggie's pulled strings with Abar and Septum Oculi. Having her here alleviates some of my trepidation and she'll manage the off-book special ops unit ordered to accompany us, twenty-one British SAS, Delta Force, and Gray Fox Operators.

I finally called Joe Abar after he tagged my beeper about a hundred times. He wanted to know how in the hell I was so quickly engaged to Lord Harrington and it wasn't what he meant when he ordered me to "get involved". Once he stopped yelling into the receiver I debriefed him just a smidge. We agreed some answers about the tribal murders may be found underground. I just never shared with him how far down. He arranged for my NOC continuation, deep under cover, he called it. Um, yea, something like that..."Just one more thing," Abar said on the phone before I left for Africa. "Samantha, watch your back. You might run into more than answers..."

Luca converses near the cave entrance with Reggie, each of their large frames casting long shadows over dancing flames. I experience a base longing to take Luca with complete abandon into me—to accept his energy and feel his muscles ripple with reflexive passion. But there's no time or privacy to pant such fantasies to life. I suppose its my nervous energy combined with the unknown, a fear of the worst, or dying with regret, that inflicts me to stand and pace. Like a good TV crime show, I expect life's problems to be solved and wrapped up, in paranormal terms anyway, in just under an hour. Unfortunately, time has other plans, and easy answers hide somewhere, but not here.

The red diamond Luca gave me radiates a luminescence on my left hand that puts star clusters to shame but it's still unfamiliar. No matter how long I gaze into its flawless detail, I'm at a loss to remember any of the lives in which he may have previously slipped it on my finger, where it's now stuck, and can't be removed, having melded to my skin, like a turtle to its shell.

And then there's Bennie. There's *always* Bennie. He's blocked any psychic connection we once shared, for our safety, I guess. I trust he has his reasons, maybe to prevent our daughter from becoming a pawn in this astral war, or to back engineer her DNA and remove the Bezaliel mist Dr. Evelyn helped spiral through her veins...or worse...to prevent me from tossing Hope into the

Source Vortex…something I'm not in any hurry to do. But if I fail to keep my agreement with Not Who, the consequences are certain death that travels far beyond my own.

"Is the stew ready?" I ask.

Barbara nods and plunges a huge wooden ladle into the big black pot and gives it a thick stir. She won't be going with us. A selfish part of me wishes she could but the reality is she's not able to traverse the highs and lows of our climbs, it isn't safe, and most importantly, Reggie cares about her too much to see her get hurt or suffer. She's headed back to Ike in upstate New York, where Ike had sense enough, this time, to buy the large farmstead adjacent to his missile silo, enough space to keep his whiskey and her Bible happily separated. Barbara thrusts a steaming bowl into my hands, its scent so heavenly I'm sure it would make Jesus Christ salivate. I dig the spoon into the stew and think some more…

…Approximately 7.8 billion humans exist on this planet. The vibration of shouting, violence, machinery, weapons, and worry diminishes little, even in the desert. I don't actually *hear* human deprivation and desperation but sense its messages carried across desert winds, tossed with the sand. I'm unable to locate water with my feet like Saratu but sensing impressions, seeing visions, good or bad, is *my* gift. And from where I'm perched, prolonged abuses nose-dive this planet into irreparable chaos, just the same as it did Atlantis and Lumeria eons ago. The land of Egypt too, with its failed pyramids, was strike three against planetary balance, an ancient last-ditch effort to fix the dysfunctional tilt of human blunders. I trace a finger around the eye of my necklace.

"Samantha?" Luca asks. "You all right?"

"Yes," I smile. It's half true. I'm here. Everything is okay at this moment. Another spoonful of heaven glides down my throat, its warmth a buffer against the fast rising chill outside.

An obsidian obelisk at the cave entrance periodically flashes hieroglyphically etched symbols, a sort of bioluminescence. No wires. Anywhere. We're in untethered territory, a wild space that hums on free energy, a gift under our noses.

"There's no reason to conserve energy underground because its freely transmitted," Luca says as he stands with Reggie, sensing my thoughts the way Camaeliphim do. "This means all of our devices and weaponry will be wirelessly recharged."

The key device responds to my rare blood and these caves, its Pleiades unfolding and refolding under my shirt. Nobody says a thing about it, not even the Sherpas or Barbara, but they notice and simply smile or fold their hands, or bow to me. I bow back. Special Forces don't ask because they have no 'need to know'.

Luca told me the key pendant is supposed to lock and twist into the underside of the Tesla coil the way a neuropeptide latches onto a synaptic deck—but I never asked for this—to be a balancer. At least I don't think I did, I can't remember. My eye necklace too, occasionally lifts itself off my chest when I face the Cave of Beasts, as if looking for something, before it rests again. The left brain side of me wants to say its due to some elevated electro-magnetic field from the caves, but the right-brain intuits its's something more—something in Tesla's papers, perhaps the ink or a coating he invented that connects with the necklace and portal key, just as it did with the Tesla coil in Port Meadow, a sort of invisible compass maybe, guiding us.

I finger the necklace and wish saving Earth and its multiverses was as simple as pushing a knob of reason—a big red SCRAM button to shut it all down. I contemplate the treason hurled upon this planet and decide that even though I mostly loathe humans, they unwittingly received a raw deal when this planet got crop dusted with enough wickedness to tip them toward irrevocable mayhem—and the thing I admire about most humans (but not all) is how they keep going even if no one believes in them—something Gods, angels, or hybrids can't do.

"There are three stages to integration," Luca says to Reggie as they inspect the Tesla coil. Reggie sweeps away minor debris at his feet with a combat boot. Luca's eyes shift between azure blue and ink black when he looks at me, the latter, a savage and unpleasant reminder of the Bezaliel mist spiraling through his Golden Blood. I haven't yet figured out a way to make that work to our advantage but I'm thinking...

Tangled orchid vines attach to elephant-sized boulders beyond our camp. They twist and coil extra-thick, gray-green tendrils to the ground. Reggie and I think they absorb and confine some of Earth's negativity, the way my mom used to do. I imagine she's here, in the orchids, reopening to youthful bloom, the way she once was—before I was born. I hope the Tall Whites gave Avril a better life, perhaps made her an orchid keeper the way they made Enoch a guardian of sacred treasures, took them both swerving into the heavens of their choice, bypassing bodily death.

Mom entrusted me with her eye necklace and left this world, I think, because she felt I was adult enough now, at the ripe age of twenty-three, to continue my mission. I don't share with anybody that I'm not so sure. I've got issues. And stress. And PTSD. But I'm a fighter too, so there's that.

Hope circles and then pounces. I play tug-a-stick with her. She isn't worse for wear after almost winding up hound meat but I've changed her name to Kitsune. It avoids confusion between my Source Guide and my daughter, whom Verity named Hope. I'd like to think there's a good reason Verity named my daughter after my fox, perhaps to assuage her guilt, but I'll never know. Kitsune (formerly Hope) now paws at Vigo's feet, a restless bundle of ignited copper and damn near impossible to manage. Vigo yawns and places his bulky head on two boxing-glove-sized front paws. Kitsune bounces around him...*boink, boink, boink...*Vigo ignores her.

I take my place before a stacked circle of blue-gray sea rocks, my nightly study. I'm supposed to focus on the space inside—but not grasp, Reggie says. I still haven't been able to levitate them—yet. But neither can Reggie or anyone else here.

Reggie says it will happen, that one day I'll stop thinking too hard and get liftoff, the same way I once flew at Plum Hook Bay, high above the trees. Being human is hard. Being hybrid, even harder. I didn't exactly jump into Dr. Evelyn's initial offer with great attitude or enthusiasm. Who could blame me? And speaking of that...anyone who makes a conscious decision to jump down a rabbit hole the way I do should also make arrangements for someone else to hold their ankles.

Tomorrow, no doubt, will be the beginning of a deadly or delightful day, a journey loaded with ultimatums or compromises, treachery or trust, and hopefully no death—just enough moral fiber and sacred spirit to keep moving us forward.

"Just for your SA, we've got unexpected visitors coming over the ridge," a Delta Operator says as he slips into the cave.

"Who?" Reggie asks.

"Hell if I know," the operator says. He spits some tobacco dip at the ground and tosses a weapon to one of his comrades. "But they sure as shit don't look human."

# ALSO BY B.A. CRISP

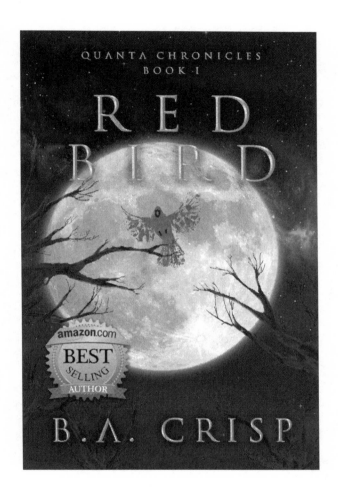

Red Bird

Available on Amazon

Made in the USA
Columbia, SC
12 February 2022

55935488R00183